D1169425

Praise for the Oak Leaves

"Drawing from her own life experience, Maureen Lang invites us to experience the honest disappointments and glorious discoveries that come from mothering a son others may see as 'different,' yet God sees only as His beloved child."
Liz Curtis Higgs, best-selling author of *Thorn in My Heart*

"I couldn't put this book down. Vivid, compelling, and deeply moving, with issues that touch the soul, *The Oak Leaves* was a story that lingered in my heart, and made me ask, just how much am I willing to accept from the Lord? . . . Every moment you spend with this book is worth it."
Susan May Warren, award-winning author of *Reclaiming Nick*

"Maureen Lang's *The Oak Leaves* is a beautiful, beautiful story of the many kinds of love and their divine author. I feel privileged to be one of the first to read it."
Lyn Cote, author of *The Women of Ivy Manor*

"This is a wonderful story—told from a wealth of experience and from the heart—of the anxiety, despair, mourning, and eventual acceptance associated with having a child diagnosed with fragile X syndrome. . . . This book offers hope and comfort, as well as a celebration of the little joys . . . of raising a child with fragile X."
Elizabeth Berry-Kravis MD, PhD, Director of the Fragile X Clinic and Research Program, Rush University Medical Center

"Readers who have children with disabilities, readers who know families affected by disabilities, and readers who are simply drawn to a rich, well-written story will be lifted up by this beautiful work."
Gail Harris-Schmidt, PhD,
coauthor of *The Source for Fragile X Syndrome*

"Maureen Lang has made the world a better place, and families impacted by fragile X syndrome, now and in the future, owe her their thanks."
Robert Miller, Executive Director, National Fragile X Foundation

the Oak Leaves

MAUREEN LANG

TYNDALE HOUSE PUBLISHERS, INC.
CAROL STREAM, ILLINOIS

Visit Tyndale's exciting Web site at www.tyndale.com

Check out the latest about Maureen Lang at www.maureenlang.com

TYNDALE and Tyndale's quill logo are registered trademarks of Tyndale House Publishers, Inc.

The Oak Leaves

Designed by Beth Sparkman

Edited by Kathryn S. Olson

Published in association with the literary agency of WordServe Literary Group, Ltd., 10152 S. Knoll Circle, Highlands Ranch, CO 80130.

Scripture quotations are taken from the *Holy Bible*, King James Version.

Library of Congress Cataloging-in-Publication Data

Lang, Maureen.
   The oak leaves / Maureen Lang.
      p. cm.
   ISBN-13: 978-1-4143-1345-0 (pbk.)
   ISBN-10: 1-4143-1345-4 (pbk.)
   I. Title.
   PS361.A554O15 2007

   813'6—dc22   2006033334

Printed in the United States of America

13   12   11   10   09   08   07

7   6   5   4

For my husband and my children,
and families everywhere
affected by fragile X syndrome

Sorrow is a fruit.
God does not allow it to grow
on a branch that is too weak to bear it.

VICTOR HUGO

ACKNOWLEDGMENTS

It seems impossible to contain within a few words the gratitude I feel toward so many people for the production of this book. When the Lord first whispered to write this story, I knew I was neither ready nor willing. But from my first gentle and encouraging readers, too numerous to name, I received the assurance needed to conquer those early drafts. From other moms who have lived through the horror of receiving a life-changing diagnosis on their child, I received affirmation of my goal: to write something that will remind us we can survive. Through all of my critique partners, I became convinced this book was more than cathartic.

My appreciation to Meredith Efken for helping me to find the focus of this story and to Jill Eileen Smith, Joelle Charbonneau-Blanco, Julie Scudder Dearyan, Karen Dale Harris and so many others from my critique groups for their unwavering belief in the value of this project.

Many thanks to my agent, Greg Johnson, and his assistant, Marjorie Vawter, whose enthusiastic report caught Greg's attention. Not only did he successfully market the proposal in record time, Greg also prodded me into imagining a sequel. Now I don't have to say good-bye (at least just yet) to the characters I've grown to love.

Finally I'd like to thank the Tyndale team of Stephanie Broene, Kathy Olson, and Karen Watson. Their wise input, friendly assistance, and ready accessibility made the process of producing this book a pleasure from the very beginning. Kathy, your insight and reassuring footnotes made editing this book a joy. My deepest thanks.

To my son Kipp and his wife, and to their children and children's children in America,

I can think of no better way for you to know me than to share with you my journal from the time in my life that revealed God's plans for me—plans far different from my own. This is my legacy to you.

I assure you each word is true. If you inherit anything from me, may it be the knowledge that love is stronger than fear, especially with faith in the One who is love: "Jesus Christ the same yesterday, and to day, and for ever."

—Cosima Escott Hamilton, 1874

1

The dull hum of the garage door sounded. Luke was home. Talie looked up from the books and papers spread across her kitchen table. She might have been tempted to stay up all night reading, but not now. Welcoming her husband home was the only thing she liked about his occasional business trips.

As the door from the garage opened, Talie stood to greet her husband. "Welcome home!"

He moved to put his briefcase in its usual spot, but finding the table covered with the memorabilia Talie had been studying, he settled it on a nearby chair.

"Hey," he said, taking her into his arms and kissing her.

Amazing how even after four years of marriage her heart still twirled at such a thing, especially when he gazed at her afterward. She read nothing but pure love in his lively blue eyes.

"Good to be home." He scanned the adjacent family room.

Talie guessed he was looking for the baby. "I tried to keep Ben awake, but he crashed about twenty minutes ago." She grinned. "You can probably get reacquainted around two in the morning, though."

"Has he been up a lot while I was gone?"

She nodded.

Luke shrugged broad shoulders out of his suit coat. "I'll look in on him when we go up."

"How did everything go on your trip?"

"Better than I expected. They offered me the job."

"They did!" Talie hugged him, then pulled away. "Why didn't you tell me when you called earlier?"

"I wanted to see your face." He kissed her, studying her again afterward. "And it was worth the wait."

Pride for him mushroomed from deep inside, spreading up and out through her smile. Once, before she'd met Luke, before other dreams had taken its place, she'd had a career vision of her own. Going up through the ranks of the education trail, from teacher to department head to curriculum director, from assistant principal to principal and on to superintendent. Now, seeing Luke's dreams going forward, she tasted vicarious living but, amazingly enough, didn't miss those old aspirations for herself. She was living a new kind of dream, one she wouldn't trade for anything.

"Congratulations, Mr. Architectural Engineering Director. When do you start?"

"Right away. I move into my new office tomorrow. They want me to restructure the department, so I'll probably have to hire a couple of new people."

"We'll have to celebrate. Get a babysitter, out to dinner—the works."

Luke loosened his tie and went to the refrigerator. As incredible as he looked in a suit, she knew he far preferred jeans and a T-shirt. He grabbed a Coke. "What went on around here while I was gone?"

"Jennifer down the street is starting a playgroup for the kids in the neighborhood. I'm taking Ben tomorrow."

"Sounds good. How many kids?"

"Five—all of them born last year like Ben."

He took a gulp of soda. "Did you have a good time at your mom's? Get a lot done?"

Talie turned back to the table. "The garbageman is going

to hate her on Tuesday, but the house looks great. I think she'll be ready to list it any day now. Look here. . . ." She held up the family Bible she'd been looking at before he arrived. "This is the treasure we found among all the trash."

"What is it?"

"A Bible that belonged to my dad's grandmother. I have a whole box of things that must have been hers. The letters are wonderful. Letter writing is a lost art now that everyone has e-mail. And look at this. I think it's a journal."

She picked up the smooth, leather-bound book. It was tied closed with a ribbon. "I'm almost afraid to touch it—the binding is cracked. It's all so incredible." Talie sighed, looking at all of the things strewn on the table. "This is like a call back, Luke."

He looked from the journal to her. "Call back?"

She nodded, her heart twisting from missing her dad. "When I was a kid our family would take driving vacations. On that first day we'd get up at three in the morning to miss rush hour traffic around Chicagoland. We'd all fall back asleep, but that's what Dad liked—to drive in the quiet. Sometimes, though, I'd sit up front with him. He used to say I was helping by keeping him company. I knew he didn't really need help. He just wanted me to feel useful."

Unexpected tears welled in her eyes. "He liked it when he could see taillights ahead. Not too close, just up the road." Instead of the kitchen table in disarray she saw a pair of round, red lights gleaming from an invisible dark road ahead. "He used to tell me that was his *call back*. The car ahead called back that the road was still there, free and clear for him to follow."

She blinked, seeing again the items in front of her. "These are like a call back. Seeing what's gone before can help us know what to expect from life. It's especially meaningful when it's your own family history."

Talie returned her attention to the Bible, opening it to the names and dates that went back to the eighteenth century.

"Is your name written in that Bible?" Luke asked.

She scanned the list toward the more recent additions at the end but then shook her head. "No, but my mom's is next to my dad's, with their anniversary date. So many names! For our next baby we can pick a name from the family. Like . . . Josephine or Sarah or Emily. Or here's one I really like: Cosima. We could call her Sima."

"What, no men in your dad's history? Aren't there any boys' names?"

"We already have a boy, silly. We need to hope for a girl next time."

"Fifty-fifty chance of it going either way, honey. Let me see." He took the Bible from her. "Matthew would be good. Or . . . wait. Branduff? Seamus? Sounds like a bunch of Irishmen. I thought your family was German and English."

"The German is from my mother's side. I guess I'll find out more about my dad's family from these names. But something awful must have happened in 1848. Five deaths are listed on the same day."

"Hmm . . . 1848. Ireland had a potato famine around that time, I think."

"That's probably it," Talie said with a nod. "Isn't it amazing that they couldn't feed themselves yet they kept birth records all the way back to the century before?"

Luke smiled. "I'm sure you have quite some family history there."

"And look at this. Dad really did have an Aunt Ellen. Ellen Dana Grayson, his mother's sister. But I'd rather not show this to Dana."

"Why not?"

"Because she's named for the mysterious Aunt Ellen. Her

full name is Ellen Dana, only my mom liked Dana better so we always called her that."

"So why is this aunt mysterious, and what difference does it make if Dana knows about her?"

"Look here." Talie pointed to an entry. *"Ellen Dana Grayson, born 1910, died 1941.* She never married, and she died in a place called Engleside. Sounds like a rest home, but she would've been too young for that. She must have been sick. I don't want Dana knowing she was named for some sick, lonely relative who never got married. You know how Dana is. She already thinks she's an old maid and she's not even thirty yet. She'll think history is bound to repeat itself just because of a name."

Luke shook his head. Talie had seen that look on his face before, the one that said she was being overprotective again. She was willing to concede she wanted the best for her younger sister, but that's how big sisters were *supposed* to be. She wasn't about to shirk her duty, even on a small point like this.

Luke was still studying the names listed in the back of the Bible.

"If I draw a rough draft and put all the names and birth dates in order, could you make a family tree?" she asked. "We could hang it in the study."

"Sure. Just birth dates, though? You're going to avoid anything morbid like when they died, even though that's the most interesting part?"

Talie hesitated.

"It's that date, isn't it?" He was watching her closely. "May 16, 1848."

"I know it's probably nothing more dramatic than the potato famine, but I guess I'd like to find out what happened before we advertise on our walls that five members of my family died on the same day."

"Don't get me wrong, Talie. I love a good mystery. But I don't think something that happened more than a hundred and fifty years ago can make much of a difference in our lives. Now let's go upstairs and peek in on that baby up there. And then—" he set aside the Bible and pulled her into his arms again, nuzzling her neck—"you can welcome me home as if I've been gone a lot longer than a few days."

Talie left their bed, knowing from past experience her movement wouldn't disturb Luke. His steady breathing said it was true again tonight.

She went downstairs to the kitchen table, where she'd left the dilapidated journal. It was old and stiff, the satin ribbon faded.

Touching one of the shamrocks engraved on the front, she untied the ribbon and opened the soft leather cover. The pages proved to be remarkably free of damage despite their apparent age. No water spots, no mold, just clear handwriting on thick paper that had barely yellowed through the years. Maybe it was a good thing her father had been so disinterested in the past; storing the items in the dry darkness of their attic hadn't done the collection any harm.

Talie instantly guessed it to be a personal diary. A stranger's, yes, but someone whose blood had flowed in her father and now flowed in her. She read the first page.

To my son Kipp and his wife, and to their children and children's children in America,

I can think of no better way for you to know me than to share with you my journal from the time in my life that revealed

God's plans for me—plans far different from my own.
This is my legacy to you.

I assure you each word is true. If you inherit anything
from me, may it be the knowledge that love is stronger than
fear, especially with faith in the One who is love: Jesus
Christ the same yesterday, and to day, and for ever."

—Cosima Escott Hamilton, 1874

Talie pulled out the Bible and turned to the records pages. *Cosima Escott, born in Ireland in the year of our Lord 1830, to Mary and Charles Escott. Married 1850 to Peter Hamilton.*

Born in Ireland? Talie's father had told her their heritage was English, not Irish. And the names Escott and Hamilton certainly didn't sound Irish. Pressing her finger along the records page, Talie found the year of Cosima's death: 1901. Though she'd died more than a hundred years ago, she'd lived to a ripe old age. Good for her; her years had outnumbered Dad's by almost a half dozen. Not bad for those times.

Strange that Cosima had chosen to write "love is stronger than fear" as her legacy.

Talie slid her finger down the death column again. There it was: May 16, 1848. . . .

Maybe Cosima's pages held the answer.

2

Ireland, 1849

Today we had an unexpected visitor, who came bearing even more unexpected news. I fear my life is about to change forever.

The day began like any other. I helped Mama straighten the bedchambers after breakfast then attended to other duties that countless servants used to do. Polishing brass kept us busy most of the morning: locks and knobs, candleholders and lamps, bedposts and curtain rods. Brass is everywhere when the time comes to clean it! To be honest, I am glad we have closed off the older wing, although it is a bit odd to have rooms of one's home dark, cold, and filled with shrouded furniture. But as we can afford the help of only four servants, confining ourselves to the new wing proves most agreeable.

Once my chores for the day were completed, I was able to rest beneath the old oak tree for a time. At first, Royboy was with me. How lovely to have him calm and quiet for a few moments. . . .

Cosima Escott idly fiddled with the amulet she wore round her neck as she watched her brother Roy playing beneath the shade of a primordial oak. They called him Royboy because he was still such a little boy of mind and showed scant hope of that changing. He lay on the ground, alternately rubbing his nose in the early spring grass and pulling bark from the tree while chattering away. Twice now she'd had to remove wood chunks from his mouth, and she anticipated having to do so again before long. All the while he jabbered, repeating words he'd heard Cosima say or recounting what he had done that morning.

On most days Cosima was barely aware of her brother's limitations. He was simply Royboy, the same as he'd always been. But today, with pages ripped and askew from her stack of favorite poems, Cosima had been reminded of her brother's penchant for mischief.

She pulled at the long gold chain hanging from her neck. Mama said the amulet Cosima wore as a necklace was too old, too large, and too plain, despite the fact that it was a Kennesey heirloom from Mama's side of the family. But Cosima rarely went anywhere without it. She squeezed the metal-edged cross dangling from the chain into her palm. No matter how hard she pressed, it left no mark upon her youthful skin. How sweet it would be to have a constant reminder, the image of the cross as close and ever present as her own hand. Then, if the family relic that meant so much to her was lost or forbidden to wear outside of home, she would have nothing more to do than glance down at her palm to remember. Remember not only the strength behind what the cross symbolized for any Christian but also that the blood flowing in her veins was that of a Kennesey. And she could survive—all and whatever.

Sometimes it was good to remember her heritage of strength. She eyed her brother again. Physically, Royboy had long ago outgrown his childlike state. At thirteen he was tall and gangly, still blond even though Cosima herself had lost her own golden flecks. It was as if Royboy's hair knew he was still a child. The curls could belong to someone the age of Royboy's mind instead of a youth only six years younger than Cosima.

And yet as Royboy tried to catch the dandelion seeds she blew into the air, it was impossible not to return his ever-present smile.

"Apple, Cosima," Roboy said.

Cosima nodded. It was time to eat.

Standing, she held Royboy's hand in her free one because she knew he would wander, hunger potentially forgotten at any moment. They walked toward the manor house, passing the gardener on their way, whose arms were laden with garden tools and a burlap bag of weeds to be carried off and burned.

"Royboy, say, 'How do you do,'" Cosima instructed as she so often did when they encountered someone.

Royboy issued a high-pitched exclamation, flapping his free hand in the air. Sometimes he belatedly repeated the phrase she hoped to teach him, but never once had he done so with anyone but herself nearby.

Cosima led the way toward the new wing, where the rooms stayed warmer with a minimum of fuel. For what should they reopen such a grand and sprawling estate? No one ever came to visit, and it wasn't because afflicted potato fields brought hard times. No. Others feared their curse was contagious.

Just as that thought crossed Cosima's mind, a carriage caught her attention. The road leading to the manor was narrow and remote, winding like a stream parting the trees. Anyone traveling the several-mile lane could easily be spotted from the front door.

Cosima rushed to the back of the manor house, where a stairwell led down to the kitchen.

Royboy followed with his slower, clumsy gait. "I want apples, Cosima. Get apples."

"We must find Mama first, Royboy," she said.

"No. Not Mama. Apples."

"But there are visitors coming, Royboy, and we must tell her."

"Apples, Cosima." Royboy pulled her toward the cupboards.

Too excited to be annoyed with her brother's typical behavior, she acquiesced. "Just bread, then, Royboy." She went to the loaf hidden beneath a towel in a basket and cut a chunk quickly, nearly slicing into her palm. The carriage had looked fine indeed, black and glistening with some sort of emblem on the door. Whoever could it be?

"Come along," she said to Royboy, luring him with a piece she tore from the corner of the bread. If she gave him the whole wedge he would stuff it all into his mouth.

He took the crust and immediately held out his hand for more. Cosima waited until he chewed and swallowed before offering another bite, then another, all the way up the stairs. By the time they reached the top, the bread was already gone.

"Drink, Cosima. I want a drink."

"All right, Royboy, only you'll have to wait until I find Mama."

"I don't want Mama. I want a drink."

"Yes, come along first, though."

Cosima found her mother in what served as their family parlor. It had once been a sewing room, and they still carried on such activity there, perhaps more so nowadays, when they wore their clothing longer. Gone was the time of sewing simply for enjoyment, designing wall hangings or table linens.

Her mother was not sewing today but at the writing table. She often volunteered her considerable talents to the church, who preferred her artful script over the local printers'.

"Mama, there is a carriage coming up the lane. Are you expecting company?"

Her mother dropped her brush and feather pen and rushed to the window. Cosima followed, keeping an unwilling Royboy nearby.

"Oh, and 'tis a fact your father is away," Mama said, as if it were a catastrophe. She turned to Cosima. "Heav'n help us; we'll have to greet whoever it is on our own."

"Shall I see if I can find Melvin? He might be of help."

"Aye! That's the way, Cosima. Only tell him to put on his jacket and be slow about showin' the guest in. I mustn't let anyone see me without freshenin' first." Mama hurried toward the door, stopping at the pier glass with beveled edges hanging on the wall between two windows. She must have seen the same reflection Cosima did: Slim and pretty, Mary Escott hardly looked like a middle-aged woman. With honey-colored hair piled loosely atop her head, large hazel eyes, a full mouth, and defined cheekbones, she was as lovely as ever.

Cosima and her mother were similar in size but different in face and coloring, Cosima being a replica of her father with his dark hair and eyes. Her face was softer at the edges, her eyes a trifle larger, lips a bit fuller. She and her father were, Cosima's mother often said, perfect examples of the same face in dramatically male and female order.

Mama frowned. "I look a fright. I should stay hidden altogether and have you greet them, Cosima. Even with your hair blown by the wind, 'tis young and pretty you are."

"Melvin will bide the time, Mama, while you right yourself. I'll find him immediately."

Cosima hastened off, tugging on Royboy, who now seemed willing to follow, perhaps guessing they were on their way back to the kitchen.

"And take Royboy to Decla at the washhouse," Mama called after them.

Royboy seemed happy to be left with Decla, who quickly gave him a drink. Cosima had little trouble finding Melvin, the man who served as butler, footman, coachman, and veterinarian. His favorite mare was due to deliver a foal any day, and Melvin was never far from the stable.

He followed Cosima hastily back to the main house. Unfortunately, despite the addition of his formal jacket, Melvin smelled faintly of hay and manure.

"Show the guest to the upstairs drawing room," Cosima said. "That's at least clean and not covered like the downstairs parlor."

"Very well, Miss Cosima." Already he was buttoning his jacket over his hard midsection. Melvin was near Cosima's father's age. The two were different from one another in manner and yet strikingly similar in build. Their stomachs protruded as if they were halfway through a pregnancy, only without a trace of softness a woman might possess.

"And wipe your shoes with a rag in the kitchen," she called.

Cosima herself hurried upstairs to see about the progress her mother was making with her attire. There wasn't time for either to change, but the old gown her mother was wearing showed the quality of fine linen edged with lace—even if the tattered lace did show too many holes upon closer inspection. Her skin now gleamed as if she'd had a good night's rest instead of having only splashed a bit of rose water upon her face and a drop of marigold oil to banish the redness from eyes too long at her calligraphy.

Cosima looked down at herself. Her gown, too, was old and nearly threadbare at the hem. She had other gowns, as had her mother, but those were yet to be brought out this year. She doubted any occasion would present itself to have new gowns made. The ones they owned probably smelled of spices and orrisroot after being stored through the quiet winter, but that was far more pleasant than finding that moths had feasted on the items.

The gown Cosima wore had been her mother's and probably very attractive when new. It was now fatally out of fashion, with balloon sleeves falling from the shoulders and an all-too-narrow skirt, weighted at the bottom with a row of fraying flounces. But it was still a beautiful shade of pink, casting Cosima's dark eyes and hair in striking contrast.

Mama smiled at Cosima's approach. To Cosima's surprise, her mother did not rush off to greet their visitor. Instead she pressed Cosima's hand into her own. "Cursed, so they say, you and I. But lovely still."

Coldness touched Cosima's heart at the pride her mother still possessed, even with that word forever attached to their names. Cursed, indeed.

Cosima looped her mother's arm through hers and led her from the room.

The wide, carpeted hallway led to the opposite side of the manor. Here the manor looked as it always had, opulent with her father's family history that few could easily discount. Images of Escotts lined the walls—English soldiers and politicians, all scholars no matter their chosen vocation. They lived just across the Irish Sea, but to Cosima, who knew little more than what the portraits could tell, they were distant strangers.

Though Cosima herself spoke like an Englishwoman due to her father's careful counsel and the English tutors and governesses he had employed from her youngest age, the English blood that ran through her veins was as foreign to her as her own speech must sound to the villagers around her.

Melvin must have pressed Cook or Briana, the scullery maid, into service, for tea was set on a small, round table before the matching settees in the center of the drawing room. The room was comfortable rather than ostentatious. Padded furniture, old drapery, worn carpets—all had the flowery theme her mother's mother had so loved. But the room needed to be updated if they were to open it to anyone beyond their own family.

Cosima and her mother were not long in the drawing room before Melvin arrived at the door and announced their guest.

"Osborn Linton, milady, employed in the household of Sir Reginald Hale, of London, England."

Their visitor was a tall and slender man with graying hair and a thin mustache over narrow lips. Melvin had removed the man's topcoat to reveal a well-made cutaway jacket and a plain waistcoat and shirt beneath, topped by a small white cravat tied at the throat. His trousers were dove colored, strapped beneath the feet and neatly tucked into black leather shoes, which were slightly pointed at the toe. For a workingman, obviously at least a valet, he was dressed to the height of English fashion.

From the corner of her eye, Cosima watched her mother smile as though she were a great lady whose portrait should next appear in the hallowed halls through which they'd just passed. At that moment it hardly mattered that she was instead the granddaughter of a wealthy Irish landlord, only married to an Englishman, and he, though of impeccable pedigree, was on his way to impoverishment if things in Ireland did not soon change. Nor did it seem to matter that this visitor was a servant instead of a man of means.

"Thank you for seeing me, Mrs. Escott," Mr. Linton said with a bow. "If I might be so bold as to ask, does the name Hale sound at all familiar, madam?"

"Hale?" Mama repeated, as if pondering the name. At last she shook her head. "Forgive me, but no. Perhaps my husband would be better suited to give an answer, as he has relatives in England."

"Yes, yes. Of course he would know a name so prominent in London business."

Cosima said nothing, yet wondered why this man would make such an assumption. Even if her father still had connections to England—and to her knowledge he did not—the business class rarely mixed with that of aristocracy. And the portraits of the Escott family were decidedly aristocratic.

"Won't you sit?" Mama asked, gesturing toward one of the Queen Anne chairs behind them.

As soon as Mama and Cosima were settled opposite him on the tapestry settee, the man swept aside the back of his cutaway, taking a seat. Cosima noticed his gaze lingering on her rather than on her mother, and for a moment she felt the tingle of chilled skin spread from head to toe. While the look was far from a leer, it was still an obvious assessment, leaving Cosima with the urge to hide.

"Your manservant informed me that Mr. Escott is away, attending to important matters. It might be best if I were to wait, but I find myself eager to impart the reason for my visit."

"I would be pleased if you did so, Mr. Linton," said Mama.

"My employer, Sir Reginald Hale, sends greetings and an inquiry regarding the subject of—" his gaze, which had left Cosima only a moment, now returned to her—"marriage to Miss Cosima Escott."

Cosima saw her mother's shock as profoundly as she felt it herself. While Cosima held back her breath, barely able to exhale, her mother's gasp filled the silence. Cosima refused to look at either her or their guest, feeling both their gazes heavy upon her.

"Your employer has offered for my daughter's hand in marriage without even having met her?" Excitement tinged each word of her mother's question.

"That is correct, Mrs. Escott. I have here in my purse a letter of introduction, so that you may know my employer. May I leave such documents for your perusal?"

"Of course."

Mr. Linton stood, his tea left untouched. "I will be staying in the village, Mrs. Escott, at the Quail's Stop Inn. Please send word to me there if you would be open to a visit from Sir Reginald."

He started to leave and Mama stood, pulling Cosima along. Mama all but hounded the man's heels toward the door, despite Cosima's effort to pull her back.

"My husband is not due until week's end," her mother said. "Of course, I cannot send word without—"

Mr. Linton paused. Cosima thought she saw a look of satisfaction on his face, as if her mother's obvious eagerness had been duly noted and welcomed.

"I shall remain at the inn until I hear from you, madam." He placed his top hat upon his head, accepting his overcoat from Melvin but only draping it on his forearm. "However long that shall be, madam. My employer is a very patient man. He will await my word."

Cosima watched him depart. He took the cool marble stairs as if he'd used them many times before, an unmistakable bounce in his step.

Mama grabbed Cosima's hand and squeezed, bringing it up to kiss her daughter's knuckles. "A proposal of marriage! From a knighted gentleman! Oh, Cosima, perhaps there will be a future after all."

Cosima's mind wasn't on her mother's words or the future. Her gaze took hold of Mr. Linton again, through the multipaned glass that afforded an outside view. Mr. Linton reentered the carriage. It was emblazoned, she could see now, with a gold *H* on its side. A family carriage all the way from England? Why send it along with Mr. Linton, a servant?

Mother and daughter watched through the window as the carriage disappeared into the trees down the lane. Either its owner was a foolhardy spendthrift, paying for transport of his crested carriage just to give his favorite valet an assuredly comfortable ride, or Sir Reginald had little doubt his proposal would be accepted. He must expect to take ownership, through Cosima, of Escott Manor at any time. The pompous cad had already begun moving his belongings across the Irish Sea.

Surely the man knew nothing of Cosima or he never would have sent his servant with such an outlandish proposal. She wanted to say as much to her mother, but Mama looked so pleased Cosima had no heart to spoil her smile.

Mama pressed Cosima's hand close, her eyes dancing merrily as they hadn't done in months. Then she let go and seemed to float down the hall, perhaps back to her work.

Cosima went to her bedroom, longing for the familiarity and solace it provided. She would find her journal.

That Mama hoped for a *future* came as no surprise to Cosima. Trouble was, her vision of the future and Cosima's were vastly different.

This wasn't the first time someone had inquired about Cosima's hand. After all, she was set to inherit the Escott property, and the income it generated was tempting. Times would improve again; the potatoes wouldn't always grow sour. . . . God would heal the land of whatever disease it currently suffered. And if not, her father sought to improve conditions through raising sheep rather than crops, and that certainly would end their hard times.

But one thing was certain: even a prosperous inheritance wouldn't outshine the shadow of a curse.

All County Wicklow knew about the curse. Two years before, the son of a landholder from County Cork had traveled through their isolated glen, and learning of the unmarried daughter who would receive an inheritance, he'd come to inquire about Cosima's hand.

But a single night had been enough to warn the young man away. He'd left before the sun rose.

It might have amused Cosima to think fear of a curse was enough to overcome greed. But because that so-called curse was upon her, she found no humor in it at all.

Perhaps, if the lad had come this spring instead, he might have stayed longer. But two years ago her uncle had been alive, whom everyone called Willie rather than William because he'd always been like a young boy. Simple.

And Percy had still been with them too. Percy was the first-born of Cosima's family, her older brother. Although Cosima hadn't come along until a couple of years after Percy, she'd guessed the questions that had filled her parents' minds during the time leading up to Percy's arrival.

Would he be like her Aunt Rowena's boy, enfeebled? Or like his uncle, unquiet of mind? Willie was loud and coarse, his language little more than the mimic of those around him. Until his sudden death at the age of forty-five, he'd been like a child—comprehending little, curious but dangerously so when it came to things like fire or fragile glassware. He seemed to crave packing his mouth with food until he gagged. It was often hard to sit at the table with Willie.

Cosima was told her brother Percy had appeared to be free of the curse for the first few years of his life. Though a pliant baby who learned to walk a little late, he slowly acquired language that went beyond that of his uncle Willie.

No, Percy was not like Willie. Nor, though, was he like other boys from other families. Cosima learned that her mother had tried to deny it for years, even through her pregnancy with Cosima herself, anticipating the birth of another child to celebrate. But somewhere during the course of the years, everyone around her, even Cosima's father, had been forced to change Mama's mind. Percy might not be as slow-witted as Willie, but he was slow nonetheless.

Decla, the servant closest to Mama, told Cosima that Mama had forbidden her husband his marital rights for years after that for fear of having any more children. But then, for reasons even Decla never knew or would not share with Cosima, Mary Escott had become pregnant again. This pregnancy was far different from Mama's delusional years when children brought her only happiness and hope. No, the months while they waited for Roy were laden with worry, murmurs of the curse rumbling through-out the town among landholders and tenants alike.

At last Roy was born, and any shred of hope Cosima's parents might have clung to all but evaporated upon first sight. Too soon to tell, Cosima's father had said. But Mama knew. She saw Roy's head, a little larger than those of the babies in the village, and the ears, so prominent on each side. So like Percy and Willie. Worst of all, when she tried to suckle him, she knew the truth. The roof of his mouth was just like Percy's, so high he had to work twice as hard to latch onto his mother's breast. The pain with each feeding reminded her all too clearly that Roy—soon to be called Royboy—would be like Percy . . . or worse, like Willie.

Two generations of males cursed under the Kennesey blood.

Mama and Cosima were not the only ones to feel the bane. Last year, Mama's sister Rowena had come to visit. How long it had been since the sisters had seen one another! But there was little joy in the reunion, because Rowena had brought two of her own children along, one a strapping young man and the other barely eight. Half-wits, both.

There had been other children in between—a boy and a girl both healthy and bright—who had not made the journey. Two days into the visit Cosima and her mother realized the curse had been far worse for Rowena despite her healthy children. Rowena, never strong of will, had suffered the same gossip about curses as Mama. Perhaps she felt it more keenly since her husband was less tolerant than Cosima's father. Rowena's husband had sent her and the afflicted boys from the home, keeping the healthy children but refusing to have anything to do with a woman so obviously cursed.

Rowena had little choice. It was either enter an asylum with her sons or die on the street. Instead, she came to her sister.

But Rowena had no intention of burdening anyone with herself and the only children her husband allowed her. No, she had a plan that was, in retrospect, obviously meant to help and not hurt as it inevitably did.

On a sunny spring morning nearly a year ago, much like earlier when Cosima had sat beneath the shade tree with Royboy, Rowena took her boys and Mama's, along with their brother Willie—indeed, all afflicted in the family—to the cottage that sat deep in the forest. It was an old hunting cabin built over a hundred years earlier by peasants serving the local lord, and now it belonged to Cosima's father through marriage to Mama.

There, Rowena shuttered all the windows, closed off the fireplace, locked the doors. And then, quite deliberately, in what Cosima had since guessed was her aunt's mind-set of martyr and savior, she set fire to the single-room cottage.

Somehow, though, Royboy had slipped away without Rowena's notice. One of the shuttered windows was found open, and when Royboy returned to the manor smelling of smoke, Cosima had begged him to tell her where he'd come from.

But he didn't have to say, even had he been able. Smoke rising from the forest soon revealed the source. Along with her parents and many of their servants, Cosima had raced to the gruesome discovery.

Rowena had tried to end the curse in the only way she could imagine.

Cosima rarely thought of that day without tears stinging her eyes. Aunt Rowena hadn't ended it, though. Rather, she'd enhanced it. Prior to that, those who called her family cursed had said it ran only in the males. But after that they began to suspect the women as well.

And *this* was the family Sir Reginald Hale wished to join?

3

Talie nearly dropped the journal, and a few pages slipped from the delicate spine. She scooped them back into place with trembling hands, her breath coming in short spasms.

This was her call back? She'd expected a family so enamored of education and history that despite poverty they'd managed to leave a family legacy. Rather than a noble, resilient ancestral line that survived the ravages of a famine, the truth involved a murder-suicide and half-wits somehow related to her. This wasn't the kind of call back her father would have wanted for her.

She shook her head, pushing away the journal as if the pages themselves were an offense. It couldn't be true.

Glancing down, she noticed the words on the cover sheet again. *This is my legacy to you. I assure you each word is true.*

Legacy. What kind of legacy? No wonder Dad had never pulled out this journal to share with the rest of the family. Some skeletons were better left in the closet.

Part of her wanted to run upstairs and wake Luke, share with him the awful words written by her great-great-great-grandmother's own hand. Adrenaline shot to Talie's limbs as if prepared to carry her, but instead she forced herself to be still. The energy turned hot from lack of use, tingling in her fingers and toes.

She placed the fragile journal back into the box, stuffing it down to the bottom, beneath her father's schoolwork, beneath all the family letters. The only item she hesitated to return was the Bible.

Talie stared at it. Did she really want to work on a family tree now? She knew Luke would make a masterpiece of whatever information she gave him, and the final product could be displayed with pride. Give him a project and he was like her when it came to scrapbooking. Perfectionist tendencies ran in both of them.

But to display something like this . . . including the dates of a murder-suicide for all to see?

Instead of placing it with the other things, she set the Bible aside on the kitchen table. Maybe she would get to the heritage record. Maybe.

She took the box upstairs, not to her own bedroom but to the guest room, a place she rarely visited except with an occasional dust cloth. She'd had enough family history for a while.

"So there I was, sitting at the top of the stairs crying a river because my husband was going back to work and leaving me alone with the baby." Jennifer Dunlap, Talie's neighbor, stirred the remnants of her tea and laughed. "I was sure I couldn't handle taking care of Alison *and* the laundry, the dishes, the house, dinner. . . . As you can see, I can't do it all if I want to take care of the baby right."

She directed everyone's vision to the dishes in the sink and the basket of laundry nearby. The other women joined the laughter while most, including Talie, admitted to their own work back home.

Talie and the other moms had spent the better part of the morning comparing husbands, in-laws, recipes, and the vacations they no longer took. Jennifer had suggested bringing a favorite book to exchange next week. All in all, it had been a mostly pleasant morning.

Talie glanced again at the babies on the floor in the connecting family room. Ben sat off to the side, occasionally watching the others play with the toys. He never played with toys the way they were doing. She thought he was just too young.

One of the neighbors stood, mentioning she had to leave.

Finished with her own tea, Talie stood along with Lindy. Each went to her child.

"I guess it's true girls develop faster than boys," Lindy said as she picked up her son, Mitchell. "Look, they're crawling already! My little guy only scoots wherever he wants to go."

Sure enough, the three girls on the carpet were getting along on hands and knees—racing, as if on cue, toward the same goal: a brightly colored overstuffed pillow shaped like a pony.

Jennifer came up behind them. "Alison started crawling early, but I've heard some babies go straight to walking."

Talie said nothing, keeping her eyes on Ben. If anyone noticed the uneasiness surging within her, Talie didn't want to acknowledge it. She didn't want to count how many ways Ben was different from the others but couldn't seem to stop herself. While Ben certainly compared favorably in size and had the most hair, his posture wasn't like the others'. He sat with a definite curve in his back, not strong and stiff like the others. He seemed . . . floppy somehow, as if his muscles didn't work the same way. And yet Talie knew he was strong. He could grip her finger tightly and certainly had the kick of a professional football player in the making.

"Wave bye-bye, Alison." Jennifer Dunlap held her eight-month-old in her arms.

Talie carried Ben to the front door. Her house was so close that she hadn't bothered to bring the stroller. She stepped outside to the sunny day. Glancing over her shoulder, she saw Alison's little hand waving much the same way her mother's did. Talie waved back.

She held Ben snug, his arms and head resting contentedly against her. "Lindy's right about boys and girls, I guess. But you'll catch up, won't you? Sure you will."

She turned at her driveway, glancing at Jennifer's house again. She couldn't ignore something heavy circling her heart, something that hadn't been there before playgroup. There was Mitchell in Lindy's arms, waving bye-bye much the same as Alison had.

Mitchell and Ben might both be behind in the crawling department, but at least Mitchell could wave.

Maybe Talie was doing too much for Ben. He'd never once expressed the ability or the interest in feeding himself the way the others had this morning. In the past if she offered a piece of bread or soft banana, he would put his mouth around it but not bite down. It was as if he didn't have the strength or knowledge of what to do, even with something as basic as taking a bite.

Back in her own kitchen, Talie gave Ben the yogurt snack she'd withheld in front of the others. She put the spoon in the cup and offered it to Ben in his high chair.

He looked around, barely noticing what she'd set before him.

Gently, Talie put her hand over his. He resisted her touch at first, so she took the spoon and fed him a bit, hoping to catch his interest once he realized it was his favorite flavor.

Instead of grabbing the spoon he knocked it over, spilling some of the yogurt.

Talie took up the spoon, not giving in to disappointment. "Guess you're just not ready to feed yourself, little guy."

She was tempted to get a slice of bread and see if he would bite into that but told herself she was being silly. So what if he liked his mother to feed him? Ben was still a baby, and she loved doing things for him. Besides, last week's sermon at church had been devoted to the frustration that inevitably came of comparisons. She shouldn't be comparing Ben to others anyway.

She jumped to the phone when it rang, grateful for the distraction. She didn't have to look at the caller ID. It was Luke's regular time to call.

"Hey." Luke didn't bother to identify himself.

"Hey back, boss man. How's the new job?"

"Great. I have my very own office—four walls and a door and everything. You'll have to come and see."

"Love to. How are the people?"

"My old boss is now a peer, and my new boss is hardly ever around. Couldn't be better. And everybody I used to work with is still here, just down the row of cubicles. I'll be interviewing next week to fill the two new spots." It sounded like he took a drink of something, probably coffee. He was an addict. "How was playgroup?"

"Nice. It'll be good to get to know the women around here better." Then she thought of something Luke had probably forgotten. "Remember to put tomorrow night on your calendar."

"Tomorrow night?"

"Our promotion celebration. Just the two of us."

"Oh yeah." His softened tone hinted he was sorry it had slipped his mind.

"It's all set up. Dana agreed to babysit, and she's coming at six."

After Talie hung up the phone she finished feeding Ben, doing her best to ignore a string of unpleasant thoughts. They wouldn't go away despite reminding herself she had Friday to look forward to—a real date night with Luke.

She should forget this morning by going upstairs and retrieving that box she'd put so hastily away. Really, she'd only meant to keep that awful journal out of sight, not the rest. She could dig into the letters, look at the old postcards. Or she could stay down here and work on the family tree. The Bible was right there, still on the kitchen table.

But when Ben went down for his nap a little while after lunch, it wasn't any of those things that drew her.

It was Cosima's journal.

4

It was a bit unsettling to sit in the sunroom this morning with Mama and Father. Before today, we had not used the room in nearly a year! I had forgotten what a lovely prospect it has, overlooking the back of our property. At the base of the hill, one can see the forest, and beyond that, acres and acres of rich farmland. Rich, that is, before the blight.

I began to think of our tenants, most of whom still live in their snug cottages through Father's generosity. What will become of them when the Escott funds are depleted? Money must come from somewhere. Yet my thoughts were not permitted to linger long on such topics. . . .

"I see no reason why you shouldn't welcome this visit, Cosima," said her father, Charles Escott.

"Of course she welcomes it." Her mother sipped tea, and her easy tone might have convinced Cosima that she was calm, except her teacup hit the saucer a bit too roughly, spilling some.

Cosima said nothing to accept or deny the pronouncements.

She looked around the room, at the furniture now revealed that had been covered for so many months, still colorful and inviting. The craftsmanship was fine, having been purchased with no thought to expense. Plush settees and polished, intricately carved side tables offered visitors what they wished: a place to sit in comfort and a table upon which to rest their tea.

The entire main floor had been reopened, a bit early since the last of winter's chill might still be forthcoming. But with their visitor due to arrive at any time, it had been an easy decision for her mother to make.

"Cosima," her father said with cajoling lightness, "have you decided not to speak until this decision is made, one way or another?"

Cosima tasted her own now-tepid tea, recoiling. She didn't like the flavor of her mother's favorite but had arrived at the table too late to state her preference.

"Of course not," she said at last. "I will speak, though my words make little difference, do they? The decision has been made . . . by Sir Reginald Hale."

Her father leaned forward and patted her hand. "Now there, child, it isn't as if we're selling you off to this man, you know. He could be a perfectly acceptable chap, one you'll grow to love. In time."

"Don't you know, darlin', if you go into marriage with the wee expectation you obviously have, it can only get better. Respect won over the years leads inevitably to love." Her mother took a bite from a biscuit and added, as if an afterthought, "Some love matches are prone to disappointment, because expectations are unreasonable. And that's the truth of it, so I've been told."

Cosima studied her mother as if she'd spoken another language. Cosima wasn't looking for love or avoiding it either. She was desperately trying to establish disinterest in the entire subject of marriage for one very good reason: she simply could not marry. Ever.

How could her mother not understand? She acted as though Cosima were drowning in the folly of her own plan, insisting on throwing her a life preserver in the form of one Reginald Hale.

Her father spoke again. "We've reviewed the man's intro-duction, Cosima. He comes from a respected English merchant family. Not aristocracy, but he's earned knighthood for benevo-lence work. It's your mother's wish, and my own, that you consider this proposal as perhaps the best that's likely to come. What with . . . well, the perceptions of people around here—"

"They call it a curse, Father." Cosima hadn't meant to sound so cold. She looked out the window, seeing Royboy laughing and stumbling after one of the dogs.

A curse. Her brother, whom she loved but sometimes resented, was the outward evidence of that curse. If she had chil-dren, it was virtually guaranteed, so said everyone who knew them, that she, too, would present a son with the mind of a permanent child. She'd seen what that had done to her father—the dashed hope, the weight of having no son fit to carry on the name or legacy. And she'd seen the way her mother had borne the guilt.

Why would either one of them expect she'd want to repeat such a cycle? And thrust it upon someone else? She had no feel-ing whatever for Sir Reginald Hale, yet even a stranger deserved to know what he was in for should he carry out his plan to marry her.

Besides, she had nearly convinced herself that God hadn't designed her for marriage. Soon, if she could trust Him a little better, she knew the last of her desire to someday wed would dwindle away as well.

"The carriage approaches, madam," said Melvin from the threshold. Gone, for the time being at least, was any trace that he'd spent much of the winter mucking out the stable. He was once again the manservant, dressed in stiff black attire, complete with spotless white gloves and shiny black shoes. Indeed, most of the servants they'd dismissed for the winter had been called back, and Cosima guessed they were delighted to be earning a wage again—however slim it would be considering the circumstances in their land. Even so, they had a roof over their head, a warm hearth at night, and more to eat at Escott Manor than they likely had at whatever alms- or workhouse they had been forced to live in the past year.

Mama was the first to her feet, and the table jiggled when her full skirt brushed the edge. One hand went to the back of her hair, which was neatly swept up into a loose bun, while with her other hand she smoothed away any wrinkles in the foulard of her gown. Their finest gowns had indeed acquired the faint smell of cinnamon, nutmeg, and orrisroot, but not a stitch had been touched by any hungry moths. A few days of airing had left the scent barely noticeable, fading altogether next to the pleasant aroma of rosewater bath both women favored.

Her parents neared the threshold before Cosima rose to her feet, and she did so only because her father glanced back and stalled, offering her his arm.

"We'll wait in the morning room," he said to Melvin.

That her father sounded like his usual unruffled self was some comfort to Cosima, but she noticed his color was slightly heightened, giving away the fact that he was every bit as eager for this proposal to prove fruitful as was her mother. Cosima followed, her hand lightly on her father's arm, but her gaze lingered behind, seeing Royboy still outside with the dogs. Perhaps it would have been better to be born like him.

The parlor was called the morning room, but Cosima had always thought of it as the blue room, for so much of it was decorated in shades of blue, from the neatly upholstered furniture and brocade curtain swags to the vases and lamps that graced the side tables.

Melvin entered just after Cosima and her parents were settled. Behind Melvin followed two figures. One she recognized as the servant, Mr. Linton. Her gaze slipped away from him, anxious to see the man who must be Sir Reginald.

He was at first glance unremarkable. No taller than Cosima herself at five foot six—tall for a woman only half Irish, but somewhat small in a man. His most attractive feature was his thick, striking blond hair. Fair skin matched the lightness of his hair, and his eyes were a vivid blue. But those eyes were small, his nose a trifle large, and he had a nearly nonexistent chin, for his face seemed to narrow straight down from forehead to neck. His lips were flat and the upper almost invisible. And yet he was somewhat pleasant, because of his hair and eyes. Surely not handsome by any measure, neither was he ugly.

If he was kind, she thought . . .

Cosima closed her mind to such wanderings. Would she so easily entertain the notion of marriage? No . . . no matter what this man hoped to achieve.

She realized her parents had already been introduced and now Sir Reginald stood before her. She offered him her hand, which he kissed after a formal bow.

"You are lovely, Miss Escott. Lovelier than I imagined."

Then her mother, in a voice that must seem obviously flustered even to a stranger's ear, offered tea. She went on to answer Mr. Linton's inquiries about Sir Reginald's belongings, as it had been prearranged that the two would stay at the manor. Mr. Linton then excused himself, following Melvin from the room.

"We've read your introduction with interest, Sir Reginald," said Father. "But nowhere could we find how you learned of our Cosima. Please, sit down and tell us."

Sir Reginald's fine, fair skin seemed to turn a bit pink.

Cosima doubted the color was from the warmth of their surroundings, though they sat in front of the fireplace. It was lit in hopes of chasing away a morning chill, but this part of the stone manor trapped cool air like the bowels of an icehouse in the middle of July.

Cosima's parents sat on the opposite settee, leaving Cosima the place beside their visitor.

Reginald addressed her father. "I am acquainted with your mother, Dowager Merit, Sir Charles. That's why I hesitated to mention the connection in my document."

Now it was her father's turn to flush. Since he had not spoken to his mother at least in Cosima's lifetime, his family was something she knew nothing about.

"I hold nothing against you for knowing my mother," he said, recovering himself quickly with a steady voice. "'Tis a sad thing that my family and I are estranged."

"They must acknowledge you in some way, Father." Cosima's reluctance to be part of the conversation was diminished by her interest in the topic. "Otherwise Sir Reginald would never have heard of us."

Her gaze, along with her parents', settled on Reginald again, this time with obvious curiosity.

Reginald looked between them, rubbed the palms of his hands on his lap, and then uttered a brief laugh that did not conceal his outward discomfort. He looked at Cosima. "You have a cousin who somehow knows all about you and your family here in Ireland, despite the fact that her own parents seem to have tried banishing all memory of this part of their family."

"She told you why, then?" Cosima wasn't sure her father would have pressed for information but knew she must.

"She supposed it was because of a general dislike for Ireland. Nothing but dissidents to be found in this land of farmers and Catholics. Oh, forgive me . . . ," he added, raising a palm to his lips as if he wished he could grab back the words and stuff them down. "I've nothing against Catholics myself, or farmers, for that matter. All this trouble between England and Ireland is none of my affair, especially since I've very little religious leanings."

"But you would be married in the church, surely," said Mama.

"Oh yes," Reginald said hastily. "I am Anglican, of course. Not a heathen at all, Mrs. Escott. Perhaps I should have said I have little *political* leanings, insofar as Catholics and Protestants are concerned. Sometimes it seems impossible to separate the two, does it not?"

"Is that all this cousin of mine said of our family? That my father was disowned for choosing to live in Ireland?"

"Well . . ." He looked around the room, as if their surroundings had something to do with the answer. "Forgive me. . . . This seems unpleasant to say the least, not at all the way I wished for you to get to know me or I to know you."

"Of course," said Mama, standing. Cosima didn't miss the glare directed her way. Nor did she miss the relief on her father's face that the subject was suddenly to be abandoned. "How remiss of us to have pressed you into a discussion better left unspoken. We shall go to the dining room for a light repast after your journey."

They were all on their feet then. Sir Reginald offered Cosima his arm, and she placed her palm so lightly on his sleevethat she hoped he felt nothing at all. He might not be comfortable telling her all she wanted to know about her father's family, but that would not stop *her* from telling him all he needed to know about her. One look into his pleasant blue eyes and she knew the sooner she spoke, the better.

Father led the way silently down the wide hall, and Cosima stared straight ahead, feeling Sir Reginald's gaze on her profile. He didn't even look around, not at the wall sconces Mama was so proud of or at the Irish landscapes her father had commissioned.

It vaguely surprised her that Sir Reginald didn't take more of an interest in the manor, if it was his hope to inherit through her. Just as well that he did not. Once he knew about her brothers, that would no doubt be the last she'd see of one Sir Reginald Hale.

Now, how to tell him without Mama's interference?

They entered the dining room, and there in the middle of the room, with a smile as cherubic as a two-year-old's, was the perfect answer to Cosima's dilemma. Royboy sat—not in a chair, but on the center of the table—contentedly scraping bread pudding out of one of Mama's favorite crystal bowls. He used no utensil, his face was covered with evidence of how he loved to fill his mouth, and his hands and shirt were lavishly smeared.

"Royboy!"

Even at his mother's surprised and angry gasp, he smiled. Even as she strode forward, taking the bowl from him, grabbing his wrist to draw him off the table, he smiled. He laughed when she called for Decla, the maid who most often had charge of Royboy.

Mama led him quickly from the room, but he grinned wide at his sister as he passed by. "Pudding."

Mama did not pause as she propelled him out. But Royboy must have noticed Reginald for the first time, and he turned, letting his mother pull him from behind so he had to walk backward.

"How do you do," he said, just the way Cosima had coached him so many times. It was by rote; she knew he had no idea that the words were a greeting or that they meant anything at all. But at the moment Cosima was inordinately proud of him. He'd used the phrase appropriately for the first time in his life.

Once Royboy was beyond sight, led down the corridor toward the kitchen stairway, Cosima looked at Reginald. What better way could there have been for him to meet her brother? to see what kind of sons she would bear him?

Reginald stood stiffly at her side, his face a mask. Well, he was polite; she would give him that. Even her father's face showed a bit of horror, and he was used to Royboy's wrongdoings. Father looked too embarrassed to speak.

No such emotion hampered Cosima. She smiled as if what had just taken place were perfectly normal. "That was my brother, Roy Escott. Did my cousin tell you about him, I wonder?"

As she spoke she stepped forward, and with her hand now firmer on his arm, Sir Reginald had little choice but to follow. They approached the table, where evidence of Royboy's misbehavior became clearer. He'd not only eaten the pudding but made a sizeable dent in the scalloped oysters, tipped over a water pitcher, and left large, colorful fingerprints on many of the plates and goblets.

"Cosima," said her father, who hadn't moved from the threshold, "let us go to the sunroom, and we'll be served something else in there."

"You know," said Reginald, reaching for one of the clean plates on the far side of the mess, "there are plenty of these oysters left, and they look rather delicious."

Cosima watched, shocked beyond belief, as Sir Reginald served himself not only oysters but a bit of salad and two frosted biscuits as well. When he looked at Cosima, he appeared perplexed as to why she wasn't joining him.

And so she did.

"Well then," said Father, as Cosima and Sir Reginald took seats farther down the table, where the contents of the spilled pitcher had not reached. He still did not move from the threshold. "I'll fetch your mother, Cosima, and have this cleaned up while we eat."

Alone with this prospective bridegroom, Cosima eyed Sir Reginald from the seat she'd taken across from him. Now she could watch him with as much interest as he seemed to be watching her.

"Royboy is my brother," she said, serving herself salad. "He's very much like my uncle, whom we called Willie. His name was William, of course, but he was so like a boy all his life that we could never call him anything other than Willie. Quite like Royboy being christened Roy, but we call him Royboy. I'm sure my father's mother—Dowager Merit, did you say her name is?—must know of them. If she isn't aware of Royboy himself, certainly she knew of my uncle Willie. He was, after all, quite grown up at the time my parents wed. I even heard that Willie made a bit of a scene at the wedding when he started to disrobe after someone slipped a pea down the back of his shirt."

If Reginald had heard of Willie, he gave no indication. He ate the oysters, looking at Cosima as if she were discussing nothing nearly as devastating as the state of the male offspring in her family.

"I also had another brother," she went on, still eyeing him, looking for some sign he'd heard this before. "His name was Percy. Now Percy was different from Royboy and Willie. Not nearly as handsome. But he could speak very well and even read somewhat. No one would suspect he was even different until at least a few minutes into any given conversation, when he would begin to talk about something entirely unrelated or ask inappropriate questions."

Reginald kept eating. Had he even heard her? Was he not distressed, dismayed, even a little afraid? That was how everyone else greeted this truth.

At last Cosima set aside her fork, glancing at the threshold because she knew she didn't have much time before both of her parents would rejoin them. No doubt they would put an end to what she must do. But she must speak so that life could go on as it always had. Without change, without surprise. Without the possibility of prolonging the curse. Therefore, without marriage for her.

"Sir Reginald—" she put away any pretense of congeniality in her voice—"this cousin of mine has done you a great disservice. She obviously had only a small portion of the facts when she told you of my supposed availability and the land I am due to inherit."

He frowned. "You are not going to inherit this lovely manor?" He looked around, then shrugged. "A shame, I suppose, but no matter."

"No, I *am* going to inherit, and most assuredly I will live here until the day I die. But upon my parents' death, the very day I inherit, this manor and all its property shall be made into a school for the feebleminded. Whatever funds are garnered from the farmlands will go to support the staff and students, so that it may be self-supporting and remain so indefinitely, for as long as there are feebleminded souls needing a place to live and to learn as best they can."

Reginald took another bite of the meal, nodding. "A noble plan indeed, Cosima. I can see you are as kindhearted as you are beautiful."

His compliment sailed past without acknowledgment. "But do you not see the inspiration for such a plan?"

He looked at her, silently waiting for her to express her unsolicited information.

"Royboy is the reason," she told him quietly. "And Percy. And Willie. And my two cousins on my mother's side of the family, for they, too, were afflicted. And another set of cousins from my grandmother's younger sister. Do you see what I'm saying, Sir Reginald? Must I tell you more plainly?"

"Tell me what?"

She held his gaze, and at last he stopped eating. "The Kennesey women are afflicted, Sir Reginald. We *may* produce healthy children, but too often we have slow-witted children instead. It is virtually guaranteed that I, like my mother, like my aunt, and like their mother before them, would produce lack-wits, especially should I have any sons."

Sir Reginald produced one surprise after another. He smiled kindly, reached across the table, and took one of her hands, pressing it gently into his. His hands were soft, his fingers long and narrow. This was, she realized, the first time anyone other than her father or brother had ever touched her in such a way. She looked down at his slender fingers and smooth nails as he stroked the top of her hand.

"Cosima," he said quietly, "if you are telling me about this supposed curse Mr. Linton learned of while staying in the village, then I must assure you immediately I believe in no such thing. You are young. You are healthy, yes?"

She nodded but quickly added, "Healthy, yes, but as sure as red hair begets red, I shall bear half-wits."

He laughed. "Nonsense, Cosima! You can prove no such thing just because . . . well, because there have been a couple of unfortunate births. If it is in the blood, as you say—and I highly doubt such a thing—how do you know it wasn't from something on the father's side? the families into which your mother and aunt have wed?"

She raised a curious brow. "*Are* there any afflicted with such a thing on my father's side of the family?"

"Well . . . no, not that I know of. But," he added, hastily holding up a hand to still her protest, "there are any number of people on the street who act very much like Royboy. It's an eccentricity. He can speak, can't he? And he isn't still wetting? Well, there you have it. I'm sure there are many people out there just like Royboy. Probably there was nothing at all wrong with your brother Percy; you just wanted to label him to mollify others and their cruel gossip."

Sir Reginald patted her hand and continued. "I'd say you listen too much to what others say, Cosima. Most of those who name-call can't even read or write. Who's to say they aren't half-wits themselves? Never put society to the test of intelligence. Most would not pass."

Cosima shook her head, knowing his words *sounded* reasonable, though perhaps a bit pompous. He did not convince her. "But my mother, her sister, my grandmother, all—"

"Now, now, then," he interrupted, "I should think the best thing for you to do would be to come to England, which I was about to propose anyway, only you've given me the perfect opportunity to do so now. Marriage is a lifelong commitment and shouldn't be rushed into, though I see no reason why we couldn't get to know one another after we exchange our vows. To give you time to think about it, my plan is to bring you home with me, to let you see where you'll be living, to give you a chance to adjust to me before the wedding ceremony."

"But you don't know it all—," she began, about to bring up the events of last spring, events that had the villagers and other landholders all speculating as to the madness that might afflict the females of her lineage.

But her mother and father were suddenly in the room, obviously having heard at least part of their conversation.

"'Tis a sensible idea for you to take Cosima to England, Sir Reginald," said Mama, with a smile so sweet that the incident with Royboy might never have happened. Royboy was nowhere to be seen. "And how generous of you to offer. Of course Cosima will accompany you. Darlin'," she continued, coming up behind Cosima and leaning down to put an arm about her shoulders, "I've no doubt Sir Reginald will make a lovely time of it. Millicent O'Banyon can accompany you as chaperone."

Cosima did not respond, did not even look at her mother, knowing all she would see was the sparkle of joy over the plans and preparations. No, she thought to herself, this would not be so easily settled. Sir Reginald Hale might discount the curse everyone else fixated upon, but there had to be a reason.

And she meant to find out why.

5

On Saturday morning Talie cheerfully greeted her sister with
a plate of steaming hotcakes while the smell of coffee wafted
among her stainless-steel appliances. Early morning sun filtered
through the red-and-white-checked curtains hanging above
the open window as Ben made his favorite noises—something
between a gurgle and a laugh—from his high chair in the corner.
He always woke up happy, just like Talie herself.

She'd already set out melon and juice, toast and jam, most of
which had been consumed by Luke, who was just pushing himself
away from the table. Dana poured syrup over her plate even as
she yawned.

"Didn't you sleep well?" Talie asked, surprised by the faint
circles beneath her sister's eyes. Dana was a morning person too,
or at least she used to be. "You look tired. Did the neighbor's new
dog keep you up? His barking is probably loudest right below our
guest-room window."

Dana shook her head and offered a belated smile. "No, it was
fine. I'm just slow today." She looked down at the steaming plate
of food. "Mom hasn't greeted me with a breakfast like this since
Dad died. Think she was trying to tell me something . . . like
maybe I should've looked for my own place a long time ago?"

Talie took a seat across from her. "No, it's been good for her
to have you around since Dad died. But I think you're both ready

43

for the changes ahead." For economy, Dana had lived at home
through college and graduate work, and when their father had
been diagnosed with cancer she had stayed on to help with all the
doctor visits and treatments—something everyone, even Talie,
was grateful she'd chosen to do.

But now Dana was a teacher in one of the North Shore
school districts with a future as limitless as Talie's had been. Talie
intended to be Dana's biggest cheerleader—whether she continued on in her career or decided to get married and stay home as
Talie had done.

She watched her sister twiddle with the food on her plate.
Marriage didn't seem on the horizon, at least not in the near
future. And yet there was something about the obvious lack of
sleep and now a decided lack of appetite that piqued Talie's interest. Dana always had the best appetite in the family, in spite of
her perpetually flat stomach.

"How was that wedding last week? Meet anybody . . . special?"

Dana's gaze shot from her plate to Talie's watchful eyes. Oh
yes, that look said something was definitely up. Talie always enjoyed
teasing her sister when there was someone new in the picture.

And yet Dana shook her head, taking a huge bite of one of
the pancakes as if to prove Talie wrong without even a word
exchanged.

Talie glanced at Luke. Maybe Dana didn't want to talk in
front of him. "Honey, why don't you take Ben up and get him
dressed? Maybe even a bath, if your grass-cutting adventure can
wait a little this morning—for the neighbors' sake, of course.
Don't want to wake anybody up with that mower."

Luke nodded, but instead of leaving, he sipped his coffee—
a cup she had just refilled. Silly her.

"I guess I should've asked last night," Dana said, "but what did
you say you were celebrating?"

"Luke's promotion!" Talie said.

"Oh, that's right." Dana looked at Luke, who was standing now to take Ben from his high chair. "How is the new job?"

"Great. My first challenge is finding a couple of new employees. A hydroengineer and an architect."

"An architect?"

Talie eyed her sister again. She had perked up and repeated the word as if it were the exact one she'd been waiting to hear.

"That's right."

"Do you know one?" Talie asked.

Dana said nothing, hiding her face by taking a drink from her large glass of orange juice. "So, how was the big date?" she asked. Her tone was polite, normal.

Talie looked at Luke, temporarily setting aside thoughts of architects and Dana's questionable reaction to everything this morning. "We had a great time. Fabulous food, wonderful company—the works."

"Yeah," Luke winked at her before plopping Ben in his lap. "Talie is still a pretty hot date, Dana." Though the words were for Dana, he'd said them in a singsong tone that made Ben laugh.

"Yuck, get *that* thought out of my mind." Dana laughed despite her protest. "I looked through the box in the guest room, Talie—the one you brought from the attic at home. The letters make it sound like Dad's family was a lot closer than you'd guess from the little contact we've had with our East Coast relatives."

Talie's heart dropped to her toes. She'd taken the journal out but put it back after reading only a little further. "That *box* . . ." She didn't have to see the surprised look on both Luke's and Dana's faces to know her tone had sounded suddenly and surprisingly stern. She tried smiling to erase it from their minds. Obviously Dana hadn't found the journal or she would have said something. Who wouldn't react to a murder-suicide in the family, no matter how long ago it happened? "It's just . . . I feel guilty about stuffing it away like Dad did, but what difference does it all make, anyway?

You said yourself we don't have any contact with Dad's relatives. Why get to know them through ancient letters? Everybody who wrote them is dead. Dad, his mom, his brother . . ."

Dana's brows drew together in either disapproval or confusion—Talie couldn't tell which. "I thought you said you wanted to know our family history. History is full of dead people, only these are people we're related to. I expected you to scrounge up some old photographs from Mom and make a sort of historical scrapbook or something."

Talie was shaking her head before Dana had even finished her sentence, refusing to listen. "Stop, will you? Forget it."

"Did you see the family Bible?" Luke asked Dana.

A surge of anger stiffened Talie's spine when they refused to drop the subject.

"No, is there one?" Dana directed the question to Talie.

"It's around somewhere," Talie said without looking at either her sister or her husband. She felt Luke's eyes on her. Concerned about her testy mood, no doubt.

"I saw it in our study," he told Dana while still looking at Talie. "I thought you were going to make a rough draft of your family tree so I can make a bigger one on architectural paper."

Talie kept her eyes on her coffee, swirling the cream into the center and lightening it from dark to light chocolate brown.

"That doesn't sound like someone disinterested in the past," Dana commented.

"Have you changed your mind about the family tree?" Luke asked.

Talie looked at her husband's baffled face, her sister's interested one. How could she tell them? Just blurt out the dismal history that belonged to her family? Of course that's what she should do; it was a hundred and fifty years ago. Surely Luke would think it had nothing to do with her family now. And Dana had a right to know.

But even as she told herself to share what she'd learned, she wondered if her father had known. Had he purposely hidden the journal away because he didn't think it was necessary for such a legacy of knowledge to be passed on? If he'd thought that, maybe that was what Talie should do too.

So she shrugged again and stirred her coffee some more. "I'll get to the family tree one of these days."

Maybe Cosima's story wasn't true anyway. There might be a way to find out about all those deaths on the same day if she saw actual Irish records or death certificates from 1848. Though how she would go about doing that, Talie had no idea.

True or not, maybe she should get rid of the journal. That past was better off forgotten. She wished her father had gotten rid of it instead of stashing it away.

"You know, I took some stuff from the attic too," Dana said. "I found a few things I'm going to hang on my wall. A basket lid with a bunch of old buttons sewn on, a clock that I think I can have fixed, and some other things I might put in a shadow box. Mom said it was all from Dad's side of the family too."

"That's nice." Talie took her dishes to the sink, determined to leave the topic behind. That and her irritable mood. She turned on the water. "Remember I asked about you joining our church, Dana? Our midweek service bulletin had a note about a singles event tonight. Maybe you should go."

"That's a good idea," said Luke, shifting the baby to a spot on his shoulders. Ben slumped forward over Luke's head but was always happy up there. Luke stood, finally finished with his coffee.

"Talie wasn't very specific about the group," Dana said without much apparent interest. "Let me guess—I suppose there are nine women and two men?"

"Actually we've heard it's a popular group," Luke said. "People from all different churches in the area attend their social events."

"I might try it out," Dana said, but her tone couldn't convince Talie that her sister was serious.

A few moments later, Luke finally walked from the kitchen to bathe and dress Ben.

Talie left the sink. She reclaimed her seat at the table across from Dana, who had barely finished half of her plateful of food. "Okay, spill it."

Dana raised what looked like convincingly innocent, confused eyes. "Spill what? You want me to mess up your kitchen?"

"No, you know what I mean. Look at that plate."

Dana did. "So?"

"Where's your appetite? You're only a picky eater when you meet somebody. So tell me, is he an architect or what?"

But Dana was shaking her head again. "No, no, no, Talie. I—"

Talie put up a palm. "You can skip the denial. Your plate and puffy eyes say it all. What's his name?"

Dana let out a breath. Victory for Talie, and it wasn't even much of a battle. "Okay, it's Aidan Walker, but he's all wrong for me."

Talie's hopes rose and sunk in that single statement. "He's not a Christian?" That was the only real line they'd ever drawn when it came to dating; beyond that, things usually fell into place.

"He says he is, but he's Melody's new cousin-in-law. Her husband says Aidan only goes to church to scope out the women. And he hit on me the first chance he got."

"Hit on you? How? You wouldn't be losing your appetite if he hit on you in the classic sense. You'd have written him off right away."

Dana shook her head. "That's just it. Melody warned me he's a womanizer, and she put a virtual protection squad around me as part of the wedding plan, just to keep me out of his sights. But then when we danced and he asked me out—right on cue, I thought at the time—I told him I wasn't a casual Christian or a casual dater, and he said something I can't really get out of my mind."

"What was that?"

"Okay, but first let me tell you he *is* an architect. He was working out of the country for the last four months. He said while he was gone he grew up—in faith. That he has a clean slate and not Melody or Jeff or even me could take away what Christ gave him."

"And he sounded sincere?"

Dana nodded.

"Okay . . ."

"But he was such a charmer I don't know what to believe about him. Maybe he just said that because he knew all the right words. Just words . . . know what I mean?"

Talie stared at her sister. There was only one thing to do, and the answer was simple. "This is what you do, Danes," she said, using the same line—and the same childish nickname—she'd used since she was in fourth grade and telling Dana how to handle her first day of kindergarten. "You let Melody or her husband tell this cousin of theirs you'll be going to the singles group at my church. If he's interested in you, he'll jump on the opportunity to go too. You get to know him under the structure of the church itself, and see for yourself what kind of faith—and lifestyle—he really has. You know you have to find this out for yourself, or you'll never be able to let it go. Right?"

A light glimmered in Dana's eyes for the first time this morning, banishing whatever fatigue she'd brought with her to the table.

Satisfied, Talie stood to take up the remaining dirty dishes. It was a mystery to her why her sister wasn't married yet, except that she was probably too picky and couldn't find anyone as perfect as Luke. But maybe that was about to change. Marriage and children might be just around the bend for Danes.

Talie's smile slipped away as memories of Cosima's journal

crept to the forefront of her mind. The suitor who came to claim Cosima had taken her away from home, away from everything and everyone familiar. An unwilling courtship at best, for reasons that were all too clear from what Cosima described.

Thank goodness Dana didn't have such problems! The way Dana worried, the last thing she needed was to read the trials about matrimony Cosima faced. That would only cement the fear that finding someone to marry was more trouble than it was worth.

Talie supposed she ought to read a bit more of the journal before deciding whether or not to pitch the pages forever.

6

Against my own better judgment, I will set out with Sir
Reginald for England tomorrow. I must trust my parents'
choice and God's plans for me. I pray that the way will become
clear; at present, I must confess it is all rather muddled.

Sir Reginald has assured us that my four trunks can
be strapped to the top and back of the Hale carriage all the
way to London. The carriage itself is to be taken on the ship
with us, across the Irish Sea. The largest of my cases
contains my best gowns; another is packed with reticules,
hats, slippers, shoes, and other accessories. (I can scarcely
believe I will need all this finery, yet Mama insists that
I must be prepared for any social gathering!) Yet another
trunk holds my finest undergarments, nightclothes, shawls,
capes, and informal gowns. Mama also insists that
Millicent accompany me, and thus the fourth trunk carries
her belongings. While I cannot imagine that I will need a
lady's maid, as Millicent is to be called, it will be nice to
have a familiar face nearby.

I will also take my small tapestry bag for those items that I cannot let from my sight. One, of course, is this journal. I have also placed in my bag the relic Grandma Josephine bequeathed to me: the iron-edged cross. I cannot leave that behind.

Only one item in my bag has more than sentimental value, and I would far rather leave it here, safe at home. But Mama was emphatic about my taking her emerald necklace—a single emerald set in gold, hanging from a braided chain. It is worth far more than any other bauble I own or ever expect to own. I can only assume that Mama wants her daughter to show that someone of Irish lineage— lo, even a descendant of Catholics—is not so backward and poor as those in England must imagine.

I have agreed to take the emerald—but I have not promised to wear it. . . .

The interior of the Hale carriage was upholstered in warm gold velvet, with matching curtains pulled aside from each window. Lap blankets and a carved wooden stool were stored beneath one seat, along with a pillow to cushion the ride more than the deeply padded seats and backrests already provided.

Cosima watched the trees on Escott land disappear, making way for rolling green hills. Escott land, so titled now, although before her mother had married Charles Escott, it had been Kennesey land. Grandma Josephine Kennesey had many children, but only three survived childhood. Several died in infancy, another at age seven when a simple cut on her foot became infected and led to a fatal fever. Josephine's oldest boy, a brilliant and promising heir, was killed in a riding accident at age fifteen. That left only the three: Cosima's mother, Mary; her younger sister, Rowena; and her brother Willie.

By English law, Irish inheritances were to be evenly split among the offspring—an old law meant to divide and conquer. But the Kennesey family, like many, resisted in any way they could. It was easy to prove Willie unfit to inherit, and once Rowena wed she signed a certificate to hand over her claim to Mary so the land would not be partitioned. A small protest, but one that made the family happy.

And so Mary had become the sole heir. Then through Mama's marriage to a Protestant Englishman, the land left the hands of Irish Catholics and passed to the English in a bloodless conquest. If there was a curse, many Irish thought it appropriate that Mama had passed it along to the English through her marriage.

The Hale carriage passed the countryside in silence for some time, and Cosima found her gaze on the man seated across from her. In the four days of Reginald's visit to Escott Manor, he'd proven to be witty and well mannered, which pleased Cosima's mother. He also engaged Cosima's father and, not as obviously, Cosima herself with his keen knowledge regarding the plight afflicting Irish farming, politics, and society.

Despite the fact that he'd made clear his intention to marry Cosima, he'd spent remarkably little energy getting to know her beyond polite conversation. She had wondered if he was saving more intimate investigation of her for when they could be relatively alone—as now. Only Millie accompanied them, but a lady's maid was expected to be both blind and deaf regarding personal matters of her mistress. Certainly now was the opportunity for Cosima and Reginald to get to know one another, before vows were exchanged.

While Reginald did not seem the shy sort, Cosima wondered if he needed help or encouragement in private conversation. She was not at all reconciled to the idea of marrying Reginald, but if he continued to be as persuasive as he had been with her parents, what reason could she give, even to herself, *not* to marry him?

"You mentioned to my parents that you lost your own parents some time ago, Sir Reginald. Will there be any . . . other family . . . expecting to meet me?"

Still studying the landscape, he spoke. "I have no family." His tone was dull, flat. At last he looked at her, and his gaze seemed the same. Though especially blue in the sunlight pouring through the window, his eyes spoke one message: disinterest.

Cosima's initial desire for conversation waned. She slid a glance toward Millie, who, true to her position, kept her eyes forward.

"You are not coming to England to gain some sort of approval, Cosima," Reginald said quietly, surprising her with his tender tone. "You need only please me, and that you have done."

She looked at him again. He seemed to have returned to the man he'd been around her parents: friendly and approachable. She smiled. "I'm glad that I do, Sir Reginald. Only we hardly know one another. I fear whatever pleasure you have in me can only be of the shallowest kind. I do hope this visit to your home will be a means for us to know one another better."

"Of course," he said, congenially enough. "What is it you wish to learn?"

She had no answer for the unexpected question. Her idea for getting to know a prospective spouse must be far different from Reginald's. He seemed to believe they could exchange a list of questions and—voilà!—know each other well enough to decide whether or not they were compatible.

But, Cosima told herself, considering marriage propos-als wasn't something in which she was well versed, even in her imagination. Perhaps his view was more realistic than the silly dreams she had tried to squelch, of intimate conversa-tion pouring out of two people like water from a fountain with two spigots, mingling as one in a great pool of shared ideas and similarities.

And so she decided she would try Reginald's way. By intention rather than inspiration. "The other day, when I mentioned my plans for Escott Manor, you didn't seem at all put upon. Have you no designs of your own on the land and holdings that will one day be mine?"

"My dear Cosima," he said lightly, "do you think for a moment that I would choose to live on this side of the Irish Sea?"

Stiffening at his clear disdain for the land of her birth, she did not reply.

A moment later Reginald must have guessed her indignation. He leaned forward and gently took both of her hands in his. "Cosima, Cosima," he said softly, "I am not money hungry, nor a landmonger. I've no designs on any of your property. It's yours to do with as you like. A school, you say? That's a noble plan, one I would encourage you to pursue."

Cosima forced a smile to her lips. Such words should comfort her. The land would remain hers to do with as she wished. Wasn't that more than she could have hoped for? Here she was, being pursued by an English gentleman—one who would allow her free use of her inheritance. What could be better?

Reginald let go of her hands and leaned back in his seat, once again gazing out of the window. He did nothing to further the conversation, though he hadn't really stymied it a moment ago.

There were a great deal more questions on Cosima's mind, but she hesitated to bring them up. Her foremost concern was Royboy's future. Once her parents were gone, he would need someone to look after him, and Cosima had always envisioned herself in that role.

Even her plans for a school to provide care and lessons for him and others like him had included her presence to ensure Royboy's safety and comfort. Could she leave him there if she couldn't hope to live there as well? That was one question she could not rid from her mind.

Far preferable would be to have him in whatever place she called home, whether in Ireland or England, if Reginald would allow it. But why should she fear Reginald's answer? Hadn't he shown himself to be tolerant of Royboy? Even when Royboy had joined them on several occasions, endlessly mimicking with his own sometimes incoherent version of speech or sitting at Reginald's feet and fussing with his shoe ties or even the luncheon fiasco, never once had Reginald complained of Royboy's presence. Perhaps he would welcome Royboy—or tolerate him, at least.

"What are your plans for your future then, Sir Reginald?" she asked at some length, like a coward putting off the real topic on her mind. "You indicated to my father an interest in politics. Is that your desire?"

He laughed. "Ho, I'd not get far with my lowly title, I'm afraid, except in the House of Commons. And I've no wish to associate myself with commoners."

"What of the work for which you were knighted?" she asked, recalling the story he told her parents of benevolent efforts in London and Liverpool.

"Oh, that." He looked out the window again. "That was mainly because of my friend Peter. He's a current baron and will be a viscount once his father passes on. Have I mentioned Peter before?"

Cosima shook her head.

"It was his idea to set up workhouses in two of the worst neighborhoods in London and Liverpool. We went there with a few of our men, to find whomever we could pluck from the gutter able to do the simplest work, and made them foremen. We provided jobs that paid workers well enough to live decently. We also set up a clinic and soup kitchen in the manner of what you had here in Ireland for a while—well, still do, I imagine, only not with the English government's help anymore. The Quakers still offer the soup kitchens, so Peter tells me. He keeps apprised of benevolent work, so he may fill a few of the niches."

"But you were knighted," she said. "You must have played an important role."

"Well, that was Peter's doing, on my behalf. I barely lifted a finger, only donated some money and went along for the adventure since I'd never been to a slum before. I wanted to see what poverty looked like from the center of it, not the fringe. Out of curiosity is all."

Cosima eyed him, baffled. Had he meant to sound so callous, or was he merely being modest by belittling his own altruism? "And Peter is your close friend?"

"Oh yes, a marvelous chap. He's always trying to get me to take the high road—you know the sort. I'm quite fond of him when I don't hate him out of pure envy for all he is and does." He laughed lightheartedly. "He'd have become a missionary, I suppose, if his father didn't have that title all ready to be handed down. Peter's younger brother is already a champion of the faith in some godforsaken place in Africa. Sadly, Peter has only the one brother. Two sisters, but we all know they don't count for much when it comes to titles. So the future of the great Hamilton legacy remains squarely upon Peter's shoulders."

"He has no children of his own yet, then, to secure another generation for his legacy?"

"Children? No, not for Peter. He was engaged once and it ended badly, so he's been hesitant to consider marriage lately." Reginald gave her a broad smile. "I was hoping that by setting a good example with you, Peter might not be so reluctant to start his own future."

"How kind of you. Is that why you've decided to search for a wife? To encourage your friend?"

He laughed again. "Well, perhaps! You must know, Cosima,

that I had designs on you before I even met you. I sent Mr. Linton to bring back his report, knowing he is a very good judge of . . . character." His laugh rang out again, as if he'd caught himself in some joke only he understood. "He returned saying you were lovely both inside and out, your reputation among the townspeople was unsullied by selfishness or stinginess, and you would, in his humble opinion, make a suitable wife for anyone in such a position as my own."

"But are there no women in England who suit you?"

"Oh yes, plenty—but none of my choosing would have me. You see, Cosima, I am a snob. I readily admit such a fault. I am but a knight—wealthy, to be sure, but for all practical purposes a commoner. Commoners do not suit me—at least English ones— and ladies of the aristocracy will not have me. You, by virtue of your father's heritage, are the closest thing to nobility I could possibly hope to acquire."

That he had looked at marriage through the eyes of social betterment should not come as any surprise, since Cosima already knew romance played no part in his interest. But to have it said so plainly, and with no obvious compunction, made her undeniably uncomfortable. More importantly though, with her family history, how could anyone think of her as being socially desirable?

Yet he had brought up a whole subject that interested her far more than she'd let herself believe to that moment. "I know very little of my father's family apart from the portraits hanging in our hall. My mother said Father hired someone to make full-size portraits from small copies he had taken with him when he left England. It always struck me as obvious that it was my father's family who disowned him and not the other way around. What is his family like?"

Reginald looked at her as if he could not believe her words. "You have no idea why your father left England?"

"No, I don't."

"You father tried to steal his older brother's wife. Well, that was before they were married, so I suppose at the time she would only have been his fiancée. She is now your aunt, actually, since she did marry your uncle. Of course this was all long before I was born, so I've only heard rumors. But it was quite the scandal. Your father seduced his sister-in-law-to-be, and the whole family was in an uproar echoing to all corners of London. Your father left in shame, promising never to return for fear of reminding everyone of the whole affair."

The story seemed completely out of keeping with the man Cosima knew as her father. Not that she'd ever thought of her father as a man, really, capable of being foolish and passionate in his youth. Could it be true? She couldn't possibly know one way or the other—but why would Reginald make up such a thing?

"I suppose I should avoid any contact with them, then, so as not to bring up such a history."

"Nonsense, my dear. We're expected to dine with them on Friday, and they're eager to meet you. The whole escapade has long since been forgotten by almost everyone, except perhaps by your father, who refuses to come home."

"My father has been invited back to his family?"

"Of course. As I said, they've kept track of him even if he's been secretive about them. And as you deduced on the day we met, how else would I have heard of you except through those who do not deny your existence?"

Her father's family. Relatives who shared the same Escott name and blood. Strangers . . . but not quite. And she would meet them in two days' time.

Family, Lord. People You've chosen for me to know. Let me know You're with me each step, and lead me along the way. Your way. Cosima's gaze fell once more on Reginald, and she added to her prayer. *And, Lord, please guide me to the future You would have for me. Whether that includes Sir Reginald or not.*

7

Talie stared at the names in the old family Bible. They were just names, after all. She didn't have to attach a history to any one of them.

From his favorite leather chair, Luke set aside the newspaper. "How is it going?"

She didn't look up. "Fine."

"I'm glad you're working on that," he said after a while.

Now she did look at him. "Are you?"

"You sound surprised." He pointed with his nose to the open spot on the wall. "Didn't I tell you I thought a family tree would look good there?"

"What about your side of the family? Where will we hang your tree?"

Luke laughed. "There aren't any family Bibles floating around my side with all of the information handy."

Despite the ease of compiling names and dates from her own side, the thought of researching Luke's heritage appealed to Talie. Maybe she should do that instead and forget all of this. Wouldn't he really rather display his own family tree than hers, anyway? They all carried his family name.

She stared at the list in front of her. The names of those who had died in the fire seemed to stand out. Was she crazy to advertise evidence that her family had once suffered in such a way?

She shook the thought away. She wasn't crazy.

Closing the Bible, she thought of Cosima's journal, once again hidden. She'd read another segment after Dana had left this morning, but Luke had found her and she stuffed it away before he noticed. She would have to move it out of the guest room in case Dana stayed over again, which was a likely possibility since she was their favorite babysitter. Talie supposed she could stuff it in her own closet, since she and Luke each had one.

"I'm going to bed," she said, pushing herself away from the desk and standing. "Coming?"

"I'll be up in a while. Not tired yet. But . . . honey?"

Talie turned to her husband. His attention was fully on her now, something she normally welcomed.

"Is it really bothering you—those dates, I mean? I noticed you didn't mention anything to Dana about it."

She shrugged, unwilling to talk about it. Not yet. "I suppose she'll see it for herself when we hang the news on our wall."

"If you don't want to . . ."

She shook her head. "Like you said, whatever happened a hundred and fifty years ago doesn't matter. Now, I really am tired, so I'll see you upstairs if you make it up before I doze off."

Talie headed to their bedroom. She knew she'd have to share the journal sooner or later if she didn't get rid of it altogether. It just didn't seem the right time, when it made marriage sound so impossible. She should wait until Dana was married before sharing it. Dana might be all grown up by legal standards, but she'd been protected her entire life. Talie wasn't about to change that now.

And Luke? She didn't worry about him. In fact, her reluctance to tell him everything was probably silly. He loved her.

She would tell him, just as soon as she was sure there was nothing to Cosima's tale. To decide that, she needed to read a little more, at least for the few minutes before Luke came up.

8

I feel very young and naïve as I prepare to spend my first night in London. I am so tired I can barely hold my pen, but before I close my eyes I simply must record the unexpected turns this day has taken.

London is far busier than any city I have visited, even Dublin. The buildings are so close that one seems to lean into the next, with nothing but a varied facade indicating the end of one building and the beginning of another. Tall shadows cast the narrow streets into near darkness, even at four o'clock in the afternoon.

Sounds and smells come from everywhere. Everything from singing and laughter to shouts and cursing stung my ears as we drove through town. And the smells are every bit as varied, from refuse and worse to various meals in the midst of preparation: familiar cabbage, roasting pork, baking bread, and other scents not so easily recognized, both sweet and spicy. . . .

"We'll be coming to our journey's end soon," said Reginald with the first hint of emotion in his voice. He sounded like a young boy approaching a toy shop. "But if you don't mind I'd like to take a detour past my friend Peter's house. Would you be agreeable to that?"

Although Cosima nodded, she realized he must have made the decision prior to asking the question, since a moment later the carriage slowed. Cosima heard Mr. Linton call out a greeting to a gatekeeper as they swept past with barely a pause in the horses' stride.

"This is the Hamilton London estate, Cosima," Reginald said with as much pride as he might have displayed had the property been his own.

And indeed the grounds were fine. Lush green lawns were interrupted only by hardy trees along the lane leading to a courtyard. Through the greenery Cosima glimpsed a high stone fence now and then, which undoubtedly spelled the boundaries of the Hamilton property.

They neared the house—a magnificent structure with a door set high in the center, accessible by a wide double staircase arching out to each side. Wrought-iron balustrades fashioned in an intricate floral design guided the way safely upward. Flowers beckoned everywhere, from inside boxes hanging on the ironware to garden beds edging the courtyard.

Almost immediately a footman appeared to open the carriage door and lay out the step. It felt good to stretch her legs. From Ireland they had taken a ship across the Irish Sea to Bristol, where horses were quickly hired and they went on their way in the Hale carriage still loaded with her goods straight from the ship.

Cosima wore the same travel suit she'd had on the day before, but despite the fine Irish linen it was rumpled and limp, every bit as worn as Millie's sturdy tarlatan skirt and jacket. Cosima suddenly wished she had not consented to stop by the house of

Reginald's friend. Surely her travel weariness would be as obvious to others as it was to herself.

But there was little time to dwell on such things. Reginald took her hand and pulled her up one of the wide brick staircases. Before they'd even reached the top, the doors opened and two servants stood aside to usher them in.

"Ah, Mr. Fisher," said Reginald gaily to the man who appeared to be the ranking servant present. He was taller than Reginald, with gray hair parted down the center. "I have a wonderful surprise for Peter. Will you summon him?"

"Lord Peter is not at home, sir," said the servant, bowing slightly as he spoke.

The animation in Reginald's face disappeared upon Mr. Fisher's pronouncement. "Not here?"

"That's right, sir," he said. "Thursday, you know."

Reginald slapped his forehead as if Thursday meant something. "Have my days mixed, Fisher. Thought today was Wednesday, without sessions running into the evening." He turned to Cosima. "Ah, well, we've wasted a half hour. Peter is at Parliament, no doubt along with his father. We shall have to wait and meet him tomorrow." He turned back to Mr. Fisher. "Unless . . . is Mrs. Hamilton at home?"

The butler nodded, eyes downcast, voice tentative, as if careful of what he said. "Shall I say you're here?"

Reginald smiled broadly. "Yes, Fisher!"

Without a word but with a barely discernable flick of one wrist, Mr. Fisher dismissed the servant at his side, and the younger man hurried off. Mr. Fisher then turned and led them through the wide, walnut-paneled entryway. Cosima caught Millie's uncertain glance, but they both followed.

The drawing room to the left was not large, though the ceilings were so high it gave the feeling of space. Cushioned chairs, wide settees, and lounging seats sat here and there, most near the fireplace. A glistening mahogany piano stood before tall windows, beyond which Cosima spotted another courtyard. She was surprised to find so much outdoor space in the middle of a thriving, dense city like London.

"Fisher," said Reginald, "why don't you take my friend's maid along with you? You might even offer her tea." Reginald looked from Cosima to Millie and back to Cosima, as if expecting her assent.

"This is Millicent O'Banyon, my companion," said Cosima. "I'm sure she would welcome refreshment after our journey."

"Go along then, both of you," Reginald said briskly before Mr. Fisher could respond. "At once."

Reginald's impatience was obvious, along with a glint of something else in his eye as he watched them go. Disdain— Cosima was sure of it.

Cosima stood silent as they left, unsure of the behavior Reginald expected of her. He had proclaimed himself a snob. Did that mean he expected his prospective wife to be one too?

When they were alone, the harsh look in Reginald's friendly blue eyes disappeared. "No wonder I'm drawn to you, my dear. You're very like Peter and his family. So kind to everyone, whether above or beneath you."

She wondered what he meant, but a moment later yet another servant came to divest them of gloves and hats while someone else brought in tea and biscuits.

In the midst of all this commotion, a woman entered who was obviously no servant despite her wide-brimmed straw hat, her garden gloves, and the broad, flat basket full of flowers dangling from her arm. Dressed in green crinoline lined with embroidered petals along the wide bodice and narrowly cut waist, the woman might have blended into any lovely garden. Flawless, creamy white skin glowed with a touch of healthy pink in her cheeks. Clear blue eyes and copper hair competed for the claim of her best feature. But to Cosima, that must be this woman's smile, with kindness so obvious in her eyes and her full lips parted to reveal stark white teeth. She was the picture of welcome.

"Reginald, how pleased I am to see you! Peter said you were traveling, and that's why you missed our little soiree the other night."

"A pity." He kissed her cheek, then drew Cosima nearer with a hand to her elbow. "But when I tell you my news you will understand." Reginald allowed a moment of silence as the two women studied one another. In that time Cosima guessed the other was older than her first impression. With little lines along the edges of her mouth and eyes and beginning to form on her neck, the woman must be close to the age of Cosima's mother.

"Lady Hamilton," said Reginald slowly, "may I present to you Cosima Escott, my fiancée."

"Fiancée . . ." Initial surprise transformed immediately to pleasure. In the next moment, Lady Hamilton thrust off her gloves and tossed them with the flower basket to a nearby side table, pulling Cosima into a warm embrace. "Fiancée! Oh, how wonderful!" Then she opened one half of the embrace to pull Reginald into the circle. Despite Reginald's smile, Cosima felt his stiffness as clearly as Lady Hamilton's warmth.

"Come, sit and tell me everything." She led them to settees near the tea service, where a maid was already pouring. "I want to know how you met, when you plan to marry, where you will be living—and oh! Reginald, I have a lovely idea. Why not be married right here, if you plan to marry in London? We have the gardens out back, the gazebo and canopy of heaven itself. I've dreamed of a wedding here for simply decades and would love to see such a dream come true."

"Peter and the girls will fulfill that dream for you, Lady Hamilton," said Reginald gently.

She nodded, still smiling but no longer looking at Reginald. Instead she looked at Cosima. "My, but you're lovely, Miss Escott. Let's see, Escott . . . you must belong to the London Escotts in one way or another, but surely not from John, since I know both of his daughters. You are related to Merit Escott, aren't you?"

"Merit Escott is my grandmother." Cosima ignored her inner reluctance to admit such a relationship. Merit Escott might be related to her by blood, but in reality the name represented nothing of the familial title "grandmother."

"Yes, Cosima is Charles's daughter, from Ireland," said Reginald. If he'd expected to shock Lady Hamilton, he failed, for the smile on her face never wavered.

Lady Hamilton reached over and patted Cosima's hand. "So Reginald has brought you all the way from Ireland. How lovely! Tell me, wherever did you meet one another?"

The woman's obvious excitement would have delighted Cosima had she more enthusiasm about the possibility of a forthcoming wedding. But their "courtship" was little more than an arrangement, a barter for whatever social betterment Reginald thought he might find in marrying her. And what was she getting out of this prospective marriage? A future, as her mother called it.

But the truth did not seem appropriate for this woman, with her romantic notions of a wedding celebration under the canopy of heaven.

Feigning shyness, Cosima looked at Reginald.

"Cosima's cousin Rachel Escott should receive all the credit, Lady Hamilton." Reginald took up the story gallantly. "If it weren't for Rachel, I might never have heard about Cosima. As it was, Rachel told me of a cousin she'd never met—how she lived in a fine old estate across the sea and how Rachel wished she could meet her someday. You know, few of us in this younger generation care about what happened before we were born.

When Rachel told me she was fairly certain Cosima was not wed, my interest was immediately piqued. I sent my Mr. Linton over to verify the story first, of course, but no sooner had he sent word with the news that Cosima was indeed free to receive my courtship than I packed my bag and set out to claim her."

"How romantic!" Lady Hamilton laughed and touched Reginald's forearm. "I've always said you're a man of action, Reginald. Peter says so too."

He glowed under her compliments, and Cosima didn't blame him. Lady Hamilton's smile of approval might come often based on the lines around her mouth, but somehow that didn't seem to diminish its value.

"Does Peter know?" she asked.

Reginald squared his shoulders, eyes twinkling as if he had a secret. "Not yet. That's why we stopped in, actually—so he could take one look at my lovely Cosima and let rivalry do its work. We'll have him thinking about marriage soon enough. Cosima and I haven't even completed our journey. We've come straight from the ferry ship here."

Immediate distress filled Lady Hamilton's eyes, and she looked at Cosima. "Reginald didn't allow you to rest after your journey all the way from Ireland?"

"We're a bit disheveled, I admit," Cosima said. "But Reginald's carriage was comfortable, and I'm not nearly as tired as one might expect after such a trip."

"Oh, but Reginald has been remiss!" Lady Hamilton scolded, hopping to her feet. "You must allow me to offer you a room, Miss Escott. Your betrothed must be so swept away with his dreams of your wedding that he's forgotten all manners."

Before Cosima could protest, Lady Hamilton sent the attending maid away to prepare a room in which Cosima might freshen herself.

"I have no desire to trouble you, Lady Hamilton," Cosima

said. "Truly, I'm perfectly fine to finish our journey to Reginald's."

"Surely you're not staying there?" Horror laced her words.

"I'm traveling with my companion, of course. We left arrangements up to Reginald."

Lady Hamilton took one of Cosima's hands in hers, directing her to her feet and looping Cosima's arm in her own. "Reginald is such a sweet, innocent boy, but you simply cannot stay under the same roof, my dear! What would people say? Unless . . ." She turned back to Reginald, who was following the conversation with what appeared to be an amused smile on his face, despite the fact that his plans were obviously being altered before his eyes. "You hadn't expected Cosima would stay with Dowager Merit, had you?"

"I suppose that might be a possibility. We plan to dine there this Friday evening, when Cosima will meet them for the first time."

Lady Hamilton patted Cosima's hand. "My dear, you must be overwhelmed with all that's happening. First Reginald whisks you away from your home with the intention of marriage, forever changing your life. Then he expects to double the size of your family in one simple dinner party. Well, I have no idea how flexible you are, but I don't assume you would like the pressure of living under the same roof as family members you've only just met."

"To be perfectly honest, I hadn't given it much thought," Cosima admitted. "That is, I have thought about meeting my grandmother, but I hadn't actually realized I might stay with her."

"I have the perfect solution," said Lady Hamilton, "and I'll not take no for an answer. You'll stay here, of course." She led Cosima from the drawing room back toward the grand foyer. As Lady Hamilton walked and spoke, she swept her palm upward to draw attention to the large expanse of the home. "We have plenty of room, and my girls will love having a visitor so near their age. I anticipate you'll get along famously."

Another surge of uncertainty rose then quickly faded. Lady Hamilton's invitation was indeed appealing. Reginald was nearly as much a stranger as this woman, but she offered sincere welcome. Reginald might be every bit as welcoming, but there was something about him. . . .

Staying here would allow Cosima to get to know Reginald from a safe distance. And this gracious woman offered that very opportunity.

"Reginald," said Lady Hamilton, "tell your lady she must stay. I can see on her face that's all she's waiting for."

Reginald studied Cosima as if to discern her thoughts. But there was something else there, Cosima thought. It was almost as if he was pleased at the development.

"Only say what you desire, my dear," he said, "and I'll see it done."

Relieved that he was so amenable, she smiled. Why did she have any qualms about him? "I think Lady Hamilton is right. Perhaps it would be more proper for Millicent and me to stay here."

Relief flickered in his eye. "I want only what is best, my dear. For you and for us."

"Then it's decided," said Lady Hamilton. "Oh, wait until I tell the girls!" She turned to Reginald, practically shooing him off. "You go on now, Reginald. Go home and have a bath after your travels; that's what I intend to offer Cosima. When you're freshened and rested, you may come back to claim her company for a time. Now off with you!"

Reginald laughed, taking one of Cosima's hands at the same time and kissing it in a polite farewell. Then he headed toward the door.

Lady Hamilton led Cosima up the stairs to a room decorated

in pristine white and cheery yellow, with flowered wallpaper repli-
cated in the bedding and curtains. As a hostess, Lady Hamilton
was obviously quite experienced, commanding every comfort for
her guest: tea and a light repast; a bed; and a bath with warmed,
scented water, fine soap, and soft, heated towels. A maid arrived
to unpack the trunks brought from Reginald's carriage, and before
long the same maid extracted a gown from one of the trunks for
pressing, taking away Cosima's crumpled traveling suit as well.

After Cosima's bath, the maid returned in time to help
Cosima with her hair, sweeping it up in a fashionable chignon.
All this was done without Millie, who Cosima was told was well
cared for and given a bed upstairs with the other maids.

Moments later, one of the Hamilton maids appeared at the
door again, standing ready to show Cosima the way to dinner.

"Cosima," said Lady Hamilton as she rose from her seat in the
small sitting room where they had met earlier. "How lovely you
look! Come and meet my family."

Cosima couldn't help but feel welcomed all over again with
Lady Hamilton ushering her farther into the room. Two young
women sat near the fireplace, and along with a tall, middle-aged
man, they stood and approached—all with strikingly similar
smiles.

"This is my husband, Lord Graham Hamilton. And these
lovely girls are our daughters. Beryl and Christabelle, meet
Cosima Escott—" she paused as if for dramatic effect—
"Reginald's fiancée."

Lord Hamilton had stretched his hand in greeting, but his
daughters swept past and grabbed both of Cosima's hands in
theirs, successfully circumventing their father's.

"Reginald's fiancée!" said the one called Beryl. She was taller than the other, perhaps older, with the same creamy white skin of her mother but dark hair like her father. "Oh, Mother said she had a surprise guest for dinner, but we had no idea!"

Christabelle, fair and pretty but on the plump side, giggled. Her laugh was infectious, and Cosima felt like laughing along. "Who would have ever thought Reginald would find such a gem?"

The girls laughed, and their mother partially hid a smile behind a raised palm, while Lord Hamilton looked on with something between amusement and consternation on his face. He was dark where his wife was pale, yet handsome for an older gentleman, with heavy brows and a full mustache. Though age drew his skin downward, he looked fit and healthy, the whites of his eyes all the more stark for the contrasting darkness in the brown centers and shrouding brows.

"A pleasure to meet you, Miss Escott," he said, and at last his daughters parted to let him extend his hand once more. "My wife has told me you've come from Ireland."

"Ireland!" said Beryl, taking up Cosima's hand again. "Oh, you must tell us all about it. Mother and Father are such bores, Cosima. Well, they're positively sweet, but bores all the same. They won't let us travel a bit, not to Ireland, not even to the Continent."

Cosima smiled. "It's been my experience that concerned parents are often bores, Miss Beryl. I'm told the world is an unpredictable place, especially far from home."

"You sound just like Mother," Christabelle said with another giggle.

"It simply isn't fair, that's all," said Beryl with a pout. She caught Cosima's gaze and held it. "They let our two brothers travel as they will. Why, one of our brothers is in Africa! Imagine being able to see such a foreign land. I think it's vastly unfair to have been born a woman."

"I've done precious little traveling myself," Cosima said, "but

I can say this about it: I believe the idea of it outweighs the reality. Seasickness and bumpy roads, stale air on trains and road dust isn't as glamorous as it might sound."

"And you're here to marry Reginald!" Christabelle sounded breathless. "I can hardly believe it. You're so pretty . . . and did you say you're an Escott?"

"That's right."

"I believe Reginald has always wanted to marry an Escott, the way he and Rachel—"

"That'll be enough talk of such nature, Christabelle," broke in Lord Hamilton firmly. "It's time to go in to dinner. Shall we?"

Lord and Lady Hamilton led the way, and the girls escorted Cosima, one on each side. Even as Cosima surveyed the large dining-room table set with crystal and china, silverware and fresh flowers, she couldn't help but wonder about Christabelle's words. Strangely enough the notion that her cousin Rachel might be more than a simple acquaintance of Reginald's didn't concern Cosima in the least.

Dinner passed in pleasant company. Beryl, whom everyone called Berrie, pressed Cosima with questions about Ireland. Cosima was only too happy to answer. She'd been gone from home a short time, yet it felt as if she'd been away far longer. She'd send a note home in the morning to let her family know she'd arrived safely.

Christabelle, on the other hand, asked questions about how Cosima and Reginald had met. "The wedding will be such fun," she exclaimed. "And Peter will be the best man, no doubt. Oh! You haven't met our brother Peter, have you, Cosima?"

Cosima shook her head just as she took another bite of beef with Yorkshire pudding. Compared to the simpler fare she was used to at home, she'd never tasted anything quite so delicious.

"Oh, you'll love him," Beryl said proudly.

Christabelle chimed in with another laugh, "Certainly, everyone does. It's a good thing you met Reginald first, or you surely would have fancied Peter instead."

"That's true enough," Beryl confirmed. "Ladies tend to like Peter, with or without a title, though I must say they can't really separate the two, can they?"

"Girls," said Lord Hamilton with a warning in his tone. "Let's direct the conversation to something a bit more edifying, shall we?"

Beryl looked surprised by the gentle rebuke. "Reginald and Peter are the best of friends, so it's a matter of fact that Cosima will get to know Peter quite well. Isn't that right, Father?"

"Yes, I suppose that's true."

"And so we should tell her something about him, shouldn't we? That he's kind and handsome and clever, even if he is a bit of a bore sometimes. But I suppose it's natural for me and Christabelle to find him something of a bore, isn't it, since we're his sisters. We've always hoped he would bring home dashing young men for us to fancy, but Father keeps him so busy between politics and charity that all he's ever done is bring home Reginald."

"Beryl!" said Lady Hamilton, the first hint of exasperation in her voice. She looked at Cosima with regret. "My daughters are outspoken sometimes, Cosima. Complaints come too easily to those who've lived a comfortable life."

Beryl's brows rose in obvious offense. "I'm not complaining, Mother. Honestly, I thought I was giving Cosima a wonderful portrayal of Peter."

"Yes, and of Reginald?"

Beryl's lids dropped to shade her eyes momentarily; then she looked at Cosima with a smile. "I was only going to add that he's quite like another brother, practically one of the family."

"That's certainly true," Lady Hamilton said. "In fact, I've invited Reginald to consider having the wedding here."

That announcement brought new squeals of delight and a

plethora of ideas for decorations and food, guests and music.
By the end of the meal, Cosima felt as though she were some
recently discovered relative—just the way she hoped to be
welcomed by the London Escotts in a few days' time.

When at last the evening ended and the girls led the way
upstairs, Beryl invited Cosima to her room to see a new gown
that had arrived from the seamstress earlier. Christabelle came
along, and the three of them chatted for another hour about fash-
ions and weddings and imagined travels, this time without any
censure from Hamilton parents listening in.

When at last the evening seemed spent, Cosima stood
and Beryl followed her to the door with an offer to make sure
Cosima found the room the Hamiltons had provided.

"Is this it?" Beryl asked when she opened the door to the room
Cosima had described. There were two halls on this, the middle
level of the home, one leading from each side of the stairway. She'd
been relieved when Beryl had offered to show her the way.

Cosima would have stepped in, but Beryl reached across
and started closing the door. "Oh, that room has the most awful
bed; you won't sleep a wink in there. Mother's forgotten. Come
with me."

"But my things . . ."

"Oh yes," said Beryl, turning back to the room. As expected,
Cosima's belongings had been neatly unpacked, pressed, and
hung in the wardrobe in the corner of the room. "We can have
everything moved in the morning, but for now just take what
you'll need for the night. And a dress for the morning, of course."

Cosima eyed the bed. It was spread with a yellow coverlet,
topped with a half dozen ruffled pillows. "Are you sure this bed is
unsuitable?"

"Quite. A dear friend of mine stayed here not long ago for a
weekend visit, and I can say emphatically that she was barely able
to walk in the morning, her back hurt so." Beryl pulled her out

of the room after Cosima had grabbed her nightgown, dress, and satchel.

They walked the length of the same hallway to a room nearer the top of the stairs. Beryl opened wide the door and scurried to a lamp on a table nearby, which she lit to reveal a pleasant decor of silver and green. This room was somewhat smaller than the other. A high, canopied bed was its dominant feature. A chaise longue offered comfort near a fireplace already set with coals as if awaiting a visitor. The wood floor, as in the other bedrooms, was dust free, adorned with accent rugs in key spots beneath the bed stool and in front of the firebox. Above the mantel hung a picture of a sailing ship, and the rough water shone silver in the lamplight.

"This bed is marvelous," said Beryl proudly. "I keep telling Mother to have the beds switched since the other room is larger, but she forgets. You'll be much more comfortable here, Cosima. The dressing room is just through that door."

"Thank you," Cosima said. Indeed, this room was nearly as lovely as the yellow one.

"Good night, then," Beryl said, but she stalled at the door. "I'm so glad to have met you, Cosima. I've always wanted another sister in the family, someone not quite as silly as Christabelle."

Cosima welcomed the words even as she was abashed for Christabelle's sake. "She's young yet, Berrie. I'm sure she'll prove to be a wonderful friend through the years."

"Yes, of course you're right. Good night, then." She closed the door.

Cosima hugged the clothing and tapestry bag to her chest, thinking she wished she'd told Berrie she'd always wanted a sister. Telling her tomorrow would have to suffice.

But for tonight . . . she was especially glad she'd brought her journal. Cosima had plenty to write about.

9

Just inside the main entrance of North Shore Community Church was a fountain of water tumbling peacefully over a graduating series of limestone slabs. Interspersed outside the water flow grew moss and ivy, creating an outdoor effect. Especially with bright morning sun shining through a wall of clear windows above.

Talie watched Luke walk ahead with Ben on his shoulders. They would go downstairs to the nursery, where volunteers took care of Ben so Talie and Luke—and those seated around them—could enjoy the service.

The usual routine was for her to find seats in their favorite section of the huge auditorium, stage left, then flag Luke down when he returned upstairs. But today she was meeting her mother for the service, and she'd agreed to wait at the fountain, a natural meeting spot. No one could get to the series of doors into the auditorium without passing this fountain, at least if they were coming from the main parking lot.

She glanced at her watch. Quarter 'til nine. Her mother should be here any moment. The condominium she would soon be moving to was less than fifteen minutes away, and even though she'd attended a small, hymn-singing church her entire life, she'd told Talie she would join them at the larger, more contemporary church once she lived so much closer.

Talie scanned the line of doors leading from the parking lot, but instead of seeing her mother, another familiar figure caught her eye. There walked Dana, not in the typical casual cotton pants she normally wore when she visited Talie's church. Instead she wore a dress that Talie had once teased her about. It was clearly meant to turn heads. A dark floral, it hugged the curves of her body even as three-quarter-length sleeves and a scoop neckline retained modesty.

But it, like the uneaten hotcakes of yesterday morning, was a sure sign of the direction of Dana's thoughts.

"Dana!" Talie called.

Dana's instantly raised brows nearly fell to a frown.

Surely her sister wasn't surprised to see her? It was true sometimes Talie and Luke went to the eleven o'clock service, but this was *her* church.

"Are you here to meet me and Mom?" Talie asked. "I thought now that you've moved out you'd make a clean break, and Mom would have to coerce you back into her company."

"No," Dana said, glancing around. "I'm meeting someone—not Mom. I didn't know she was coming."

Talie smiled knowingly. "So Melody's cousin-in-law came to the singles event last night? Aidan—wasn't that his name? Is he who you're meeting?"

Dana nodded, accompanied by what looked like friendly exasperation. "I am meeting him, but Talie, do me a favor. This is just too soon for him to have to meet my whole family. Could you not let Mom know I'm—?"

"There's my two girls!" Val Martin came up behind Dana, and as clearly as the sudden distress appeared on her sister's face, pure pleasure sprouted on their mother's. In her midsixties, Val Martin had always been older than most other mothers of the friends Talie had growing up, but only chronologically. Physically she looked at least ten years younger than her real age, with the sandy hair she'd given both her daughters, smooth skin, and perpetually smiling blue eyes. "I was worried about missing my old church, but I won't have to if I can sit here beside my kids."

As Dana wiped the frown from her face, Talie tried to think fast. She took her mother's arm. "Let's go find some seats," she said, hoping a plausible explanation for Dana not sitting with them would come to her along the way.

But Val didn't budge. "What's the hurry? I just love this fountain! Every time I see it, I can't help but think of that engineer husband of yours, Talie. Didn't he volunteer his expertise to design it?"

Talie didn't let go of her mother's arm. "He was a volunteer consultant. He didn't design it, just lent another opinion on whether or not the contractors knew what they were doing. Come on, Mom."

Still, Val didn't move. "My, Dana, you look so pretty today. Not that you girls don't always look pretty, but that dress is one of my favorites on you. Talie, where's Luke?"

"Taking the baby to the nursery. We really need to find seats."

"All right, all right. My goodness, I thought church was a place to slow down and contemplate?"

Talie pulled her mother along, but they weren't far before her mother stopped. "What's the matter, Dana? Aren't you coming?"

"Danes came here last night to the singles group and will be sitting in the service with them," Talie said. It was sort of true.

Disappointment crept up on Val's face. "Oh. Well, how about brunch after? Now that we're not sharing the same roof, we have lots to catch up on."

"I think she'll probably be going out with at least one person from the singles group; won't you, Danes?"

Dana nodded, looking a bit uncertain. Uncertain about letting their mother think it was a group, or uncertain about her availability after the service?

"Then we'll have to set up dinner this week."

Dana nodded again, this time more eagerly.

Talie led the way, but by the time they found three open seats together, Luke was already behind them.

"I saw Dana in the lobby," he said. "I was going to say hi, but I don't think she saw me wave. She was with some guy."

"Just one?" Val asked.

Luke glanced between Talie and her mother. "Why? Should there be more?"

"She's meeting her singles group," Val said as they took their seats.

"Actually I'm not sure how many will be there," Talie said carefully. This was beginning to feel like outright deception. "Maybe . . . just one person."

"Oh?" her mother said. "Is that why you shuffled me away like that?"

She didn't sound perturbed, even though Talie conceded she probably had a right to be. "She just met the guy, Mom. She didn't want to subject him to the whole family until she knows if she's ever going on a real date with him. That's all."

"Meeting for church sounds like a date to me," Luke said.

That was enough to inspire Talie's mother to launch a visual search. The auditorium might seat three thousand, but it was still possible to get a good view of the two-story room without missing much. When even Luke turned to get another possible look, Talie couldn't help herself. She wanted to see what the guy looked like.

She should have warned Dana not to sit on this side of the church. With the three of their necks craned to scan the room, they'd probably be hard to miss.

"If she wants us to meet the guy, she'll bring him around," Luke said, the first to give up. He turned in his seat and took up his program.

"You're right," Talie said, righting herself as well.

"There they are," said Val.

To his credit, Luke didn't look up. However, it took Talie less than a second to turn around again. She followed her mother's line of vision, spotting Dana as she led the way to the risers in the back. Those seats were always the last to fill. The rest of the auditorium had packed in fast.

Talie first noticed that Aidan was tall, probably around the same height as Luke. Where Luke was lighter in hair and skin, this man was dark. His hair was brown, his skin tan. She wondered what color eyes he had but conceded it probably didn't matter. The guy was, without a doubt, what Dana's middle school students would call a babe.

"Well, we can't very well walk past them as if we don't know them, can we?" Talie said to Luke as they filed out of the crowded auditorium after the service.

"Of course we can't," said Val, answering for Talie's husband.

"Yes, we can," Luke said. "We can all go downstairs and get Ben."

But when they reached the lobby, Talie saw Dana standing in front of the fountain, talking and laughing with the man she'd met.

"No, you go on, Luke," Talie said. "Maybe Dana is hanging around because she changed her mind about wanting him to meet us."

Luke looked skeptical, hesitating to leave. "Go easy on the guy, will you? No third degree before they've had their first date?"

Talie pretended to be offended, shooing Luke off then following her mother toward the fountain. Thankfully, Talie noticed that Dana caught sight of them coming and seemed neither alarmed nor unwelcoming. Before they'd said a word, Dana put one hand on Aidan's arm and drew out her other toward Talie and their mother.

"I mentioned my family was here," Dana said. "Aidan, this is my mother, Val Martin, and my sister, Talie Ingram. And my brother-in-law is here somewhere—getting Ben from the nursery?"

Talie nodded.

Val shook Aidan's hand, and if an assessment could be accurately judged, Talie guessed her mother at least thought Aidan good-looking. It was impossible not to. His eyes were blue, his teeth a stark white against his tan skin.

"This is Aidan Walker," Dana said.

"How did you like the service, Aidan?" Talie asked. That didn't count as a third-degree question, even though she had ulterior motives in asking. If the guy hadn't been listening, maybe he'd attended just to "scope out" Dana.

"Great!" he said. "I've heard of this church, but I've never been here. I liked it."

"Do you usually go somewhere else, then?" Val asked.

Talie smiled; her mother could always claim she hadn't heard Luke's admonition.

Aidan nodded. "It's smaller, more traditional."

They chatted for a few moments about the pros and cons, likenesses and differences of contemporary versus traditional churches, a subject Talie's mother was interested in since she was about to make a switch herself. No easy decision, Talie knew— one she made only to see Talie, Luke, and Ben every Sunday.

But Aidan didn't seem to have the same reservations about leaving behind something so familiar. Talie had to admit he seemed interested in North Shore Community—hopefully not only because of Dana and the singles group.

"We'll be going out to brunch," Val said. Talie shot a worried glance Dana's way, who looked back with what was probably a better hidden sense of alarm. "Care to join us?"

But if Val entertained any real hopes of a quiet family brunch, they were forgotten a moment later when Luke arrived with Ben in his arms. Ben was red faced and in obvious distress. Talie offered to take him but instead of handing him to her, Luke put Ben on his shoulders. Sometimes Ben's favorite position was enough to calm him.

Not today.

Dana made introductions over Ben's noise, and Luke and Aidan shook hands. Aidan tried to shake Ben's hand too, obviously not put off by his noise, but as usual Ben kept his hand tightly fisted and didn't respond to anyone's calm voice, not even a stranger's.

"Ben has these moods every once in a while." Talie raised her voice with the heightened sound of Ben's cries. "We call them meltdowns. It'll take a while for him to quiet down, so it looks like we better take him home."

"Yep," Luke agreed, then turned to Aidan. "It was nice meeting you."

He turned then, and Talie knew she would have to follow. "I'll call you later, Dana, okay?" She looked at her mother. "Coming, Mom? You'll meet us at our house? I can throw brunch together there."

Her mother nodded, saying good-bye to Dana and Aidan and following Talie toward the parking lot. Not without a few glances back.

Much as Talie wanted to see her sister happily wed, she felt surprisingly cautious of the idea now that a potential husband had appeared on the scene. Even as she reminded herself that Dana had seen him at the singles ministry event Talie recommended, she couldn't help but think there must be a way for all of them to get to know each other.

Talie wondered if her mother's curious glances might mean

she felt the same way. Maybe she was just worried Dana would be blinded by the guy's good looks; he certainly had that going for him.

Once Ben was buckled into his seat and the car was running, he quieted somewhat. Nonetheless Talie sat in the back with him rather than up front next to Luke.

She wasn't sure what made her think of it. Would it be too meddlesome? But it could work out for everyone's benefit. Why not? She had to voice the thought, at least.

"Luke, have you begun the interview process for your architectural position?"

"There's no reason not to at least mention it to him," Talie said to Dana on the phone the next night. "Maybe it'll work out for both of them—Aidan and Luke."

"I can think of plenty of reasons not to mention it. Dating isn't a lifelong commitment, Talie. What if this leads absolutely nowhere? Then Aidan will be left working for the brother-in-law of a former . . . whatever. I can't really call myself his girlfriend after only one brunch date and two lengthy phone calls."

"I don't see why that should be awkward, if he likes the job. If it doesn't work out and he continues to work for Luke, why would you ever have to see him, or vice versa? I rarely see anyone Luke works with."

"I don't know. . . ."

"Just mention it to him, Danes."

"Why are you interested in having him work for Luke, anyway?"

Talie was sitting on the edge of her bed, having set aside the journal she'd been reading again. She stroked one of the pages with a fingertip. Maybe it was the way Aidan had looked at Dana at church on Sunday morning . . . or the way Dana looked back.

Or maybe her hormones were out of whack. She'd been feeling so strange lately.

"It was just an idea," said Talie. "Forget it."

"No, I'll mention it. He'll probably call me tomorrow, and I can bring it up then."

Talie smiled. "Then let's see what God has in store, shall we?"

10

Earlier tonight, this bed looked every bit as inviting as Berrie promised. Sheltered under a leafy canopy, it is larger than the one I left behind at home. Sheer material stretches across the top, dangling attractively at each of the four posters in swags that touch the floor in gentle folds.

But I could not have foreseen how very little sleep I would get in this bed, no matter how comfortable it is in comparison to either the one at home or the one from which Berrie rescued me in the yellow room. I simply cannot slumber after what just happened.

It all started innocently enough, as I doused the light and prepared to retire for the night. . . .

Cosima doused the light beside the chaise, then went to the window and untied the loops of the heavy silver-and-green drapes. The room fell into darkness without stars or moon to cast a shadow. Feeling her way along the wall, she found the far side of the bed and knelt. Tonight's prayer would not be written, but that made no difference to the heart of the Lord; of that Cosima was certain.

From the familiar position on her knees, she automatically closed her eyes for prayer but opened them a moment later. The room was so dark it made no difference whether her lids were up or down.

"Father in heaven," she said aloud, then decided to continue without disturbing the silence.

Once again she asked the Lord's guidance but also His forgiveness for her suspicions of Reginald and caution with her lovely hostess, at least so far as discussing wedding plans. She asked for heavenly wisdom yet again, wondering how she might serve God best: at Reginald's side or back home alone, to see the vision of a school become reality.

The door clicked.

Cosima's thoughts fell from heaven back to earth. Still on her knees, her gaze flew to the threshold, but she saw nothing in the darkness. She hadn't thought to lock the door; no one at home ever did such a thing. Indeed, she hadn't even checked to see if this door offered any sort of latch.

Fear crept up her spine, surpassing the initial surprise. Whoever—or whatever—was at the door seemed of strange intent. A sliver of light passed in from the hallway, but there the door stopped for a long, motionless moment.

And then it moved again. Cosima cowered in the darkness, hiding in the shadows behind the canopied bed. At last she saw a figure, darkly clad and large, holding what appeared to be a heavy and unwieldy bag.

"Too many this time," the person said, evidently to no one in particular. Had the broad shoulders not already revealed this visitor a man, his deep voice would have given him away. The figure deposited his burden on the floor before the unlit firebox before pulling something from his pocket. A match. He struck it and lit the coals awaiting use, illuminating that portion of the room and sending the scent of sulfur as far as Cosima. Then he returned to the door and closed it. Evidently this door did offer a lock. Cosima heard it snap into place.

Heart pounding, she slunk beneath the bed altogether, too timid to watch. If the invader never suspected her presence, she would keep safe. But what sort of invader *brought* a full sack of goods?

She heard what sounded like rocks, bricks, or stones sliding against one another. Venturing from beneath the bed's frame, she stole a quick peek over the edge of the quilt-covered mattress. With his back to her, she could see nothing more than one strong hand pulling out rock after rock, placing each one in a neat row before the light of the coal fire.

Cosima had seen Royboy do such a thing before—line up stones in a straight row. He had done it with sticks as well and once with his food, though that was only after he'd eaten far more than anyone thought his stomach could hold. Was this visitor like Royboy, then, trying to create order in some mysterious fashion, with items of no possible value for anyone else?

Unwilling to find out, she sank back under the bed. The bottom of the bed was high enough from the floor to afford her a low view as far away as where he knelt, and she saw the stripe he created lengthen with rocks of all shapes and sizes. Every once in a while he would tap two against one another, and dust would flicker in the meager light or a spark might catch hold of the flame only to instantly disappear.

Soon Cosima's fear abated, and she wished only that he would leave. Instead he looked at the rocks as if they were some rare treasure, now and then grunting an indecipherable phrase as he studied them in the fire's glow.

At last he stood; Cosima could tell when his knees disappeared from the floor and she saw only his shoes, a pair of sturdy black boots that were as dusty as the rocks he'd toted.

She offered a quick prayer of thanksgiving, glad he seemed finished inspecting whatever sort of hoard he'd pulled out of that sack.

But he did not go to the door. When she heard more movement, she dared another peek. Her heart sank as she saw the man take off his coat, drape it on the back of the nearby chaise longue, then sit to remove his boots.

Surely he wasn't planning to stay!

Suddenly his stockinged feet headed her way, and a moment later the bedsprings sighed and sank to accept his weight. Oh! What could she possibly do *now*?

She must leave. She would wait until he fell asleep, then let herself out and find another room in which to pass the night. Hopefully she could find her way to Beryl's room or perhaps back to the yellow room. A lumpy bed didn't seem as unappealing now as Beryl had made it sound earlier.

Soon Cosima heard the man's even breathing. Keeping herself to a crawl, knees and palms to polished wood, she made her way along the dark side of the bed, occasionally tugging on her long cotton nightgown when it hampered her progress. Nearer the door, eerie shadows danced from the light of the coal fire, making the chaise longue in front of the firebox seem huge. Even the rocks placed before the fire seemed larger in the shadows, like a living landscape along a shoreline.

At last she reached the door and clutched at the knob. Twisting it in her fingertips, it moved as though unfettered—and yet the door did not budge. She looked for the lock, seeing nothing in the vicinity of the knob that would prevent the door from opening.

Then she saw it, placed high near the corner of the door. A slide lock. She eased herself to a stand, uncertain she could reach it even on tiptoe.

"What's that?"

In a burst of panic, Cosima stretched but her reach fell just short of the lock. Bedsprings ground again, and too fearful to look behind her, Cosima jumped. She hit the mechanism with the tip of her longest finger, but it did not easily slide and she managed to move it only partway.

"Who's that?"

She jumped again, hearing the man's approach. This time she fell back, only to be caught in the arms of the invader. Immediately she squirmed free of his touch, even if he had prevented her from falling altogether.

"How did you get in here? And who are you?"

"I wish to leave—if you would open the door, please." Her voice sounded tremulous and downright silly, which would have been how she felt if she weren't so frightened. The magnitude of her vulnerability had the best of her, and she couldn't bear to raise her gaze to him.

"Not until you've told me a thing or two, such as who you are and what you're doing in this room."

"I'm a guest," she whispered, folding her arms across her chest as if to protect herself. Her heart thumped so badly she felt it clear through her forearms.

"And your name?"

"Cosima Escott."

The man turned away, heading toward the firebox, where he retrieved a long match. He approached the lamp on the corner table.

Panic erupted in Cosima again when she realized light in the room would do nothing but illuminate her state of undress. The nightgown might cover her from head to toe, but it was thin and entirely inappropriate attire in which to make introductions. "Please don't!" she requested, breathless from her fear but firm nonetheless.

He stopped, turning to her. With his back to the fire he seemed larger and darker, and his shoulders, even minus the overcoat, still broad. He was far taller than she was—well over six foot, she guessed—with long, strong legs that seemed about half of him. He looked like a farmer or a soldier or an American cowboy she'd seen drawings of once, but his features and clothes were so dark she could not make out if he was gentleman or rogue.

"You're an Escott girl?"

"Cosima Escott," she repeated, feet still frozen to the floor. She took some comfort that he'd listened to her plea and not lit the lamp.

"Cosima," he said, as if by saying the name it might suddenly sound familiar. Evidently it did not. He shook his head. "I know all the Escotts here in London. Where are you from?"

"County Wicklow."

"Ireland?"

He sounded so surprised, yet it suddenly struck her that this conversation had gone on long enough. She glanced around, spotting the bed stool that would serve well enough to reach the lock without this man's assistance.

"Let's see," he said, evidently perfectly content to continue conversing as long as he pleased, "I've not heard of any Escotts in Ireland. But you're related to John and Meg Escott, here in London?"

Pulling the stool toward the door, Cosima said over her shoulder, "Yes, they're my aunt and uncle."

"Then why on earth are you staying here and not at their home? Are they having some sort of festivity, that they're so full up they couldn't make accommodations for their own niece?"

Stepping up and reaching for the lock, she answered without looking at him. "I've never met them, actually, though I believe I will shortly."

The lock slid apart, and she was awash with relief.

As if belatedly observing her actions, the interloper was at her side and took her hand to aid her back to the floor. "Pardon me," he said. "I should have done that. I must have a few cobwebs in my brain, what with the surprise of finding you in here."

"Yes, well, not more surprised than I when you first entered." She pulled her fingers free, since he still held her hand although she was safely on the floor. She put her hand to the doorknob then, drawing it toward her.

"Where were you when I came in? I saw no one, and the bed is undisturbed. I thought the room empty."

"I was beside the bed."

"On the floor?"

Cosima folded her arms before her again, feeling a chill enter through the door she'd just opened, though she stood behind in its shadow. "If you must know, I was on my knees at the far side of the bed and would have been abed shortly."

"On your knees?" he said. With the light from the hall shining only on him, Cosima could see his face now. Stark black brows hovered over dark eyes, separated by the bridge of a nose well set on his face, barely widening just above a mustached mouth. His was a handsome face, beneath ruffled hair every bit as dark as his eyes.

Just now he looked at her intently, as if trying to see something not readily discernable even in the improved lighting. "Were you looking for something on the floor?"

"Because I was on my knees?" she asked, slightly offended that such a thought was the first to come to his mind. She shook her head. "No, sir, I was praying. Kneeling is the best way to keep my mind on God and not fall off to slumber."

Whatever light had seeped into the room suddenly seemed to come from his eyes. His brows rose, and his mustache widened with his lips into a broad smile. "That's *my* favorite way of going to bed."

She stiffened, and the arms clasped before her tightened.

"Forgive me for saying so, sir, but I noticed no such action before you got into *that* bed."

He laughed. "Oh, that's not my bed. I was only going to stay a few moments because I was so tired I wasn't sure I'd make it to my own. There it was, looking so inviting. But when I'm in my own room, nearly every night my knees touch the floor before my head touches the pillow." He folded his arms now too and leaned casually against the doorjamb with a smile as easy as his laugh had sounded a moment ago. "Come now, Cosima, you don't think I'd lie about something like that, do you?"

She wasn't sure what she believed so late at night and in such extraordinary circumstances. "I don't know you a'tall, sir, therefore I cannot decide."

"Well, let's see," he said, stroking his chin with his hand. Such a large hand, she noticed, with fingers that could easily envelop her own. "I can think of a way to convince you. What goes along better with prayer than study of the Bible? Name a book and I shall try a quote. I'd say I could quote any given specific passage you might bring up, except I'm not that bright. But I think I might have at least one verse from any named book of Scriptures."

She lifted one skeptical brow. Surely anyone who could recite from each book of the Bible must not be too dull. She took the challenge. "Zephaniah."

He laughed again, and she found herself wanting to smile, but held back until hearing if he would pass or not.

"'For then will I turn to the people a pure language, that they may all call upon the name of the Lord. . . .' I think it goes on a little after that, but I forget soon after those words about a pure language. What a verse! I heard a sermon once that explained this foretells the gospel."

Cosima felt her single, skeptical brow rise higher, ready to protest his obvious shift from completing the quotation to what seemed a diversionary tactic.

He held up a hand as if in surrender. "I said I could name a quote, but I didn't say I could name an entire quote. From Zephaniah? Can *you* finish the verse?"

She smiled at last, shaking her head. "No, of course not. The test was for you, not for me. Of your own choice, I might add."

"Well, you could have been kind and asked for something from one of the Gospels. Perhaps the verse 'Jesus wept'? I never get that one wrong, from beginning to end."

Laughter welled up, banishing any trace of the fear this man had inspired only minutes ago. "Did you say this was not your room?" she asked.

"That's right. I only come in here when I have a bag of fossils. This room isn't used . . . well, not regularly, anyway. I usually bring the fossils here first because they can sit for days without disturbing anyone until I have a chance to sort through them. Servants don't have to clean around them if they're left here for a while."

"Why did you lock the door?"

He still lounged so comfortably against the doorjamb that he might have been at a Sunday social. "Are you an only child, Cosima?"

She shook her head, confused by his counterquestion.

"Your siblings must be less bothersome than mine. Usually when I bring a sack home, they're into it before I get a chance to examine my find properly. Not that they have much interest in fossils—they don't. In fact, they call me a dragon hunter and laugh at me most of the time. But they insist upon seeing every single rock, as if I might bring home gold by mistake. And so I installed that lock, so high none of my inquisitive siblings can reach it. And I use it, no matter the time of day. Out of habit, I suppose."

Cosima's gaze went to the rocks in front of the fireplace. "Fossils? They look like rocks."

"They are. There are new sciences of geology and paleontology. Have you heard of such things? They're the study of rocks. If you look closely enough at the ones I've broken just so, you can see the outlines of creatures."

"Creatures?"

"Not living creatures—not anymore. Well, except for a spider or two that might have crept into the bag. Fossils are amazing evidence of God, Cosima. He's created many wondrous things. We're the pinnacle, I believe. The pinnacle of His creation, and all of this——" he motioned toward the rocks that might have been just that, except she could see they were so much more, at least to him—"all of this is for us."

Cosima surveyed him much as he had surveyed her a moment ago.

Then he bowed and stepped into the hallway, nearly closing the door only to peek back in and say, "I'll remove the rocks in the morning, if you don't mind. Early, though, before any servants may suspect I've been here at all."

"I'm an early riser," she said.

"So am I." His gaze lingered as he spoke, but then he leaned away, gently closing the door behind him.

Cosima turned toward the bed, easily seeing her way in the glow of the firelight. From the pillow, she eyed the landscape of rocks. Even thoughts of a stowaway spider couldn't take away her gladness at having met the late-night visitor.

11

"So, how did it go?"

Luke had barely had a chance to walk in the door. Dinner was ready, but Talie couldn't wait until they sat down to start this conversation.

The interview with Aidan had been that morning, two weeks since Luke had first made the call. She'd already exercised patience in not calling Luke at his office that afternoon. Of course, that was because she didn't know how long the interview would last, thinking the longer it went, the better.

Luke left his jacket and briefcase near the table, then went to Ben, who was seated in his high chair. Talie had already fed him and he was content, so while Luke tickled him she filled their dinner glasses with water.

"Luke!" Talie called his name with some exasperation, watching her husband leave their son's side and go to the kitchen sink to wash his hands before finally sitting down at the table.

He looked up at her and laughed. "I'm going to hire him."

Talie raised her brows. "You are?"

"He's already got my vote and my boss's. Aidan will have to come in one more time, but only to meet the owner and we'll officially offer the job. Aidan has an impressive résumé. He's done well freelancing, but he said he's ready to settle in to one place now. I think we're lucky to get him."

"Settle in . . . as in settle down?"

Luke shrugged. "Maybe."

"What's he like?"

"He's a nice guy." Luke sounded surprised.

"What's hard to believe about Dana dating a nice guy?"

"I just thought he was a little too good-looking, but he doesn't act like he knows it." Luke looked at the table, set with dishes and so far only garlic bread. "Are we eating now or later?"

"Oh," Talie said, scooting over to the stove top, where she'd left the spaghetti. "I know you can't ask a bunch of personal stuff during an interview, but did you get any feel for what kind of guy he is? Faithwise . . . womanwise?"

Luke frowned. "I'm not going to screen the men Dana decides to date, Talie. Or be responsible for a breakup if I read things wrong, one way or the other. I agreed to interview the guy because he really is an architect and I happen to need one. His credentials are great, and he's smart. That's all I know; that's all I need to know."

"But what was your impression?" Talie persisted. "I mean, sometimes you get a feel for someone's lifestyle just by talking to them."

"Let's just say I didn't have a bunch of red flags waving in my head, okay? Dana can find out what she needs to know about him without our help."

Just then Ben fussed and Talie picked him up. It wouldn't be the first time she held him during dinner, and he might even want a taste of her noodles.

When Luke asked about her day, she knew she couldn't press for more details about Aidan. Maybe it was just as well; she'd been looking for something to worry about, and Dana's love life was certainly handy. But Luke was probably right; Dana would have to find out for herself if Aidan's faith was sincere. So far, it appeared so.

Not that having him work for Luke wouldn't give all of them plenty of opportunity to get to know him. Having Dana and Aidan over for dinner to celebrate his new position was the least she could do.

"I've decided to put together a scrapbook of those old post-cards my dad collected when he did all that traveling before he met my mom. It'll be quite a project, since I'll have to cut and reinforce the pages so you can see the front and back, but it'll be fun. I'll give it to my mom for Christmas, so she can read all of the notes my dad wrote about different places and what he did."

"Sounds great. So you've abandoned the family tree info? Or is that ready for me to start on?"

Talie fed a spoonful of noodles to Ben, who coughed just as he took it in. Grabbing a handful of napkins, she wiped his face, her shirt.

"Talie?"

"What?"

"The family tree info?"

"I've been so busy with this new project, but I'll get to it."

She felt his eyes on her but kept her own on Ben. The ances-tral line reminded her of Cosima's journal. Even though the pages no longer seemed to emphasize the supposed curse, the underlying reality remained with it . . . something Talie was still reluctant to acknowledge. It was hard to read without worrying.

She should go back to worrying about Dana's love life instead.

At four o'clock in the morning, after singing Ben back to sleep, Talie left his room feeling an oddly familiar sense of nausea. But this was no flu; she was almost sure of that. She would go to the drugstore today. There was one sure way of finding out if this queasiness was familiar for a reason.

12

Today I finally made the acquaintance of the much-admired Lord Peter Hamilton. Of course, we had met before we were formally introduced, but no one must ever know of that indiscretion. And no one ever shall, so long as this journal remains in my possession. . . .

After a fitful night's sleep, Cosima rose just as the sun sent a tentative ray of light through the gap in the middle of the curtains. Quickly splashing herself with the cool water left in the pitcher in the dressing room, she shed her nightgown and stepped into the petticoats, camisole, and dress she had brought with her from the yellow room the night before. The bow at the back gave her some trouble, but she managed well enough. She combed her hair, used tooth powder from her tapestry bag, and slipped on her shoes. Then she returned to the bed to set the covers aright. Better to have the fossil collector thinking her like common folk to do such menial labor than to have him looking at the covers she'd mussed.

With the curtains wide and the sun pouring in, the room looked bright and inviting with its silver-flecked green designs. The chaise longue before the firebox was upholstered in green

103

leaves and silver branches, with a light cream-colored background. She sat on it, staring at the rocks at her feet. Picking up a broken one, she ran a finger over ridges that formed an image of a small, lizardlike creature.

"I don't know why You've left behind such evidence for us, Lord," she said, "but 'tis a wonder indeed."

A gentle tap sent her heart racing. She popped to her feet, opening the door and peeking around its edge.

Last night's visitor filled her vision, so large did he appear in the doorway. He was taller than her father, lean at the waist but with muscular legs that filled the riding breeches he wore. He seemed a little like the giant she'd pictured David having fought all those years ago, a strong soldier who could intimidate any enemy.

But Cosima hardly felt like an enemy, even if having him come to collect his rocks at this time of the morning might be considered risky to her reputation. His mustached mouth smiled in a reflection of the smile she offered, and without a word she stepped aside to let him in. She did not close the door, though, in spite of a wish for no one to see him.

"I see you're studying the fossils," he said.

Cosima remembered the rock she still held. "Oh yes," she said, handing it to him. "I hope you don't mind."

"Not at all. That's why I collect them—for people to look at. Once I clean and document them in my records, I usually donate the better ones to the history department at the museum. That way everyone can see them."

She helped him pack some of the rocks from the far end of the line he'd created the night before. "I believe we have a great deal to learn about God's creation," she said, "but I think all of it will point to the same thing as Christ's death on the cross: how much we're loved."

In that moment he stopped what he was doing, and Cosima

felt him study her, even as she held out one of his fossils for him
to replace in his bag. Instead of accepting it, he caught her gaze
and held that. She wanted to look away, to break what seemed
to be a merger, at least of thoughts and interests, but she found
herself unable to cool this instantaneous affinity. She *should* but
simply didn't want to.

At last he did accept the proffered rock, placed it with the
others, and stood up, holding the full sack.

Just then someone tapped on the frame of the open door.
Fearing a maid had discovered them, Cosima looked, wide-eyed,
only to see Beryl Hamilton standing before them with a broad
smile on her pretty face.

"Good morning, Cosima. I see you've met my brother Peter."

Cosima eyed the man before her once again. So this was
Peter Hamilton. Somehow his identity came as little surprise. He
was the brother both Berrie and Christabelle extolled—and best
friend to Reginald.

"Good morning, Berrie," said Peter as he fastened his bag. "I
was just leaving for a ride in the park and was going to drop off
these rocks but found the room occupied."

Instead of eyeing them suspiciously as she might have done,
since he had obviously just closed his bag and left a circle of dust
at his feet inside the bedroom, Beryl laughed. Not a little giggle
but a laugh so large she had to cover her mouth for propriety's
sake.

"Beryl," said Peter, and his tone took on a new dimension,
almost as if he were a father figure and not an older brother.
He took two long strides closer to his sister. She stood barely as
high as his chest, and Peter, with one hand still on the sack, took
his free hand and pulled one of hers into his. "This was a prank,
wasn't it?"

"And it worked!" She laughed again, though with Peter
so close this laugh was considerably more demure. At last she

looked from her brother to Cosima and took a step farther into the room, closer to Cosima.

"I owe you an apology, Cosima," she said, and even though her words sounded sincere her eyes were still full of mirth. "I was fully expecting my brother to come home last night, and I hoped he would stop here as he often does when he collects fossils. That's why I recommended this room. Tell me, you did meet last night, didn't you?"

Peter gave Cosima no chance to answer. "Beryl, if I didn't have Miss Escott's best interest in mind, I'd drag you downstairs to Mother this minute and have you confess your whole sordid trick." Lord Peter's voice was sterner than Cosima would have expected. "Do you know you could have had her screaming in the night, fearing for her life?"

Beryl grabbed one of Cosima's hands in hers. She still had a recalcitrant smile on her face, but the look in her eyes showed the first hint of contrition. "I didn't think of that, I suppose. I just thought it might be a fun way for the two of you to meet. No harm done?"

Cosima patted Beryl's hand. "Well, I suppose if I'd known it was your doing while I cowered in the corner waiting for your brother to leave I might have been peevish. But no real harm done."

Beryl laughed again. "But it *was* fun, wasn't it? Even cowering in the corner?"

"You're as bad as Christabelle," accused Peter. "I always thought she was the prankster."

"No, she's only the one who gets caught."

Cosima eyed Lord Peter again as he hoisted his bag over his shoulder. She knew he was about to leave, but something told her she couldn't let him go without telling him why she was here. She must tell him because there had been something in his eyes. . . or maybe she'd imagined it because she wished it to be there. Whatever the truth, she felt compelled to speak.

"So you are Reginald's friend, Lord Peter."

He eyed her as if surprised she'd mentioned Reginald's name. "Reg? Do you know Reginald?"

"He brought me here from Ireland . . . to wed him."

"Wed him," Lord Peter said quietly. Had he repeated her words with some disappointment, or was that just her own silly, eager imagination?

He adjusted the bag on his shoulder and glanced from Cosima to his sister with what looked like briefly narrowed eyes. Then he smiled Cosima's way, so quickly that Cosima thought she might have imagined any fleeting discomfort on Lord Peter's part. "Congratulations, I should say. Reginald is a champion, a great friend, and a good fellow. Smart, that one. And I must say," he added softly, "his taste in choosing a fiancée is flawless. Now if you'll excuse me, ladies, I will be off before anyone discovers Berrie's mischief. Good day."

And then he left.

Beryl laughed again, turning fully to Cosima. "Tell me, what do you think of him?"

"Well . . . he's very nice. . . ."

"Nice?" Beryl repeated, obviously disappointed. "Is that all?"

Intent on hiding any hint of her confusing feelings, Cosima put one hand on her hip. "Now, Berrie, you really ought not to have done that. Have you forgotten why I'm here to begin with? To marry Reginald Hale?"

Beryl's face twisted as if she'd bitten into a sour fruit. "Oh, Reginald. He's not for you, Cosima."

"And why not? He's been very kind to me, and besides—" Cosima stopped herself short. She didn't want to go into details as to why her prospects were so few. Beryl herself would regret any action to throw Cosima together with her brother if she knew about the curse.

Beryl took up the conversation as if she hadn't noticed

Cosima's unfinished sentence. "Cosima, sit with me a moment, won't you? We can talk here without being disturbed, especially at this hour of the day."

They took seats on the chaise longue. Cosima leaned forward, for whatever Beryl wanted to share Cosima felt eager to hear, especially if it had to do with Lord Peter.

"My brother is a wonderful man," Beryl said. "Now I know I have a biased opinion, because he *is* my brother, but perhaps that makes me a better judge. Who could know him better than someone who lives under the same roof? Two years ago he was engaged to be wed, and the woman hurt him badly by being unfaithful. For that reason he's shown remarkably little interest in women, even avoiding the balls where there are so many eligible girls eager to be noticed by him. But I believe it's been long enough to get over Nan. Both Mama and Papa want him to be wed, of course—he is the heir. But I just want him to be happy."

"We all wish that for someone we love," Cosima said gently. "But I cannot help him, Berrie. You must know that."

"Why? Your engagement to Reginald isn't known. It hasn't been announced and certainly banns haven't been posted. From what I gathered last night, I believe Reginald is a relative stranger to you. You should feel no obligation whatsoever to wed him."

Cosima shook her head. How quickly Beryl's wishes would cool if Cosima simply revealed her family history. But she couldn't. Whether it was the same pride that ran through her mother or something else, Cosima didn't know, but at that moment she could not tell Beryl all the reasons she was unsuitable for her brother.

"I came here under the agreement to get to know Reginald better, Berrie. I cannot go back on that agreement."

"Well, once you know him better I doubt you'll want to wed him."

Curious, Cosima asked, "Is there something about Reginald you would like to tell me?"

Beryl brushed her palms on the pale pink silk of her morning gown. "I know my brother and parents are fond of him. He can be charming, I'll admit. But there is something about him. . . . I've never really trusted him, I suppose."

"Trusted him?"

Beryl stood. "I shouldn't say more if you are intent on getting to know him yourself. I've no wish to cloud your impression, and to be honest, I believe Reginald cannot help but reveal his true self to you. I just hope it will be sooner rather than later."

Cosima smiled sympathetically, tempted to press the matter but thinking there could be only one reason for Beryl's words. "Not everyone can live up to the example your brother sets, Berrie."

Even Cosima knew that, and she'd only just met him.

13

Talie spent the day pulling her thoughts back to her responsibilities and hobbies, away from anticipation over using the item she'd bought at the drugstore that morning. She worked on her new idea for the scrapbook of her father's travel memories, designing each page before making any cuts. She played with Ben, dancing to their favorite children's music and twirling him around until he laughed. She made dinner and even lit candles, but Luke called and said the owner wanted to offer the job to Aidan over dinner at the Chop House, so he wouldn't be home. Talie fed Ben and ate her own meal under the candlelight anyway. He seemed to like it.

The phone rang just as they finished.

"Hey, Danes," Talie said after spotting the familiar number on the caller ID.

"I suppose you know where your husband is."

"Sure do. With your guy."

Dana's laugh sounded like it did on Christmas morning, excited and happy. "Did you know they were going to offer him the job?"

"Only that Luke thought it would go that way. The final decision was the owner's, so I didn't want to say anything until it was a done deal."

Dana's sigh came clearly over the phone line. "I can't believe it. If you'd asked me when we were cleaning out Mom's attic a few weeks ago if I thought I'd be seriously dating someone in a month, my answer would've been a very sad no."

"So . . . it's serious?" Why this wash of caution? Dana knew what she was doing; she was all grown up now.

"I guess it's still a bit early, but to tell you the truth, if we haven't learned something about dating by our age, both Aidan and I are in serious trouble."

"Oh, you're both so old."

"He's thirty; I'm nearly there. And I'll tell you this: we're both tired of dating."

"So the reservations you had about what your friend said—about Aidan being a skirt chaser—those are gone?"

"He's changed, Tal. Even Melody's husband thinks so, and he's known Aidan his whole life. Do you know what we did the night before he went on the interview with Luke?"

"Do I want to hear this?"

Dana laughed again; apparently laughter was in endless supply these days. "We prayed together. There's nothing more intimate than that."

"True," Talie agreed. Her heart should be dancing, nearly the way Dana's must be. Talie wanted her sister to be happy. Maybe if she acted that way, the emotions would follow. "I'm happy for you, Danes. I really am. I pray God will direct this relationship all the way through."

"He is, Tal! He is."

When it was time to tuck Ben in, Talie changed him into his most comfortable pajamas and put him in the crib. She slid the mobile hanging over his crib back to the center, where he could easily see it. Why had she ever pushed it aside? It was a cute, colorful collection of ducks wearing Uncle Sam hats, but for as much attention as it had received, she might as well have never taken it out of the box.

"See this, little guy?" Talie said with a smile. "See these ducks? Here you go, touch one. They're so fuzzy."

Talie wiggled one of the ducks Ben's way, and he glanced at it as he put his favorite finger in his mouth. A moment later when she quacked and made the duck dance, the suction around his finger smacked loose for a smile.

"See how soft it is, Ben?" Talie coaxed. She pulled the duck downward, stressing the plastic from which it hung.

But Ben just sucked his finger again, never reaching for the object.

Talie stroked his hair, wondering why he didn't do what seemed to come naturally to other babies at playgroup. But nothing was really wrong; she was sure of that. He smiled all the time and ate so well. And he *looked* so healthy. Sure he cried, maybe more than some at two in the morning, but he had his reasons.

Besides, nothing could mar her mood today. She was almost certain she had reason to glow.

"I love you, buddy; you know that?" Talie covered him with a duck-printed blanket and left the mobile hanging in his line of vision. She turned and saw Luke at the bedroom door.

"He looks happy to be in for the night." Luke approached the crib and kissed Ben's forehead.

Talie watched, a catch in her breath at the burst of love she felt for them both.

"Maybe he'll sleep through the night tonight," Luke commented.

She nodded. "I hope so." Talie looped her arm through Luke's as they left the room. "So how did the dinner go? I assume Aidan accepted the position, or you wouldn't have made it past hors d'oeuvres."

Luke loosened his tie. "It's all set; he starts next week."

"Great."

"What, no whoop and holler? You're the one who orchestrated this whole thing."

"I did not. I just suggested you find out if he was interested in filling the position you needed. The rest was up to you and Aidan."

He shook his head. "Your spy system is all in place, honey. I thought you'd be a little more excited."

She silently admitted she should be; however she felt an element of caution she couldn't shake.

Talie grinned. "Guess I have something else on my mind. There's something I was going to talk to you about tomorrow, but I'm not sure I can wait."

"Oh? What's that?"

"I bought something today."

"Uh-oh."

She laughed. Normally she consulted him on major purchases, but this one had cost only eight dollars. "Let's go in here, and I'll show you."

He followed her to their bedroom. "Not in the jewelry box, I hope? Your birthday is . . ."

She shook her head. "Nope. It's in the bathroom."

He looked perplexed but not for long. His brows rose. She never could keep anything from him for long; he was too good at figuring things out.

Talie pulled the pregnancy test from the bag hanging on the doorknob. "I bought this to use tomorrow morning. I'm late. And you know I'm never late . . . not unless . . ."

Luke pulled her into his arms with a grin.

She laughed as he held her close. Over his shoulder she saw Cosima's abandoned journal peeking out from beneath the bed, but even that didn't dampen her mood.

Talie had a plan for dispelling her silly worries. She intended to see if there really was one hundred and fifty years between her and Cosima's so-called curse. It was time to contact her East Coast relatives and learn a little about them. If they were all fine, she would know she had nothing whatever to worry about.

Maybe then she could share the journal with Luke and Dana.

14

The saying goes "Blood is thicker than water," but this is not always true. I believe God can turn friends into families, but sometimes, sadly, families are not always friends. Tonight I met my Escott family, and there was so much emotion roiling in my stomach I was certain I could not eat a bite. . . .

"Oh, Mama, it'll be too crowded!"

"Yes, I suppose you're right, Beryl," said Lady Hamilton as they stood in the cool evening breeze just outside their front door. She looked at her husband. "Berrie certainly has a point. If the four of us get in with you, we'll be nothing but a pile of petticoats."

Lord Hamilton hardly looked concerned. "Peter isn't down yet. Beryl, you may accompany him to the Escotts'. Come along, darling," he said to his wife.

"Papa, couldn't Cosima wait here with me for Peter? I'd so love her company."

Cosima looked from Beryl to Lady Hamilton. Beryl's cheerful presence on the ride would start the evening right. Cosima allowed herself little more than a passing thought as to whether or not sharing the carriage with Lord Peter had anything to do with her willingness to comply with Beryl's invitation.

"I'll have the second carriage brought round. But," Lord Hamilton added, his black cloak swinging open when he turned to them from the third step, "if Peter isn't down in precisely five minutes, you are to leave without him. Better for him to ride over on horseback than to make Cosima late."

"Very well, Papa," Beryl called after him, her smile now aimed Cosima's way.

Once they were gone, Cosima whispered to Beryl, "This isn't another of your schemes to throw me together with your brother, is it?"

Beryl's eyes twinkled. "If it is, I didn't see you trying to get out of it, did I?"

Cosima knew the early evening light was still bright enough to reveal the blush she felt rise to her cheeks. Beryl put an arm about Cosima's shoulders and laughed.

"Waiting on me?" said a masculine voice from behind.

Cosima turned in time to see a footman step aside to allow Lord Peter passage out the door. He loomed dark and large but so handsome he inspired more awe than fright. A black cloak clasped at his chest opened to reveal black trousers, waistcoat, and cutaway beneath. White gloves and cravat were the only contrast.

"I thought women were supposed to keep men waiting, not the other way around?" Beryl teased as they made their way down the stairs to the carriage.

A footman pulled out a foldaway stair from the plush, black phaeton. Beryl stepped up first, followed by Cosima, who took the seat next to her.

"Wouldn't it make more sense for you to sit—?" Beryl began, only to cut herself short at Cosima's frown and shake of her head.

"I was only thinking of our dresses," Beryl said with a pout.

With Lord Peter already taking his place opposite them, Cosima did not have time to respond. Once the footman shut the door and hopped up to the rear board, the coachman signaled the horses, and they rumbled forward on the pulverized-stone lane.

"This is your first visit to London, isn't it?" Lord Peter asked. Cosima nodded.

"You should have Reginald take you on a tour," he suggested. "Westminster Abbey, the Tower, St. James's Palace. You could walk if you have a good constitution."

"I would enjoy the exercise."

"First have him take you through Hyde Park. There." He pointed out the window.

"Is that where you went riding this morning?" Cosima asked, too late realizing she should probably not mention their earlier meeting, even though it was certainly no secret from Beryl.

"Yes. There's a ladies' mile if you wish to ride. Beryl often goes midmorning."

"I would like that," Cosima said.

"Your grandmother lives closer to the old city of London." Peter's voice was as cordial as if he were a guide giving her his suggested tour.

"Oh yes . . . Grandmother Escott." Cosima felt Peter's gaze on her, wondering if he guessed her nervousness.

"Let's see," said Beryl. "If every Escott is in attendance tonight—and one can only assume they will all want to meet you—then there will be quite a crowd. Dowager Duchess Merit Escott, your grandmother, first and foremost. For a matriarch, she has quite the iron hand. Your uncle John will be there—he's the duke now—and his wife, Lady Meg. Then there will be aunts, uncles, and cousins. Oh, you'll have a time keeping them straight. I know I do. Have I thoroughly confused you yet?"

Cosima tried to laugh. "Yes, but I hope once I meet them face-to-face this will serve as a helpful foundation."

"Just don't mistake a butler for a cousin, and you'll be fine," said Lord Peter in his even, deep voice, which she found instantly soothing. "At our house it's acceptable to talk to a servant as if he is a person. Not so at the Escotts'."

"I have a lot to learn, haven't I?"

"Not at all," he told her. "You have one thing going for you that none of the rest of us have."

"And what's that?"

"You're an Escott, whether they like it or not."

As the carriage turned down a cobbled street leading alongside a row of wide town houses, Cosima silently prayed, *Lord, an Escott I may be, but for these past nineteen years I've been a Kennesey by culture and habit. Help me tonight to honor one family without dishonoring the other.*

When she opened her eyes, she saw Lord Peter looking at her, and he offered a smile that seemed to indicate he'd guessed she was praying—and approved.

"That's the way," he said softly.

"What's that?" inquired Beryl, looking between them as if she'd missed something.

And indeed she had.

"Miss Cosima Escott," announced the butler as she was shown into a large drawing room. She stood alone at the threshold, unsure what to do next. Thankfully a moment later Lord Peter and Beryl were presented, so Cosima stepped away to make room for their entrance behind her.

"I'll take you to your grandmother, since Reginald isn't here yet." Lord Peter's rich, quiet voice and warm hand on her arm brought instant comfort. She let him direct her path through the ornate furniture. They skirted brocaded ottomans and doily-covered occasional tables upon which sat lamps and dazzling gold knickknacks or ceramic matchboxes.

Cosima tried to take it all in, but little registered through the dozen or more faces still staring at her curiously.

"Dowager Merit," Lord Peter said once they reached an elderly woman seated in a thronelike, winged chair, "may I present Miss Cosima Escott, your granddaughter."

Merit Escott, dowager duchess, was at first glance similar to Cosima's image of the queen. Small in stature but dignified. Of course, Cosima's grandmother was much older than Queen Victoria, an age not hidden with a bit of powder. Wrinkled but fine boned, the heart shape of her face was accentuated by twin puffs of hair emerging from a part at the middle of her head. Her mouth formed a permanent frown, as if a testament to the gesture most familiar. Triangular eyes with lids sagging along each outer corner revealed brown irises but only a bit of the fading whites.

Cosima felt her grandmother study her as if she were an imposter trying to fool her way into an inheritance.

The dowager leaned forward, and her age-spotted trembling hands gripped the small golden globe at the top of her cane.

"You are like him," she said.

Cosima knew to whom her grandmother referred.

"Sit," the dowager ordered, and from somewhere behind a footman immediately appeared, bringing a chair. At some point Peter had backed away.

"You've had a happy life in Ireland?" Dowager Merit asked.

Cosima wondered what her answer could honestly be. Happy to have been raised in a household viewed by others as cursed? And yet Cosima had never wanted for any basic need. Her mother and father had loved her all her years, and so had they loved Percy and Royboy as well. It was all she had ever known; certainly that must play a part in her answer. Her life had not been unhappy.

"Yes, I've been happy," she said.

"And your father?"

She nodded again. "He's been a good father to me, a good husband to my mother."

"Yes." The dowager leaned back. Cosima saw a sparkle of a tear in one eye and wondered if it was age or emotion that caused it. "He would be such."

Cosima had myriad questions she wished to ask but knew this was neither the time nor the occasion. She would let her grandmother determine how this evening—and perhaps their relationship—would progress.

Moments later the butler announced Sir Reginald, who came dutifully to Cosima's side, bowing formally before them both.

"Reginald Hale?" said Dowager Merit, as if her vision were fading and she wasn't sure it was he standing before her. "I know little of you, sir. I understand it to be your desire to marry my granddaughter."

Cosima took note of the reference to herself. It sounded as if they'd taken possession.

"Yes, milady," Reginald said. "To marry an Escott—to marry Cosima—would be a great honor."

"Sir Reginald and I are getting to know one another, milady," Cosima said. She didn't want everyone thinking the wedding was as certain as he made it sound.

Her grandmother lifted one brow, which diminished somewhat the triangular shape of that eye. "In matters of marriage not pertaining to English land or title, as it will be with both of you, it is generally left in the hands of the parents or even the individuals themselves. In this case, however, since we know so little of either of you, caution is advised. I suggest no banns be posted yet, until I have considered this matter."

Reginald bowed again. "Of course, ma'am."

Cosima glanced at Reginald. If he was disappointed at yet

another reason to delay their possible nuptials, he showed no sign.

Dinner was announced then, and each couple proceeded down to the dining room, starting with the current duke and his wife and the rest following according to rank.

The meal was far more lavish than any Cosima could remember, even before Ireland's blight. Tomato soup and shellfish, peppered roasts, venison, vegetables and whitebait, cheese, confectioneries, and fruit-flavored ices, which was only a trifle soft considering the room was warm from a roaring fireplace. Every taste was met, from salty or spicy to tart or sweet. Ten courses, she counted by the end, and had she taken more than a taste of only half she would have been sick indeed.

Cosima sat between two of her cousins, daughters of her father's sister. Neither of them had known of her existence until the day before, so they were understandably curious.

At last the meal ended and Dowager Merit suggested the younger people be excused to the music room to pass the time without a hovering older generation nearby. Almost at once Reginald invited Peter to come with Cosima and the rest of the cousins.

Coffee and tea were served in the music room. A moment later a group of younger children entered, obviously cousins who had been served dinner in the nursery. Their ages ranged from barely more than a toddler to ten or eleven years old. Two nurses accompanied them, each evidently having charge of certain children.

"You must tell me what you think, man," said Reginald to Peter as he smiled Cosima's way. "Haven't I outdone myself in finding Cosima?"

Lord Peter smiled and looked at Cosima. She wished she could ignore her quickened heartbeat and the warmth stirring in her breast at the sight of him. But she pulled her gaze to

Reginald instead. He seemed perfectly at ease, happy to have their company.

As if reading Cosima's thought, Reginald placed one hand on Peter's shoulder and the other on Cosima's forearm, linking the three of them together. "You are the two most important people in my life. I'd like for us to spend time together."

From behind Peter came her cousin Rachel with her fiancé at her side. He was a bit taller than she, but Peter towered above all the other men in the room. Rachel, Cosima decided, favored their grandmother. Not a classic beauty but appealing with high cheekbones, a full mouth, and a heart-shaped face. Her narrow nose was her only unfortunate feature, but that could be easily overlooked when she smiled.

"Cousin." Rachel took both of Cosima's hands in hers and kissed her cheek. "We meet at last."

Reginald leaned closer to Cosima. "If it weren't for Rachel, I might never have had the opportunity to meet you, Cosima."

Cosima looked at Rachel. "Yes, I was curious about that, since it appears none of my other cousins knew of my existence until a few days ago."

Rachel laughed. Her laugh was not infectious like Christabelle's nor spontaneous like Beryl's but rather practiced.

"You'll find, of all your English cousins, Cosima, I'm the most resourceful. There is a portrait in the hall of your father with mine, and I always wondered what happened to that little boy who looked so much like our grandfather. And I found out."

Cosima wanted to learn how, but others came forward, eliminating the opportunity for individual conversation.

Soon Rachel was at the piano, accompanying herself in a series of popular songs. Reginald stayed by Cosima, but between rounds he engaged more in conversation with Peter than he did with Cosima. She was glad when Beryl came to her side, helping her quietly match names with faces from afar.

Everyone clapped when Rachel finished her repertoire—until she stood, her gaze a warning to where she headed, coming face-to-face with Cosima. Though she smiled, there was something in her eyes that Cosima had never seen directed her way before. A steady, level gaze that appeared friendly and yet challenging at the same time.

"It's your turn, Cousin," she said. "Will you show us what they teach the young women of Ireland?"

A snicker sounded from somewhere in the room, and Cosima wanted to look around to see from whom the disrespectful sound had come, but she dared not take her gaze from Rachel.

Rachel took one of Cosima's hands, leading her to the piano. "You do play, of course? I cannot imagine an Escott untutored at music. Even if your father did abandon the family, I'm sure he didn't abandon proper etiquette. Come now, sit and let us hear what Ireland can do."

Had Cosima been warned she might have to perform, it could very well have ruined her evening before it began. Sitting down, she paused a moment to decide her choice of music. Complicated pieces to showcase her Irish teacher's best student came instantly to mind, but another thought, not her own, emerged as she looked past Rachel to Lord Peter, who was not far behind. *Pride serves no one.* Certainly not the One she ought to be serving.

And so she chose a simple old ballad, haunting in its melody but rising gradually to a cheerful note. Cosima closed her eyes, pretending she was home again, cocooned in the family drawing room with her parents and Royboy. Royboy rarely stayed long at her side, except when she played the piano or pianoforte. It was one of the few things that made him sit still.

Clapping greeted the end of Cosima's music, bringing her back to England. She smiled, glancing first at Peter, who looked pleased. Belatedly, she looked at Reginald, who was exuberant in his applause.

She started to rise, but Rachel stepped forward again, waving her back to the piano bench. "You have a delighted audience, Cosima! Of course you must play another. And can you sing?"

Reluctant to be the center of attention much longer, Cosima did not take the seat immediately. Instead she looked again to where Peter and Reginald stood. She knew a wise woman would seek the approval of the man claiming an interest in marrying her, but somehow her gaze went first to Peter. In that moment she saw only warmth, a desire to hear more music.

Cosima sat once again, just as Rachel bent over her with an arm about her shoulder. "Who would have thought Ireland could produce such a pianist?"

"Ireland didn't," said another voice from behind Cosima. She didn't have to look this time; Cosima knew the voice belonged to Walter, Rachel's older brother, the future duke. "She's half English, you know."

Rachel smiled as if the words were light and harmless, but Cosima felt the cut to the land of her birth. Immediately she knew which song to sing.

Her voice was clear and steady, accurately following the tune that flew from her fingertips across the piano keys. If she'd allowed herself more time to consider which song to perform she would have chosen another. But the Gaelic words meant nothing to them, so she sang with assurance.

The applause at the end seemed louder than before, and when Cosima glanced up she saw they'd been joined by the rest of the dinner guests. She stood, avoiding eye contact with Rachel, who might implore her to sing again.

"Cosima."

Though the room buzzed with conversation, she approached her grandmother at the call.

"You have a lovely voice," her grandmother said. "I should like it if you would visit again and sing for me. But that song . . . in the language of your homeland. We prefer English, for little good comes from Ireland."

Cosima swallowed hard. "I believe such words were once said of a Nazarene."

She heard a gasp from somewhere behind.

The dowager lifted one of her brows, stiffening in her seat. "What did the words of your song mean?"

Cosima folded her hands, letting her gaze fall to the floor. For the barest moment she was tempted to lie, to say she'd been taught the words but not the meaning. She shouldn't have chosen that song, and now she must pay the price.

"'Tis a lament, milady."

"Lament? Why should someone your age sing a lament?"

"The song is a prayer, beseeching our loving God to remember the outcast, the downtrodden, because our Savior Himself was cast down by those in power."

The political ramifications were not lost on the dowager, whose triangle eyes opened wider ever so briefly, as if in shock. But the song had never been political for Cosima. Rather it was a plea for God's protection of her brother Royboy and others like him, against those healthy society members who tried to take advantage of them. Even if the composer of the lyrics had some hidden political agenda, Cosima knew they had served more as a personal expression.

"Who taught you such a song, child?" demanded Dowager Merit.

"'Twas the composer himself, milady."

"A dissident, no doubt. Who was it, girl?"

Cosima squared her shoulders. Dissident, indeed. "My father."

The heavy lids closed altogether for the barest moment, and when they opened again, Dowager Merit looked fatigued. "I had thought to have you stay here with me. But I can see that you need to think about what it would mean for you to have the privilege of living here. For now, it is best for things to remain as they are until I summon you. This visit has come to an end."

The dowager stood, leaning heavily on her cane, and made her way from the room, leaving an awkward silence in her wake.

The Hamilton cloaks were brought first. It must be as clear to others as it was to Cosima: she had ruined the evening.

"We'll go home the same as we came?" Beryl asked as they made their way to the foyer. Her voice was light as ever, as if nothing unpleasant had taken place.

"No, Beryl," said her father. Lord Hamilton glanced Cosima's way. "I would like a word with you, Miss Cosima. Beryl, you and your sister will take the carriage that you and Peter arrived in. I should like to have Peter's company as well."

Cosima was ushered into a carriage beside Lady Hamilton. She barely had a chance to say good night to Reginald, who politely patted her hand but his tone revealed his disappointment.

In the carriage, the silence was interrupted only by the pounding in Cosima's ears, blood pumping too fast and too hard. She realized she'd displeased her grandmother but somehow felt little remorse. However, if she'd also displeased the Hamiltons, that was something she *would* regret. "I am very sorry if my actions have embarrassed you or your family in any way, Lord Hamilton."

One corner of his mustache twitched. "No, Cosima," he said gently. He looked more sorrowful than offended. "It's you who were disserved. First by your own father and then by Reginald and lastly by my family."

Surprised, Cosima said nothing. How had so many failed her when it was she who'd proven to be an embarrassment?

"I can only surmise your father had his reasons for sparing you the details of his life here in England. Reginald, of course, might be excused from having warned you because he may not be familiar with the family, as certainly I am, or even my wife.

Though I must pardon my wife, as she is hesitant to broach topics of the serious sort. Therefore, Cosima, it's I who must apologize for allowing you to go into a lion's den, so to speak, ill prepared."

"I'm afraid I don't understand," she said, and indeed she didn't.

"My son and I," said Lord Hamilton, glancing at Peter beside him, "have long been a pair of gnats in your grandmother's ear."

Lord Peter, directly opposite Cosima, offered her a smile. "We should have asked what you knew of your family, not simply thrust you into their midst and expected you to come out unscathed. Your family is—" He suddenly stopped himself, looking from Cosima to his mother, then to his father and finally back to Cosima. "Here you have it, Cosima—the reason none of us said anything. It's hard to present information in a gracious light when you've few kind words to use."

"My grandmother can be difficult?"

Lord Hamilton laughed. "Your song, even if only to entertain, *could* have been interpreted with a political tone. And the dowager is staunchly in favor of English supremacy wherever the Crown extends."

"Your grandmother," Lord Peter interjected, "once called my father—let's see if I can recall it correctly—a single, nagging straight hair among a luxurious abundance of curls. She was fairly right in her assessment in that my father will stand for what he believes even when it's unpopular, but that she spoke in public put a rather visible line in the sand. She likely thinks one of us heretical Hamiltons put you up to singing a song that might be construed as shedding a bad light upon our glorious England."

"Oh . . . I'm so very sorry to have caused any—"

Lady Hamilton squeezed her hand. "We're not looking for an apology, my dear. We should have realized that having you stay with us would put you in an uncomfortable position."

Cosima sighed. "If I'm in an uncomfortable position, then I would say my father set the foundation."

"We needn't talk about it any further," said Peter's father. "Tomorrow someone else will do something for people to talk about."

Lady Hamilton nodded. "Yes, put it from your mind, my dear."

Cosima knew that was far easier said than done.

15

Talie and Luke shared a celebratory breakfast before he went off to work with an especially handsome smile that morning. In about eight months they would have a new addition to the family. After Luke left, Talie made an appointment with her obstetrician, then went about her regular routine: fed and dressed Ben, cleaned a room or two, read him a book, and took him for a walk in the sunshine.

When they returned at midmorning, she changed his diaper then turned on some classical music for Ben to enjoy from his blanket on the floor. As usual, she surrounded him with plush toys and rattles, but he preferred to suck on his finger.

It was time. Time for something she'd planned to do days ago but had put off.

Talie hadn't mentioned anything to Luke, had even used a bit of subterfuge to collect the phone number she was about to dial. Her mother thought Talie only wanted to check on a few names from the family Bible, verify a date or two.

That was certainly true.

Pulling the scrap of paper with the number on it from a drawer in the kitchen, she noticed her trembling hands. Why be nervous? This was Aunt Virg's phone number. Her father's sister-in-law, the woman who'd been married to Talie's uncle Steve for over forty years, until his death nearly fifteen years ago.

Contact between the two branches of the family remained limited to a Christmas card. It was from one of those that Talie's mother had scrawled Aunt Virg's phone number.

Although Talie had met Aunt Virg and Uncle Steve on a couple of occasions when she was a child, she only vaguely remembered them. A dozen years had separated her father from his elder brother, and both age and distance prevented Talie and Dana from getting to know them or their cousins very well.

Talie swallowed once, noticing with some annoyance that her hands hadn't stopped shaking despite her calming thoughts. She really did want to verify a few names and dates. Besides, she would have something to offer Aunt Virg once Luke made the family tree. Talie could send her a copy.

So why was Talie nervous?

There was no question about it. She had one question for her aunt that she wasn't sure she wanted answered. Were any of her grandchildren . . . slow?

How could Talie possibly ask such a question?

And yet, touching her flat middle where the miracle of new life was already working, she knew she needed to ask that very thing . . . somehow.

Talie didn't believe in curses, but she did believe in genetics. If there had been something in Cosima's genetics a hundred and fifty years ago, could it somehow have survived all these years?

Talie shook her head. Of course it hadn't. She and Dana were living proof that nothing was wrong genetically. Her father had been fine as well, and so had his brother. And although Talie had only met her cousins a few times when she was a child, she didn't recall any of them having cognitive problems. Each one was proof that Cosima's so-called curse had died a long time ago.

Aunt Virg would probably be delighted to talk about her family. And she would likely welcome any information Talie could give about her husband's family line . . . provided Talie left out details of Rowena and what she had done.

Talie dialed the number.

"Hello?" The voice sounded frail but loud.

"Aunt Virg? This is Talie Ingram . . . although you might remember me as Talie Martin, your niece from Chicago."

"Chicago? Oh, Talie . . . Natalie, is that you?"

She closed her eyes in relief, remembering Aunt Virg calling her by her full name, the way she'd called her own daughter Elizabeth instead of Liz, as everyone else addressed her. At least Talie wouldn't have to introduce herself as if she were a stranger.

"Yes, it's me. How are you?"

"Oh, fair to middlin', as they say. Can't complain since I'm seventy-eight and still kicking."

"I'm glad to hear that. My mother said from your last Christmas card that it sounded as if you liked your new place. I hope that's still true?"

"I do. Don't tell anyone, but it's really an old folks home." She laughed and the sound was instantly familiar. It pierced Talie's ear. "Watch yourself, sweetie; it happens before you know it. Old age! But, still, it's nice here. If I don't feel like cooking, I just go downstairs to the cafeteria. Of course, the food isn't very good, but the people make up for it. We complain together. Suffering's always better in community, you know."

Talie laughed. This wasn't so hard, was it? Aunt Virg was as friendly as ever.

"I'm calling because I'm putting together a family tree from my dad's side. A genealogy record. I have quite a few names from past generations, but I don't know many details from Uncle Steve's branch. I'm looking for birth dates for your kids and spouses' and children's names too."

"Goodness! I know the names, but I'm not sure I can get all the dates straight on any of them except my own. I'll have to ask Elizabeth to help me on that, and we can send a list to you. Would that be all right?"

Squashing her disappointment in the reasonableness of the request, Talie knew she had to find a way to keep the conversation going. "That would be great . . . but just so I know how much room I'll be needing, could you tell me a little about your family? I know you and Uncle Steve had four children—two daughters and two sons. Did they all marry?"

"Yes, some time ago now."

Surely if her cousins were responsible enough to marry they were as healthy as Dana and herself. That was a good start. "And did they have children?"

"Oh yes. I have seventeen grandchildren, last count." She laughed again, and Talie held the phone a little farther away before pressing it back when Aunt Virg started talking again. "But that's not likely to change since my children are all done having their own kids. They're grandparents themselves."

"So of the seventeen grandchildren, some of them are great-grandchildren?"

"Oh no. I have four great-grandchildren and another on the way."

Talie doodled a rectangle around Aunt Virg's phone number to keep her fingers employed, even though they were no longer shaking. She was calmer by the moment. "Sounds like the Martin branches will be bigger than I expected. Would you like a copy of the information when I've compiled it?"

"That would be lovely. I'm sure the family would like to see it too."

A new thought struck Talie. "Perhaps I could compile a note-book of some sort, listing some of the occupations for the adults and activities that the kids are involved in. I could name hobbies . . . awards . . . that sort of thing."

"Marvelous, Natalie! What a lovely idea for family posterity. I'm sure Elizabeth could help you in that area, too. My, my, it would be too hard for me to remember all of the things my grandkids are involved in. Of course they all love sports, boys and girls alike. Baseball, basketball, soccer—you name it. They all played one thing or another."

Talie's heart floated. Hand-eye coordination didn't come naturally to everyone. "Sounds like a healthy bunch."

"Oh yes. Our family has been blessed with excellent health, thank the Lord. Though I think one grandson had asthma, but he grew out of it and now he's on his college volleyball team."

"College, yes . . ." Eager to continue in this vein, she tried to keep excitement from her voice. "Let's see . . . I suppose I could list various educations. Have all your grandkids gone on to college, then?"

"All but one, and he's graduating high school this year."

"Does he plan to go?"

"Yes, he's been accepted at New York University. Won't this be quite some family ledger if you plan to include all that? Very generous of you, Natalie. And what about Uncle Henry's bunch? Do you recall your father having an Uncle Henry?"

Talie's mind raced at the unexpected help. Maybe she could save herself another phone call. "I never met him, but I do have a Henry Grayson listed, and I was going to ask if you knew someone I should call. He passed away . . . some time ago."

"Yes, over thirty years ago now. He had three young ones as far as I know. Well, they're hardly young anymore! Did you know one of his kids went on to be a congressman? One of your father's cousins. Retired now, though."

"Perhaps Elizabeth can send me information on them, if you have any."

"I'm sure she can. They haven't been as numerous as my bunch, but between politics and big business ventures I guess they were too busy to have so many kids."

"But they're all healthy, as far as you know?"

Aunt Virg hesitated. Maybe Talie had gone too far, been too obvious.

"Oh yes. Well, other than poor Abigail, your father's cousin from Henry. Lung cancer, you know. And young when she died—just fifty-eight."

Talie had never before welcomed the word *cancer,* though at the moment she found herself doing just that. "There is one more name I'm not familiar with, Aunt Virg. Did you know Ellen Dana?"

"Hmm . . . oh yes, of course. Such a sad story there, really."

Talie's buoyant heart refused to be stilled. Sad story? How sad could it be if every other member of her extended family was healthy?

But Aunt Virg was talking, and Talie made herself listen again. "Ellen Dana was your grandmother's sister. When their mother died, your grandmother was around seventeen, with plans for college. Ellen Dana was younger, maybe around ten or so; I'm not sure. Their father didn't think he should have such a young girl in the house without a mother. Things were different in those days, you know. When your grandmother went off to college, he sent Ellen Dana to a boarding school. I really don't recall the details, and she died rather young. Pneumonia, I think. Or was it polio? That was before I came into the family. I never met her. Did your father ever mention his aunt Ellen?"

"Only that my sister, Dana, is named for her."

"Ah yes, I'd forgotten. That was a lovely sentiment."

"So you never met Ellen Dana, then? Or knew where she went to school?"

"No, I'm sorry I don't. Steve never spoke of that aunt. To be honest I'm not sure he even met her."

Talie looked down at her list. "I have the date of her death . . . 1941. I think that's the same year my father was born."

"I'm sure you're right, Natalie. He was twelve years younger than my Steve, and he was born in '28." She sighed. "I suppose that's why Martha mentioned the name Ellen Dana to your father. Maybe she thought they had some kind of connection . . . you know, her dying and him being born the same year."

"Maybe she did." Talie knew she'd found out all she could for now. She cleared her throat. "I suppose it would be a lot of work for Elizabeth to compile some of this information. Will she have time to do such a thing?"

Aunt Virg's laugh punctured Talie's eardrum again. "If you knew Elizabeth, you wouldn't even ask. That one is so organized I'm sure she has every name and date, hobby and college recorded on that computer of hers. Whatever she doesn't know offhand she'll get through that e-mail you young folks do all the time."

"Sounds perfect," Talie said.

"Let me write down your address and have Elizabeth send you what you're looking for. What a nice call, Natalie! I'm sure Elizabeth will be thrilled to help."

Talie wouldn't call herself thrilled, but *outrageously relieved* was close enough.

16

I have long been known to friends and family alike as one who detests secrets. And now I find that I have reason to keep a few myself.

Here I am, quickly and easily developing the most wonderful friendship with Berrie, and yet I have told her little about myself. But how can I ever reveal the truth? About Royboy, Percy, Uncle Willie? I can only imagine Berrie would be aghast. Too kind, perhaps, to treat me much differently, but how could her opinion of me not change? I am, most certainly, peculiar in my circumstance. Once such a secret is known it will be known forever, impossible to forget or ignore. At first, she might wonder if my curse is contagious. After that she might wonder if I am bent toward instability myself. Worse than either of those, she might pity me.

And so I keep silent. . . .

Cosima followed Beryl along the hallway, wondering why her step was unusually quick, her voice unusually animated. But

Cosima convinced herself she didn't know Beryl well enough to assume she was up to anything. She was often lively, which made her company so enjoyable.

"I want to show you the single most interesting thing about this home."

"The single most?" Cosima repeated, eyeing Beryl with surprise. "But there are many interesting things here, Beryl. The tier gardens, the painted ceiling in the dining hall, the aviary . . ."

"I suppose to someone who hasn't spent *every* London season of her life right here this isn't the most boring place on earth. Perhaps I misspoke. There are actually two places of interest. One that I'm about to show you, and the other is downstairs. Although I wouldn't call that room downstairs actually *interesting* . . . rather I'd call it fascinating, the way something might be ugly like a carriage accident yet we can't quite look away. But this—"

"Do you know you sound like Christabelle right now, the way you're going on?"

Though Beryl smiled, she said, "No need to insult me, dear. Will you tell me what time it is?"

The oddly placed inquiry surprised Cosima, but nonetheless she looked at the watch pin attached to the bodice of her beige-and-white striped day gown. "Almost four."

"Almost, but not quite?" she clarified, as if it made a difference.

Cosima nodded.

"Perfect. Come along to the library then."

Cosima shook her head at Beryl's curious but lighthearted behavior. She couldn't imagine why Beryl was taking her to the library. She'd been there already with both Beryl and Christabelle, and although the room was lovely and well stocked, it was hardly new to Cosima.

The library was situated at the back of the town house. Like the rest of the home, it was long and narrow with the height of the ceiling giving a feel of space. Even the shelves rose to the top of the room, with a ladder allowing access to the books up high.

Though the open door beckoned anyone to enter, once they were inside Beryl closed it tight. She turned to Cosima with a gaze that looked at once excited and serious. "You must promise what I'm about to show you will remain a secret."

"You're being so mysterious, Beryl!"

Beryl grabbed one of Cosima's hands. "Promise me, Cosima."

Cosima eyed her friend, sensing her earnestness. "Of course, Berrie. God is my witness; I've no need to say more than that for you to know I'll keep my word."

"I'm about to show you something only my family knows of. I'm not sure my father would approve of my showing you, at least not yet, but he doesn't have my foresight or quite understand that I think of you as my sister."

"You're like a sister to me too, Berrie."

"Come with me."

Still holding Cosima's hand, Beryl went to one of the shelves at the rear of the room. She touched a heftier volume, but rather than withdraw it she tilted it to its side and reached behind to slide something aside. It sounded like brick or stone, not at all like the simple wood that should have been there. She did the same to another book at the opposite end of the same shelf.

A moment later she stood back and pushed on the frame. To Cosima's amazement the entire shelf, wide enough to accommodate both of them at the same time, opened as if it were a door rather than a wooden panel of books.

"My grandfather had this room added after the turmoil in France back in '89." Beryl whispered, as if mindful of her parents' disapproval of her if they knew.

Cosima caught the caution and spoke up. "Berrie, if this is

truly some sort of family secret, then you really ought not be showing me. Let's come away, and I shall forget all about it."

Beryl tugged on Cosima's hand, still firmly in hers. "There's no harm in it, really. I want to show you."

"But—"

With Beryl already moving forward, Cosima had little choice but to obey, especially when Beryl took a candle from the wall, lit it, then closed the panel behind them. Cosima had no idea how to open the panel again. She was thankful she had no fear of closed-in places, for if she had, this would no doubt be the right spot for a panic.

They descended steps along a narrow stone corridor remarkably free of dust though it was a bit dank. Cosima couldn't tell how deep the passageway might be since the candle's light reached no farther than a few steps ahead. She stayed close to Beryl, unable to quell her own curious excitement. She felt like a child, exploring some place meant only for a club of which she was decidedly not a member.

"Outside the family, only Claude Seabrooke, my father's valet, knows about this room. He's fifth-generation valet for the Hamiltons and thus trusted. Claude comes down here once a month after the other servants are abed, to tidy up and put fresh water in the urns."

"But . . . why?"

"My grandfather feared an uprising here, like in France. I remember the stories, how he took in many of the aristocracy who fled. They told such terrible tales my grandfather decided to build this secret room. Actually he enlarged an original secret place . . . but I'm not supposed to talk about that, either, though I shall tell you."

Cosima was intrigued but interrupted Beryl anyway. "You've told me too much already, so keep at least one family secret, won't you?"

Beryl's laugh echoed off barren, dark walls. "The original room was a priest hole. It's positively silly not to acknowledge that our early forebears might have been Catholic or at least sympathetic to the priests who were banished so long ago by our Protestant kingdom. By building this room, all evidence of what it might have been was forgotten. Grandfather killed two birds with one stone, so to speak."

The stairs seemed to lead upward until at last they stepped into a room, complete with a lamp Beryl lit, revealing a comfortable settee, blankets, and pillows stacked upon a mattress stored to the side. In an opposite corner were the urns Beryl had referred to and a large tin box.

"Claude puts bread in there and closes it tight against any mice that might find a way in here. I suppose I should be horrified to eat something I thought was at risk of being nibbled first by a mouse, but Father said one can eat anything if hungry enough."

"It is indeed an interesting place, Berrie," Cosima admitted. "And I will always honor my word and never tell a soul about it. But I believe we should be going before anyone discovers you've shown it to me."

"We needn't hurry off. I've told Mama we'll be on our own this afternoon and not to look for us. Christabelle would never think to look here."

Cosima couldn't help but lift a brow. "Of course not; she is the obedient daughter."

Beryl gasped. "You simply cannot believe that! She'd have no compunction about bringing you here. I only excluded her so as not to get her into trouble if we're found out."

Cosima looked around. "I doubt anyone can hear us from here."

"Precisely true. Come along; there's more."

Beryl went to the wall where she found a doorknob Cosima

hadn't noticed before. She pulled open another door, this one revealing steps leading upward again, though not nearly as many as those they'd descended. At the top of the sixth stair was another door, which Beryl pushed. It was as if a seal had been broken. Light from outside rushed in along with fresh air and the sound of birds.

All Cosima could see was green. Tall yews in every direction.

"This exit spills directly into our garden maze. It's not much of a maze, since we have so little room here in the city, but enough to befuddle someone who might be on the trail of any fleeing members of the aristocracy long enough for us to get away."

It might not have been much of a maze to Beryl, but a few steps into it Cosima was thoroughly confused. Not Beryl, who walked along as if the path were marked.

"I'm glad you know the way so well," Cosima remarked.

"My parents played a game when Christabelle and I were little. The first one to the center earned a piece of candy. Of course Christabelle was always first between the two of us. I'm convinced that's why she's developed such a sweet tooth and is plump today. But I learned my way eventually. I could do it with my eyes closed now."

"I'm glad to hear it, since I'm utterly lost already."

"Not to worry." A moment later the green colonnades opened to a garden center, complete with flowers of every color and a curved bench upon a circular mosaic of smooth white and purple stone. "Sit, will you?"

Cosima was glad to follow Beryl's invitation. The colorful spot was lovely, accompanied by a gentle breeze and the symphony of birdsong from every direction.

But Beryl did not sit with her. "Oh, dear, I think I left the lamp lit in the secret room."

Cosima started to rise.

"No, I shall go and put it right. You stay here; it's such a lovely day."

Cosima rose anyway. "Perhaps I should accompany you. I've no idea where I am."

"I'll be right back, goose." And then she scurried away.

Cosima was half tempted to follow anyway but decided if Beryl trusted her enough to show her the secret room, the least she could do was trust Beryl enough to return for her. So she settled back on the bench, closing her eyes and smelling the lavender that was planted along the edge of the garden.

A few moments later she heard the crunch of Beryl's footfall on the pebbled pathway. Without opening her eyes, Cosima smiled and spoke. "If I sit here just so, with the sun on my face and the scent of flowers so delightful, I can imagine I'm anywhere at all. Back home or in heaven or right here . . . which surely must be nearly heaven itself."

"Except the paths would be lined with gold instead of stone," said a surprisingly deep voice, "if this were truly heaven."

Cosima's eyes shot open, and she sat ramrod stiff. Peter Hamilton stood before her, minus a formal topcoat but resplendent in dark trousers and a white shirt and cravat.

"I . . . thought you were Berrie."

He smiled easily, as if he weren't at all surprised to have found her. "I surmised as much. It's obvious she's put us together again. She sent me a missive to meet her here at four o'clock."

Cosima stood, folding then unfolding her hands. "She is quite the prankster, isn't she?"

Peter did not move, merely watched her as she paced and wrung her hands. How foolish she felt in comparison to his calm perusal. She stopped, demanding her hands and feet to be still.

And yet it did not help. She could do nothing but look at him, and while her body might be outwardly still, inwardly her mind played havoc. Was there a way he could see inside, through her eyes, and guess at the effect he had upon her?

"I . . . will speak to Berrie." She was relieved her voice was steadier than her heartbeat. "Tell her she mustn't play such tricks on us. She should be right back."

Peter's smile slowly widened. "Perhaps not, since she left us here."

Too quickly, thoughts of Beryl disappeared. Instead she contemplated Peter's face. He was indeed fine. His nose on another might have appeared sharp, but his mustache softened the look. And his eyes, shrouded by matching brows so like his father's, were keen and set intently upon her. But it was his mouth that fascinated her most, barely visible beneath that mustache yet enough to glimpse his smile.

"I'm afraid I haven't the slightest idea how to find my way back," she said. Somehow her voice was little more than a whisper, though she hadn't intended it to be.

"It isn't hard. I'll show you."

Despite the polite offer, neither one moved to leave.

He stepped toward her. "I wanted to tell you I enjoyed your music the other night. *Both* songs, in spite of your grandmother's reaction."

"Thank you." Still her voice was quiet, as if the privacy of the maze's center wasn't intimate enough. "I used to enjoy singing at home."

"I hope you feel free to do so here as well."

"Yes. I shall."

He looked away for the first time, glancing back at the path he'd taken, perhaps looking for Beryl if he thought she might arrive the same way.

"And how are your latest fossils proving to be, Lord Peter?" Cosima knew as well as he that they should go, yet the stalling question left her mouth anyway.

"Splendid, actually." His tone said he was pleased to keep the conversation going. "I've come across a type I haven't seen in quite some time. A fish, I believe, that was devoured by something larger. The museum curator will welcome them."

She wished she could think of more to say, wished she had some knowledge of fossils so she might ask an intelligent question. But none came to mind.

"Perhaps we could pay a visit to the museum," he suggested.

She held back an immediate and boisterous agreement, saying demurely instead, "I would like that. I was so surprised by the fossils I saw from your bag. Amazed that something could be hidden away for so long. How many wonders do you suppose our Creator has for us?"

Peter took yet another step closer, so that he stood within arm's reach. "I believe we'll never know the full extent of God's creativity—at least not this side of heaven."

She found her gaze swept up in his. "I'm sure you're right."

"Your interest in fossils is refreshing, Cosima," he said. "Everyone else quickly finds another topic whenever I bring them up."

"Oh, but why, when they show God in them?"

He smiled. "Evidently the rest of the world doesn't see it as you and I do."

Cosima knew they could have been speaking of something far less profound than God and she still would have been fascinated. And he felt the same. She saw it though his brows tried to hide his eyes and his mustache the smile.

Something she could not, of course, allow. She looked away, reluctantly aware of what she must do. "I suppose Reginald is as intrigued by nature as you seem to be, Lord Peter?"

"Reg?" In the instant it took to be reminded of his friend, something changed. Cosima glimpsed a veil come over those dark eyes, one that erased whatever it was she had wanted so much to see before.

Peter stepped back to the edge of the circular mosaic pattern. "Reginald is more practical than I," he said brusquely, "without much time for God's creation. His interests lie in business, in a job well done."

Cosima wished she hadn't felt compelled to mention Reginald's name, since it banished the intimacy that had sprung up just now, the same intimacy that had erupted the night they'd met. But how could she encourage whatever it was that seemed so eager to form between them? There was Reginald . . . and so much more. So much that Lord Peter didn't know.

Peter brushed something from his forearm, a petal that had fallen from the magnolia tree nearby. "I'm surprised Reginald isn't here this afternoon."

"I suppose he must catch up on his business ventures, since he took time away to . . . fetch me."

Peter looked at her again, perhaps having noticed the catch in her words, the reminder of why she was here at all. For a moment he held her gaze, and she let him. How could she not? Looking at him seemed all she was capable of doing whenever he was nearby.

"Cosima . . ."

She longed to hear what he would say, so much that she stepped forward, silently urging him to continue.

But at that moment a call summoned their attention.

"Oh! I've bungled it!" And there stood Beryl, looking flustered with pink cheeks and wide eyes. "Papa is looking for you, Peter, and now Christabelle is wondering where you are, Cosima. It wasn't supposed to be this way. You were to have a solid hour to get to know one another privately."

Peter's dark brows sank into a frown, with what looked like a touch of anger in his eyes. And then surprise. "Where . . . did you come from, Beryl?"

Beryl tried to smile, but it looked like little more than a twitch. "From . . . there." She pointed in the direction of the maze that led to the secret room.

Peter looked between them both.

Cosima couldn't help but feel a twinge of guilt, no matter that she'd initially been reluctant to see Beryl's revelation. "I-I'm sorry, Lord Peter, but I know about the room," Cosima said. "I've given my word not to tell a soul, of course."

"No need for you to apologize, Miss Escott. My sister is consistent in one thing: her impetuosity. May I speak to you, Berrie? Alone?"

Beryl looked anything but willing. She pointed toward the green corridor that led to the rest of the yard, the way Peter had arrived. "I really should take Cosima to Christabelle, and don't forget Papa is waiting for you."

"This won't take long."

He led Beryl away, but they must have stopped in the very next aisle of yews, for Cosima heard his voice clearly when he spoke again.

"Beryl, I'm disappointed in you. I cannot let you—"

"You do not believe she would betray the secret room?"

"I'm not talking about that, Berrie. I'm sure you're right, and what does it matter? We've no need for that antiquated notion of security. I'll trust God instead. What I'm disappointed in is the fact that you've once again made me the fool by pushing my company on her."

Cosima realized she should step away, at least move out of hearing range. She was clearly eavesdropping. But she couldn't seem to move.

"A fool! I don't see it that way at all, particularly when I look at either of you. It's obvious you *both* enjoy each other's company."

"That doesn't matter. Do you think I want to do to Reg what was done to me? I won't have it, Berrie, and you mustn't orchestrate any such thing again."

Silence. Cosima vividly imagined Beryl with a pout. But she

really must listen to her brother, not for the intriguing reason
he gave but for a far more important reason, one Cosima had no
intention of sharing.

Beryl might be willing to share all of the Hamilton secrets
with Cosima, but Cosima wasn't yet ready to reciprocate.

17

Three weeks later, Talie peeked around the door to their study. Luke was bent over his drafting table, illumined in the light suspended from the uppermost edge. The table was old and heavy, a near dinosaur in the world of drafting tables. Luke's father had purchased it at a high school auction for him when he was eight years old. Perhaps more than anything else, the gift had nurtured his dream to become an architectural engineer.

"Want some decaf?"

"Sure."

In a few minutes Talie returned with a steaming mug. She settled for a glass of skim milk for herself, mindful of the new baby.

"Working late?"

Luke pushed himself back but not far from the table, motioning her closer. As he accepted the mug, he slipped his arm around her waist. "It's your family tree. See?"

She'd left the family Bible on his desk. Luke must have begun the project on his own without telling her. She knew they'd get to it eventually—she'd promised Aunt Virg as much. She just hadn't thought it would be so soon.

"You don't like it?"

Maybe he'd felt her stiffen, or maybe there was something on her face when she recognized certain names at the bottom: Willie, Royboy, Rowena . . . Cosima.

"No . . . Luke, it's . . . fabulous. It's lovely, really. I just didn't think you would start it without telling me."

"I wanted to surprise you."

That he was both pleased and proud was obvious. And there was plenty of reason to be proud. Talie marveled at her husband's talent despite her aversion to the subject. Before her was a work of art, a strong and vibrant tree of meticulously placed leaves and sturdy branches. Names were neatly printed along deep veins of foliage and limbs, starting with *Kennesey* drawn near the sinewy roots.

Luke brushed the edge of the oversize paper where it curled away from the clamps holding it down. "I heard about an old tradition of having males bearing the family names on the branches and the female names on leaves."

The penciled coloring was ingenious in itself, using rich browns for older male names amid the contour of the bark. Deep forest green enhanced the women's names of previous centuries. Gradually the colors lightened toward tan branches and virescent leaves to indicate a more recent age, a hope of budding new life and life yet to come.

"Here you are," Luke added. He pointed to a gently shaded leaf toward the top. There, in bold and clear lettering was her full name: Natalie Martin Ingram. A leaf of similar size and color nearby belonged to Dana. He'd even incorporated all of their cousins on Uncle Steve's and Uncle Henry's branches from Elizabeth's list, which she'd received the other day. When it came in the mail Talie had stuffed it in the old Bible and forgotten about it.

Below the fullness of the tree and off to one side was a more traditional family line indicating names with spouses and children, giving birth, marriage, and death dates.

"I can blot out the death dates," he said in a low voice, "if you really want me to."

That he was reluctant to do so was all too clear. And really, what reason could she give for making him? The truth?

Seeing her name and Ben's linked not only to Cosima but also to Royboy and Willie, Talie felt a shudder run down her spine. She lifted her glass of milk sheepishly at Luke as if it were nothing more than a chill from the cold drink affecting her. "No, Luke, don't change a thing. I can take it to the print shop and have a copy made on one of those machines that handle this size. My aunt Virg will love it." She smiled. "You've done a wonderful job. Thank you. It's . . . a tribute."

Yes, a tribute. If only she didn't know what that tribute entailed. She should have been gratified that her lineage had been preserved by ancestors who cared enough to keep track and pass down such information, should have been struck only by the creativity and detail Luke had given the project, with its color and symmetry. He wanted—no *expected*—her to be proud of her heritage and of his work.

Talie wished she could live up to that expectation.

18

*This time I felt like a coconspirator, even though
Beryl assured me we would be invited to Peter's special
room—she calls it his laboratory—had he been home.
Perhaps that was what bothered me so—that he was not
home, and he was not the one showing me instead of
Beryl. . . .*

"I've already assured you: he's at the evening session." Beryl's whisper did little to ease Cosima's mind as they tiptoed farther along the basement corridor.

"And how late do evening parliamentary sessions normally run?" Cosima persisted.

Beryl let out a loud, obviously exasperated sigh. "Heavens! You'd think we were breaking into the royal vault with all of your questions. Peter won't mind, I tell you, even if he were to walk up behind us."

Cosima touched Beryl's arm, effectively stopping her. "I want your assurance this isn't another of your pranks."

Beryl laughed. "I'll stay with you the entire time we're down here. And he *isn't* home."

"I must tell you, Berrie, I overheard what he said to you in the garden last week. Your brother seemed adamant about not repeating against Reginald something that was done to him."

"Humph," Beryl said, moving forward again.

"And that's all you have to say on the subject?"

Beryl stopped, facing Cosima and holding up the single candle as if to better see the subject of her scrutiny—Cosima's face. "I shall tell you everything. Only it has a rather unpleasant side, and you may not welcome what I have to say."

"I want the truth, Berrie."

"Do you recall my telling you about Peter's broken engagement?"

Cosima nodded.

"I suppose Peter doesn't want Reginald hurt by the possibility of his fiancée's preferring someone else. Peter will not believe the truth of what happened to him. We all shunned Nan after she was seen being kissed by another, but she nearly accosted me one morning on my ride along the ladies' mile in the park. She was desperate to speak to me away from the others in my party, to explain what had happened."

Cosima waited.

"Nan said she'd been fooled by a man whose sole intent was to cast her in a bad light in Peter's eyes. He was paid by someone to dress the part of a gentleman, charm Nan, and do his best to steal her away. Of course the fact remains she was seducible . . . but someone deliberately wanted Peter's engagement to end. And I suspect I know who."

Again Cosima waited. She wasn't sure she should be listening to such talk, but curiosity made her incapable of stopping Beryl.

"Reginald."

Cosima could not believe her. "But why?"

Beryl lifted one shoulder, then continued on their way. "Sometimes when I see Reginald looking at Peter I think he hasn't a bit of affection for him. I think he is using my brother

simply because he is part of the aristocracy. That and of course
for the betterment of his business ventures."

Cosima was so surprised by Beryl's words that she didn't at
first move; then she hurried after Beryl. "But . . . they're friends!"

"So everyone seems to think."

"Do you know what *might* be true, Berrie?"

She slowed long enough to look Cosima in the eye.

"That you simply don't like Reginald and are eager to believe
the worst of him. And this Nan person might not have wanted
you to think badly of her and drew up the story of someone
being paid to sully her."

Beryl humphed again and kept walking. "You're as trusting as
Peter, blind to another's faults. Can I help it if the Lord gave me
more discernment than others?"

The single candle in Beryl's hand flickered until she slowed her
gait and they entered a small room. She touched the flame to the
wick of an oil lamp on a rough wooden table in the center of the
room, which illuminated the small basement chamber.

The sight before Cosima chased away her desire for more
conversation. On one side stood shelving that reached floor to
ceiling, full of rocks, odd-shaped objects, and something rather
sinister like bones or skeletons. All were tagged with white scraps
of paper. Another wall housed a shorter shelf, this one piled with
books, papers, and drawings of skeletal remains.

"I'm not afraid to come in here," said Beryl, even though her
tone was still rather hushed. "It's the one in our country estate I
don't like."

"Why is that?" To her dismay, Cosima found herself whispering too. There was something about the room with its obvious
connection to death that touched her. Not in fear but rather in
awe to be surrounded at such close range to the unimaginable.

"For one thing, Peter's country laboratory smells horrid.
Here there are only fossils, and they don't stink."

"What's the source of the smell in the other laboratory?"

Beryl, hands now free of the candle she'd placed beside the lamp, folded her arms against the chill in the room. "You promised not to think ill of Peter when I brought you down here. Do you hold to that promise, no matter what I say?"

Cosima grew more mystified by the moment. "How can I agree to that, Berrie?"

Beryl stepped to the shelf and picked up what looked like a leg bone of the largest chicken Cosima had ever seen. She held it out for Cosima, who touched it with one fingertip. It was dark and hard, nearly like rock. Beryl replaced it and wiped her palms on the skirt of her gown.

"In order to identify *these* bones, Peter must compare fossilized skeletons to those belonging to animals alive now. What better way to know if an animal is old or different than by studying what animal bones look like today?"

Cosima nodded. It made sense to her and was far less dramatic than Beryl had intimated. Why should she think ill of Peter for analyzing animal bones? Unless there was more.

"And that's all he researches . . . animal bones?"

"Isn't that enough? He pays hunters and zookeepers to send him *carcasses*!"

"It's only that you expect me to be repulsed. Now if he were digging up cadavers, I might find *that* repulsive."

Beryl laughed. "You've a strong constitution, Cosima Escott. I believe your aunt Meg and cousin Rachel would both swoon in this room. Lady Meg won't even allow a boar's head to be served at her table; she can't tolerate the look of it."

"I might agree with her there, actually." Cosima looked at the line of shelving, nearly full of objects from side to side, top to bottom. "What are all these tags?"

"Identifications," Beryl said. "Peter won't bring a thing into this room until he's tagged it for fear of getting one thing mixed up with another. That's why I knew he'd go to the upstairs bedroom that first night you were here if he had any fossils with him."

"You seem to know his work," Cosima said. "Are you interested in fossils too?"

"They don't fascinate me as they do Peter. He seems to view each one as some sort of evidence of God's love. He thinks that about all of creation. Of course, I think it too, but I'd much rather thank God for a lovely, unimaginably scented red rose than some ugly old bone."

Cosima's heart warmed as she pondered the variety of God's gifts. "But isn't it wonderful, Beryl, the way God has created things that appeal differently to each of us?"

She couldn't help but think of Royboy then. In his slowness so many thought of him as nothing more than an aberration, a mistake. But in his smile and willingness to please another if he could, Cosima saw a reflection of innocent goodness. Yes, he often made messes or tore pages from her favorite journal, but Royboy never acted with malice. It simply wasn't in him.

"Do I have company?" said a deep voice from the threshold, startling Cosima and Beryl as well, for she gasped then laughed like a guilty child.

"I was showing Cosima where you bring your fossils," Beryl said. "I hope you don't mind that we didn't wait for an invitation?"

Stepping into the light, Peter's tall form cast a giant shadow that slanted across the shelves behind him. "Not at all." He smiled broadly at Cosima but a moment later turned a frown on his sister. "You weren't planning on abandoning her down here until I happened to come along? Because if you were, it might have been quite a wait. I had no idea I would be home so early or stop in here for that matter."

"Nor did I, Brother dear, which is why I claim complete

innocence this time." She smiled. "Honestly, I only wanted to show Cosima your fossils. She doesn't seem bored by the topic at all."

Peter turned to Cosima. "I'm glad you were interested enough to take a look."

"Cosima was just saying how gracious is God for providing us with a wide range in creation, things that appeal even to you with your complete disregard for beauty."

"Disregard for beauty!" The melodramatic offense in Peter's tone made Beryl wink Cosima's way. He turned toward the shelves, picking up one of his fossils. An intricate leaf pattern showed in the center, perfect in symmetry and design. "What artist could create such a thing? And this . . ." He searched the shelves a moment, coming up with what looked like an oddly bent bone. "This is magnificent. This animal had an impediment of some kind. Either he was born that way or an accident befell him that didn't heal properly. I'm not expert enough to tell the difference. And yet I do know this animal lived with his impairment a long time. It's an amazing testament to the tenacity of life, making do with what one's given, a representation of life being productive, even with limitations."

Cosima stared at him, tales of her brother Royboy on the tip of her tongue. Surely Peter would understand. And yet she kept the words to herself, remembering too well the stares, the whispers, the repulsion that accompanied too many "aberrations" in one family.

"Where did you get so many fossils?" she asked instead. "Surely not here in London."

He replaced the bone. "Mostly from quarrymen. I have a few who contact me when they find anything interesting. In fact, I'm going to the Bristol coast in a few days to meet one of my best suppliers."

Beryl's brows suddenly lifted. "You're going to the seaside?"

Peter nodded.

"Then we must all go. You and I and Cosima." Beryl turned to Cosima, taking both hands in hers. "Oh, it'll be lovely . . . a holiday."

"I was only going for a day or two—that's all I can spare," cautioned Peter. "And you'll want to be back in time for the regatta."

Beryl laughed. "No, *you'll* want to be back in time for the regatta. I only go to watch the people, not the event."

"In any case, I can't be gone long from Parliament." Peter looked at Cosima. "The seaside is several hours by train and carriage, and that's if we can get on the express and not the penny-a-mile. In the past we've rented a cottage, but it's little more than that. You'd have to share a room with Berrie and probably Christabelle, too. She won't be left behind. But," he added, a new smile growing beneath his mustache, "I could show you a cave I've been exploring. At low tide we can walk right up to the entrance."

Cosima had never been inside a cave. She couldn't recall ever having had a desire to do so before, but as she looked at Peter, the thought suddenly sounded so appealing she knew she must go. "Sounds fascinating."

Beryl clapped her hands as if she could barely contain her excitement. "Let's go and tell Mama our plans." Beryl pulled Cosima along.

"She'll want to accompany us," Peter called after them, then added, "And Reginald as well."

Cosima, letting Beryl direct her path, glanced over her shoulder at Peter's reference to Reginald. Peter was looking at her, his smile from moments ago now gone.

19

Talie watched the newest member of their playgroup pick up her daughter from Talie's family-room floor. Maybe it was the pregnancy hormones, but so far prayer hadn't chipped away the hardness that had begun forming around Talie's heart during playgroup weeks ago. A new neighbor, Kenna, had plopped her daughter, Addison, down next to Ben and laughed over the fact that Ben was almost two months older yet obviously behind in playing with toys like blocks and even trucks.

Talie kept telling herself that Kenna hadn't meant to be offensive. Kenna was young and outspoken. She often talked before considering the impact of her words, as everyone in the group had noticed at one point or another. Whether she was pronouncing a perfectly enjoyable movie an insult to her intelligence or a political figure too extreme to be effective, she had an opinion about everything and didn't hesitate to voice it.

"I have to skedaddle, girls," said Kenna. "We have a doctor's appointment to see if Addison's ear infection has cleared up." She passed Talie, who had risen from her chair. "Thanks for the coffee and treats, Talie. Next week is at my house, right?"

Jennifer, the unofficial coordinator by virtue of founding the group, answered for Talie. "We'll be there."

"You know, Talie," said Kenna, "I was telling Addison's doctor about Ben, and she said perhaps you ought to have him looked at.

You know, to see why he's not doing some of the things the rest of the babies are doing."

"Oh?" The single word was all Talie could choke out.

"Like patty-cake and 'so big.' You want to know if something's wrong, don't you?"

That Kenna made it sound as routine as finding out the day's weather was not lost on Talie—or on Jennifer, who looked as horrified as Talie felt inside.

"It was nice of you to think of Ben, Kenna," Jennifer said as she came up behind Kenna. "Why don't you let me walk you to the door?"

Grateful for Jennifer's intervention, Talie turned to the table where the other two neighbors still sat. She was relieved to see they were immersed in their own conversation and probably hadn't heard the brief exchange with Kenna.

Talie's gaze went to Ben, who was still sitting on the adjacent family-room floor. He wasn't playing with toys the way the rest of the babies were. Rather, he was sucking his thumb, content to watch the others in their side-by-side play.

Who was Talie kidding? Jennifer wouldn't have been horrified by Kenna's words if she didn't think there was some truth to them. Suddenly Talie wanted to be alone, to forget everything and everyone around her. Especially other babies and the way they compared to Ben.

Jennifer returned a moment later and made herself at home in Talie's kitchen by pouring herself a cup of tea at the stove top. "You know, Talie, Ben is the most contented baby I've ever seen. You're lucky to have one so even tempered."

Talie didn't mention the meltdowns Ben frequently had. Somehow he'd never had one at playgroup . . . at least not yet.

"Let's hope your next one is as calm," said Lindy.

How easy it was to change the subject, to think about the

new baby with hope and love. To ignore what Jennifer seemed to want to ignore as much as Talie did: Kenna's words.

No subject lasted long, however, and soon Talie pushed away some of her worries as they talked about the next book they planned to read as a group. Somehow the children's play-time was evolving into a book-and-movie club, a therapy group for life's complaints, a cooking club to introduce and exchange recipes.

Nonetheless, even as she laughed with the others, something dragged at Talie's spirits. The underlying fear in Cosima's journal. Curses and grown-ups with the minds of little boys. People who were related to her by blood.

She thought she'd alleviated her worries. She'd found no one in this generation or the one before or the one coming up to indicate anyone was affected the way Cosima's relatives had been so long ago.

Even if Cosima's story was true, it was a hundred and fifty *years* ago. Nothing that happened so far in the past could have an impact on Talie today. If she'd inherited anything from her father, it was intelligence and reason. Certainly he'd given her nothing but the same to pass on to Ben.

Eventually playgroup ended, leaving Talie alone with Ben. In the new quiet, she gathered her son in her arms and headed back into the kitchen.

Ben made his typical baby noises, sounds Talie never tired of hearing. She withdrew sliced strawberries from the fridge, cut a banana from the bunch on the countertop, and chose a jar of baby food for toddlers from the cupboard. Not that Ben was toddling yet, but he certainly enjoyed a variety of food.

He was such a pliant, happy little boy most of the time. Yet how could she ignore that other babies stared up at their mother's face as if her countenance was the only sight each baby wanted to see? Ben barely looked at Talie, even now as she tried to draw his attention with a happy description of his lunch.

At Ben's last checkup, Talie had casually mentioned to the doctor her concerns about Ben's being late reaching a few milestones like picking up cereal to feed himself. The physician had patted her shoulder and said not to worry, that babies were on their own schedule. He'd tracked Ben's progress every time she brought him in for a checkup. Ben held his head erect, could sit up and roll over. Besides, he was a happy infant with such subtle delays that the doctor assured her he wasn't far behind the normal range. Ben would catch up. The doctor claimed his own son had been a late bloomer, and now the boy was a straight-A student and on the high school basketball team.

Talie wanted that future for Ben.

She made choo-choo trains and airplanes of spoonfuls of fruit and vegetables. Eventually her sour mood faded. It was easy to forget how Ben compared to others when they were alone. He was all smiles and adorable, and she enjoyed every minute of caring for him.

Ben *would* catch up and be a perfect big brother to his little brother or sister.

Talie couldn't wait to hold the next one in her arms. There must be a hormone released at conception that guaranteed a mother's love. It was already working the same way it had worked with Ben.

The phone rang just after Ben finished the last bit of fruit.

"Hey," Talie said, recognizing Luke's number on the caller ID.

"Hey back. I was going to call earlier but I thought you said you were having playgroup today."

"Yeah."

"I thought you might be too tired since Ben was up last night."

"I was." She wiped Ben's chin as she spoke. He'd finished lunch but was a drooler. "I decided to host it anyway."

"And?"

"And what?" If there were hormones for baby love, there were also ones for snippy feelings, especially when it came to unaware husbands.

"I thought you were going to quit the group because you end up feeling like you do right now. Much as I love you, honey, you're cranky and you know it, especially on Thursday mornings."

The fact that he hadn't dropped the topic once her tone had sharpened irritated her, even though she knew he was right. He was, after all, only concerned about her. But she didn't need to be reminded of the obvious.

Despite her thoughts, Talie heaved a great sigh, letting go of the anger so willing to show itself. Why ruin Luke's mood? Besides, the thought of dropping out of the playgroup appealed to her after this morning.

"You're right," she admitted. "I guess I'll call Jennifer later and tell her I won't be coming for a while. Just until . . . you know . . . Ben catches up."

"Yeah," Luke said, his tone cheerful. "It won't be long and that little guy will be passing up all of them."

Talie prayed that was true.

With worries over Ben's development surging again and a new baby coming, she knew she had to stop ignoring these fears, as tempting as that was. How easy it had been to stop her search with Aunt Virg's good news.

But it wasn't enough.

There was one other person who might provide a clue.

Ellen Dana Grayson. The mysterious relative for whom Dana had been named.

20

I have often pondered whether more travel helps us learn about ourselves. I believe it might be true.

Our traveling party left the confines of London this morning, taking the express train heading west to Bristol. The train coaches, at least for first class, were like long, comfortable carriages. Travelers sit on cushioned seats with wide, curtained windows overlooking the view. I saw a yellowish cloud of coal dust hover over the city we left behind.

Our group almost filled one of the first-class cars. Though Lord Hamilton declined to accompany us, Lady Hamilton and her two daughters are in attendance, plus Lord Peter, Sir Reginald, and myself. Several Hamilton servants are traveling with us in second-class carriages. Millicent stayed behind because of limited space at the rented cottages.

I found myself watching Reginald and Peter, who sat opposite me. The two sometimes seem as close as brothers, as Reginald once claimed. They have an easy camaraderie, but

Reginald looks first to Peter for his opinion rather than the other way around. . . .

When the train stopped for fuel and water, everyone made a dash for the privies in the nearby inn, including Cosima. She was one of the first to reboard and found Peter had already taken his seat.

With a moment to contemplate him alone, she suddenly wondered if Reginald had consulted Peter as to whether or not he should follow through with his plan to marry her. Wouldn't it be logical for a friend to consult another about such an important decision? Especially in view of her circumstances.

She determined to ask Reginald if he had done so and if he had not, would counsel him to be utterly frank with Peter about all that marriage to her might mean. Watching Peter enjoy the easy fellowship of those around him, she somehow felt no fear of Peter knowing the truth. She was cursed, so they said. What would Peter say about that? She unequivocally wanted to know.

Soon they arrived at their destination, where a trio of hansom cabs was hired to take them to the rented cottages. The land between the station and the village was low, marshy country, with the waters of Bristol Channel and the gray-blue coast of Wales in the distance. The country scent of fresh-cut hay and the sound of bleating sheep from the fields made Cosima think of home.

Closer to the water's edge they came upon a row of cottages, most of them painted yellow and with shingled, not thatched, roofs. The cottages themselves sat just beyond the sand on more solid, higher ground. Rocks and pebbles littered the beach, nearly outnumbering the sand.

By teatime they were refreshed and presented with tea and biscuits on the porch overlooking Bristol Channel.

"Ah," said Lady Hamilton, taking a deep breath, "I know Peter comes here for his sciences, but I do so love to tag along and smell this fresh, salty air."

"Absent a southwestern wind and heavy seas, yes," Beryl said. "We were here for one such storm, remember, Mama?"

Lady Hamilton, taking up a teacup of her own, nodded. "Yes, and as I recall Peter was thrilled. He could hardly wait to go along the gullies and chalk cliffs with his hammer and chisel the next morning, to see what God dug up for him."

"There he is now," said Beryl.

Cosima resisted the urge to swivel in her seat, eager to catch sight of Peter. Instead she remained still and waited until she heard his sure footfall on the steps leading to the porch. Then she turned to greet him with a smile, immediately aware he wore casual dark trousers; a white linen shirt, loose at the collar; sturdy boots; and a pouch slung over his shoulder. He appeared to be on his way somewhere, hardly having arrived for tea in such sporty clothing.

"I see you've settled in." Peter stopped behind his mother and placed an affectionate hand upon her shoulder.

"Are you off already? I thought we were all going tomorrow."

"Tide's low now," he said. "I can get in a visit today as well as tomorrow."

Cosima leaned forward. "You're going to the cave?"

He nodded, adding, "I assumed you would rest from the travel, but if you'd—"

"Who needs rest? I've already waited nineteen years to see the inside of a cave."

"And one more night won't do?"

Standing, Cosima said, "Exactly." She looked down at Beryl, who hadn't moved. "Beryl? Aren't you coming?"

"I only came for the diversion, to tell you the truth," Beryl said. "I've seen the inside of that cave, and between spiders and horseshoe bats, I don't need to see it again."

"But it's why we came!"

"No, it's why Peter came—and you, apparently. Why don't the two of you run along?"

Cosima looked from Beryl to Lady Hamilton, alarmed at what she thought might be yet another blatant matchmaking effort on Beryl's part.

But Lady Hamilton appeared not to have noticed. "It's only up the shoreline a little way," she said. "How long do you suppose you have until the tide rises?"

Peter looked out at the water. "A couple of hours." He studied Cosima, and she wondered if he'd guessed her uneasiness about going off alone with him. If she weren't so attracted to him it wouldn't make a bit of difference.

"I'll find Reginald," he said quietly, then strode down the steps.

Cosima dared not look at Beryl, afraid she, too, would guess her thoughts. Keeping her gaze downcast, she hoped at least to hide such feelings from Lady Hamilton.

"Let me see your shoes," Beryl said, assessing Cosima's overall appearance.

Cosima lifted her skirt and petticoats to reveal kid slippers, fashionable yet obviously unsuitable for any kind of walking. Cosima had a pair of sturdy leather work shoes she wore back home when gathering herbs in the forest and gardens, but she hadn't brought them to England.

"Just as I thought." Beryl rose. "It's a good thing Christabelle came along. Mother just bought her a new pair of boots. You can borrow them. Come with me."

Soon Cosima wore Christabelle's boots, which had been specially made for just such outings as accompanying her brother or walking the rough Bristol beaches. Christabelle didn't seem to mind in the least that she couldn't accompany them.

Back on the porch, Cosima saw Peter with Reginald at his

side. Reginald was dressed similarly to Peter, with trousers and boots.

As eager as Cosima was to see the cave, sudden caution struck her and she faced Beryl. "Are you sure you won't accompany us, Berrie?"

"It's only down the coast; see there?" Beryl pointed to a hill that rose gradually, grass growing at the modest peak like a line of green hair over craggy shadows resembling a face with a large mouth—obviously the entry to the cave. "You'll be in full view. It's perfectly safe."

Lady Hamilton stood and put an arm about Cosima's shoulders. "I think she's more worried about what we might think than safety, Berrie." She hugged Cosima close. "Go along, Cosima. It's fine."

With a grateful smile to Lady Hamilton, Cosima placed her bonnet on top of her head and tied it beneath her chin. The stiff, rounded-poke style modestly shaded not only her face but also her view of anything except what was straight ahead. She left the porch, all the more eager now. Christabelle's shoes made the walking easy.

Stopping before the two waiting men, she paused when neither moved in the direction of their goal.

Peter had an odd look on his face. "I'm afraid I must see your shoes," he said at last.

Cosima laughed away the awkward concern on his face. "Berrie already thought of that. I have on Christabelle's, which were made for just such a trail. Shall we go?"

He nodded, and the three set off down the beach. Cosima's gown, though one of her best, was one she would not worry over if it was splashed with water or sand. In shades of blue and green, it was made of lightweight but serviceable gingham. Snug sleeves traveled only as far as her elbow, the skirt was decorated with a single flounce halfway down from her waist, and the smooth weave of the fabric was spread full and round thanks to a half dozen petticoats.

"Your mother asked about the tides," Cosima said. "How do you know when the water will rise again?"

"I'm here a few times every season. I've observed the cycles," Peter said. "It's starting to rise now, but it takes a few hours to affect the cave."

Before long the trail rose steeply over rocks and crags. Reginald was lithe on his feet, skirting the rocks with ease. He soon went ahead. More than once Cosima nearly slipped and wished Reginald wasn't setting such a quick pace, but she managed to keep a fairly reasonable distance between them.

Stuck in between was Peter, who seemed capable but reluctant to follow Reginald's stride. Instead he slowed when Cosima did, keeping an even distance along the way. "Reginald," he called.

Cosima looked up to see that the gap had widened embarrassingly between her and Reginald's lead. She tried to move faster, but between narrow cavities that grabbed at her footing and petticoats in her way on the uphill climb—plus a corset preventing her from breathing as she wished—she simply could not move quicker.

Instead of backtracking, Reginald waited at the mouth of the cave, shielding his eyes from the sun, evidently to watch Cosima's approach.

Peter was closer, having hung back.

"I'm sorry to delay you," Cosima said. "Perhaps I shouldn't have interfered today, since you have limited time with the tide on its way back."

Without speaking, Peter approached, a familiar smile reshaping his mustache, and reached for her hand.

"Thank you," she said.

With Peter to lean on over the rocky pathway, Cosima made

better progress, and in short time they met Reginald at the cave's black opening. It was a wide, diamond-shaped portal into the earth, high enough in the center to accommodate Cosima's height without her bending.

Just inside, Peter pulled a small lantern from his pouch and lit it. The floor of the cave was damp, rocky, or muddy in various spots.

As they probed farther inside, Cosima sensed a rise in temperature despite the dampness. "It's warmer in here than outside," she said, the sound of her voice hollow as it bounced off the encrusted walls.

"Caves usually stay around the same temperature year-round," Peter said. "So it feels warmer on a cool day and cool on a hot day."

Cosima wanted to ask about the bats and spiders Beryl had mentioned, but guilt at holding them back made her refrain from displaying weakness yet again. She planned to keep an eye out for either of the creatures that must love the dark, isolated confines where humans so rarely visited, yet soon the cave itself cast out any cautions.

Peter pointed out stalactites from the cave roof, stalagmites from the cave floor, and limestone, which grew like fungi on the walls. He showed them where the floor ascended above the tide-marks, the spot he'd found the most interesting rocks.

Farther inside, where the roof descended, he'd discovered bone specimens coated with limestone, and told them there was another entrance from the back of the hill just large enough for a wild dog or a hyena to have once used. Peter had removed a few of the bones but some still remained. He pointed them out with his lantern, and Cosima saw how they stuck up through the mud bottom like bizarre headstones at an abandoned grave site.

"This is where our tour ends," he said. "When I'm digging I don't mind crawling through the mud, but you can just as easily see what I bring to the comfort of the cottage or fossil room back home."

Cosima felt Reginald's gaze on her. "Looks like we're being sent home for our own good."

Cosima was sure Christabelle's boots were now coated in mud and the bottom of her dress no doubt matched, yet she was reluctant to leave. The cave was magnificent, even with its dampness and darkness. She'd read about exotic animals that lived in all the reaches of the earth, from mountaintops to the deepest oceans—at least, those observed by experts. And now here she was, in a place most people never visited, where only God Himself could see the creatures in such crevices.

"I'm glad I've seen this," she whispered, and even though her voice was quiet it was easy to hear in the utter silence of their surroundings. "The Creator really is everywhere, isn't He?"

Peter nodded. "My light isn't bright enough, but the walls and the floors sometimes glimmer under the right circumstances. All these formations, from the floor or the ceiling, are like a garden, cultivated by God's laws of nature, not man."

"Meant for whose enjoyment?" Reginald asked, evidently not caught up in their reverence over their surroundings. "No one is supposed to see any of this; it doesn't matter what it looks like."

Cosima smiled. "Just more evidence of the details God offers for our benefit then, isn't it?"

"I suppose." Reginald started back toward the cave's entrance.

Peter stayed where he was. "You'll be all right finding your way back?"

"We can manage," said Reginald easily.

"Maybe you can match your pace to Cosima's then, Reg," Peter said. Was it only her imagination, or was there a touch of reproach in his voice?

"Certainly," said Reginald, and although Cosima couldn't see his face, he sounded like he was smiling. As she neared him she saw it was true, and he bowed gallantly.

Outside the sun was bright, and Cosima took a moment for her eyes to adjust. As promised, Reginald stayed by her side the entire walk back to the cottage, even steadying her when she slid on a moss-covered rock.

"The moon shines bright on the water at night, Cosima," said Reginald before they approached the cottages. "Perhaps I could persuade you to view it later."

"Yes, Reginald, provided Lady Hamilton approves. A maid might accompany us if we'd like to take a walk."

"She'll approve," he assured her. "We'll be in plain sight—no need to bring a chaperone."

"Very well." But even as Cosima agreed, she glanced back at the cave, now smaller in the distance. How much more exciting would it be to meet Peter by the water?

She squelched that thought as quickly as it presented itself. Besides, perhaps time alone with Reginald would allow her to suggest he receive Peter's counsel about his wedding plans.

Joining Berrie and her mother on the porch, Cosima permitted one more thought of Peter. She hoped he didn't get so caught up in his digging that he forgot the rising tide.

21

"I was just wondering why you named Dana after an aunt you'd never met," Talie said to her mother on the phone while Ben was napping. She'd carefully choreographed the conversation about choosing a name for the new baby, but this was what she'd been secretly getting at all along.

"Your father and I were having such a hard time agreeing on a name. It was actually his mother who suggested Ellen Dana. We both loved it—well, the Dana part anyway."

Talie sat at her kitchen table, Cosima's journal and the family Bible in front of her. She gripped the phone that almost slid out from between her shoulder and ear. "From the records page in the family Bible, Ellen Dana was Grandma Martha's sister."

"Is that right? For some reason I thought she was your father's great-aunt. But I suppose your grandmother was thinking of her deceased sister, not an aunt."

Talie glanced down at the records page again. "Ellen Dana Grayson, born 1910."

"Hmm . . . she *must* have been Martha's sister then, since I believe your grandmother was born around then too."

"I wonder why Grandma never spoke of her. Or Dad."

"Your father never knew her. And we barely saw your grandma Martha while she was still alive, you know, being so far away."

Talie stared at the names in front of her. "So you don't know anything about Ellen Grayson?"

"Nothing more than the name. Why?"

Talie pursed her lips, hesitating. "She died young. Aunt Virg really wasn't sure why, whether it was pneumonia, polio, or something else."

"Haven't a clue, dear."

"Thanks anyway. I just thought I'd ask."

"I guess I'm about as history oriented as your father was, huh? But I'm glad you're interested. I don't think the past should be forgotten, after all." She sighed. "I suppose my opinion has changed now that I'm closer to becoming part of the past myself."

"Oh, Mom," Talie said, but she had nothing to offer besides that gentle protest. Her mind was too full of other things. She wondered again if her father had read Cosima's journal, at least the beginning, and buried it away because he had a reason to forget the past. The same reason she wanted to forget it.

She talked to her mother awhile longer, about her new place and other things, but her mind was elsewhere. There must be a way to find out more about Ellen Grayson.

Talie looked again at the entry. *Ellen Grayson . . . Engleside.*

22

*If good character is formed in the quiet only to show itself
in the tempest, then I maintain that some of my parents'
lessons for the good of my character have not been wasted
after all.*

*I was interrupted last evening before I could record the
outcome of Peter's visit to his cave. I suppose I should be
embarrassed to record the dreadfully silly mechanics of
my mind. But if I am anything in this journal, I am
honest. Sometimes that includes allowing my foolish side
to show. . . .*

Cosima shaded her eyes from the setting sun. The sight might
have been lovely, an orange-and-purple sky ablaze over a reflect-
ing sea, but she could think of only one thing. Where was Peter?

Lord Peter. She silently corrected herself for being too familiar with his name. Yet where was he? Still in the cave? In the time
it took her to change her shoes and gown, she'd expected to see
Peter traipsing along the beach toward the cottages.

There was no sign of him.

She didn't want to raise an alarm. Peter was familiar with the cave and the tide. Besides, if she voiced her worries, Beryl would take full advantage of her obvious concern and tease her, especially since no one else seemed the least bit troubled.

Lady Hamilton, Beryl, and Christabelle sat at the table, still enjoying the fresh air while they played a game of loo. Cosima had never played cards. Her father never approved of such things, especially where stakes were involved. But rather than money the ladies used small, polished stones, which, they told her, Peter had given them over the years.

Were they so caught up in a silly game that they completely forgot about Peter? Cosima glanced again at the water's edge. There was no doubt about it; the line had definitely shifted and the water was much higher.

"I see the tide's made quite a rise," Cosima said, hoping her voice sounded as casual to them as it so falsely did to herself.

No one looked up from the cards, not even Lady Hamilton.

"The sun is nearly touching the horizon." Cosima hoped to gain at least a glance and take advantage of their attention after that. "'Tis a lovely sky, don't you think?"

Beryl, who was losing if Cosima could judge from the meager pile of pebbles nearby, gave her a scowl. "Yes, lovely. It's getting dark, Mother. I'll call for a lamp."

"We really ought to stop playing and find something Cosima would enjoy with us," said Lady Hamilton.

"Yes, just as soon as I've won back some stones." Beryl went to the cottage door to call for a maid.

Moments later a housemaid appeared with two lanterns, which she placed on small tables close enough to give the women ample light.

Swallowing once to banish any sign of nervousness, Cosima spoke up. "Did Lord Peter make it back from the cave? I wonder."

No one seemed to hear. Each gaze appeared glued to the cards in her hands. Cosima began to suspect a reason her father had forbidden such games at home. It knocked sense right out of one's head.

"What did you say, Cosima?" asked Lady Hamilton after a while.

"I wondered about Lord Peter's return, with the higher tide."

Lady Hamilton barely glanced toward the water's edge. "Oh, I'm sure he'll be back soon."

Cosima wanted to shake her head—or one of the women. How could they be so nonchalant? Peter could be trapped! Cave exploration might be exciting, but it was something no one should do alone, no matter how experienced.

"That's another win," said Christabelle with one of her familiar giggles.

Beryl pushed herself from the table. "I think I've had enough for one afternoon."

Her mother gathered the cards. "I thought you wanted to win back your stones."

The older daughter glared, not at her mother but at her younger sister. "I'll try again tomorrow." Beryl looped her arm through Cosima's, who was relieved the game had finally ended. They both faced the colorful sky. "It *is* a lovely sunset."

"Yes." Cosima wondered how to phrase her next words without making her anxiety too obvious. "How high does the tide actually get, do you suppose? In the cave, I mean?"

"Oh, it's risen about its highest now, I believe—" Beryl cut her words short and faced Cosima squarely, an intent look on her face.

Cosima returned the gaze, wondering at the complete lack of distress on Beryl's face. Her brother could be in quite a predicament in that cave, at least until the tide receded, and all his loving family had done was play a game while it happened.

"Let's walk a little, shall we, Cosima?" Beryl asked, in a voice more firm than friendly. "I've been sitting so long I'd like to use my legs a bit."

"We'll be called in for supper before long," her mother cautioned.

How could she? How could Lady Hamilton be thinking of supper when the tide was as high as it was going to get and Peter wasn't back? And why was Beryl willing only to take a walk, not call for help to see if there was a way they could get to Peter?

"We'll stay on the grasses and not try the beach," Beryl called over her shoulder.

"Beryl," Cosima said as they left the last step of the porch behind them.

"Don't say another word, m'dear." Was that a foreshadow of a smile creeping to Beryl's lips?

They walked around to the back of the cottage, out of range of both sight and sound of those left on the porch. Cosima followed, agitation growing beside her worries.

"Unless you want both my mother and sister to suspect you have feelings for Peter that should be reserved for your fiancé, you'd best follow me."

"I don't know what you're saying, Beryl. What I do know is that the tide is high again, and no one seems to know for sure if Peter is still in the cave."

"He's perfectly fine, I assure you," Beryl said. "Didn't he tell you about the inland entrance?"

Cosima breathed a sigh of relief she could not withhold. "Someone might have mentioned that."

Beryl laughed, but after a moment her pretty face grew serious. She pulled one of Cosima's hands into hers. "You do see what's happening, don't you, Cosima? You came to England hoping to fall in love with Reginald, only it's Peter you're starting to love."

"Oh no, Berrie, that's not true! I was only concerned about your brother's welfare, as I would be for anyone who might be in danger."

Beryl shook her head at each of Cosima's protests and folded her arms. "I've seen the way you look at him. Furthermore, I've seen the way he looks at you."

"What way?" Cosima bit her lip when her voice trembled. She shouldn't encourage such a subject—certainly not—but the words had escaped before she could catch them.

"You might not recognize it, but I do. I'm not sure I've ever seen him so smitten, not even with Nan. I think Peter is ready to start trusting again."

Thoughts and emotions surged in Cosima like the tide she'd just watched come in, rising and bubbling and impossible to stop. And yet she knew she must. There was too much both Peter and Beryl didn't know.

"Berrie, you mustn't talk this way. Reginald is the one who's asked me to marry him, and he knows me far better than Peter. There are things you don't know, things that might make a difference."

"What kind of things? If you're talking about your family history, then I suggest you put that right out of your mind. It means nothing."

"What do you know of my family history?"

"About that unfortunate rift between your father and Dowager Merit, of course. Perhaps once you're married to an Englishman, your father will have the opportunity to come face-to-face with his family here. Then they can repair whatever's happened in the past."

"Perhaps," Cosima agreed, unsure whether she was relieved or disappointed that Beryl did not know the rest of Cosima's family history. Should she tell Beryl the truth? At least then she would stop trying to pair Cosima with Peter. It was far too appealing to be thrown together with him, and Cosima could no longer allow it. "There's something I must tell you."

Just then, rounding the second cottage they'd rented, which

housed Peter and Reginald and the male servants, came the slight shadow matching the shape of Reginald. "I came to fetch you for dinner before our walk later, Cosima," he said as he approached, taking one of her hands in his.

Cosima, flustered over his interruption, followed nonetheless, noting that Beryl did the same. Once inside the cottage, Cosima found herself nearly giddy when Peter came in just moments after their arrival, bending somewhat to fit through the low doorway. His gaze scanned the small parlor, stopping at her. She allowed herself only a brief smile his way, knowing if she didn't keep a tight rein on her behavior, Beryl wouldn't be the only one who guessed her secret.

The spring moon was nearly full, casting sparkles of white light to dabble across the waves as Cosima and Reginald walked along the beach.

Cosima stepped cautiously on the shifting, pebbly sand, feeling her shoes fill with each step. Glancing back at the cottage, where light shone so cheerfully from each window, she wished she'd stayed with the others. But she smiled at Reginald. "'Tis a lovely moon," she said quietly.

"Only you are lovelier."

She looked away upon hearing his words, embarrassed. Reginald could be so charming, and yet there was something odd about his courtship. Even now, on a path as unsteady and insecure as sand, he didn't offer a hand at her elbow, though no one would think him too bold if he did.

"How are you finding England?" Reginald's voice sounded stiff.

"Wonderful," she admitted. "A bit more industry than at home, which I suppose is good for the country, but aside from that it's lovely."

"And the Hamiltons?"

"They're marvelous. I believe Berrie and I will be friends for life. I hope so, at any rate."

He nodded. "Yes, Beryl is a fine young woman."

"I haven't had many friends," Cosima admitted. "Most people are afraid it might be catching."

"What's that?"

"The curse," she said, nearly in a whisper.

He made a scoffing sound.

"Why are you bothered so little by it, Sir Reginald?"

He clasped his hands behind him. "Because it's ridiculous. Such things as curses do not exist."

"Perhaps not, yet there must be some explanation for Royboy and Percy, my cousins and my uncle."

"It's still something of an uncertainty as to whether or not your brother Percy was feebleminded. Even your father admitted your older brother was better off than Royboy. And the others . . . well, I have no explanation, of course, but there's always you, Cosima. You're of sound mind—quite bright I would say. It's my guess you'll have only healthy children. Your mother and your aunt . . . perhaps they never were as healthy as you. Certainly your aunt wasn't, from the tale you told me during our travel here to England."

Cosima didn't want to argue about her aunt's mental stability, even though she felt Reginald judged her too harshly. Aunt Rowena had been dealt a heavy blow, banished by her husband and forbidden to see half of her children, losing her home and facing nothing but a grim future without help in caring for the two needy sons she had left. Anyone might have snapped under such strain. But Cosima was convinced her aunt's unstable mind had been only temporary, and had she lived longer, she surely would have adjusted to her life and accepted the offer of help Cosima's father had extended.

"Still," Cosima said at last, "there remains a good chance I shall produce children like my brothers. I know that you are willing to take the risk because of your hope to gain influence through the Escott family. I also know my parents are eager for us to marry. Yet I can't help but be cautious for both your sake and mine. Perhaps you should seek counsel as to whether or not to take such a chance as marrying me."

"I already have."

"You . . . have? Whose?"

"Why, Peter's, of course!" Reginald beheld her a moment before returning his gaze to the sea. "I talked with Peter yesterday, following his afternoon session in Parliament. He sought me out to inquire about accompanying you and the family here. We spoke at some length, Cosima. I told him everything about you, including the silly rumors of the curse. He thought I'd be a fool not to marry you if I have the chance."

Cosima stared at Reginald, her heart bouncing around in her chest. Peter knew? He knew everything? If he'd known since yesterday, shouldn't it have affected his behavior toward her? Not that he wasn't always mannerly, keeping a proper distance between them. Yet he'd been continually solicitous toward her. Even tonight, when he'd entered the large parlor where a dining table had been set up, he'd greeted her with a smile that seemed to have been reserved for her.

Or perhaps she'd imagined his gaze stopping at her, as if he needn't look any farther for what he wanted to see. Perhaps she'd imagined *everything,* and Peter wasn't the least bit interested in her. Perhaps that was why the curse made no difference to him.

"There's no need to talk about it, except between the two of us, is there, Cosima?" Reginald asked quietly.

"I don't care to talk about it," she admitted.

"Very good," Reginald said quickly. "I'm glad you agree. It's no one else's business, after all. Ah," he added, eyeing the cottage, "I see Peter has missed us."

In spite of herself, Cosima's gaze flew to the cottage. There he stood, on the porch looking out at the water. Or was he watching them?

She squelched the thought. Why must she automatically hope Peter's every move had something to do with her?

Cosima faced the water again, but to her dismay just as she turned she saw Reginald smile broadly and lift an arm to beckon Peter near. *Oh no. How am I to avoid him when everyone, including Reginald, seems to be pushing us together?*

"I think you've found the best spot to pass the evening," Peter said as he approached.

"That's probably true," Reginald said, "but I can guess what happened while your mother was reading for the family. Whose work did you insult by falling asleep this time? Austen or Goldsmith?"

"Can I help it if her voice is soothing as a lullaby? She's my mother, after all." He smiled at Cosima, who couldn't resist looking back at him.

Reginald's laugh was followed by a yawn. "I can see why you fell asleep, chum. I'm nearly done in myself. Must be all this fresh sea air. He yawned again, afterward apologizing. "I'm afraid I'm not much company. I don't know which would be more rude— to stand here yawning in front of you or to excuse myself early."

Cosima couldn't restrain another glance toward Peter. On his face was a look of disapproval evidently caused by Reginald's words.

"I don't mind going in if you'd like to retire for the evening, Sir Reginald," Cosima said.

"Oh no," Reginald insisted. "Why don't the two of you stay out here for a while? Take advantage of air you won't get back in London."

Did he mean to leave her out here, alone with Peter? Shouldn't she protest? Or Peter—perhaps he should say something. But she found no words; nor did Peter, for neither voiced any objections. She only said good night when Reginald bowed her way.

Cosima looked up at the moon, then out at the sparkling water, glancing once over her shoulder to see Reginald's steady progress to the second rented cottage.

"Reginald told me you spoke at some length the other night," she said carefully.

"Yes." His gaze turned from the moon to land on her.

Wondering if the moonlight was enough to reveal a blush rise to her cheeks, Cosima didn't dare let him see her eyes. "He told me he spoke to you about my family history."

"Yes, we talked for some time about you. Of course, I lent an all-too-willing ear, I'm afraid, and he took advantage of that."

A smile crept to her lips, but she kept her gaze averted.

Silence. Cosima brushed a stray strand of hair that had escaped from the chignon at the nape of her neck. She watched the water lap the sand, ever changing, hypnotic. Little whitecaps formed one after another, building until a higher wave seemed to push each smaller wave forward. Then it would start again, several smaller followed by a larger wave behind. She dared not speak.

Peter bent and picked up a pebble. There were so many along the coast. He studied it, then threw it far out to sea. He did it again, and Cosima watched, seeing his fingers touch the stone, smooth away any sand, then grasp it and toss it farther than she could ever hope to throw. She didn't even try.

She should excuse herself, go inside, and join the ladies. But somehow she couldn't get her feet to obey. She watched Peter instead.

At last he picked up a stone, but rather than launching it

into the ocean, he held it, rubbing his thumb over the wide, flat center. It reminded Cosima of the way she sometimes caressed the relic her grandmother had given her, the center of the iron-edged cross that already had an indentation where others had caressed it just so.

It became clear Peter had no intention of casting that one out to sea. He wasn't even facing the ocean anymore. Instead, he faced her. "A few days ago, when I said I was coming to the coast, do you want to know why I was intent on leaving London?"

"To find more fossils?"

He shook his head. "I wanted to get away from you."

His words might have seemed harsh, but his tone was gentle, intimate. So news of the curse had affected him after all. And he was going to admit it now.

He stepped closer and she didn't move away, even though part of her wanted to. He was going to tell her he was sorry about the curse but she should have faith in a future designed by God. She knew his faith was as strong as her own, and that's what she would say to someone if faced with the same predicament.

He was so close behind her that she heard him take in a deep breath. But he didn't seem to be breathing in the ocean air. Rather, it was as if he'd taken in the scent of her hair. She dared not move.

"I hoped, by getting away, I might return happy for Reginald instead of envying him. He is my friend, and I want the best for him."

Cosima's heart pounded and blood rushed to her temples, her pulse racing louder in her ears than the entire ocean. Was that all he would say? Nothing of what he knew?

Still eyeing the water, she barely trusted her voice not to tremble but spoke anyway. "And I invited myself along, didn't I? I'm sorry."

"No, don't be. I've enjoyed it far more than I would have

alone." He breathed in again, and then he took a step back, glancing toward the cottage as if afraid someone might spot him standing too near. "I must seem very disloyal to my friend."

"What do you mean?"

Peter tossed the small rock in the air, catching it in his palm. At last he held the stone and turned his gaze fast on hers. "I mean that I shouldn't be standing here alone with you, despite the fact that Reginald himself obviously set it up—for what reason I cannot fathom. If you and Reginald are determined to go through with a wedding, then I wish you both much happiness. I want that, if you are best suited for one another."

"It's really up to Reginald, isn't it?" Cosima said.

"You could refuse him," he said, then surveyed the water again and threw in the very stone she'd guessed he would save. "If you don't believe you suit one another."

Staring at him, his white linen shirt rippling in the gentle breeze off the water, his hair mussed, she could barely make out any color in his eyes when he looked back at her, only darkness. But even in the dark depths she spotted a glimmer, the way he stared at her so intently, as if willing her to speak the truth.

She wanted to. How she wanted to speak the truth of her heart. As incredible as it seemed, she believed at this moment he wanted her to say she would refuse Reginald. That it would be impossible for her to agree to wed another when there was something growing between the two of them. Something uninvited yet real. It had been there nearly from the moment they'd met.

Yet even as she stared, wanting to tell Peter she would refuse Reginald and become free to accept Peter's attention if he desired to offer it, she knew she couldn't. A vivid picture of Royboy came to mind, Royboy whom she missed. But even while she missed him, she enjoyed not having to guard her things from him—jewelry he might wander away with and lose or shoes he had a penchant for tossing over the balustrade. She enjoyed being free. Free from restraining him from the messes he liked to make. Free from worrying at every meal that he might stuff his mouth too full and gag, bringing up the contents of his stomach. Free from worrying that he might wander too far and end up in a village only too ready to mock him.

Those were the thoughts that made her still unsure about accepting Reginald's proposal, no matter what her parents thought. Certainly she could not accept Peter's interest, even if he cared to give it. What would he gain by marrying her except the possibility of ending his legacy? Only to face the same fears she faced?

Both Reginald and Peter might think the curse a matter of foolishness, but she did not. How could she marry either one of them, knowing what kind of children she would undoubtedly produce? Reginald might be willing to take the risk in order to gain a step up into society by marrying the niece of a duke. She could understand that.

But Peter? He had everything already: a title, money to go with it, land, a family who loved him. And intelligence. Surely he would want to have a son with whom he could share all the blessings he'd been given.

Cosima looked away, knowing if she stared at him any longer the words wouldn't come. Words to make it clear that she might be persuaded into a bartering marriage with Reginald but would not allow Peter to risk everything for her.

"I won't refuse Reginald if he decides to go through with the wedding," she whispered. She hoped the Lord would forgive her if she accepted Reginald without love and gave him only feeble-minded sons in exchange for the social standing he desired. And that the Lord would bestow upon her the strength to endure such a life.

Peter stiffened. He stood taller than a moment before when

he had been so close, breathing in the fragrance of her hair. "I understand." His voice sounded stiff as well. Rigid. Formal. Polite. "I admire a woman of her word as much as a man of his. You are correct, of course, to be so loyal. More correct than I."

He started to turn away, to walk toward the cottage, but something made him pause. He turned back to her, and she thought she saw the intensity there once more.

"It is that, isn't it? You've given your word, and you won't go back on it?"

It was so much more. But Cosima simply nodded. Keeping her word to Reginald would have to be reason enough.

Peter walked away, heading to the second cottage.

She didn't want to watch him but couldn't turn from the sight.

He never looked back.

23

Talie opened the door, having been watching out the window for her sister's car. "Thanks for coming on such short notice."

"I'm not teaching summer school this year, so it was no problem," Dana said. "What's up?"

"Nothing's up," Talie said as she grabbed her purse. "I just need to run a few errands. Do you have anything on your agenda tonight? a time you need to leave by?"

"Middle of the workweek for Aidan. Nondate night," Dana said, adding, "but I thought you could feed me at least."

Dana's gentle humor registered somewhere in Talie's mind, but she couldn't even muster a smile. "Sure, yeah. I was planning to stop by the grocery store anyway."

"Okay. How about filet mignon then?"

"Funny," she said, knowing her mood didn't match the word or the humor Dana was obviously trying to provide. "I'll be back in a couple of hours."

"Hey . . . what's wrong?"

"Nothing, just busy. Gotta go."

"Do you want me to wake Ben up at a certain time?"

"Oh! Yes, in about a half hour or I'll never get him to bed tonight."

Talie turned toward the door leading to the garage, but Dana touched her arm. "Are you sure everything is okay?"

"Of course. What could be wrong?"

"I don't know. Is everything all right with . . . you know, the new baby? What kind of errand are you running? Going to the doctor?"

Talie shook her head and forced a smile. She knew it was that same fake gesture she gave when their mom asked if she could bring sweet potatoes to Thanksgiving dinner. Only their mom and Luke liked them.

"Okay," Dana said slowly, "then are you going to the dentist for a root canal or what?"

There. Almost a real smile. "Just tired, I guess. Ben was up at two this morning, ready to go for the day. I didn't get him back to bed until after five, and a half hour after that Luke's alarm went off so I was up again."

"Maybe *you* should take a nap and forget the errands."

"No, no. I'm all right. I'll see you later."

Then Talie was out the door.

24

I believe it was the great poet Shakespeare who counseled, "Give thy thoughts no tongue." This, at times, is exceedingly difficult—no matter how noble the motive.

For the last two months I have seen little of Peter. (And is it not significant that I have found little of which to write in this journal? More so, perhaps, than I care to admit.) Beryl tells me Peter spends his days at Parliament and his evenings at Pall Mall playing cards, billiards, or some other waste of time. Anything but coming home, at least until well after everyone is abed.

Beryl makes it clear she finds her brother's behavior unusual, repeatedly inquiring if we had some sort of row while at the coast. She calculates that to have been the changing point, when Peter began avoiding home—or me.

But of course I have admitted nothing. I cannot tell Beryl the entire truth and still honor Reginald's wishes not to talk about the details of my family curse. Besides, what would it serve to share everything with Beryl, except perhaps to bring about a quicker end to any hope she carries for Peter and me to find a future together? Beryl must come around to that conclusion on her own, sooner or later.

My relationship with Reginald becomes more puzzling by the day. Indeed, it seems hardly necessary to have brought Millie along as chaperone, since Reginald never calls to take me anywhere on our own. He rarely visits, citing business concerns taking most of his time. He has been a faithful escort at various social events, but even at soirees he seems to pay as much attention to Beryl or Christabelle as to me.

On one of the rare occasions he was here, Lady Hamilton urged him to set a date for the wedding. She hinted at the idea that a date might be all Dowager Merit needed to give her final blessing. But Reginald seemed strangely indecisive as to when we will marry. It was clear he wanted to marry me, but having him agree to the slightest detail has yet to happen.

I could not deny my relief, if only to myself.

There is another element to my hesitation, something I cannot ignore no matter how hard I try to believe the best of Reginald. While he claimed to my parents that he was active in the Church of England, that he was anything but a heathen, I see little evidence of anything beyond the shallowest faith. Once, when I suggested we pray over the matter of matrimony, I saw a look in his eye that disturbed me. Intense feeling but hardly a passionate reverence. Until he laughed away the mood I knew a moment of confusion—almost fear. I was left not knowing how he felt about prayer—whether he thought it intensely foolish or a matter for laughter. Either is profoundly disturbing.

I often wonder if Reginald's vacillation about marrying me stems from my strained relationship with Dowager Merit. Is he waiting to make sure marrying me would be worth it? The dowager is cordial to me in public. But never once has she invited me back into the Escott fold.

Yet of all the things vying to fill my mind, it is Peter whom I allow to settle there most often. As absent as he is in person, he is forever present in my dreams. When I do happen to catch a glimpse of him either coming in or going out the door, my eyes follow him like magnets to metal. If his gaze meets mine, I cannot look away.

I have decided I must ask Beryl to speak to her brother, urge him to stay at home one evening and spend it as he used to, with the family. But first I must somehow make it known to Peter that I will keep to myself during the evening. Surely that will help. . . .

Cosima found her way down the stairs to Peter's fossil room. She was sure she wouldn't find him there at this time of the day, just after three o'clock, and she intended to leave him a letter he would find. Short but honest, it stated her desire that he should spend more time at home. If he would let Beryl know the occasions he would allot for his family, Cosima could find something to occupy her in the library or elsewhere so she would not interfere.

It was a simple, impersonal note that she had rewritten several times. Once her hand trembled so that her penmanship was nearly illegible. Another time she'd inadvertently splattered ink across the page. Finally she'd been especially careful and reread it several times to make sure she'd gotten it right. She intended to leave the letter and return to her room, and no one but Peter would know of it.

The room was still and dark, the candle in her hand the only light. She easily found the table in the center of the room, a spot he would notice near the lamp. She left the letter there.

Turning back to the door, Cosima paused. The room so represented Peter's presence that she couldn't hurry away. He was here in essence and nature, like an invisible fragrance she'd connected to him from their very first meeting.

Holding her candle high, she looked at the shelves that were full of his treasures. She wished once again that she knew what some of the fossils were. In truth she wanted to discuss everything that interested him.

But of course she couldn't have such a conversation. She mustn't. She'd told him she would choose Reginald . . . and she must. It was for Peter's own good.

She should leave, of course. Yet there was so much here, so much knowledge, not just of what fascinated Peter but of Peter himself. She held the candle toward various stacks of paper, finding one labeled "Fossils from Bristol Cave." The cave she had visited with him? Flipping beneath the first page, she noticed various drawings. Was Peter himself the artist? They were simple charcoal renderings yet intricately detailed.

Cosima studied page after page, noting the bold printing

identifying each picture. One stack after another, of the fossils and bones. Everything from his artwork to the tags on each item bespoke Peter's meticulous organization. He was, she was quite sure, brilliant. How she wished she could know him better in person rather than only through his work.

"Cosima."

Her heart leaped into her throat, where it lodged and made her gasp. She dared not move, afraid she might drop the candle from suddenly unsteady hands. Had her ears deceived her? She hadn't known, hadn't let herself hope he would arrive at this moment . . . and yet how long had she been here? Had she dawdled not only because of the subject but because she longed for Peter to appear?

It hardly mattered. If a person's wish could conjure someone, then he was here because of her.

At last she turned to him. He stood in the shadow, his broad shoulders outlined against a dim light from the corridor outside the room. Her candle was barely enough to illumine his face, for it, too, had shadows. She saw no smile and felt rather than saw his gaze upon her.

"I . . . came to deliver a note," Cosima said, and the candle-light flickered as she motioned to the table. "It's there."

Peter stepped closer, passing her for the table.

"I'll leave you to it, then."

"No, wait. Let me read what you've written."

He did so after taking up a match and lighting the lamp nearby. It took only seconds to read the few lines she'd written. When finished, he looked at her, standing not three feet away.

In such proximity and added light she could better see his face, and now she saw his mustache-shrouded smile. But it wasn't a happy one. Rather it seemed vaguely sardonic.

"So you think you are standing in the way of me and my family."

"Aren't I?" she whispered.

"How I spend my time is my own choice."

Cosima looked away, embarrassed. "I wanted only for you to know your mother and sisters miss your company." She neared the door.

Peter's footfall sounded behind her. She should not hesitate, should not even have paused. The truth was here, in his nearness. Surely she was the reason he stayed away.

His hand barely touched her shoulder, but like a shock on a dry day, it coursed beneath her skin. Unavoidable. Real.

"I won't have you leave me believing a lie, Cosima."

She wanted to turn around, to see him face-to-face, but couldn't. She was sure if she did he would see her desire for him to take her into his arms. Surely she could not allow that. So she was still, staring at the floor with her back to him.

"You are a mystery to me, Cosima," he murmured. "I see in your eyes a welcome I've not witnessed you give anyone else, not even Reginald. And yet your words, your actions, always turn me away. I wish I understood."

How she wanted to show him that welcome now and accompany it with words she longed to say. But she bit them back, intent only on the truth that mattered above all else. She wasn't for Peter. She couldn't be. Not her.

She started to go, but his hand did not leave her shoulder. Instead she felt it press more firmly. She stilled but did not turn to him despite wanting just that.

"You are like one of my fossils, Cosima," he whispered. "Something wondrous but barricaded and hidden deep inside a rock. The greatest challenge in opening a fossil is not to damage the treasure inside. I wish I could do that with you, but I find myself unable . . . ineffective."

He paused and the silence extended, though his hand remained upon her. "I know I mustn't say such things to you. I despise myself for doing so. You are Reginald's and have yourself reminded me of such."

She heard a deep intake of breath, sharp and momentarily unsteady.

"I am wrong to try coaxing that welcome from you, Cosima. Forgive me."

Tempted yet again to look at him, her neck ached from the battle to keep her face from his. "There is nothing to forgive, Peter. I . . ." She pinched her lips shut. How foolish she was, how weak to want to give in when she knew she mustn't.

She must leave—and quickly.

If it were only Reginald keeping her from Peter, Reginald her lukewarm suitor, she could allow herself to be weak. But because it was more, she did not turn around. It didn't matter if Peter was able to ignore whatever Reginald had told him of her family. She knew enough to be convinced his legacy could not afford someone like her to be admitted into the pristine Hamilton line.

Cosima walked unsteadily, silently, from the fossil room, the candlelight sputtering in her quivering hand.

25

"I received a call that a book I requested through interlibrary loan is here."

The woman behind the counter at the Glenview Public Library smiled and asked for Talie's last name, then turned to a shelf behind the counter where books were tagged. "Here you are. Will you be looking for other books today, or will this be it?"

"This is it." Talie presented her card as she noted the size of the book she'd ordered. Old and small, hardly bigger than a pamphlet. But it wouldn't take much to find what she was looking for.

Instead of leaving the library when the transaction was completed, Talie went to the reference section and took a seat. She'd spent a week online and calling New York records offices trying to find details of a place called Engleside, a school for girls that had closed more than forty years ago. Here it was before her. The school connected to the manor house where Ellen Dana Grayson had died.

The cover of the Engleside pamphlet was hidden by the interlibrary loan paperwork, which Talie gently slid aside. Beneath was a black-and-white photograph of a girl. She was seated on a chair and looking ahead, her hands folded demurely in her lap. Her long, dark hair was pulled neatly away from her face and fell past her shoulders. Dressed in what must have been white or some other light color, she appeared to be the picture of genteel youth.

Talie looked at the caption describing the old photograph.

We shall call the subject of this report Mary Thornton, although her actual name is confidential. In Mary's story you will see the success of Engleside, for Mary is the triumph of how far the feebleminded may go.

Feebleminded. The word stuck in Talie's brain, echoing as if the inside of her head were as empty as a canyon. *Feebleminded.*

Engleside was a home for children no one else wanted. A thinly disguised institution. A mental ward for the feebleminded.

Talie scanned the pamphlet's brief table of contents: Observations of the Feebleminded; Average Length of Stay at Engleside; After Engleside, Returning to Family.

She flipped through the pages, barely breathing as she skimmed some of the text.

The healthy infant finds a human face, whether his mother's or otherwise, to be an object of some fascination. While he will study the whole face, he will peer directly into the eyes of someone smiling and speaking gently to him. One of the earliest signs of a feeble mind is a lack of direct eye contact, lack of this fascination for the human face.

Talie raised a fist to her lips, pressing hard to keep back a cry. She forced herself to glance at another page.

Most common observations: In infants, lack of coordination, difficulty rolling over and/or crawling, late walker, clumsy gait. In older children, difficulties with language production, both receptive and expressive. Often agitated, accompanied by flapping of hands.

Talie put the pamphlet down, pushing it closed as if the words were an affront, a conscious attempt to prove everything she longed to deny. Obviously Cosima's curse had found its way to the twentieth century.

Had it found its way to the twenty-first as well? to Ben?

Talie rushed from the reference section toward the door, pausing only long enough to shove the pamphlet into the return slot. She'd learned more than she wanted to know.

In the car, Talie tried to slip the key in the ignition. The key chain fell from her unsteady grasp, but instead of reaching for it somewhere near her feet, she clutched the steering wheel. Sudden, unstoppable sobs erupted.

She didn't know how long the tears racked her body, but eventually they eased. Talie wiped her face with her hands, looking for a tissue but finding none in her purse. She grabbed a paper towel she kept in a bag beneath the passenger seat and blew her nose. Then, aware her car wasn't as private as she wished, she found her keys at last.

This had nothing to do with Ben. How could it? Everyone else in her family was fine, along with all those first *and* second cousins on her uncle's side of the family.

Forcing herself to breathe easier, she patted her middle, where tiny new life grew. "Guess I'm just a little vulnerable to emotional upheavals these days," she said as if the baby could hear and understand. "But I'll stop being so silly now. I know what we have to do. We have to face this head-on. No more denying what might or might *not* be there. Your daddy will agree it's best to have your brother looked at by a specialist. See if there really is something wrong or if Ben's just the late bloomer our pediatrician claims him to be. That's the only way to put an end to this roller coaster."

She drove out of the library parking lot. "Besides, I don't have time for all this crying. We have more errands to run. The grocery store, but first . . . the frame shop." Luke had dropped off the finished family tree a month ago, and the shop had called nearly a week ago to say that the job was complete.

Talie wasn't sure what had helped more—releasing all the tension through her tears or making the decision about seeing a specialist. Whatever it was, she felt better already.

At the framers, Talie gasped when she saw the finished product, complete in the double matting. Luke had teased her about the oak tree being the strongest wood available. An oak frame for an oak family tree. Durable, the best to represent such a long family line. In this frame his work was true art.

Her gaze was drawn to those names near the base of the trunk. Royboy. Willie. Was it her imagination or did certain leaves stand out? Rowena . . . Cosima . . . Ellen . . .

Talie paid the framer and let him wrap it, then left the shop and carefully placed the picture in her trunk.

An hour later, Talie stood in the grocery checkout line, absently looking at the magazines on the rack while she waited her turn. With so many groceries in her cart, she knew the self-checkout lines would be a disaster, so there was little choice but to wait.

A woman took the spot in line behind Talie. She had a little girl clinging to her leg and a baby strapped into the attached seat on the cart. All three of them were impeccably dressed, from ribbons in the girl's hair to designer shoes and socks on the baby boy. Judging by the wear on the little leather shoes, the boy could walk even though he was obviously younger than Ben.

Out of the corner of her eye, Talie noticed the mother had the same bored look common to those waiting, except when her daughter whined and irritation replaced her blank stare.

"Get off of me, Dorrie," she said, but the child didn't move. In fact, she seemed to adhere tighter, until the mother peeled her away.

"I want a candy bar, Mommy. And so does Sam. That makes two candy bars. 'Cause I get one, and he gets one. And one plus one equals two. Did you hear me, Mommy? One plus one equals two. So can I get two? Can I?"

"No, Dorrie. Now be quiet."

Talie heard rather than saw the exchange. The little girl couldn't be much older than three, but she was already adding. No fear anyone in her family might be feebleminded.

And that mother didn't rejoice in her daughter's accomplishment one bit.

Rage surged in Talie. *It's not fair, Lord. She gets two healthy kids, two kids who can walk and cling. She doesn't have a worry in the world about their futures. And she doesn't even appreciate it!*

Talie swallowed hard and pressed her stomach again, squelching the urge to shake the woman. Demand she be thankful there weren't any bad genetics in *her* family.

Instead, Talie lifted yet another prayer that both her children would be okay. That a visit to the doctor would prove this to be true.

Then she finished unloading her cart, blinking away her tears.

26

I suppose I am a bit odd in my penchant for remembering the past. At least, I know of no others my age who seem to do so as often as I do. Yet I feel that those who went before us have so much to teach. Lessons that I must remember for myself and for, God willing, any children I may bear. If I have one who is capable of learning, I shall at least be equipped to pass on something of value. At times, as now, it is clear to me that I do want children, and yet it is that very possibility that frightens me most.

Much of the time I refuse to dwell on what I shall do with my penchant for recording what I have learned. Instead, my days pass in the pleasant company of Beryl and Christabelle and their mother. Yesterday morning I sat in the upstairs parlor sharing tea with Lady Hamilton while Beryl and Christabelle were busy with a final fitting with their seamstress. A servant arrived, in his gloved hand a silver tray, upon which sat a pair of embossed envelopes. I had seen many social announcements delivered

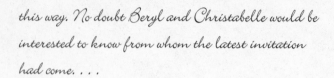

this way. No doubt Beryl and Christabelle would be interested to know from whom the latest invitation had come. . . .

"This one is for you, Cosima," said Lady Hamilton, and Cosima looked up in surprise. On all of the occasions Mr. Fisher had delivered invitations, nary a one had been for her. Until now.

She recognized the Escott name immediately. She saw it was a handwritten card requesting her presence for dinner the following night, Wednesday, an evening free of parliamentary sessions. Without the customary phrase *hoping for the pleasure of one's company*, the note was little more than a summons.

"For dinner with Dowager Merit," she said somewhat tremulously. The thought of facing her in her formidable home again made Cosima instantly meek.

"Mine as well," said Lady Hamilton, waving it once in the air. "For all of us."

"May I respond for you, Lady Hamilton?" Cosima inquired. If they were all invited . . . would they *all* attend?

"Of course. No one refuses the dowager," she added with a grin.

Excitement found its way to Cosima's heart, despite herself. Surely that included Peter.

And yet Cosima wished the invitations were from someone else. If Lady Hamilton couldn't refuse Dowager Merit, neither could Cosima. This was undoubtedly the very thing Reginald anticipated. Perhaps this was enough sign that marrying her would pay the dividends he hoped.

Cosima had been saving a favorite gown for a special occasion and decided to wear it to the Escott dinner. She told herself it

was because she wanted to look her very best for her grandmother. If there was a rift between her and Cosima, it was due
to Cosima's unacceptable behavior on the first night they met.
She was determined to make up for it and would begin by
presenting herself in the best possible manner, starting with her
favorite gown.

Rather than the customary white reserved for formal balls,
this silk was neither blue nor green but somewhere in between
and shimmered in candlelight. The color reminded Cosima of
home, of endless rolling hills that glowed after a rainfall. The
high, straight neckline was modest while still exposing her shoulders. A narrow waistline came to a point in the center, accentuat-
ing her feminine figure. Below that the top layer of silk opened
from waist to floor, revealing an underskirt embroidered with
tiny blue flowers and green leaves.

Cosima added the single emerald her mother had insisted she
bring.

Millie worked tirelessly on Cosima's hair until each curl
obeyed her fingers. Then, with only a touch of clear powder,
Cosima was ready.

"You are lovely, miss," admired Millie.

"Still, I'm taking this along to remind me of the other blood
that flows in me—the best of the Kenneseys'." Cosima held up
her reticule, in which rested the ancient wood-and-iron cross
that reminded her she could withstand anything so long as her
trust was in the right place. All and whatever.

Soon she was in a carriage with Lady Hamilton and her two
daughters. No interference from Beryl tonight as to how they
traveled to the Escott town house. Beryl had merely smiled at
Cosima and hugged her, whispering something about how courageous she was to wear such a lovely color gown.

The Escott town house was lit from top to bottom, aglow in
the dim light of dusk. Footmen appeared from both directions to

assist them from the carriages and lead them through the open doors.

Cosima had barely noticed the foyer the last time she had been there, too nervous over meeting her relatives for the first time. Now she saw that the entryway boasted wealth and history. Gold was the dominant feature—gold knickknacks on carved side tables, gold candelabras hanging from above, gold edging on the woodwork.

Peter and Lord Hamilton arrived, Reginald trailing them by mere moments. They had all made it precisely on time, as if they were as aware as Cosima that tonight was a second—perhaps final—chance for her to please Dowager Merit.

Once their party was complete, the butler showed them to the same large drawing room they'd been presented in weeks ago. The room wasn't full, as some cousins seemed to be missing. Dowager Merit sat in her familiar thronelike chair and received their greetings graciously, even if her manner was a bit tepid.

Cosima chose each word carefully. She purposely avoided Peter the same way he seemed to avoid her. It wouldn't do to lose her head and say something silly because of being flustered by a man who was not her intended.

Soon more cousins arrived, and Reginald stayed dutifully by her side, eventually putting a hand to her elbow to draw her forward. Once, when he seemed to be heading Peter's way, Cosima stood still, and he looked at her questioningly. She merely shook her head, hoping he didn't ask why she was reluctant to join Peter.

"I imagine you haven't seen much of Peter these past few weeks," Reginald said. "He's spent more time at my house or Pall Mall than he has at home."

Cosima did not need to confirm his words.

"What happened, when we all started out so friendly?"

Unsure how to respond, she said nothing.

"Whatever is rankling my friend must be settled," Reginald

declared, albeit softly. Evidently he wasn't willing to share his concerns with the entire Escott family.

"He's busy and trying to enjoy his evenings, I imagine," said Cosima.

Reginald shook his head, his gaze on Peter, who stood across the room, now speaking to Cosima's uncle, the duke. "No, it's something else. I asked him to tell me why he's spent so little time at home lately, but he shrugged off the question." Reginald now looked at Cosima. "Do you have any idea? Did he have an argument with someone? his father? mother? Beryl, perhaps? Or you?"

"Me!" Her voice sounded breathless and guilty even to herself. She spared little more than a quick glance Reginald's way. "Why would you ask? We may reside under one roof, but 'tis a very large roof, Reginald. I barely see him."

"Precisely what I want to change," Reginald said. "I once mentioned you and Peter are important to me. I want the three of us to be as comfortable together as any family, one made by a bond since there is no blood between us."

"Yes, you've said that before, sir; only I find myself wondering at the sentiment. Marriage is for two parties alone."

Reginald's pale skin deepened in color, and his gaze flew away from her. "If you and I are to wed—" his tone belied anger rather than embarrassment—"Peter will no doubt be like a member of the family, as he's like a brother to me now."

"And I would not seek to change that. Beryl and I are as sisters, and yet I see little reason for you to become so close to her. Why do you think it important that Peter and I become friendly?"

"Why should anyone be friends? For a richer quality of life, of course. Not to mention that Peter has been instrumental in helping me gain acceptance within the circle of people to whom I wish to belong."

"Peter has been a fine friend to you, and I shall never come between you." She hoped that was enough said, for she dearly wished to move on to another topic. But when she looked up at Reginald's face again, his eyes were colder than she'd ever seen them before.

"You will mend whatever rift has occurred between you, Cosima." The words were so low they resembled a threat.

Then Cosima's cousin Rachel greeted her with a kiss, and several other cousins followed suit. Cosima was glad to ignore Reginald as her Escott cousins chatted about mundane things, dresses and the weather and how quickly the summer was winding down. Surely she'd imagined the menace of Reginald's voice. It made no sense for him to threaten *her*. He wanted to marry her.

Rachel told Cosima about the next season ahead. Soon the parliamentary sessions would be over for the year, and the peers and their families would return to their sprawling country estates for other pastimes: weeklong house visits and lavish balls, riding through the countryside, enjoying the gardens, playing outdoor games like tennis or croquet, and, of course, hunting. The way Rachel laid it out, the year seemed as structured as any occupation, except to Cosima it seemed that the aristocracy worked as hard at leisure as others did at more productive pursuits.

She began to enjoy herself despite the dowager's scrutiny. The reticule containing her family relic hung from her wrist, and she knew the cross was tangible proof of the Lord above who accepted her even if others did not. The thought eased her nerves as she began to understand perhaps some of the reasons her father might have left England altogether.

Soon they were called to the dining room, where the long, damask-covered table sparkled with silver and intricately cut glassware. A footman carved a roast at the sideboard, delivered as each guest desired. Other maids and footmen brought lobster and roast fowl, mullet cooked in wine, vegetables, venison, lamb with asparagus, plovers' eggs in aspic, sweetbread, fruit, and meringues, with wine in between.

Reginald seemed preoccupied and sullen, despite the fact that he sat at one of the most exclusive tables in London. Cosima had little idea how to ease his mood. What more did he want of her? Wasn't it enough she did her best to be accepted, thereby laying the path for *his* acceptance?

At last the meal ended and the men were excused. Dowager Merit offered no separate respite for the younger cousins as she did last time. Rather, once she finished her tea and the gentlemen returned from the library, the entire party went to the conservatory, where more beverages and a light dessert were laid out.

The room boasted a high glass ceiling that revealed a lovely evening of moon and stars. The glass walls were supported by a rough stone foundation, in front of which stood plants of every shape and size. Tall palms and flowering hibiscuses dominated one corner. Enameled pots and mosaic urns housed all kinds of flowers, from narcissi to orchids and exotic Roman topiaries. Cosima was sure the room dazzled the eye in daylight, yet at night, with only candlelight revealing its cultivated wonders, the room seemed a jungle, making her feel as if they'd traveled farther than just down the hall.

Reginald seemed intent upon talking to Peter, so Cosima, keeping true to her intention to avoid him, pulled her arm from Reginald's and whispered that she wanted to talk to some of her cousins.

And so she did. Children had appeared again, along with their nursemaids. Ignoring the fact that older cousins seemed to think the young ones invisible, Cosima went to the midst of the toddling youngsters and tickled a chin for a smile. She received and handed out hugs as easily as the older ones exchanged stories of recent sporting events or sailing trips.

One child, barely walking, took hold of Cosima's reticule and tossed it to the floor. The sole object it held, the old relic, slipped to the Italian-tiled floor with a ping. Cosima picked it up, and when the infant reached for the cross, she held it in front of him, letting him touch the smooth center.

One of her young cousins, a boy called James who couldn't be much older than ten, approached. "Cousin Cosima," he said, obviously unshaken by the looks he received at his close proximity to the older cousins' territory, "may I see what you are showing little Chessie? It looks . . . old."

Cosima turned. "'Twas my great-grandfather's—all that's left of a boat that saved his life."

"A boat that saved his life? How so?"

Cosima handed the relic to the boy, who, like everyone before him, was drawn to caress the center with his thumb.

"I'll tell you a tale if you'd like to hear one." Cosima was glad for the reprieve from having to join the others.

There was a settee nearby, and she took a seat with young James beside her.

"'Twas the year of our Lord 1748," Cosima began, letting her voice take on the lilt of her mother's and grandmother's who each told the story so well with their Irish cadence. The conservatory of lilies and ferns seemed to disappear, and Cosima's home took its place, along with a man she'd never met. Her great-grandfather. "This is the cross of Branduff Kennesey. You see it's fashioned from wood that's worn—beaten by years at sea. He told his daughter—my grandmother—this story. She told me, and now I shall tell you the tale of Grandfather Kennesey and the cross he held so dear.

"Young Branduff Kennesey was alone on his fishing boat—his first venture out by himself—when a tempest rose. Aye, 'twas a wind so fierce nothing could fight it, straight from the ice breath of evil itself. Any other boat but his would have splintered under such a gale, but not his little *Selah*. She held fast like a warrior in battle. The storm had a life of its own, come to claim victory over his puny form and send him to the bottom of the sea.

"But *Selah* held fast, and Branduff clung to her with his spindly arms, at the mercy of where the gale would take him. Many hours he clung to the bow, though it seemed like days. He knew neither hunger nor pain nor weakness, dreamed only of life and seeing his dear ones again."

Cosima watched James caress the center of the cross again and knew well what it felt like, for she'd done so herself many times. "Finally even his *Selah* was beaten as the last bellow of the storm spewed its great torrent and hail. Grandfather heard the splinter and thought surely he would face the Lord God.

"And yet," Cosima went on after a deep intake of air, as if she felt the suffocating storm whip the breath from her, "even as *Selah* broke into pieces, the Lord let the little boat bring young Branduff to safety on the bow—all that was left of her. When the wind calmed and the rainbow came, as is God's promise, Branduff saw the land at last and *Selah* carried him there on the hand of God. Aye, 'twas a sweet boat, that one, so it's said. And here it is—" she motioned to the relic—"all that's left of her you hold in your hands, fashioned into the cross of the Lord who plucked me great-grandfather from the jowls of death."

"Why do you have it and not him?"

"He died many years ago," Cosima said.

"Why didn't he give it to a son, like a title to the oldest boy?"

"Nearing the day of his death when he was very old, he gave it to my grandmother. 'Your brothers need no reminder of the strength in their blood,' he said. 'They use their strength ever' day. But you, my child, you will need the sum of their strength together to live in this land a woman. You will work as hard as any of your servants if you want the work to be right. You will bear children and bury some, weep with other mothers and sisters and daughters when the men go off to war. Life comes with tears, child, because we serve a God who knows suffering.'"

Cosima took the cross gently from James. "And my grandmother gave the cross to me on her own deathbed. I took it in my hands, just as I do now, without fear but rather awe, because it reminded me of the blood that runs through me, blessed and chosen by God to survive all and whatever comes my way. I remember when I hold it that I have the strength of the Lord on my side, and I can survive just as my grandmother Josephine did, and my grandfather Kennesey before her. All and whatever."

"All and whatever," James repeated softly, staring at the cross Cosima now held.

"Interesting story," said her cousin Walter from behind her.

Cosima looked up, suddenly aware that it wasn't only James who had listened to her story. Everyone in the room had quieted somewhere along the way.

"But tell me," Walter added. "Your Irish family actually *works*? I mean, alongside the servants, the way you mentioned in the story, or was that just the older generation?"

Cosima could have listed a great many tasks, from gathering herbs for medicine to cleaning up after Royboy when necessary. But before she opened her mouth she caught sight of Dowager Merit and amended her answer.

"No, that was for my grandmother's ears, many years ago. But I believe life comes inevitably with sorrow, sooner or later, no matter one's station in life."

"Something most young sprouts have yet to learn, the way these youngsters are coddled," said Dowager Merit as she slowly rose to her feet. She approached Cosima, putting a hand to Cosima's chin and directing her face upward. "You have a fine voice for storytelling, child. You must hear some of the Escott tales so your education of family history is not limited to one side. You'll come back tomorrow afternoon."

Dowager Merit turned to leave the room, pausing to lean on her cane only a few feet from Cosima. "And at the next dinner, Cosima, you will wear white, as is customary. You may miss your Emerald Isle, as the poem calls your Ireland, but you do not need to remind us of such in the color of your dress."

Cosima felt her heart sink and looked around the room at all the faces staring at her. So much for stepping outside custom, if only for a family dinner. "Yes, Lady Merit," she said, eyes downcast.

"I wish everyone to enjoy the rest of the evening," said the dowager as she continued her slow progress toward the door. "But I must say good night."

Cosima breathed deeply. Would she never be able to please her grandmother?

Cosima saw the dowager nod toward Lord Hamilton before exiting. He followed Dowager Merit from the room. Cosima found this odd, considering her grandmother's feelings for Lord Hamilton. Would they have a private meeting?

Slipping the cross back into her reticule, Cosima watched James wander off, and a moment later Beryl took his place beside her.

"Don't let that old hag ruin your mood, Cosima," Beryl said. "Your gown is the loveliest here tonight."

"I shouldn't have worn it. I don't know why I did."

"Because white is a boring theme! And coal dust is everywhere in this awful city." Beryl brushed away a black spot on her own snowy skirt. "I much prefer the day events, where we're free to wear any color we like."

"We don't host many evening parties back home." Cosima spoke before she could catch the words back. She couldn't talk about the reason.

"Oh, because of the blight, you mean?" Beryl said, and with relief Cosima nodded. "Well, don't worry about it another moment. Your grandmother not only invited you back for tomorrow afternoon; she said at the *next* dinner you should wear white. There wouldn't be a next if she didn't intend having you back."

Cosima was instantly soothed by Beryl's presence and words. Soon she put any discomfort from her mind. The children were taken back to the nursery, and Cousin Walter invited everyone remaining to the billiard room. Cosima was more than a little curious about the room normally reserved for the men. There more beverages were served, and Walter daringly challenged the women to a game. Rachel consented for them with a giggle. The entire room watched as one by one each of the women took a turn.

Cosima shot carefully during her chance and knocked a ball in, and everyone hooted. But on her next turn she proved her lack of skill, making Rachel smile her way.

Soon there were more serious games on the table, first between Walter and Reginald. As the winner, Reginald challenged what looked like a reluctant Peter, who was forced to play amid dares to prove a reputation rumoring him to be an expert.

Cosima had vowed not to watch Peter, but everyone seemed riveted to the game. She tried to talk to Beryl, but she was eager to see if her brother would win and didn't engage in much conversation.

Making each shot look easy, Peter won in short time.

Although the evening hadn't been perfect, it was an overall success. Surely Reginald could rest easier now. She would have to contend with whatever came with that.

Cosima should have welcomed the end of the evening but didn't. It meant the resumption of Peter's exile from her life.

27

"Can you find the duckie? Where's the duckie?"

From behind a one-way mirror, Talie and Luke watched the doctor with their son. Ben was on the floor in the middle of a playroom full of colorful toys, mirrors, mats, and balls bigger than he was. Dr. Karen Cooper knelt in front of him. Considered an expert in childhood development, Dr. Cooper had been trying to engage Ben in play for the past five minutes. And having little success.

Talie had watched three therapists with her son in the past hour, each of them assessing Ben's developmental level from their own areas of expertise. While they "played" with Ben, they jotted notes or checked boxes, then handed Dr. Cooper a single sheet of paper upon completion of their evaluation. Seeing how little Ben cooperated, Talie was suddenly struck with how odd Ben's behavior must seem. Obviously they expected him to do far more than Talie would have guessed any child his age capable. Why else would they test him on certain functions? Each scribble on their papers was a jab to Talie's maternal spirit.

Dr. Cooper was the last to spend time with Ben.

Ben sat with his typical poor posture, looking at everything except the doctor, who had just hidden a small yellow duck beneath a red-and-white bandana.

"Here's the duckie!" She pulled the toy from its hiding place and gave it a squeeze. The noise startled Ben and his lower lip quivered, but he didn't cry, for which Talie was grateful. Sometimes it took a while for Ben to calm once he became upset.

The doctor put the duck on her head and gave Ben a smile. He looked at her but the eye contact lasted no more than a moment.

"One . . . two . . . threeee . . ." She stretched out the last number and tipped her head to let the duck sail to the floor in front of Ben. He laughed and reached for the toy.

Before Ben could touch it, the doctor shrouded the duck with the dotted scarf once again. "Find the duckie, Ben. Where's the duckie?"

Ben put his forefinger back in his mouth and looked away, disinterested now that the duck was out of sight.

Leaning back, the doctor rose from her knees to her feet and motioned toward the glass where Talie and Luke observed from the darkened room.

Luke was the first to the door, and Talie followed slowly. The pediatrician didn't look at either Talie or Luke; she just made more notes on her pad.

All morning Talie had denied what she felt inside. Now her long-held fears would be either confirmed or relieved. Something tightened the pit of her stomach. Cold and hard and unwanted. This doctor thought there was something wrong with Ben, and it wouldn't be long before Talie must hear what she had to say. Talie's gaze sought Luke's again, but he was focused on the doctor.

Talie reached for Ben.

"Let's go into one of the examination rooms, where we can all have a seat."

Was Dr. Cooper stalling? Why couldn't she say what she had to say right here? Talie followed them, her gaze straight ahead, holding Ben close. He squirmed, but she held on tighter. When

Ben squealed, Luke took him and put him on his shoulders, where he calmed.

The room was typical for a pediatrician's office, decorated with bright colors and shapes that would appeal to any child who noticed his or her surroundings. One wall was lined with a cushioned bench seat, and in the corner a few playthings were neatly stacked. Talie had brought along Ben's favorite toy, one that lit up and played music when he pushed large, colorful buttons. It was the first toy he'd played with appropriately, and Talie had chosen it to show he could do some things right, even though she knew the age recommendation for this particular toy was three to six months. Far younger than Ben at fifteen months.

"I'm not going to tell you anything you don't already know," the doctor began, placing the folder under her arm. She took a seat on a small, round stool as Luke placed Ben on the floor. Ben slipped his finger into his mouth, ignoring the toys.

Talie looked at Luke again as they took seats on the bench nearby. They'd talked about coming here today, about the possibility that something was really wrong with Ben. Luke had said all along he hadn't been around enough babies to know much, but if Ben wasn't doing things other babies his age were doing, it was logical to have him examined. And while Talie ignored the feeling that she'd put this examination off too long already, she reminded herself how easy it had been to be persuaded by a pediatrician who didn't see anything drastically wrong. And by her own wish that Ben would catch up.

But facing a specialist who saw only kids with something more serious to consider than an ear infection or sore throat, it was all too easy to think she'd been wrong.

"Your son is well behind in development. Speech in particular, but also in general cognitive ability." Dr. Cooper pulled out the folder and glanced again at some of her notes. She looked at it rather than at either of them. "And he doesn't engage—by that

I mean he isn't interested in other people. He makes little or no eye contact, doesn't interact even when invited to play."

At last she looked up at them, but neither spoke. Talie waited, and so did Luke. The silence seemed to go on forever, like darkness during a sleepless night.

Finally the doctor spoke again. "He's young yet, but old enough to be recognized, I believe, as autistic."

Autistic. Talie felt Luke reach for her hand. She registered nothing except the physical sensations that came with hearing a specialist tell her there was something wrong with her son: Her head felt instantly light, almost dizzy. Her throat dried, and the heavy weight in her stomach wrenched at her. If she stood she would fall, so she stayed put, even though what she wanted most was to scoop up Ben and flee somewhere. Anywhere but here. Take Ben and the new baby far, far away.

Lord God, what is happening? Are You here? Can You hear me? Tell me what's happening.

She'd heard about those with autism, about those who were described as living in their own world, like a bubble they didn't want to penetrate—or have anyone invade.

"But Ben likes to be around us." Perhaps Talie could convince the doctor she was wrong. "He doesn't want to be alone. He smiles all of the time."

"I'm sure that's true, Mrs. Ingram," said the doctor, not before glancing down at the paperwork in her lap. Perhaps she'd forgotten their names and had to check before addressing Talie. "But at this point you need to be aware you're not imagining his delays. He needs speech therapy, occupational therapy, perhaps some sensory integration therapy, as well as physical therapy. . . ." She went on, describing successes made in one-on-one teaching with autistic children that followed an intensive schedule and routine.

But Talie couldn't listen. Somewhere during the course of

advice she felt herself slip away. She looked at her son, giving him the only toy he loved, the one meant for infants instead of toddlers. He pushed the buttons. . . . Couldn't the doctor see he did that right?

But it didn't matter that a fifteen-month-old child who couldn't walk or talk could play appropriately with a toy meant for a three-month-old.

All Talie heard was that word. *Autistic.*

Then Luke was speaking in his normal, calm, intelligent voice, and she had to listen again.

"My wife is almost four months pregnant, Doctor. What are the chances of this baby being autistic too?"

The doctor looked at Talie. "You're pregnant?"

Talie nodded. The loose cotton shirt she was wearing hid the slight protrusion in her middle. Talie felt the tingle of perspiration pop into her palms. She pulled away from Luke, unwilling for him to feel it.

Dr. Cooper jotted some notes, studied the other papers in the stack, and then looked at Talie again. "Are there any other kids in your family with learning disabilities? Or maybe an uncle somewhere along the way, one you thought was maybe a little slow, but otherwise okay?"

Talie couldn't speak. Ellen Grayson came instantly to mind, a woman Talie had had no knowledge of before reading the family Bible. And Willie, Royboy, Percy . . . but they'd lived *generations* ago.

"I have an uncle who's kind of strange," Luke volunteered. He turned to Talie. "You know, my uncle Wade." He addressed the doctor again. "He sold everything he owned to live in a van. Painted all the back windows black and is traveling the country somewhere, living out of that van."

The doctor smiled, but the gesture looked shallow, polite. "At this point I'm more interested in Mrs. Ingram's side of the family." She looked back at Talie. "Is there anyone with delays or mental disabilities in your family?"

Talie knew what she should say. She should tell them. But the last known person in her family to suffer developmental delay had been dead for over sixty years. Talie had convinced herself Ellen's condition could have nothing to do with Ben.

Talie shook her head. "Not in my immediate family. My sister and I are both fine."

"Ben is the first grandchild born to your parents?"

She nodded.

"What about cousins or uncles?"

"I . . ." She started to tell her about Ellen Grayson, started to reveal everything. But her throat constricted, and she had to force out her words. "I have several cousins a little older than me and second cousins a bit younger. . . . They're all fine. Just fine."

The doctor scrawled a prescription and handed it to Talie. "This is an order for a blood test on Ben. I recommend that you stop by Dr. Benson's office in the genetics department here at the hospital before you leave today."

"Today?" Talie repeated, and her voice cracked. Hadn't they been through enough already today?

"There are some disorders known to be genetic that can cause developmental delay. Since you're pregnant, it would be best to eliminate all the worries." She turned to Luke. "To answer your earlier question, Mr. Ingram . . ." She glanced again at the paperwork in her lap. "I should say, *Dr.* Ingram. I see the nurse wrote on your referral that you're a PhD."

"That's right," he said, "but I only use the title in business."

"Well, at any rate," Dr. Cooper went on, "they don't know yet exactly what causes autism. Genetics might have something to do with it, and some families seem to have a somewhat higher risk of having multiple affected children, but it's not dramatic in the occurrence of classic autism. My advice to both of you is to go home, engage your son as much as possible, love him, love him, love him, and don't think about blood tests. I will add, Dr. Ingram, we have a lot of genes that we pass on to our children. Your son may not be able to present the level of intelligence you might hope for your offspring, but you'll find he's still your son. A diagnosis doesn't change that."

Though the doctor wasn't speaking directly to her, Talie listened to every word, each spoken in a businesslike tone. Luke was smart; of course he expected to have smart children. What other genes meant as much as ones that had to do with the brain? What did this woman know about *anything*? It wasn't her child who had just been given a life sentence.

Talie knew one thing. If Ben was autistic . . . or feeble-minded . . . she knew through whom he'd inherited it.

Her.

A few minutes later they left the multistory medical building that housed some of the leading children's experts in the state. Luke held Ben, and when they reached the car in the attached garage, he placed him in the car seat before sliding behind the wheel. Talie was already seated on the passenger side.

Luke sat still. He had the keys in his hand but didn't put one in the ignition.

Talie waited.

"Was it just my imagination, or is that woman about as cold as a fish?"

Talie leaped on his bandwagon. Feeling anger toward the messenger was easier than facing the message itself. "How anyone can say 'love him, love him, love him' so many times without any warmth is beyond me."

Talie put from her mind every name in the old family Bible, refused to think of any one of them. She turned around to check on Ben. He was already leaning back in his car seat. He hadn't

slept well the night before and would probably be asleep before
they left the parking garage.

Luke started the engine but glanced at Talie before pulling out. "She could be wrong, you know. It's not like there was
a blood test with some kind of evidence. Autism is just her
opinion."

But Luke wasn't dealing with all the facts. Maybe autism was
more genetic than they thought. Maybe it could last through
generation after generation.

"We'll have to look up some facts on autism before we buy
what she's trying to sell. The Internet, books, maybe a second
opinion."

"Right," Talie said and tried to summon a courageous smile
but didn't think she succeeded. The smile felt almost like a sneer.

Luke reached over to her lap and took one of her hands. "It
doesn't change anything, you know. He's still Ben."

Her heart squeezed with love, and she pinched her eyes shut.
When she opened them again, she looked at Ben in the backseat,
sitting so contentedly. "I know."

"We'll definitely get another opinion. I didn't like her much
anyway."

Talie wanted to agree, wanted to say something—anything—
to concur, but she bit her lip instead. Her voice would tremble,
and the sound might break the dam holding back her tears.

Luke glanced at his watch. "Ben was the only one who had
lunch back there. Are you hungry?"

The thought of food made her stomach lurch, but she knew
she had to eat. She had another baby to think of, and besides, it
might help to settle her thoughts if they went about their normal
activities.

At least that was what she told herself.

28

I have always been an early riser. When the sun brightens the horizon something in me wakes. Beryl and Christabelle, and even Lady Hamilton, have no such malady. They have told me when I become more accustomed to London society I shall put aside this habit, since so many of the parties we attend last well into the night.

So far, my awakening time remains fixed, whether I like it or not. I often read or write in my journal in the upstairs parlor, well before breakfast. But today I was joined unexpectedly early by Lord and Lady Hamilton, who arrived together. . . .

"Good morning," Cosima greeted Lord and Lady Hamilton. Lady Hamilton often sat with her husband before he left for the day, only to return to her own bedroom once he was gone. To Cosima, knowing Lady Hamilton would rather stay abed yet shared his company at such an early hour was another sign of her devotion to him.

But the somber look on the faces of both warned Cosima that this was not a normal morning.

Cosima stood. "I don't mean to be in the way. I shall come back later, when the girls are up and about."

"No, Cosima, you may stay," said Lord Hamilton. "There's no reason we shouldn't speak to you first about our plans, since they affect you as well."

"Plans?"

Lady Hamilton approached, reaching for Cosima's hand but then awkwardly pulling back before touching her. Instead she motioned Cosima back toward the settee she'd just abandoned.

"The parliamentary session doesn't end for another week," Lady Hamilton said. "Normally we don't return to our country estate until after that, but Lord Hamilton has decided to send us to the country a bit early."

Cosima looked from Lady to Lord Hamilton and then back again. "Is anything wrong?"

Lord Hamilton cleared his throat. "There's been a rather nasty outbreak of cholera here in the city. Now there's nothing unusual in the disease; it happens every year. But this year it's especially prevalent, and I don't want any of you exposed."

"We should like to extend the invitation for you to accompany us, Cosima," Lady Hamilton said, but her tone was hesitant, ambivalent. "Only we're uncertain as to what is best for you. With Reginald here in London and your plans still undecided, we wondered if perhaps you would rather stay behind and transfer residence to your grandmother's home."

Thoughts clicked through Cosima's mind one after another. Leave London or live with her dour grandmother? If she no longer lived with the Hamiltons, there would be no chance of seeing Peter again.

At Cosima's lingering silence, Lady Hamilton spoke again. "We're quite certain your grandmother would be pleased to have you spend time with her. She said as much to Lord Hamilton last night."

Surprised, Cosima eyed Lady Hamilton's face. Though she was smiling, there was something different about her today, as if for some reason she had a sense of sympathy in the reserved glances directed Cosima's way.

"And they're planning to stay in London until the end of sessions?"

"Lady Merit is, and the duke of course. I'm not sure if she's sending any of the family home sooner than next week. Perhaps in that time you and Reginald can determine what your future will hold."

Cosima clasped her hands together in an attempt to keep them steady upon her lap. "When will you be leaving?"

"As soon as the girls and I can be packed."

Cosima raised her gaze to Lady Hamilton, trying to read meaning into the words and tone and expression. It seemed there was more, and yet Cosima had no idea what it could be. "You think it best for me to go to my grandmother's then?"

Lady Hamilton exchanged glances with her husband, who remained silent. "Yes, dear, we do."

To her own horror Cosima felt her eyes dampen and sting. Hurriedly she brushed away a fallen tear. "I shall miss Beryl." She felt as if she were being sent away, even though she knew it was silly.

Lady Hamilton sat beside Cosima and drew her close. The simple gesture invoked more tears, for a moment ago it had seemed as if Lady Hamilton did not even want to touch her. "But you shall still see Beryl! I've seen your friendship grow, and it's warmed my heart." Her voice shook and Cosima looked up, wondering at the extent of Lady Hamilton's distress.

Lord Hamilton cleared his throat, and Cosima felt Lady Hamilton stiffen and pull away. She stood beside Lord Hamilton.

Cosima gripped the lace of her gown, wishing she had a handkerchief. She forced herself to her feet. "I shall summon my maid and begin my own packing, then." Another tear fell even as she offered a quavery smile. "My grandmother was expecting me this afternoon. Only I didn't know my visit would be with bag and baggage as well."

An hour later, with Millie beside her and her trunks half full, Cosima heard a loud tap at the door. Before Millie reached it, Beryl pushed the door wide, a look of alarm lighting her brown eyes.

"Mother told me," she said, putting her hands on her hips and surveying the disarray in the room. "This is not acceptable, simply not acceptable." She took two strides closer to Cosima, who stood beside a large trunk with a folded nightgown in her arms.

Beryl's face was flushed. "You can't mean to move in with that old . . . well, your grandmother! She's . . . she's . . . oh, I can't say a word without sinning." Taking the gown from Cosima and placing it carelessly on the bed, Beryl put her hands on the trunk as if to close it. "Why would you want to go and live with her when you could come to Hamilton Hall with us?"

Cosima retrieved the discarded nightgown and refolded it. She couldn't look at Beryl. "It seemed the most logical option, as your mother presented it to me."

"Mother is acting so strangely today, but I know her, Cosima. I know she cares for you like another daughter. I'm sure she doesn't really want you to leave us. Perhaps she's only following an order from the dowager."

Cosima shrugged. "If that's the case, all the more reason I should go to the Escotts. I've disappointed my grandmother enough without refusing to live there if she expects it of me."

Beryl plopped down on the chaise longue near the unlit fire-box. "This is unacceptable."

"You're leaving London only a week early, Beryl," Cosima reminded her. "Things would have changed then anyway."

"Yes, but only to the extent of where we were all living." She leaned forward. "You're like a sister to me now, Cosima. Closer than that, since Christabelle and I don't see things half as similarly as you and I. And besides . . ."

Cosima faced Beryl. "Besides what? You had plans for me? With your brother?"

Beryl stood, nodding and looking thoroughly self-assured. "Yes, that's right." She glanced from Cosima to Millie in what looked like a brief moment of uncertainty, then back at Cosima. "And I'll say it in front of your maid, too. I don't care who knows. You and Peter are right for each other, Cosima. I knew it the first day I met you. And you know. So does Peter. If you leave our family now, how will that ever progress?"

Cosima grabbed Beryl's hands and squeezed them in her own. "Oh, Beryl, Beryl, it isn't meant to! There's nothing between your brother and me except what your imagination has conjured."

Impulsively, she gave Beryl a hug, knowing an added benefit of such closeness was that Beryl could no longer see into Cosima's eyes. It wouldn't do to have her friend suspect with one look that every word Cosima spoke was a lie. "It's better this way, Berrie. I'm sure we'll be able to visit back and forth, especially once Reginald and I wed . . . if we do. You shall be my favorite houseguest."

Beryl pulled away. "At this moment my own maid is packing my bags too. Oh, it's all such a mess."

"But you've seen how little time he's spent around me most of the summer."

"Yes, avoiding you because you're supposed to marry his best friend. He's too loyal to Reginald to do anything about it until you give him a reason. And you must, Cosima. Before Reginald sets a date, now that you're on good terms with your grandmother and even considering living with her."

"What do you mean by that?"

"Oh, posh, Cosima. Anyone who knows Reginald doesn't have to wonder long what his real motives are for marrying you. Not that he mustn't be fond of you, because frankly, who wouldn't be? But he has an ulterior motive: to gain the attention and acceptance of the aristocracy. Who can help him better than the dowager? One nod from her and you're on everyone's guest list."

Cosima felt her knees wobble, and she sank to the chaise Beryl had vacated moments ago. None of this came as a surprise to her, of course, but the fact that Beryl knew Reginald's plans as intimately as Cosima did came as a surprise.

"I must be quite the pity of everyone who knows us, mustn't I?" Cosima whispered. "To be used in such a way."

"Oh, for heaven's sake," Beryl said, nearing Cosima. "No one thinks anything of it because it happens every day. But it doesn't have to be that way for you. Peter is obviously interested, and if you would only give him a word of encouragement, I'm sure he'd speak to Reginald, and Reginald would be the gentleman and excuse himself."

Cosima shook her head, returning to her packing.

"I don't see why you won't follow your heart," Beryl said sullenly.

Cosima watched her friend leave, feeling as bereft as Beryl looked.

29

Talie placed Ben in his favorite chair, the one that spun around but stayed safely in the same spot. She held out a toy for him, but he didn't reach for it. She smiled and called his name, but he ignored her. He started spinning.

She turned at the sound of the garage door opening, and a few moments later Luke announced his homecoming with a good imitation of Jimmy Durante.

But Talie wasn't in the mood for charm, either Luke's or the long-deceased Mr. Durante's. Since receiving the diagnosis of autism, Luke's mood had been steady and unflappable. Talie couldn't understand him. Why wasn't he worried? How was he able to function, to work, to create office buildings, homes, and skyscrapers just like he always had before?

She suspected he somehow still hoped Ben would outgrow his delays. They'd had the blood drawn at the hospital as the doctor had recommended, but they hadn't gotten any results yet. She hadn't made an appointment for a second opinion and wondered if Luke didn't push doing that because he wanted to believe the first doctor's opinion had been wrong. Why risk seeing another doctor who might tell them the same thing?

Though Talie longed to cling to such hopes too, she couldn't. Not anymore. She had to tell him the truth. And she had to do it now.

Instead of a greeting, instead of their customary kiss, Talie stopped short in front of Luke. "I need to tell you something, Luke. Something I've been keeping from you."

She turned from him to the kitchen table nearby, where the journal now sat. She had tried hiding it away like a secret, pushing it to the back of her bedroom closet and pulling it out only now and then. But it haunted her all along.

She'd been ignoring the journal for what it was. The call back she didn't want it to be.

She faced Luke with the book in hand. "It's about my family, and it's all in here."

"Isn't that the journal from the box?" Luke looked curiously confused, but not nearly as concerned as he ought to be.

How implicitly he trusted her. Surely nothing she'd kept hidden could be all that important.

Confirmation of that assessment came when Luke's calm gaze left her for the mail, off to the side of the kitchen table. He might even have reached for it, but Talie placed herself in his line of vision.

"They used to call it a curse. Today it's genetics."

A full two seconds went by before Luke looked at Talie. "What did you say?" He sounded more baffled than alarmed, so she knew her point still hadn't been made.

"Here," she said, pushing Grandmother Cosima's writings at him. "Read it for yourself. And then tell me our son isn't just like Royboy . . . and Willie and Percy. . . ."

Then she fled the room in tears.

30

How is it, Lord, that the curse I thought I could bear seems too heavy a burden? I have never pleaded with You to remove it . . . until now.

I fear that I am being sent away for some reason I cannot fathom. I try to assure myself that everything Lord and Lady Hamilton said this morning makes perfect sense. But it does nothing to change my mood. Servants have arrived to take my trunks to the carriage awaiting me and Millie. I must say my good-byes momentarily, particularly to dear Beryl and Christabelle.

And yet, even in the midst of knowing I have no hope for love, I would not say I would have been better off had I never left Ireland. . . .

"Oh, Cosima!" cried Christabelle, stepping forward to pull Cosima into a hug. "I feel as though I'm losing a sister."

Cosima squeezed Christabelle.

Beryl joined their hug, and no one seemed to care there were

servants around to witness Cosima's undignified and tearful departure. Lord and Lady Hamilton were not there to bid caution.

With Cosima's arm looped through Beryl's, they made their
way outside.

"I don't know what's come over Mother. She's not even here
to say good-bye."

"I've left a note expressing my gratitude for your parents'
generosity in keeping me so long," Cosima said. "It doesn't seem
enough."

"It's more than enough, if you ask me," Beryl said with an
irritated edge.

"Berrie, 'tis no fault of your mother's that I should spend
time at my grandmother's," Cosima whispered.

Beryl nodded just as a tear slipped down her cheek.

A footman helped Millie into the carriage first, and after one
last embrace from Beryl, Cosima followed. She waved, forcing a
smile to her face as the carriage rolled down the lane.

Cosima settled back, her heart so heavy she could barely
breathe. Just as the carriage approached the gate leading to the
public street, it halted. Cosima leaned out again to see the last
trace of Beryl and Christabelle then looked ahead to see the cause
of their unexpected stop. Nothing seemed amiss, but she heard
voices from the opposite side.

The footman alighted from the rear of the carriage, and
she saw him pass toward the front. Cosima barely had time to
exchange puzzled looks with Millie before seeing that same footman lead a horse around to the back of the carriage, where it
sounded as though the horse was being tethered.

Then the door opened, not by the footman but by Lord Peter.

"The driver tells me you're going to your grandmother's," he
said as the carriage jostled to accept his weight. A moment later
he was in the seat beside her. "And I can see from the trunks atop
that you plan to stay."

Throat instantly dry, hands atremble, Cosima wondered if she could speak. "Have your parents not spoken to you?"

"They mentioned something about returning early to the country—well, neither Father nor I would do so until the session ends—but I assumed you would be accompanying my mother and sisters."

The carriage lurched forward again, much to Cosima's surprise. Did Lord Peter plan to accompany them to her grandmother's, then? Her heart had not found its usual place since the moment he'd opened the door, and now it bounced a bit faster. She cast a quick glance toward Millie, ever the dutiful servant, who looked out the window, pretending for the moment she didn't exist.

"Since my plans . . . with Reginald . . . are still uncertain and he resides here in London, it was decided I should stay with my grandmother for the time being. She expressed an interest in spending more time with me."

Cosima looked away from Peter's gaze. If she allowed herself to glance at him more than the briefest, most polite moment, she might not be able to look away.

"Why is it, I wonder," he said, and suddenly his voice was lower, more intimate, "that those plans with Reginald are still unsettled?"

She clasped her hands tighter together, feeling the tremble that had been confined there threaten to spread throughout her body. "I . . . cannot say, milord."

"I can." Peter leaned back on the seat, farther away from her. "But I won't."

They rode in silence, and Cosima wondered at his presence. All summer he had avoided her, and now he sat beside her as if it were his rightful place. Myriad thoughts shot through Cosima's mind like lightning bolts, electrified with emotion. What would he have said if he'd chosen to speak of her uncertain plans with

Reginald? Was he disappointed she would no longer reside with his family? Did he regret spending so much time away now that it appeared they would have no further opportunity to spend time together?

The carriage slowed at a corner, and Peter rapped on the roof for the driver to stop. He extended his hand, and Cosima slipped her palm into his. "I bid you farewell, then, milady," he said cordially, barely looking at her.

Cosima couldn't help herself. With his hand so strong and firm around hers, every ounce of sense evaporated. She clung to his warm palm as no lady should, even when he began to pull away.

Peter did not miss the simple movement, subtle yet obvious. His gaze rose immediately to hers and fastened steadily.

Cosima lost all courage. She looked away.

Peter still held her hand in his, but with his free hand he touched her chin, tipping her face toward him so she had little choice but to look at him. If he searched, she knew she couldn't hide her feelings for him.

"Cosima," he whispered.

She'd never loved her own name so much as hearing him say it. With all her being she wanted to feel his arms around her. Little did she care that Millie, with her outward effort to blend in with the upholstery, could see all that Cosima desired to do.

But she couldn't. She mustn't. It wasn't Reginald that Cosima thought of just then. She thought of Royboy. And Percy. And Willie.

And she knew she couldn't give such sons to Peter . . . or maybe she couldn't give them to herself. Not for Peter.

Stiffening, she averted her gaze as she pulled her hand free. "Good-bye, Lord Peter." Her throat felt so tight the words were barely audible.

Peter seemed as attuned to the language of her movements as to anything verbal. As quickly as he'd discerned her reluctance to have him depart, he must have perceived her sudden rigidity.

He lowered the hand she'd let go, then left the carriage.

Cosima closed her eyes. She heard the footman untie the horse from the rear of the carriage. Not a word was exchanged between lord and servant. All she heard were hoofbeats carrying Peter away.

Although her grandmother's town house was as comfortable as the Hamilton city estate, Cosima immediately missed the Hamiltons. All of them.

After her bags were settled and Millie assigned to unpack, Cosima shared the afternoon with her grandmother, listening to the Escott military lineage. Dowager Merit talked of kings and queens, British Whigs and Tories, Chartists and revolutions, mingling family history throughout Britain's.

Cosima tried to keep the information straight but found her mind wandering more than once. She wondered if Peter would be safe in the city, if there really was an unusually high incidence of cholera this year. She wondered if he would spend more time at home now that she was not there anymore. When would he join his mother and sisters in the country? The town house would be quiet with only a few servants and the two Lord Hamiltons in residence. She wondered if Peter would miss his family . . . if he would miss her.

She knew it was foolish to allow herself such feelings but was powerless to change the way her heart behaved. She supposed she would stop caring for Peter someday. After all, if she married Reginald, she must squelch such feelings for anyone but her husband. She would be the dutiful wife, and maybe, if she prayed very hard and acted like the loving wife she ought to become, her heart would follow in due course.

If she didn't marry Reginald, she would return to Ireland unwed. She would continue with her plans to convert the Irish

Escott Manor into a school. Surely that was a far more valuable future than marriage and this endless social circle Reginald seemed so eager to join.

Reginald was expected to dinner on Friday night. He had respectfully waited for an invitation from the dowager, and now that he had it Cosima believed his proposal would soon be forthcoming.

Although the dinner was not expected to be as formal without the entire extended Escott family in attendance, the next evening Cosima chose her gown carefully: pure white with a single vine of roses embroidered from the waist across the front of the skirt.

To her surprise, Reginald was already in the drawing room when she came down, along with Lord and Lady Escott.

Cosima always marveled how warm were Lord and Lady Escott when Dowager Merit wasn't in the same room. They chatted for a few minutes, and Cosima found herself enjoying their company. While Lord John was a bit quiet, often when he spoke—or instantly when he laughed—he reminded Cosima of her father. She told him so, and when he looked at her with a frown, she regretted having mentioned it.

Soon the dowager joined them, and Cosima successfully survived the evening without causing a single outward frown upon the dowager's face.

But Cosima was not only exhausted after having carefully chosen each word and move; she was relieved when Reginald prepared to leave. She longed to return to the privacy of her room, let her thoughts be her own instead of a slave to the rules of Dowager Merit.

When she bid Reginald good evening, however, he lingered over his polite farewell. "Will you see me to the foyer, Cosima?"

She looked to her grandmother, who gave a tacit nod of approval.

"See that you're not alone," the dowager said. "Let the footman tarry."

At the door, the footman with Reginald's top hat and gloves stood at the ready.

"I want to be sure you're aware of the upcoming Hamilton garden party and ball."

Unbidden, undeniable hope rose in Cosima's breast. She hadn't seen an invitation. "When?"

"In two weeks' time," Reginald said. "Peter leaves tomorrow to join his mother and sisters, and I may go along for a few days then come back in time to escort you. Their party is one of the highlights of country life, and they invite everyone."

"Oh! I do miss them." She smiled at Reginald. "Thank you, Reginald, for letting me know about the party so I may look forward to it."

He kissed the palm of her hand and sent her his most charming smile. "It's the least I could do for all concerned."

He took his leave, and Cosima found her way back up to her room, considerably happier than when she'd left it earlier.

Two weeks. Two weeks until she would see Peter again.

31

"Did you read all of this, Talie?"

From their bed, Talie looked up from the mystery she was reading to see Luke approach. He wore the flannel shorts he slept in and carried Cosima's journal. Reading was Talie's only escape . . . but not the kind he held in his hands.

She turned her attention back to her book. "I didn't have to. I read enough to know whatever is causing Ben's delays is from my family. Through me."

"A curse from 1849." He spoke as if the notion was to be derided instead of respected or feared the way all the Irish villagers feared it in Cosima's journal.

She shrugged.

"You realize how ridiculous this sounds, don't you? And how faithless?"

"Okay." The word was curt, but she couldn't change the feelings instigating that tone. Pain and fear and guilt and . . . faithlessness.

"Talie." Luke's tone was gentle now, and it made headway to soften some of her prickles. "We're talking about genetics and you know it. We live in a world full of diseases and decay. It's not because one family or another did something to deserve bad genes."

"Do you really believe my family has been carrying around

bad genetics for one hundred and fifty years? How was my dad spared? Or my dad's brother and his family? Everybody was spared except *my* son?"

"I don't know. That's why I'm calling Dr. Benson tomorrow."

"The doctor who took the blood test on Ben?" Although they still hadn't received the results, both of them had been impressed by the geneticist's friendly compassion.

"Maybe she can tell us what kind of disorder we're dealing with."

"What difference will it make?" Talie whispered. "A new label? Ben won't be any different whether we call him autistic or something else."

"I just think we should have all the facts."

Talie dropped the book she'd been reading and snapped off the light on the bed stand. She punched the pillow behind her in a feeble attempt to rid herself of frustration. When she lay back at last, she turned her face away from Luke.

"And Talie?"

"Hmmm?"

"I think you should read the rest of this."

"Why?"

"Where did you leave off?"

She shifted position to look at Luke again. Even in the darkness he was fully visible from the moonlight shining through the window. She'd forgotten to shut the blinds. "It doesn't matter. The curse—okay, the bad genetics—didn't die with her, because it's still alive today. In me. I don't want to read about it."

He held out the journal. "Read it, Tal. I'm glad I did, even if I can't live up to the man your great-great-great-grandmother married."

Talie tilted her head to one side. "What do you mean?"

"Read it and find out."

Reluctantly Talie accepted the worn-out journal. She was half tempted to put it on the floor and get to it some other time. But Luke would probably stand vigil until she gave it some attention tonight or he fell asleep—whichever came first. She reached for the lamp beside the bed and clicked it on again.

Before searching for the page where she'd left off, Talie looked at her husband. "I don't believe in curses any more than you do, Luke. But there's something here. It points to whatever Ben has. I don't know if I can read any more. . . ."

Luke sat beside her, cross-legged. "I'm not ready to believe anything yet, Talie. Not in curses and not in some genetic disease that's been hiding in your genes for so long. If Ben does have something and it's the same thing described in this journal, then we have to know. It'll show in his blood test; don't you think? Since nothing has come back so far, maybe nothing will."

Talie felt hot tears gather on the rims of her eyes. "It came from me."

He put his hands on her shoulders, pulling her close. "You don't know that, but it doesn't matter anyway. We can't choose our genes, Tal. It's no one's fault."

A pair of tears slipped from each eye. "Then why do I feel so guilty?"

"That's why you have to read the journal," he whispered. "Don't you think your ancestor Cosima had a reason to write this journal? Maybe she felt guilty too, but by the time she wrote this she'd learned enough to know that wasn't right. Remember what it said in the beginning? That love and faith in Christ are stronger than fear? Is fear all that different from guilt if you're the one feeling responsible for the fear?"

Talie pulled away to reach for a tissue from the nightstand. The journal felt heavy in her lap, and she wanted to push it away.

As if reading her thoughts, Luke stared at her. "Read it, Tal."

"I really, really don't want to."

"You won't regret it. It made me think that if Ben does have something, maybe we can face it after all. If we can live up to them."

Luke leaned back on his own side of the bed. Reluctantly, Talie turned the pages. But no sooner had she read a word than Luke spoke again.

"When you're done you ought to give it to Dana."

Talie stared at him. The very thing she'd been protecting Dana from all this time . . . he wanted to tell her? Just like that? There was no proof any of this affected her. Why bring her into it at all?

She looked back at the journal without saying a word.

32

Cervantes said in Don Quixote that honesty is the best policy. I thought I held to such a policy, and yet what have I done? Kept from my friends the truth about myself.

The last two weeks have dragged so slowly I wondered if they would ever pass. Long days spent under the scrutiny and tutelage of Dowager Merit have brought my spirits down. I have felt only the slightest peace upon my pillow each night as I count another day gone.

Dowager Merit finds my education for running a household somewhere between woefully lacking and downright delinquent. She drills me with questions, most of which I fail to answer properly. What should the mistress of a house do if a servant is found derelict in his or her duty? Find the reason and address the problem. Which is, of course, incorrect. Unworthy, unskilled, or uncommitted servants are to be sacked immediately, without references.

However, while my grandmother is fastidious and firm, I have also learned she is generous in wages. Hopeful applicants *for a position in the Escott home never dwindle. Nearly every morning I spot a plain-clothed man or woman either approaching or retreating from the yard.*

I have also experienced the dowager's generosity firsthand. A dressmaker was summoned to "complete my wardrobe." In an amazingly short span of time she produced for me a dozen new gowns for day and evening, two new cloaks, and even a striped burnoose inspired by an Arabian seamstress, plus many hats and countless pairs of gloves, petticoats, and shoes. Bundles and baggage of every shape and size have been packed and sent ahead to the Escott country house or marked for later transport.

Because Reginald has been absent since the week after my arrival at the Escott town house, Dowager Merit has frequently addressed the topic of my possible nuptials.

"Until the man proves himself more attentive than he has done so far," she said to me one morning, "all plans for a wedding are out of the question."

I do not care how long it will be before I am able to plan my wedding with Reginald. Instead I am counting the days until I leave London for the three-day stay at Hamilton Hall. Only within these pages will I admit that impatience proves love, as the old saying goes. . . .

Reginald arrived early on the day of departure. His bright blue eyes were happy and light, and Cosima felt a genuine fountain of happiness spring up when she saw him. He had sent two notes during her stay with her grandmother, telling Cosima about preparations the Hamiltons had made for their upcoming garden party. Reginald seemed to be looking forward to the event almost as much as Cosima herself.

It rained most of the way out to the country, and when they arrived at the proper station, they hastened from the train coach to a borrowed Hamilton carriage one at a time, a footman holding open a huge umbrella. Baggage was transferred to a separate, tarp-covered wagon, while the two servants in their party waited for a hired carriage.

The grounds at Hamilton Hall glistened in shades of green that Cosima hadn't seen since she left home. Sprawling lawns, patches of trees, flowering hedges, and far-off gardens attested to the meticulous care of every inch of land God had entrusted to this family.

The home itself stretched out with two wings balanced from a taller middle, where six white columns enhanced a circular portico. Built of light brick with white shutters at the countless tall windows, the residence was imposing and inviting all at once. Three stories high and twice the size of the ancient manor house Cosima had left in Ireland, it was by far the stateliest home she had ever visited.

Cosima peered through the wet glass at other carriages arriving with them, toward the open front door teeming with guests and footmen with black umbrellas. Not seeing the one she sought, her gaze scanned the home's windows in hope of spotting him there.

That Peter was nowhere to be found among the influx of soggy visitors shouldn't come as any surprise, though she couldn't deny a certain disappointment. But what did she expect? Why did she think he would want to seek her out, to keep looking for a message she would not send?

Before long, Cosima stood in a crowded foyer. She barely noticed any of the decor, just a sparkling chandelier hanging from a high, domed ceiling and a marble-and-alabaster staircase lined with mahogany railings. She watched guests greet each other while servants lingered to take away their sodden garments or direct them to assigned rooms.

"Cosima! Oh, my friend! Welcome!"

The call came from Beryl, making her way through the throng followed closely by Christabelle. Beryl pulled Cosima into a tight embrace.

Christabelle's hug quickly followed. "I feel like saying welcome home; only you've never been here before, have you?"

Cosima shook her head, laughing and looking beyond the people to their surroundings. "It's splendid!"

"Let's go upstairs, away from the crowd," Beryl said.

But Cosima held back. "I've become separated from Reginald."

"He'll expect you'll want time to yourself after the journey, and besides, he's probably looking for Peter. They have some bridges to mend. Come along."

Her statement about mending bridges intrigued Cosima, but Beryl was already leading the way upstairs. She led Cosima to a large bedroom, and even with dull weather outside, the room seemed full of light from many windows. The walls were covered in red-silk wallpaper, with a fringed canopy atop the bed. Scattered occasional tables were laden with books and oil lamps.

"I'm glad the weekend is finally here," said Beryl. "And I'm especially glad you're here. I wish you were here to stay."

Cosima squeezed Beryl's hand. She wished it too but didn't think she should say so. "You said something downstairs about Reginald and Peter mending bridges. What did you mean?"

Christabelle spoke up. "The two of them had an awful dispute the other day. They were outside in the pavilion, and we heard it all the way to the veranda." She shrugged one shoulder. "Peter wouldn't say what it was about, but I have a notion it was about you, Cosima."

Cosima felt her eyes widen and her heart drop. Even Beryl looked surprised. Cosima looked across at Christabelle.

"Oh, you both think I'm some kind of ninny, don't you?" Christabelle said with a frown. "Just because I'm two years younger, you think I don't see things. But I do. I see more than either of you might guess."

"All right, Chrissy," coaxed Beryl, "why don't you tell us what you think you've seen?"

Christabelle leaned back on the settee and folded her arms in front of her, looking at Cosima rather than at her sister. "I think you're not in the least bit interested in marrying Reginald, and he knows it. I think you're in love with my brother, and moreover, I think he's in love with you."

A tremble coursed through Cosima, mortified that Christabelle knew the truth without their ever having exchanged a word on the subject.

But even as Cosima felt so vulnerable, Beryl exuded an amused laugh. "How do you know so much, Chrissy, when Peter was absent much of summer?"

"That in itself is evidence. It was quite easy to figure out, even if I hadn't seen the way he looked at Cosima on those rare occasions they were together."

Beryl laughed again as though she was thoroughly enjoying herself. "There, you see, Cosima? If even little Christabelle has figured it out, the truth is obvious. You know what you must do, and you must do it immediately. You must go to our brother and tell him how you feel. You're the one supposedly engaged. He won't come to you first."

Confusion engulfed Cosima. Desire warred with logic. She couldn't marry Peter, no matter what any of them believed or even wanted. Perhaps Beryl should know why, and then she would give up her efforts to throw them together.

"It seems to me Reginald must suspect something if their argument concerned Cosima," Christabelle said. "Perhaps he won't give her up . . . and they'll fight a duel!"

Beryl rolled her eyes and Cosima's stomach twisted, even though she knew no one fought duels anymore. She stood, turning her back on the sisters, wringing her hands. If Christabelle had guessed Cosima's feelings for Peter, she probably wasn't alone. Perhaps Reginald really did suspect Cosima cared for Peter in a way that should be reserved for Reginald alone.

But if that was the case, why bring her here? Why make sure she was included in the invitation and go to the trouble of escorting her? Perhaps to prove to himself—and to Peter—that even if she did harbor feelings for Peter it was Reginald she would choose to marry.

"What's the matter, Cosima?" asked Beryl, coming up behind her. "Surely you don't believe Christabelle! Only silly Frenchmen would consider a duel these days, or perhaps a wild American."

Cosima forced a smile. "No, it's not that. It's . . . something else. Something you don't know."

"What don't we know?" asked Christabelle.

Cosima faced them, offering a quick prayer for the Lord to guide her tongue. Truth was the answer. She knew Reginald preferred she didn't speak of the curse, but she no longer felt honest without Beryl's and Christabelle's knowing.

"I am in love with your brother," she admitted, and both girls' grins widened.

"Well," said Beryl, "that's something we do know. You said there is something we don't."

Cosima nodded, took a deep breath, then walked around them to retake her seat before the fireplace. With the dampness of the day, a low fire had been set and she welcomed the warmth.

"I will tell you why I cannot marry your brother, even if he asked me."

"What?" Christabelle said.

At the same moment Beryl took her seat next to Cosima and put a hand on her shoulder. "I knew there was something troubling you. Tell us, Cosima. It's high time."

Cosima looked from one sister to the other, welcoming their concern. Would they still look at her with such affection after they knew? "I should have no real wish to marry any man. And no man should wish to marry me. Not even Reginald, who has so much less to lose than Peter."

"Now you're making absolutely no sense, Cosima," Beryl said. "What should Reginald lose if he marries you?"

"A future generation," she told them, looking down at her hands instead of at them. "I'm . . . cursed."

She hadn't meant to use the word she so hated, but in that moment it was the only one that expressed it so succinctly.

"Cursed!" Christabelle repeated.

Beryl looked exasperated. "Do you know how medieval that sounds?"

Cosima rubbed her palms together in an attempt to still their unsteadiness. She avoided Beryl's penetrating gaze. "'Tis true—at least so says everyone who knows the Kennesey women."

"Kennesey . . . that's your mother's side of the family, the side that handed down the cross?"

Cosima nodded. "Yes. Only it seems the Kennesey legacy isn't just a family heirloom." She paused, wondering how best to tell them. "Starting with my grandmother and her younger sister, and after that my mother and my aunt . . . all the Kennesey women who bore children . . ."

"Yes?" Beryl probed, filling the hesitation Cosima left.

"All of them . . . had children . . . sons in particular . . . who . . . who were . . ."

"Oh, for heaven's sake, Cosima, just tell us!" Beryl insisted.

"Feebleminded," Cosima whispered at last. There. She'd said it. She'd told them the truth.

Cosima watched Beryl and Christabelle exchange uncertain glances.

"All of the men on your mother's side are feebleminded?"

"Not all. But I had two brothers—one of whom has gone on to heaven and one who remains with my parents—both dull witted." Perhaps it was better for her to explain in more detail before she allowed too many questions. "My surviving brother is Royboy, and no sweeter boy can be found. Mischievous, I should add, but there's not a trace of malice in him. He . . . he just doesn't learn. He talks only a little, though he chatters quite a bit and does odd things, like chewing on clothing or leather or paper. Anything, really, if he has the chance to put it in his mouth. He remembers some things, like events of long ago, but something said a moment ago or an instruction given is immediately forgotten."

She smiled then, remembering Royboy. She had spoken so little of her family for fear of giving away the secret that blocked memories now flooded in one after another. "He loves animals and loves to eat, though he's so slim you wouldn't guess it. He loves music and the game of pantomime—just to watch, mind you, not to participate—and he smiles from the moment he wakes to the moment he goes to sleep. Except . . . well, sometimes things upset him, like sudden noises. And at times he'll cry for no reason at all—at least no reason we can see. He might go from tears to laughter in a moment."

Cosima looked at Beryl and Christabelle again, and she could tell she had their avid attention. "But never would a mean thought cross his mind—not like the rest of us. He's pure to the core, even when others are mean or impatient with him. His smile makes me remember what's important when I become caught in my own troubles. He's here as the smile of God, I believe, because he has one for everyone."

"He sounds easier to love than most brothers," Christabelle said. "At least brothers who sometimes ignore you or tell you you're silly."

"I do love Royboy," Cosima admitted, "but sometimes 'tis hard. He gets into things, makes messes, and breaks things because he doesn't know better. He's restless much of the day, simply cannot sit still. But if he's kept busy and watched over, he can accomplish some small tasks. He never complains."

"How many such boys are in your family, like Royboy?" Beryl asked.

"Percy was my older brother who died." She wouldn't tell them the details of that death, at least not yet. She'd horrified them enough. "And I had two cousins and an uncle and two distant cousins who moved to Dublin with their family long ago."

"Do they die younger? Is that why your older brother is gone?"

"No . . . he died in a fire. The boys in my family are healthy, except they can't learn."

"But you're so smart, Cosima! How could this be in your family? Is your mother . . . ?"

Cosima shook her head. "She's very much like me. In fact, she's a talented artist. I did hear long ago of a child who would have been my aunt, who died of a fever. She might not have been very clever, but then women are accepted with lower expectations than men, aren't they? I suppose we'll never know if this . . . curse . . . can pass to women as well as men. Not if the curse dies with me."

A long silence passed, and Cosima eyed her two friends, who looked suddenly spent, as if they'd just returned from a walk that had gone on too long. "You see now why I cannot possibly marry your brother, no matter what we might feel for one another."

Beryl shook her head. "I don't see that at all. It's obvious some of the babies born to Kennesey women aren't feeble-minded. You, for example. I'm sure if you counted all of your relatives, there are quite a few who are sound minded."

"Yes, of course, but where most families might have one or two children with some sort of flaw, my family has more than its share."

Beryl hugged Cosima close and Christabelle quickly followed.

"Thank you," Cosima whispered, seeing her friends' faces lacking all horror after what she'd just told them. She brushed away an escaped tear, then with one arm around each of them, eyed them earnestly. "You'll help me, won't you? help me now to avoid your brother? rescue me when I think of him and help me to ignore these feelings?"

The sisters exchanged glances.

Beryl spoke up. "I don't know what to do, Cosima. I've imagined you as my sister-in-law since the day I met you. I'm not sure this is enough reason to think otherwise. You should speak to Peter, tell him what you've told us, and decide together."

"Reginald already told your brother about my family background," Cosima assured her. "He knows everything."

"He does!" Beryl said, and her brows lifted. "And he loves you anyway."

"He's never said such a thing—"

"Oh, please, he doesn't have to say a word," Beryl said.

Christabelle nodded. "It does seem to me he wouldn't look at you the way he does if the truth bothered him very much."

Cosima shook her head. "Neither of you is helping in the least. How can you think I might be a suitable wife for your brother after everything I've told you? He is the next viscount, with title and land to hand down. If he has no proper male heir—"

"And who, may I ask, can guarantee presenting a 'proper male heir' to her husband? Don't you know anything of English history, Cosima? How many wives did Henry VIII do away with in search of a woman to give him a male heir?"

"And our own queen, don't forget, inherited the crown instead of a son," Christabelle reminded Cosima. "We all love her!"

"But I have no wish to bring disappointment to a long line of Hamiltons. I may have feebleminded daughters as well as sons. Who knows?" Cosima sighed. "And besides, I've seen my parents struggle. I'm not at all sure I'm strong enough to follow such a path."

"But surely if you're forewarned, you can manage? If you're prepared?"

Cosima looked away. "I don't know. I know my mother's love, but I don't know what it's like to be a mother, to feel someone grow inside and hope that child might one day be a valuable member of society. People who know my family would look at me and think I have no right to bring another half-wit into the world."

"Who determines the value of any child God gives? Obviously you love your brother; you didn't even have to say so."

"Of course, but what if the only children I bear are like Royboy? 'Tisn't fair, not to a husband or myself or even to the children who might be better off unborn."

"Oh, so we're talking fair, are we?" Beryl asked. "I need look no farther than the slums of London to see life isn't fair—me with my comforts and full belly at the end of each day. My dear Cosima, if good things only happened to good people and bad only to the bad, which might seem fair to us with our limited minds, then where would the Lord God come in? What faith would it take to believe in a God who doles out blessings only to those who deserve them? And who does deserve them, anyway?

Certainly not me, with my loose tongue and so many unchari-
table thoughts. Yet here I am, with abounding blessings. Perhaps
God wants to bless you with a family. You mustn't discount it
without allowing Peter to have some say in the decision."

Tears pricked Cosima's eyes, but she blinked them away. She
didn't want to hear such words, words that brought hope. Hope
for a life she'd tried to deny herself ever since she was old enough
to know she was different.

Beryl hugged Cosima close. "I don't know what's right,
Cosima. I've never met Royboy and so I don't really know
what living with him must be like for you or your mother, who
faced this before you. I only know I love you as dearly now as I
did a half hour ago, and I would welcome you and a half dozen
Royboys if that is what you and my brother want. As far as I'm
concerned, the Hamilton line could use a little flavor. We're a
boring lot, really."

33

"Funny how we can worry about all the wrong things," Talie said to Dana as they retrieved plates, napkins, and soda from Talie's kitchen. The foursome was looking forward to the latest of the many take-out dinner nights they'd shared since Aidan had begun working for Luke a couple of months ago.

"What do you mean?"

Talie put a napkin on each of the plates, stacking them. "Just that we once worried Aidan's faith might not be strong or that he might be too good-looking for his own good. But he's a great guy."

Dana nodded with the smile that always made the features of her pretty face glow with pleasure. "Yeah, he is." Then she turned more serious. "But you said we were worried about the wrong things. What *should* we have been worrying about?"

"Ben." Talie didn't want to reveal just how good she'd been at denying all the reasons she should have been worrying about him.

"Worrying in advance wouldn't have helped, even if you had reason to. But you didn't. You're a good mom, Talie."

Talie pinched back tears. Those might be the words she wanted to hear, but they were words she hadn't lived up to. How long had it taken her to face what she'd tried to deny?

"This has all been so hard on you," Dana said. "For all of us, really—me and Mom too, watching and feeling helpless. But hardest on you and Luke."

"Mom's been trying to put on a happy face ever since the diagnosis. Believe it or not, it does help." Talie took a deep, steadying breath. "You and Aidan coming over helps too. If I don't keep to some kind of normal routine, all I do is obsess about how bad the future might be."

"We'll keep your mind on other stuff for a while. You have to think of the new baby, right? So here's your water and Luke's Coke. I have our pop. Let's go join the guys and wait for the pizza with them."

Luke and Aidan were in the adjacent family room, and Talie heard their discussion about a project from work. She envied Luke that; he had demands on his attention that distracted him from futures with a diagnosis. Everything Talie did revolved around Ben and his new therapies.

Ben was in his chair, spinning and laughing. He'd soon go down for the night—hopefully to sleep through—but Talie wanted to keep him up a bit longer. She couldn't help but watch him more closely, looking for telltale signs of autism.

She handed Luke his drink and sat on the couch beside him.

"Sorry to interrupt your shoptalk, boys," said Dana as she took a place beside Aidan. "But now that we've joined you we'll bring the conversation around to something more aesthetic. You'll have to come over to my place soon, Talie. I finally had that old clock fixed, and Aidan hung my arrangement. To be perfectly honest—in all modesty, of course—I should win an award for decorating on a budget. The whole thing cost less than fifty bucks, and it looks terrific."

"The stuff you found in Mom's attic?" Talie asked.

Dana nodded. "I also had some black-and-white photos of Mom and Dad blown up and took some color photos of us as kids and converted them to black-and-white. Then I put them inside a four-paned window frame Mom was going to toss and hung it up. In between that and the clock, I put up shadow boxes hold-

ing some mementos from one of Dad's old trunks, and presto—
a wall of family history and nostalgia."

Talie wondered what the mementos might be. Irrationally
she wondered whether taking home the trunk instead of the
box with the journal might have prevented her from ever having
worried about curses and delays in Ben and made everything
okay. Maybe she'd just picked the wrong box.

"I don't get into decorating much," Aidan said with a laugh,
"but I have to admit it looks pretty good. Like a museum wall,
only more personal."

Talie wanted to keep the mundane conversation going, to
stave off other thoughts, other fears. But anything ordinary
escaped her. She noticed Luke was quiet now too, without business to talk about.

Talie watched Ben. "You know, he seems a bit too social for
this diagnosis," she said at last. "Some of what we've read about
autism says it's hard for autistic kids to be around others. Ben's
not like that."

"He doesn't make eye contact," Luke said gently, taking her
hand. "We know something's wrong."

"Something—yes. Just not autism. He's delayed, but he
might still catch up."

"He might," Luke said. He didn't sound convinced.

Quiet settled over the room again. Even Ben stopped making
noise for a moment, as if listening. Talie wished she'd succeeded
in carrying on with the small talk. Now it felt as if they were at
the funeral of a loved one, sharing the face of grief.

Talie looked between Dana and Aidan, sitting on the adjacent
love seat. They were holding hands.

"I suppose we don't portray a very bright picture of family,"
Talie said. "Maybe the horror side of it—a reminder that things
can go wrong even if you try to do everything right. Even if
you're trusting God."

"I haven't seen anything that qualifies for horror," Aidan said. "Dana and I have talked about families. We both want kids some-day. She knows more about them than I do—she's around kids every day. But I don't think I have many illusions. Being a parent is hard, even with healthy kids. I don't think I made it very easy for my own parents."

Dana smiled at him. "You? I thought you represented what every father wants. A normal, productive, responsible member of society."

"I wonder how many people think they've met their parents' expectations." Aidan shrugged. "Maybe more than I think . . . maybe not. When I was a kid my dad was my Little League coach. Man, I didn't want him to be the coach. I thought the guys on the team would treat me differently because of him. I knew I wasn't that great, and I thought I'd either embarrass him or, if he gave me a good position, they'd think I was his pet."

With his free hand Aidan rubbed the back of his neck. "The very first day of practice, he called me up to the pitcher's mound so he could demonstrate—through me—what he wanted the others to do. I was embarrassed to be the first one called. So I went right up to my dad and kicked him in the shin. Then I went back to the bench."

Dana giggled, and even Talie felt a mild sense of shock at the admission.

Aidan shot Dana a half smile, as if still abashed by the memory. "I remember the look on my dad's face. I might have been the first to be embarrassed, but I did a quick job of transfer-ring that feeling to him. There were a couple of other coaches who saw the whole thing, not to mention all the boys. What were they supposed to do? If he couldn't get his own kid to follow him, how was he supposed to get the rest of the team to fall in line? Yep, I think I let him down pretty thoroughly that day. But you know what he did?"

"What?" Dana asked.

"Nothing. Grace, I think God would call it. My dad went on as if I wasn't the biggest disappointment in the whole wide world. He treated me like any other kid on the team. I think that was the first time I was old enough to realize he loved me, even though I wasn't the sports-crazy kid he wanted me to be. The way God loves us, whether we deserve it or not."

"Sounds like your dad was an example of what fathers should be," Talie said.

"I think so. But my point is that even healthy kids don't live up to what parents want. My dad was good at anything he tried, and I wasn't. He wanted a sports-loving kid. He got me instead."

"I guess nobody gets everything they want," Luke said. "Not in this life anyway."

Just then the doorbell rang, and Talie went for her purse to pay for the pizza. Aidan's story might not have taken away her pain and worry about Ben, but it did remind her how genuinely she would welcome Aidan into the family if she had the opportunity.

34

The Bible says, "There is no fear in love; but perfect love casteth out fear." Sometimes, though, this is hard to believe. Fear can be so dark it seems to blot out all the light in one's life.

I shall always recall tonight, for so many reasons. Each moment must be preserved here in my journal as an example of how darkness and light may come in their turn. But as my father once told me, the only constant in life is God's love. And there is no fear in that.

This night for which I had waited so long began with the bright hope of honesty. Beryl convinced me I should at last reveal my true feelings to Peter. How effervescent it made me feel to contemplate speaking to him of the love that grew in me. My heart danced with the orchestra. . . .

"No polka?"

Cosima didn't have to look to know who was speaking. Peter's voice was as effective as his smile, powerful enough to make her heart go one direction and her stomach another.

She hadn't seen much of either Peter or Reginald since the ball began several hours earlier, though her dance card was nearly full even without them. But now, finally, Peter was at her side. She knew she hadn't smiled so merrily in the last two weeks, knew her gaze hadn't been so eager to meet another's, and knew if anyone glimpsed her just then, they might very well guess she took pleasure in his company as in no one else's. But she didn't care. She'd missed him too much to know how to hide it.

"This is one dance I'd rather watch," she admitted. "At least tonight."

He took a spot beside her, folding his arms in front of him. "I have been trying to welcome you since yesterday." Like her, he still eyed the dancers. "But one thing after another has been in my way."

Cosima had thought her heart couldn't float any lighter than the moment she'd heard his voice. She was wrong. "I imagine it's been quite demanding, helping to host such a large gathering."

"My mother doesn't usually worry over her parties, but this time she is especially fidgety. She's had me running faster than an echo on a cold day."

"She needn't have worried," Cosima said. "Everything is perfect."

"Yes, so I and half the staff assured her."

"I'm sure she appreciates you."

Cosima welcomed the trifling conversation. It calmed her pulse. "Cosima . . ."

One word, her name on his lips, was enough to send that pulse racing again. She looked at him. His voice had changed from the socially acceptable tone to something quieter, more intimate.

"I'm glad you're here." His voice was still soft.

"So am I." A smile tugged and twitched at the corner of her mouth.

"Would you care to dance? Do you have any waltzes free?"

"The final of this first set before the supper break." She was glad she'd obeyed her reluctance to assign a partner to every dance.

"Keep it open."

She nodded.

"Peter."

Cosima heard Lady Hamilton's voice and guessed Peter had too, but he didn't look away. His mother approached them from behind, and Cosima broke their mesmerized gaze at last, having sensed worry in Lady Hamilton's tone.

"Good evening, Cosima," she said politely. "I've come for Peter. Do you mind?"

Cosima watched Lady Hamilton place her hand on Peter's arm. He bowed to excuse himself and exchanged one last smile with Cosima. After a few more waltzes, they would meet again. That is, if his mother could spare him.

Each dance after that seemed longer than the last, but Cosima floated around the floor as if angels carried her, only half listening and rarely speaking but constantly smiling.

She did not see Reginald. He hadn't requested a single dance, hadn't approached her all evening. She had barely seen him since he entered the ballroom with Peter some time ago. Obviously whatever fences needed mending had been mended . . . with Peter. Had he now some offense against her?

She chanced to see Beryl and Christabelle, each busy with her own steady line of dance partners. They were right, she reasoned. Right to have counseled her to let Peter be part of the decision about their future. She couldn't deny it any longer.

When the second-to-last dance of the set ended, Cosima glanced down at her card although she knew the line was blank.

Finally.

Standing beside the wall, she perused the room for the tall figure so easy for her to find. But he was nowhere to be seen.

Heart thumping, not doubting he would come if he could, she waited and watched the other dancers take their places.

It will be wonderful to have Peter's arms about me.

"I'm sorry I'm late."

The words spoken into her ear banished every thought except to register his presence. Peter took her into his arms, and they twirled into the midst of the other dancers.

"Berrie says you're seldom on time."

"Normally I admit my guilt, but this time I claim an excuse. My mother committed me to look for a guest's lost trinket."

She'd barely noticed, but he seemed to be leading her against the flow of other dancers, closer to the open doors of the veranda. The air coming in was dry but cool for August, and Cosima welcomed it on her shoulders.

"The dance is about to end already," he said, "but I'd like to request your company longer to make up the time I missed due to my good deed. Do you mind?"

Cosima shook her head and they left the ballroom.

They were not the only ones outside. Couples of all ages strolled the garden lit only by moonlight or a rare torch to warn of a step. On the veranda, potted roses had been placed along the edge, and their fragrance filled the air.

Cosima breathed in, knowing she would never forget the scent . . . and would always associate it with tonight. She had never allowed herself to relax in Peter's company before, but tonight was different. The dam had burst, the one holding back her true feelings.

The music ended, and Cosima heard the hushed rumble of conversation as those inside and some from the veranda moved through the ballroom in search of supper. Whatever the menu boasted, Cosima was sure it would be plentiful and delicious. She had no desire to join them.

"Would you care to walk a bit?"

She nodded, and they stepped down to the stone pathway leading toward the flower gardens and a vine-covered pavilion in the distance. Tall, lacy arborvitae formed a wall behind the structure, separating the pavilion from the rest of the lawns.

"Forgive me for saying so, Cosima," said Peter, strolling beside her in no apparent hurry, "but you seem . . . exceptional tonight." He stepped ahead and turned back to stand in her path. "I like it."

Her laughter competed with the chirp of crickets hopping out of the way.

"I hope you're not hungry," he said as they neared the pavilion. "We're missing supper."

"I don't mind if you don't."

"Not in the least. I'd rather spend time with you while I won't be missed. My mother will be busy because no one can eat until she does, so I don't think she'll need me for a while."

The pavilion felt like a conservatory with its arborvitae walls and foliage-covered supports. In the center of the shelter were stone benches erected in a square, following the shape of the roof.

"Does your mother always depend on you so for the galas?"

"My mother usually allows the staff to handle the parties once she's told them what she wants. I don't know why she is behaving so strangely tonight, and to be perfectly honest I hope it isn't a permanent change. I don't mind helping, but I'm considering asking for a butler's wage if she keeps this up."

Cosima felt his gaze on her, watching her, perhaps pleased she found him amusing. She eyed him in return, not at all shy tonight.

"Why are you different, Cosima?" he asked gently.

That he was suddenly serious was not lost on her. She wasn't sure what to say, wondering if she could admit aloud the feelings she'd denied so long.

"I suppose part of it is that I've missed you—your family— and I'm glad to be with you again."

"I'm glad you're here." His quiet tone kept the feeling of intimacy intact. Though there was no one around to hear, he spoke in a low voice as if for her ears alone.

Peter raised one foot to the bench in front of them, resting his forearms on his knee. Standing close to him, she viewed his profile as he looked ahead. He mustn't be able to see far—just the full moon winking through the branches of the arborvitae.

"I suppose Reginald told you about the argument," he said at last.

"No. Actually, I've spoken very little to Reginald since he escorted me here. To be honest I've found his behavior somewhat distant since we arrived."

"Just since you've arrived? That is what we argued about. If he's going to marry you, he should have announced himself as your intended by now."

"Perhaps he's changed his mind."

Peter shrugged. "He didn't say that, if it's true."

Cosima frowned. "I hope the argument has been settled. I would hate to be the cause of a rift between two friends."

"We'll weather the storm. Reginald and I have locked horns before. Evidently neither one of us has learned how to avoid our disagreements."

"He has much to weigh in marrying me, as you well know. It may take some time for Reginald to adjust to the idea."

"You make it sound as if it would be beneath him to marry you."

"Being an Escott doesn't cancel out the other worries. About my family background, that is."

"He's not worried about that," Peter said. "And he shouldn't. Every family has something to deal with."

"Not yours. I've never met a happier, more cohesive family."

"We're compatible, I suppose, but like everyone else. Good and bad in all of us."

"Yes, it's true there is good and bad in everyone. I was afraid of Dowager Merit because I saw little kindness in her. But after spending these past weeks in her home, I see she's firm but fair. And she's generous. I think she isn't so frightful."

"There, you've already started to mend that family you're so worried about."

She looked at him, wondering at the statement. Her father's mother was such a small part of the troubles in her family background, yet Peter saw even this as a hopeful start. *Perhaps that's the way optimists think.*

Perhaps an optimist was the only type of person hopeful enough to face a curse and not run.

"I'm glad you agreed to come out here with me, Cosima," he said quietly. As he leaned slightly forward on his raised knee, his face was nearly level with Cosima's. "This is the longest amount of time we've spent alone together."

The seclusion and intimacy seemed more obvious all of a sudden, with only the moon and stars surrounding them. Something she had no desire to change.

"It makes me wish I could go back," he added. "Start the summer again and spend most of it with you."

"We might not be able to go back," she said, "but at least we can go forward. Differently."

Peter stood tall again, bringing his other foot to the ground. He moved one hand as if to touch her but stopped. "I do want it to be different." He stood closer, much the way he had weeks ago on the Bristol coast, when he'd breathed in the scent of her hair. He did so again, closing his eyes and inhaling. Cosima did not move, though she wanted to take the tiniest step forward and place herself within the realm of his embrace. "Your hair," he whispered, "smells like honeysuckle."

"'Tis the soap." She was barely able to breathe with him so near. "I . . . brought it with me from my home."

His fingers grazed her shoulder, and the contact sent a shiver across her back. Placing the tip of his finger on her chin, he gently brought her face toward his. "May God forgive me, Cosima, but I want to kiss you."

Just as his arms went around her, her own crept up around his neck. "Then God forgive us both. I want you to."

His lips came down on hers, covering her mouth, and Cosima thought she understood for the first time why silly girls might swoon. Dizziness overcame her, so that if Peter's arms weren't so tightly holding her she might have done that very thing. His mustache pressed above her lip, as inviting as the warmth of his touch. This was Peter at last—so close, kissing her as she'd dreamed of a thousand times.

"Cosima," he said her name tenderly, as if it were a kiss in itself.

At last he pulled away, his fingers sliding down her arm to take her hand in his. He urged her with his touch to sit on the stone bench, and once she settled he joined close beside her. He still held her hand and studied it in the moonlight, discovering her skin, the lines of her palm, the veins of her wrist. Could he see her blood pounding and rushing through that vein? Could he feel her pulse wildly racing? He'd kissed her as no one had ever kissed her before, and she'd never wanted it to end.

Then, enveloping her single hand with both of his, Peter looked at her. "You cannot marry him."

She nodded. "You're right, of course."

"I'll speak to him."

She placed her hand on top of his and held steady his gaze. "We shall speak to him together."

He raised his hand to her chin again, tipping her face to accept another kiss. She felt his lips, smooth beneath the mustache, welcoming and unfaltering all at once. This was a powerful force, this love she felt.

God be praised. Only a blessing such as this could overcome a curse.

Peter lifted his lips from hers but did not move away. With his face so near she studied him, much as he seemed to study her, close for the first time. God had created perfection in him, she thought. Even if he had a flaw, she couldn't see it.

Then she saw something from the corner of her eye. A figure approaching the pavilion. Blond hair showed light beneath the moon.

Stiffening but remaining still, she said, "'Tis Reginald."

Peter looked over his shoulder, slowly rising to his feet and pulling Cosima behind him as she rose as well.

"Reginald." It was impossible to tell if he was surprised or taken aback by Peter's presence. Both appeared calm.

"Good evening, Peter." Reginald's voice, too, was even and undisturbed. He took a step closer and peered around Peter's shoulder at Cosima. "Good evening, Cosima."

She stepped out to Peter's side.

"Reginald," said Peter, "there is something you should know, and you ought to know it immediately. Cosima and I have no wish to hurt you, but we've admitted we have feelings for one another that will prevent her from marrying you. Not that you've announced any intentions."

"I can see why you might be relieved I haven't posted banns yet, my friend," said Reginald lightly.

Cosima wondered at his behavior. Wasn't he upset at all, having come upon what was obviously a private moment between his fiancée and his best friend?

"I can only assume you've had doubts, for whatever reason I cannot imagine," Peter said. "As I said, neither Cosima nor I have any wish to hurt you, but you cannot expect her to feel much loyalty to a relationship as uncertain as the one you've offered."

"Oh, I don't hold it against her." Reginald spoke as if Cosima weren't even there. "The heart isn't something we can control, is it?"

"You . . . you're not upset, then?" she asked. "That I obviously cannot marry you?"

"Upset?" His eyes, light even in the darkness, glinted something in them she'd not seen before. Jealousy? "If I said I wasn't upset, you would think I hold no feelings for you whatsoever. Perhaps I am, a little. But since I've lost you to my best friend, what can I say, except to give you my blessing?"

No, it wasn't jealousy she saw in those eyes. His tone was too light, too unhurt. It was something else, something Cosima was unfamiliar with.

"Just like that?" Peter asked. He sounded as suspicious as Cosima felt.

"Of course. Never let it be said I stood in the way of love. Not when we're to let love rule our lives. Isn't that what you always say, Peter? God's love and all that?"

Peter nodded, but his face was watchful, perhaps wondering at Reginald's oddly affable reaction.

"So, do you intend to post the banns I should presumably have posted long ago?" Reginald could have been inquiring after a stranger's upcoming wedding.

Cosima eyed him curiously. She knew he held no real feelings for her, certainly none of the attraction she'd felt for Peter from nearly the moment she'd met him. But at the very least Reginald's pride might have suffered a blow. Why was he so cavalier?

"We haven't discussed marriage," Cosima said.

"But isn't that what we're talking about?" Reginald said. "Isn't what you were doing on that bench meant only for people who plan to marry?"

Cosima's gaze fell to the ground, glad the pavilion shaded her face from the moonlight. She should feel embarrassed but couldn't, not when kissing Peter had meant so much.

Peter slipped his hand around Cosima's. "I have every intention of asking Cosima to marry me and setting a date right now if she'll agree."

"There you have it, Cosima," Reginald said. "I don't think he's merely defending your honor or showing me up for the way this ought to be done. He must mean it."

Cosima had no doubt of Peter's sincerity. She knew him to be a man of his word. If a proposal under such circumstances seemed sudden to Reginald, it somehow didn't seem that way to Cosima. She'd felt Peter's kiss; she'd looked into his eyes. She'd been aware all summer that they had a rare affinity. Commitment was the next logical step . . . if they were stronger than the curse.

"Well, Cosima?" Reginald pressed. "He's just proposed. Do you accept?"

"Peter knows my feelings mirror his," she said. "I would marry no other."

Reginald took yet another step closer. Now his eyes were strangely gleeful, without a trace of the disappointment or anger a spurned fiancé might be expected to have. "Then may I make a suggestion? Marry tonight. Leave here and take the train to Gretna Green. You can make it by morning and be married before the day is out."

"You've hesitated about marriage all these months but now think Cosima should elope with me? Why should *we* hurry?"

Reginald laughed. "I know you, Peter. I know with your honor you won't touch the girl until you're wed. I'm merely trying to save you several months of waiting. If the two of you don't plan on changing your mind, what's to stop you from marrying privately now and returning home for a public celebration later?"

"We won't change our minds." Peter's firm voice wrapped itself around Cosima's soaring heart. How right he was!

"Then do it," Reginald urged.

Peter turned to Cosima. "I would do that," he whispered. All the surprise and mistrust he'd aimed Reginald's way were gone as he looked at her earnestly.

"Peter . . ." Thoughts and desires, hopes and dreams assailed her. Was this real? Was she really standing here with Peter's hands on her shoulders, and was he really inviting her to elope?

"You should say yes, Cosima," Reginald counseled. "Ease the poor man's mind. He's been through an engagement once already. Do you recall hearing of that? Of course he's willing to wed you right now, to prevent a repeat of what's happened in the past. He's eager to have you before you can be spoiled by some-one else."

Peter turned from Cosima to face Reginald again. "Reginald, I don't welcome the inference in those words. In fact, you've acted oddly from the moment you found us here. If you're angry with me, just say so and we'll deal with this honestly instead of sparring with words at Cosima's expense."

Reginald lifted both palms. "No offense intended, my friend. If I'm acting strangely it's because you've won the lady and I've lost. I shall recover, since neither Cosima nor I had any of the personal interest in each other that the two of you obviously have. Nonetheless, I care for her and I care for you as well. I want only to see you happy."

Peter turned back to Cosima. "I'll marry you today, Cosima, or I'll wait for the kind of gala my mother will want to plan. So long as you become my wife, I will do either . . . or both."

"Peter, how can you be so sure?" She thought of the doubts that had plagued her all summer. Not of her feelings for him or her desire to marry him but thoughts of everything he might lose if they did wed.

"Why should I have any doubts? I love you, Cosima! I love your faith and your interest in all God created, your humor and your loyalty and your courage when you faced the wrath of no less than Dowager Merit. I know we have more to learn about each other, but plenty of marriages begin with the husband knowing far less of his wife. We have a lifetime ahead to discover the rest."

"But my family—"

"Will welcome Peter into your fold as eagerly as they did me," Reginald interrupted. "More so, since I'm but a lowly knight."

Cosima studied Peter's earnest face. "Are you sure, Peter? Are you very sure you want to marry me? Knowing what it could mean?"

He pulled her into an embrace. "What could it mean, except that we'll be happy? God Himself brought us together; of that I'm certain. The way we met, that you should be here all the way from Ireland, the way we fell in love . . . it seemed against our will, but it happened anyway. We're well matched. In faith and in a desire to honor God with our lives. That's all we must do, and we can do that better together than alone."

Tears welled in her eyes and she stayed within his arms. "Peter . . ."

"I hope that's an embrace of congratulations!" said a new, deep voice from beyond the pavilion.

Cosima's gaze followed Peter's past Reginald to the two figures coming rapidly up the path: Lord and Lady Hamilton.

Somewhat out of breath, the older couple joined them under the canopy of the pavilion.

Lady Hamilton gasped for air. "Peter, are you congratulating Cosima on her engagement to Reginald at last?"

Reginald turned to Lord and Lady Hamilton, and Cosima could no longer see his face as he stepped back to take a stand behind her and Peter.

"Congratulations are definitely in order." Reginald reached up to place a hand on Peter's shoulder from behind. "But not for me. Rather it's all of us who should congratulate your son and Cosima."

The fatigue upon Lady Hamilton's face changed before Cosima's eyes—to blatant alarm. Even Lord Hamilton, usually so placid, had a dark look, his brows nearly meeting in the middle and his mustache, so like Peter's, turned downward in a frown.

"What do you mean?" Lady Hamilton said to Reginald. But she looked at Peter. "Tell me, Peter. What does Reginald mean?"

Peter took Cosima's hand in his and smiled. "We're going to be married. She hasn't agreed on a date, but I think she'll have me."

Cosima wanted to smile. She wanted to rush to Lady Hamilton and be received into the family.

But stark horror showed on Peter's mother's face now, even as she grabbed her husband's arm as if she might fall. "This cannot be."

"Mother," said Peter, taking a step closer. He, too, must have been afraid she would faint. "What is it?"

"You . . . cannot marry Cosima, Peter. I—we, your father and I—forbid you."

Peter looked back at Cosima, appearing every bit as confused as she felt amid the pain of Lady Hamilton's outright rejection.

"Father," said Peter in a voice far more calm than Cosima could have mustered, "what is Mother talking about? If it's because of Reginald, rest assured he's given his consent."

His parents' grave faces did not change.

"You've known Cosima all summer," Peter went on. "Both of you have cared for her. There is no reason I *shouldn't* wed her. Even Reginald has given his blessing. Why can't you?"

"Son . . . ," began Lord Hamilton, "there are other factors, her family—"

"If you're talking about the feud between Dowager Merit and Cosima's father, that's ridiculous. No one cares about rifts in families, and I have little doubt it can be mended now that Cosima has made progress with her grandmother."

Cosima stepped forward, searching Peter's face for more. He was so convinced, so sure of his words. Words that meant nothing.

Suddenly it all made sense.

His parents knew.

And Peter didn't.

"Peter." She could barely breathe. The sting of hot tears gathered in the corners of her eyes. "Peter, you know that is the least of the worries regarding my family."

Peter looked from his parents to Cosima, a new touch of confusion beginning to mar his happy, earnest face. "I told you—it's nothing!"

She nodded, and the first of her tears began to fall. "Yes, Peter, that *is* nothing. Nothing compared to . . ." She looked away, suddenly losing courage. Her gaze rose to Reginald, accusing. "You *didn't* tell him, did you?"

Reginald, his face somber, did not move from several paces behind Peter. Now she knew what she saw in his eyes, something she'd never seen firsthand. Cruelty. Unmistakable, utter cruelty.

"Tell him what? About a curse? And have him thinking I was crazy for taking such a risk in order to forge a path into higher society? It isn't as if I *believe* in curses, anyway. It's all rubbish."

"What is?" Peter asked. He looked from Reginald to Cosima, and at that moment she knew her dreams hadn't really come true after all.

She wanted to flee, to hide from his face when he learned the truth. She took a step forward, but Peter caught her arm, preventing her from leaving.

"Please," she begged through tears that wouldn't stop no matter how much she longed to shed them in private. "Please, let me go. Reginald knows everything. Ask him. Or," she added, looking at Lady Hamilton, who, to her credit, no longer looked horrified but rather upset, "your mother obviously knows. Ask her."

Cosima pulled her arm away and fled the pavilion. She heard Peter call her but didn't look back, not even when she heard footsteps followed by a scuffle.

Lord Hamilton's voice echoed after her. "Let her go, Son. Hear us out and you'll know you *must* let her go."

35

After Talie's morning routine of spot-cleaning the house, planning lunch and dinner, and attending to Ben's needs, the music therapist arrived with her bag of instrumental toys and a guitar. Ben loved the ocean drum best, with tiny silver balls that were visible through the sturdy plastic top rolling from side to side. The movement sounded amazingly like a series of gentle waves. Ben always quieted for that.

Talie sat on the floor with Ben in her lap. She didn't sing along with the therapist, knowing she'd rarely hit the right keys, but hoped showing her own enjoyment might increase Ben's. It was still easy for her to maneuver on the floor at almost five months pregnant. This was one of her favorite half hours spent, because Ben seemed to listen to the words though he had yet to say any himself.

The phone rang just as the session ended. Talie would have let the call go to voice mail, but with the therapist busy packing maracas, tambourines, and rain sticks and with Ben content on the floor, Talie decided to check caller ID. The medical center. She picked up the phone.

"Mrs. Ingram?"

"Yes. Hello, Dr. Cooper." Talie took a quick breath. Though the pediatric specialist hadn't inquired about Ben, Talie decided to offer some information anyway. "Ben's music therapist is here," she said. "Of all the therapies, we think he enjoys this one the best."

"That's great," Dr. Cooper said. "Mrs. Ingram, the reason I called is to let you know I received the results on Ben's blood test."

It had been weeks since Talie and Luke had taken Ben to the geneticist for that awful blood test. She had put that from her mind long ago. They'd poked him on both hands until they found a vein and taken four full vials. He'd screamed the whole time while Luke held Ben's head and nurses at each leg pinned him down. Talie had fled the room like a coward. Ben's screams made her head spin and her stomach knot. That couldn't be good for the new baby. But waiting in a nearby conference room hadn't helped. She still heard Ben's screams.

Her heart began to pound, and it had nothing to do with the memory of that day. "I thought those results must have come back weeks ago and we'd get something in the mail eventually."

"This test often takes a little longer because not all labs do the specific tests we needed, and they wait to batch together the ones they receive. Our policy is to mail negative results, Mrs. Ingram. But Ben's fragile X test came back positive."

Talie might never be able to forget the blood draw, but she couldn't recall the name of any specific disorders they had tested for. Myriad thoughts rippled through her brain. A blood-test result meant a genetic disorder. That's what she had expected, wasn't it? Bad genes passed down from Cosima? Why even be surprised?

But she was. Undeniably. Her heart began to sputter her blood instead of smoothly pumping it where it needed to go. "What was that?"

"Fragile X. I could go into a long explanation, but it would be better for you to meet with Dr. Benson, where you had the blood drawn. She's a top geneticist and can explain everything in greater detail."

"We're seeing Dr. Benson tomorrow." She didn't want to admit Luke had made the appointment weeks ago; she still had trouble acknowledging everything pointed in the direction of a genetic disease.

"Oh?"

"We . . . wanted genetic counseling." Dr. Cold Fish didn't have to know all the evidence supporting her latest diagnosis.

"Before receiving the fragile X diagnosis? Is there some reason you might have suspected this before now?"

"I . . . I'd rather not talk about it right now, if you don't mind. But what about the diagnosis of autism? You were wrong about that?"

"He has fragile X. Some people refer to it as 'autism of known cause,' since so many of the symptoms are similar."

Talie could remember nothing about the disorder this doctor kept naming. All Talie knew was that blood-test results were far different from one doctor's opinion about autism. Her heart sank and raced at the same time. Talie could deny a simple opinion—in fact she had been doing a remarkable job at that very thing, despite her family history. It was easy to listen to a pediatrician who said Ben might grow out of his delays. But a blood test . . .

She took a deep breath. "Ben is slow; of course that's true. But even though he doesn't make very good eye contact, he seems to want to be in our company—"

"Mrs. Ingram," interrupted Dr. Cooper, "autism was a diagnosis based on the symptoms I saw, symptoms I've seen in countless other children your son's age. But now I have the results of a blood test that give the reason for your son's delays. There's no question about it. He has fragile X syndrome."

Talie's head filled with cotton. She could not comprehend the doctor's words. "What does this mean? I don't know what fragile X is."

"Physically there are a few complicating factors, none of them life threatening. No one can tell what level of cognitive ability Ben will achieve, Mrs. Ingram. I know you would like to see his future; wouldn't we all. But for now, the best thing for you to do is see Dr. Benson. In the meantime, I can send you what literature I have on fragile X."

Talie's gaze fell on Ben, still contentedly sucking his finger. She was aware of the music therapist lingering nearby, as if wondering if she should stay or leave. Talie didn't know what to do—point her toward the door or burst into tears.

Instead she spoke into the phone. "Dr. Cooper . . ." She had to ask, even though every fiber of her being knew this blood test only supported what she expected. "Is there any chance you could be wrong? Maybe this blood test is wrong."

"This is an accurate test, Mrs. Ingram, and the diagnosis fits Ben's symptoms. He's delayed physically as well as cognitively, which points to fragile X. You should be relieved to get a firm diagnosis."

Relieved? Relieved, when she'd done nothing but try to convince herself that Ben would somehow be all right? Relieved to hear there was a blood test telling her he would never be "all right"? never be normal?

She ignored her thumping heart. "What is fragile X, exactly?" She knew the answer but asked the question anyway. It was a modern-day name for an age-old curse. But she needed to know more.

"The X chromosome, when viewed under the right circumstances, appears 'fragile' on the long arm of the X. It often results in mental retardation."

Talie registered only the words *mental retardation*. The cotton in her head spread to her heart and lungs. She couldn't breathe, couldn't feel. This could not be happening. Talie saw the concerned look on the music therapist's face but could do nothing to assure her or hide the upheaval erupting inside.

Talie gripped the phone receiver. "I want to know what this means for my son."

"It means messages in his brain probably aren't connecting properly. He's missing one specific protein that is responsible for dendrites and synapses to—"

"No, Dr. Cooper, I guess you didn't hear me. I want to know how this affects my son."

"I don't know what to tell you, Mrs. Ingram, except that he is probably affected cognitively. Approximately 90 percent of frag-ile X boys are intellectually challenged at least to some degree. The level of retardation can't be predicted. It varies in every patient."

Retardation. The term sounded archaic, like some kind of disease that should have been cured a long time ago. *Cured.*

"And there's no cure, no treatment? If they know what this disorder is, can't they . . . fix it?"

"The brain is probably the most protected organ in our bodies. Getting a synthetic protein up there, in proper levels and at the time of learning, is something that in reality is even more complicated than it sounds. That's not to say they're not trying, though. It's a single gene disorder, attracting top-notch research-ers. But for now you're doing exactly what Ben needs. Speech therapy and all the other therapies will help him learn."

"But if he's . . ." *Mentally retarded.* Talie couldn't say the words aloud. He was the same as Willie and Percy and Royboy. Feeble-minded. How desperately she wanted to cling to her denial. "*Can* he learn?"

"Of course. But only time and Ben himself can tell you to what extent."

Talie had no tears, only panic slowly making its way through the numbness. She moved to the nearby kitchen table. Suddenly her knees weren't strong enough to hold her. She wanted this conversation to end, but the doctor seemed to have more.

"You should realize this condition is genetic. It's on the X chromosome, which means you're the carrier, Mrs. Ingram."

Genetics again. She'd guessed she was the carrier, had prayed the new baby would be all right. But she had to know more, even if she wasn't ready to hear what the doctor had to say.

"Are there . . . statistics? What are the chances of having another child with this . . . fragile . . . X?"

"You have two X chromosomes. One is probably good, the other bad. That means each of your pregnancies has a fifty-fifty chance of producing a fragile X child. That's why I'm glad you've already called Dr. Benson. You need to know the child you're carrying now might be affected as well."

Fifty-fifty.

Talie couldn't keep the numbers from repeating in her mind. *Fifty-fifty.* She was no gambler, but she knew those were stakes only the reckless accepted.

She heard the garage door open. Luke was home. She'd called him the moment she'd gotten off the phone, just after seeing the therapist to the door. Talie couldn't speak, couldn't explain what the phone call had been about—couldn't even cry at that moment. But as soon as she heard Luke's voice she'd burst into tears. He told her he'd be home within an hour.

Talie sat on the floor in the family room beside Ben. She'd avoided holding him, thinking he might sense her trauma. But could he? He wasn't like other babies who could read social cues. Perhaps he wouldn't even be aware his mother couldn't stop crying.

But it was lunchtime and some things couldn't be ignored, at least for Ben. He'd always been able to tell her when he was hungry, and he was beginning to fuss now. She picked him up and brought him into the kitchen.

Luke stepped in and without a word pulled Talie close, with Ben in between. Then he took Ben from her arms. "So this has a name. What he has, I mean. Fragile X."

Determined to control her tears, Talie nodded. "I need to feed him lunch."

She watched Luke lift Ben higher, the way Ben liked. Ben smiled wide, every tooth in his mouth visible. As Talie prepared his meal, she watched Luke carry on as if nothing so devastating as an irrefutable blood test had just been returned. At that moment, she envied him. How could he be so unflappable?

Luke put Ben in his high chair. "This doesn't change anything, you know."

"Maybe not for Ben. But for the new one?"

His face was grim. "We suspected it was genetic—"

"Fifty-fifty, Luke! Fifty-fifty."

Luke approached her. But it wasn't until he placed his two steady hands on her arms that she realized how pervasively she trembled. "I have one thing to say to you, Talie." Though his voice was grim, it was also calm. "And if you've read very far in Cosima's pages you'll know what I mean. All and whatever, Talie. All and whatever. Both of us need to remember that, and maybe we'll make it through."

36

I stumbled on the stairs leading to the veranda, catching myself. The ballroom doors were before me, and I dared not glance around for fear of seeing someone looking my way. Breathing deeply, I paused. Why had I retraced my steps here?

It was the quickest way back into the house. I had no choice except to walk through the ballroom.

Wiping away tears stalled only by fear of having someone spot them, I stepped forward, determined to find my way upstairs. No one could detain me, not even the gentleman whose name was listed next on my dance card. Thankfully, the music had not yet resumed after the supper break.

Staring straight ahead so I would catch no one's eye, I walked steadily through the crowd. To linger might draw attention, yet going too fast might do the same. And so with careful steps I wound my way through the room, barely breathing until nearing the interior doors leading to the hallway beyond. . . .

"Cosima!"

Cosima pretended she hadn't heard. Surely the call was from Beryl, and much as Cosima needed a friendly face, she knew she couldn't slow. She must go, and quickly, before tears, trapped only temporarily, escaped once again.

In the hall beyond the ballroom, a shadow thrust itself at her. Beryl flung her arms about Cosima in an instantly firm embrace. "Oh! I'm having the most wonderful time. I've been looking all over for you." Beryl spoke into Cosima's ear, holding her close. "There is the most wonderful man here, someone I've met only briefly before. His name is Lord Robert Welby, and he's put himself on my card three times. He's remarkable; wait until you meet him!"

Pulling back at last, Beryl looked at Cosima and her face changed from excited to concerned. "Cosima! You've been crying. Whatever is the matter?"

"I . . . can't. . . . Please, I must leave. I'm sorry."

She tried to turn away, but Beryl held her in place. "Leave the ball? But it's barely half over."

"No, not the ball," Cosima said. "I need to leave your house entirely. I must leave England and go home."

Beryl opened her mouth to speak, but no words came. She looked over Cosima's shoulder, and for the first time Cosima noticed a steady stream of guests coming in from supper. People now filled the hallway, parting like a stream around an island to bypass Cosima and Beryl.

Beryl took one of Cosima's hands and dodged the crowd heading in the opposite direction. She led Cosima past the conservatory and through a doorway she hadn't noticed before. It opened to a narrow, unadorned stairway, and from the lack of decor, Cosima assumed it was only for servants. In a moment they were in the upstairs hall, not far from Beryl's room.

"Thank you," Cosima managed to say, knowing she couldn't

maintain control much longer. She didn't know what she wanted most: to be alone with her tears or to flee. But how could she? She had only the money the dowager had given her to tip Beryl's maid since her own maid had stayed at the Escott estate to avoid adding to the congestion of the gala. Cosima would need to send for Millie at once and arrange passage home. She had no idea how to do that in the middle of the night, but somehow she must.

Beryl closed the door behind them and lit several lamps.

Drawing a deep breath, as if she'd forgotten how to breathe and needed to catch up, Cosima turned to Beryl. She needed to be strong only a few moments more.

"Don't stay, Berrie," Cosima said, glad her words were clear if a bit unsteady. Perhaps she could be coherent after all. "You were enjoying the ball, and I don't want to spoil it for you. I'm fine; I just need to be alone."

"But you said you want to leave England! Do you think I'll abandon you now, knowing how upset you are?" Beryl closed in, taking Cosima's clasped hands in hers. "Have you spoken to Peter? Is that what this is about?"

Hearing his name shattered what tenuous hold Cosima had on control. She pried her fingers from Beryl's and covered her face, letting the tears out at last.

Beryl pulled her into an embrace, this time far gentler than her happy one downstairs. "Oh, Cosima," she whispered. "I cannot imagine what he said to you. I am certain he loves you."

"He . . . does . . . or did. . . . I don't know what he must feel now."

Beryl led Cosima to one of the settees. "Tell me everything," she entreated. "Whatever happened? If he loves you, I don't understand why you're crying."

"Oh, Berrie, he didn't know!" Cosima's tears replenished themselves. "All this time I thought he knew."

"Knew . . . about the supposed curse, you mean?" As she spoke, Beryl rose and went to the bureau in the corner, returning with a handkerchief and handing it to Cosima.

Cosima wiped her face. "Reginald said he told Peter everything. He specifically said he told Peter about the curse."

"Reginald lied to you?"

With the handkerchief held under her nose, Cosima nodded.

"But why?"

Now Cosima shook her head, dabbing more tears. "I don't know! He said something about not wanting anyone to dissuade him from marrying me, since he wants so much to gain acceptance into society through my name. Perhaps he thought Peter would discourage him, or perhaps he was ashamed of the lengths he was willing to go in order to achieve his goals. All I do know is that Peter had no idea he was falling in love with . . . with . . . someone like me."

"But he does love you."

Cosima shook her head again. "No, not really, Berrie. How could he, since he didn't know all he needed to know about me? I'm sure he never would have been the least bit interested from the beginning if he'd been told the truth."

"Did you talk about it tonight? Is that how he learned of your family's . . . situation?"

Cosima stood and faced the cold fireplace, away from Beryl's sympathetic gaze. She wrung the handkerchief in her hands. How could she tell Beryl of Lady Hamilton's certainty that Cosima was not fit to be her daughter-in-law? Both of Beryl's parents had been obvious in that opinion.

"If I'd been aware he didn't know, I certainly would have told him long before today," Cosima whispered.

Beryl came up behind her. "Perhaps he just needs time to adjust, to ponder the risk and decide what he really wants. I'm sure if he loves you, Cosima, he won't give that up."

"Your parents made it very clear they would never give their blessing if he still somehow wanted to marry me."

"My parents? They know?"

Cosima nodded, swiping at more tears that came with recalling the look on Lady Hamilton's face.

Beryl sank to one of the settees as if toilworn. Cosima was exhausted as well but knew rest would elude her. Not with an emotional upheaval invading her mind.

"None of us should be surprised," Beryl said, staring ahead instead of at Cosima.

Curious, Cosima said, "Why?"

Beryl looked up at her. "I mean that we shouldn't have been surprised Reginald lied. He's as self-centered as they come, Cosima, and if anything good has come of this, it's that you have reason to never speak to him again. At least you won't marry *him*."

Cosima moved to the settee opposite Beryl. "I should have stayed in Ireland. There I had a future that didn't seem so lonely until now."

"A future as a spinster?"

"Yes, but I planned to open a school for children like my brothers. I never really wanted to abandon that plan. Only I hoped . . . well, I hoped I could have shared my time between the school and here. If Peter and I . . ."

New tears fell, and she raised the wet handkerchief to her face once again.

Beryl must have noticed the condition of the cloth, for she rose and fetched another. "I think a school is an admirable plan," she said gently, handing Cosima the unused handkerchief. "Perhaps I could help you. We can be the spinster schoolmarms, giving our lives for the betterment of those less fortunate."

Cosima tried to smile at Beryl's illustrious tone of voice, knowing her friend had hoped to achieve a lighter moment.

But Cosima failed in her attempt to smile and smoothed away another tear. "What about your Lord . . . Welby, did you say? The one with three dances on your card."

Beryl waved away the name. "Oh, we'll just break each other's heart. This past season in London was my second, you know. One more without a proposal and I'll be labeled a failure. I rather like the idea of your school, Cosima. I didn't know I had any options other than accepting some fop."

"It didn't sound like you thought Lord Welby a fop."

Beryl shrugged. "At the moment, love frightens me. I think I shall let Lord Welby wait."

"Don't let my experience color your thinking, Berrie. If I didn't carry a curse, your brother and I would likely be planning a wedding right now."

The statement brought yet another round of tears, and Beryl moved to the settee on which Cosima sat, putting an arm about her shoulders. "I wouldn't give up on my brother so quickly, Cosima. Give him time to think things through. And won't you both let God in on whatever decision you make?"

Cosima's heart felt like ice. God. He alone held the power to remove a curse . . . and hadn't.

She shook her head. "No, I was foolish to believe, even for one evening, that I might be suitable for Peter. I've been right all along to discourage him. It was clear on your mother's face. She couldn't bear thinking the Hamilton legacy might end with Peter."

Just then a tap sounded at the door.

Cosima's heart jumped, and she exchanged surprised glances with Beryl.

"Who is it?" Beryl called.

"Peter."

Cosima sprang to her feet, not knowing if she wanted to rush toward or away from the door. Beryl looked at her, silently motioning for permission to let Peter in.

"I . . . don't know . . . ," Cosima whispered.

"You must speak to him. You simply must." Beryl moved toward the door. "Just a minute, Peter. Don't go." Then she stepped closer to Cosima and whispered, "You must hear him out, no matter what he says. And you'll not be alone. I'll stay if you like, but if not, the Lord is with you always."

"Oh, Beryl . . . I don't know what the Lord could have been thinking to let things become so dreadful!"

"I don't know, Cosima, but I do know He's promised to be with us through whatever He allows our way. *All and whatever.* Remember your grandfather's words."

Cosima closed eyes that burned with an apparently endless supply of moisture. *All and whatever, Lord. All and whatever.*

One last dab with the handkerchief and she nodded to allow Peter entrance.

He stepped into the room, his gaze finding her in the shadows behind the settee. "Cosima," he said.

Never before had his gentle tone been so welcome. She wanted to run to him, to put her arms about him.

But she couldn't. A gentle word could mean good-bye as easily as anything else.

"Beryl," said Peter, still looking at Cosima, "would you leave us alone?" Beryl moved around him to exit, pausing only when he spoke again. "If you happen to see Mother, don't tell her where to find me."

"I . . . believe it's too late," Beryl said softly.

Cosima's gaze followed Beryl's to the door. There, at the threshold, stood not only Lady but Lord Hamilton as well.

Peter turned to them, a hardness in his jaw that Cosima had never seen before. Stepping aside only long enough to let Beryl pass, he then stood stiffly with one hand on the door, the other on its frame, allowing no passage.

"You cannot mean to be alone with Cosima without a chaperone.

And in Beryl's bedchamber!" His mother's tone was so shrill Cosima wondered if she'd ever truly known Lady Hamilton.

"Yes, Mother, that's exactly what I intend." He resumed closing the door, but Cosima heard the thump of Lady Hamilton's slight hand on one of the panels.

"This simply isn't done, even in a home as progressive as ours!"

He closed the door to the width of his broad shoulders. "Progressive, Mother? If tonight is an example of progressive behavior, I fail to see how it differs from the most narrow-minded of your guests downstairs."

"Peter," his father said, his voice calmer than his wife's, "I see no reason why we shouldn't all sit down together and discuss this situation."

"No, Father, not until I've spoken with Cosima alone." He brought the door toward the jamb, adding, "Return to your guests. You've probably been missed by now."

"See here, Peter." Now it was his father's palm upon the door instead of Lady Hamilton's. "You can't leave us out of this matter. You're my heir, like it or not, and we have a say in the decisions you make that affect the future of this family. Now step aside and let us in."

"Unless you want to create a fracas, which might have your guests line the stairway to investigate, I suggest you both leave."

Then he closed the door altogether. Unlike the silver-and-green bedroom in the London town house, there was no lock to guarantee this door stayed shut. Peter must have considered that; he slid the chair from Beryl's vanity and propped it beneath the doorknob.

He turned to Cosima, who had not moved. "Are you all right?" His tone was quiet, solicitous.

She folded her arms against a shiver, not knowing how to answer.

He approached, and she wanted to back away, afraid if he

came too near she would throw herself at him whether he welcomed her or not. She took a step back.

At her retreat, he stopped as if he were a hunter and she the frightened prey.

"I'm so sorry, Peter." She kept her voice low in the feeble hope he wouldn't hear the tremor that accompanied each word. She stared into his eyes, wishing she could see into his mind. She saw only concern, but whether it stemmed from love or pity, she wasn't yet sure. "I thought you knew."

He nodded. "I guessed that from the look on your face." He took another step closer, then paused when she stiffened. "You have nothing to apologize for, Cosima. You were as much a victim of Reginald's thoughtlessness as I."

He took another step, but Cosima's back was to the wall and she couldn't move any farther away. She was no longer sure she wanted to, the way Peter was looking at her. It was as if he hurt as much as she did.

"I want to hear about your family from you," he said. "I've heard what the others have said, but I want to hear it from you."

"I'm sure whatever they said is true," she admitted. "'Tis a near certainty I will bear offspring with unsound minds, incapable of learning beyond the level of a child."

Peter heaved a great sigh, as if he, too, had been holding his breath. He looked from her to the settee behind which she stood, then back to her again. "Will you sit?" he asked, adding, "Beside me?"

She hesitated only a moment before nodding. When he held out his hand, she placed her own, still trembling, in his. He held hers tight, and the trembling disappeared.

They sat, and almost immediately Peter put his arms around her. The touch of his fingers brushed one shoulder, pushing away her hair, which had tumbled forward. With the same hand he lifted her face to his and caught her gaze with his own, not letting go.

"I love you, Cosima," he said. "And I will not believe the Lord brought us together only to have us part because of fear. That's what it is, isn't it? Fear of a future no one can really foretell?"

"But based on the past . . ."

Held so securely within the comfort of his arms, she regarded his profile. He hadn't disregarded the gravity before them, but it was equally obvious he was not fleeing as another man might.

"All of this has come as a surprise—that others think of you in such a way. I wouldn't be honest if I said I was unconcerned, Cosima," he said. "But part of me wonders if it was meant to be this way, to have met you first without being tainted by knowledge of something that might have unfairly skewed my thinking."

"But 'tis a fact and cannot be dismissed, Peter. It's unfair for you to have thought of me as if I were like any other woman."

He looked down at her, his arm still about her shoulders, and smiled. "I've never thought of you as being like any other woman, Cosima."

She caressed his cheek, grateful for his words. "Peter, I do love you."

He kissed her, letting his lips linger on hers. She longed for his kiss to last, even while part of her cautioned that sharing such intimacy might be a different sort of skewing to taint their thinking.

"Then that settles it," he whispered into her ear. "We'll be married."

Cosima pulled away, shocked by his words. "What?"

Peter captured her hands as if afraid she might leave him alone on the settee. With a confident smile, he said, "You love me. I love you. People who love each other get married, Cosima."

"But . . . your legacy. Your parents. Feebleminded children, Peter!"

He shook his head. "What is the alternative, Cosima?"

Releasing her hands, he raised his palms to each side of her face. "I won't let you go. Not for anything. The Lord brought us together—I see no reason why we should part."

"But how do you know it was the Lord, Peter? There was certainly nothing noble in Reginald's bringing me here."

"Does it really matter why we met, Cosima? The fact is we have, and we've grown to love one another. Remember the day we rode in the carriage to your grandmother's, when you were to meet her for the first time? I sat across from you and watched you lift your fears to the Lord. Why can't we do that now? Both of us?"

"I do want to do that, Peter," she said, breathless.

"Right now," he said firmly and took hold of one of her hands again. "We'll give our fears to the Lord and ask guidance from Him. Together."

Sitting near the edge of the settee, Cosima bowed her head, just as Peter did. He began to pray, thanking God for the gift he'd received in knowing Cosima. He asked for heavenly, not earthly, wisdom, acknowledging they sought to do God's will and not others'.

Then Cosima spoke, tears welling in her eyes as she praised God for the love He'd given her through Peter. She asked forgiveness for thinking, even for a moment, that God was somehow to blame. "We ask you to touch the hearts of Peter's parents, Lord God. Without their understanding," she finished, "without their consent, I don't see how Peter and I can marry with Your blessing."

Cosima opened her eyes, finding Peter's somber gaze on her.

Three firm taps at the door demanded his attention.

"Peter, I suggest you open this door," said Lord Hamilton's angry voice. "We've waited long enough."

Peter stood and, despite his prayer for wisdom just a moment ago, impatiently shoved aside the chair. But he seemed to collect himself then, and with a smile aimed at Cosima, assuring her his momentary lack of control had passed, he opened wide the door.

"Come in, Father," he said. Cosima watched as Lady Hamilton entered first. "Mother," added Peter.

Cosima stood, looking toward the threshold, hoping Beryl was with them.

But Peter closed the door. "Where is Berrie?" he asked.

"We sent her downstairs so at least part of the family might be represented." Lord Hamilton led his wife to a settee.

Peter and Cosima sat opposite his parents. "Do you know what we were doing just now, Father?" Peter's tone was almost challenging.

"We can't imagine," answered his mother for his father. "Which is why I had your father rap on that door. It became far too quiet."

"We were praying. Asking God for His wisdom and guidance."

"Very well then," said his father. "I commend you. Been doing the same thing myself, actually."

Peter smiled, his hand still on Cosima's. "Good, then if we all listen to God, we should be able to settle this without any misunderstandings."

Cosima did not miss Lady Hamilton's gaze flying to Peter's hand covering Cosima's. She was tempted to pull away to ease the worry on his mother's face, but desire to feel Peter's strength outweighed desire to appease her.

"Cosima and I wish to be married," Peter said.

"Oh, Peter." Lady Hamilton raised a hand to her mouth. Tears dampened her cheeks, glistening in the light from the oil lamp on the table nearby.

"In spite of what we've told you?" Lord Hamilton asked. "In spite of all her grandmother explained, about the condition of the women in her mother's family?" His tone was as calm as Peter's, but one corner of his mustache twitched.

"My grandmother?" Cosima repeated.

"The dowager told me about your family, Cosima," said Lord Hamilton. "She's kept abreast of your family for years, through letters from a man living on your estate. Your father and his mother may not have spoken for years, Cosima, but the dowager does still care for her youngest son. A parent's love, you see. We all want the best for our children."

Lady Hamilton's brows rose. "You do see that, don't you, Cosima? I know you're a sweet child! I've come to love you, and I'm heartsick that you should have this cloud upon you. But no matter how affectionate we may feel, we simply cannot allow you to marry our son. His future is quite important. Generations of Hamiltons have fought and shaped our laws and society, in service to queen and country alike. We cannot have such a line end with . . ."

"Lackwits," Cosima finished, her voice hushed. She pulled her hand from Peter's. "I do understand, Lady Hamilton. I've only respect and admiration for your family and no wish to bring any of you harm or disappointment."

"Then you'll not marry our son?" Lady Hamilton asked.

"I love him."

"Then you'll want what's best for him, of course," said Lord Hamilton.

Cosima nodded, looking at Peter's father, whom he so resembled. "I do want that. Without question."

"It's very good to say all that," Peter said matter-of-factly. "But what is best for me is to marry the woman I love."

"You say that now, Peter," his father replied, "but in time, once the fervor of emotion has faded—"

"It will not fade," announced Peter with such conviction that Lady Hamilton brought her hand to her mouth once again and fresh tears shimmered in her eyes.

Cosima stood without a word, going to the bureau she'd

seen Beryl visit and withdrawing yet another handkerchief. She handed it to Lady Hamilton.

"Thank you," Peter's mother said in little more than a whimper.

Cosima took her seat again, next to Peter, who instantly reclaimed her hand.

"I will not change my mind, Father," Peter said. "You do realize that fear is making this so difficult for you? Fear of something you cannot know. How can you believe with such certainty that Cosima will produce only feebleminded offspring?"

"And I say how can you think otherwise, given the last two generations in her family? Think, boy! Imagine yourself in ten years, with only impaired children in your nursery. I'll forget, for the moment, the history to which your mother has just referred. Forget the long line of Hamiltons who have helped to make this empire what it is today. I'll suggest that you consider instead all you'll miss if you have no one to inherit your abilities and strengths, no hope to see your child do better, perform better, live better than yourself. Instead you'll have servants coddling children who will need to be coddled all the days of their lives. You won't know the hope that comes with children. You won't receive their love because they'll be incapable of giving it. Is that what you want? Do you think you'll still love Cosima after the years have passed and you've lost so much?"

"I will still love her," Peter insisted without hesitation. "I'll love her then as I love her now, perhaps more after we've learned and grown together and known what it's like to be sharpened by God's own hand. I won't let fear dictate to me, Father. Or you."

"Peter!" Lady Hamilton scolded. "How can you say such a thing? The Bible you profess to believe in commands you to honor your father and mother."

"I am no longer a child, Mother," he said stiffly. Then he looked down at the floor and his shoulders slumped.

Cosima put her hand on one of them, those strong shoulders that bore so much tonight.

"I do wish to honor you, Mother." Peter looked up at his father. "And you, Father. But for me to marry Cosima is not outside of God's will, and it's His will I seek first."

"Peter," Cosima said gently, her hand still on his shoulder. "They're right."

He looked at her, brows drawn in confusion. "What do you mean?"

"We do need to honor your father and mother."

"Even when they're acting without faith?"

She touched his face. "I love you, Peter. Images of being married to you far outweigh my own fears of our future. But . . . I cannot marry you."

"What!" He turned to her fully, taking her hands in his and holding them tight. "You cannot be convinced by them."

"Your father's words make sense," she told him gently. "Did you truly listen? I've no wish to wake up in ten years with the knowledge that I've brought you heartache."

"You won't!"

"It's what I've feared all along, everything he said. It's why I've fought so hard not to love you or hope that you could love me."

"But we do love each other! You see how the hand of God must be in this, when neither one of us sought to love each other. How can you think, even for a moment, that we can abandon that love now?"

Cosima shook her head, confused. She wanted nothing more than to love him, but the fear was already returning, so soon after their proclamation. How could she ignore it?

"Listen to her, Peter." Lady Hamilton said. "I believe she does love you enough to want what's best for you, even if it isn't her."

Peter stood, facing his parents. "I think you both should go.

We've made our statements. We understand one another's point of view. There's nothing more to be said."

Cosima stood as well, placing a hand on his forearm. "Wait, Peter. There is one more thing we might consider."

He looked at her. "If our wedding is the outcome, I'm willing to listen."

"I don't know the outcome," she admitted. "But I do have a suggestion."

Lord and Lady Hamilton both stood. "We'll hear what you have to say, Cosima," said Lord Hamilton, and beside him his wife nodded.

"I shall return to Ireland—"

Peter shook his head, facing her and putting both hands on her shoulders.

But she didn't stop. "No, Peter, listen to me. If I return home and give you time to consider the repercussions of our marrying, perhaps your decision will be more logical than emotional."

"Sounds like a reasonable plan, Son," said Lord Hamilton.

"All right." Peter spoke with a smile and a look of triumph in his eyes. "But I propose one small alteration. If it's logic and information rather than emotion you wish me to consider, then there's only one thing to be done. You may indeed return to Ireland, Cosima. It's an excellent idea. Only I'm coming along."

37

Talie raised her hand to knock on the door to Dana's apartment but stopped. She looked up at Luke, who held Ben perched on his shoulders. Ben was content sucking on his finger, his posture slightly hunched over his daddy's head.

Talie gripped Cosima's journal. She'd finished reading it last night and knew the next person to see it must be Dana. And then perhaps Aidan, *if* . . .

Luke's face was solemn, as she guessed her own must be. He waited grimly for her to carry through on the knock. She did so, because she had to.

A quick "Be right there!" sounded almost immediately.

Talie glanced at Luke again. Dana's tone was so happy Talie wanted to savor the moment. She doubted any of them would be hearing her voice quite like that again, at least for a while.

But she didn't have time to mention such thoughts to Luke. The door swished open and there stood her sister, smiling her own particular smile. The one that said this world was a gift full of hope and happiness.

Talie pushed away another surge of grief and anxiety. *Breathe, just breathe.*

"Come in!" Dana held the door wide and stepped to the side. "As soon as you called I ran down to the bagel shop. I bought some of that fancy coffee you guys like. Did you have any trouble finding a parking spot?"

Dana's Rogers Park neighborhood was usually crowded with cars parked on the street, but this was Saturday morning and they'd had no trouble.

Talie eyed her sister closely, wishing they'd come with other news. Dana's cheerfulness probably stemmed, in part, from wanting to cheer them up. But she still trusted the misinformation that Ben's delays were due to autism, a condition that affected only him. Talie swallowed hard. Classic autism would have been a better diagnosis, at least as far as Dana went.

Dana neared the dining nook, where her table was set with a colorful pink-and-orange tablecloth, green glass plates, and Talie's old white coffee cups. Beside a stack of bagels was a tub of whipped cream cheese.

Ignoring their grave silence, Dana chatted on as she poured coffee. It probably smelled good, although Talie's stomach had ceased demanding food since the phone call two days ago. Yesterday's visit to Dr. Benson's office had done little to alleviate her anxiety. The doctor had armed her and Luke with information, information that had sent them here but hadn't done a single thing to make Talie feel better. She forced nourishment upon herself only for the sake of the new baby, and even with such a pure motivation it was difficult to eat.

Since the dining nook was an open area, Ben was easily visible on the blanket Talie spread upon the living-room carpet. She surrounded him with toys—not that he played with any. She had remembered to bring the one he did know how to use and placed it in his lap. Soon classic childhood melodies announced there was a baby in residence.

"I guess you'll be seeing Aidan tonight?" Talie asked as she took a seat.

"Sure. We're going to a movie."

Talie had tried to rehearse, but whatever words she'd once thought acceptable now escaped her. How could she tell her sister she was a carrier for fragile X, the same as Talie?

She must remember that nothing happened outside of God's design. In all things, trust Him. All and whatever . . .

With her silence, Talie found Luke's gaze. She needed him here today. She knew Ben's diagnosis was as devastating to him as it was to her, but through his ache he remained calm—the only rock in her life these days. She'd tried depending on her faith, but Luke was the best tangible evidence of that faith.

He looked from her eyes to the journal still in her hands, as if reminding her about its significance in all of this.

She spoke. "Dana . . . we have something to tell you, something about Ben. And us. Us as in you and me . . . not me and Luke."

Dana had taken the chair next to Talie. She set aside her coffee now, giving Talie an intrigued look. Her eyes looked very blue today, bright with happiness that Dana always seemed to have on hand.

Talie breathed in once deeply. "It turns out the diagnosis of autism was wrong."

She knew she'd chosen the wrong words when Dana looked pleased. "That's great! I always hoped this was just a delay thing, that if you give him enough time . . ."

Talie shook her head. "No, he has a new diagnosis. Results of a blood test came back positive for fragile X syndrome."

Dana's brows, a moment ago so hopeful, now drew together. "What's that?"

Talie looked at Luke, who took the cue. "It's a genetic disorder on the X chromosome," he said. "Basically this condition is responsible for the brain not producing enough of a specific protein to function . . . to learn."

"We spoke to a geneticist yesterday, Dana." Talie was amazed

311

her voice was steady. Inside she was anything but calm. "She said I'm the carrier. And that fits with what we know about our family history."

The confusion on Dana's face expanded to surprise. "What do we know about our family history, except that everybody is fine? Is it possible someone else has it in the family, but we never knew? Because Ben will outgrow his delays too?"

Talie shook her head, closing her eyes against new tears. "No. I'm sorry I'm not doing a very good job at explaining this. First of all, the geneticist told us that it must have come from me because Ben is what's called a full mutation, and only mothers can produce full mutations."

"What makes him a . . . full mutation?"

"The protein in his blood is so limited it's indicative of what's going on in his brain. Without the protein, he doesn't learn. His brain will never work the way it's supposed to."

Talie saw Dana look at Ben. It would have been easy to think he was perfectly fine; he was still so little. But they all knew that wasn't true. At sixteen months he couldn't walk, couldn't feed himself, made poor eye contact, had low muscle tone . . . the list held so many items Talie was amazed she'd been able to deny there was anything wrong for so long. Even with cousins on Dad's side of the family being perfectly fine.

"I called Mom last night, Dana. She said she'd meet us here."

Dana looked at Talie. "Here?"

"I told her we'd be telling you this morning."

Confusion again. How long would it be before Dana realized this diagnosis affected her, too? Right now, other than that faint confusion, all Talie saw on Dana's face was sympathy.

"I'm sorry," Dana said. "I think we all wanted the diagnosis to go away. I guess it's only changed."

Talie nodded, knowing she had to forge ahead. "The thing is, this most likely came from Dad." She swallowed hard, taking a sudden shift from the direction she knew she ultimately had to go. "We think Dad gave it to me because . . . well, there *were* others in his family like Ben, only we never met them. The baby I'm carrying now has a fifty-fifty chance of having fragile X as well."

Dana's eyes rounded—whether in horror or deeper sympathy it was hard to tell. Either would have been appropriate.

"Is there any way of knowing if the new baby is all right?" Dana asked. "I mean, now? Before he or she is born?"

Ben dropped the toy from his lap and fussed when it landed with a thud. Talie rose to pick him up, letting Luke take up the conversation.

"We could have an amniocentesis. The geneticist recommended it, but . . ."

"But what? Don't you want to know? I'd be dying to find out."

With Ben in her arms, Talie fished in the diaper bag for the juice bottle she'd brought. "We want to know too, Dana, but the more we think about it the less we've been able to justify it."

"The test has a small risk to the baby," Luke said.

Talie took her seat, putting the bottle in Ben's willing mouth. "What if this baby is fine? And we lose it because of a test we didn't need to take? We're not going to have any more kids after this, not with the odds we're dealing with. We know God made this baby, same as He made Ben. What would an amnio do for us? It's not as if we'd act on whatever we find. We couldn't end this pregnancy one way or another; it's a baby God wants us to have—fragile X or not."

"Maybe it would help prepare you . . . one way or another."

"I'm prepared enough." Talie's voice sounded hard, harder than she'd ever heard from herself. She took a deep breath, hoping the edge would go away. She had more to say . . . words that would affect Dana far more personally than everything that had been said so far. Evidently Dana had forgotten the basic biology facts she'd learned in school, or she would have figured it out for herself by now.

"There is something else you need to know." Another lump lodged in Talie's throat. "If this came from Dad, you and I . . . we're *both* carriers."

"What?" If panic was about to erupt beside the sympathy, Dana hid it well. Except for a slight tremor in the word, she looked almost normal, only a slight dimming of the brightness of her eyes.

"It's passed on the X chromosome. Remember biology? Women have two Xs, but men only have one. They have an X and a Y. Men give the Y chromosome to their sons, not an X. They give the only X they have to all their daughters, and if it's affected by fragile X, then every daughter a male carrier has is automatically a carrier."

Dana shook her head, the first hint of a frown forming. "Wait a minute; you're talking too fast." She leaned over, rubbing her temples with her fingertips.

"We're all having a crash course in genetics in the worst way possible. It means both of us inherited the fragile X gene from Dad. If we'd been boys the problem would have ended because he'd have given us Ys and not Xs. But because we're girls, he gave us the only X he had. A bad one. And we're not full mutations because it's never been documented that a male carrier can produce a full mutation. Only mothers can do that to their kids." The word *curse* came to her lips, but she bit it back.

"*Mutations* . . . sounds like science fiction." Dana gave a little laugh that sounded anything but happy. As predicted, her earlier tone had entirely disappeared. The sparkle in her eyes was fading. Talie wished there was a way to get it all back, but she didn't have anything to use as inspiration.

"It's just starting to sink in for me," Talie said. "It was easier to convince myself everything was fine after talking to Aunt Virg.

If it was genetic, it stands to reason their side of the family would be affected too, doesn't it?"

"But they're not," Dana said, then shot Talie a suspicious glance. "Or are they?"

Talie shook her head. She deserved that question after the secrets she'd kept. "Dad's mom must have been a carrier just like you and me. Every baby she had was born with the same fifty-fifty chance of getting her good X or her bad. The bad one doesn't automatically produce someone like Ben. Dad got the bad X, but he was just another carrier. And Uncle Steve must have gotten the good one, since nobody in his family has a problem."

"Lucky him," Dana whispered.

But Talie knew her sister didn't believe in luck any more than she did. This was all by God's design. Talie's heart twisted at the reminder.

Just then the doorbell rang, and Dana popped up as if the noise had startled her. Talie watched her sister walk to the door as though she were one of Ben's windup toys, stiff and unnatural.

Oh, Lord . . . be with us now.

But instead of receiving a heavenly peace, all Talie felt was a cold, leaden weight.

Their mother stood at the door. On her face was a look Talie hadn't seen since the day she'd returned from the hospital after Dad's cancer diagnosis.

Val entered saying nothing, passing Dana and going to Talie. Ben was finished with the juice and sitting upright. Val took the baby and patted his back as if she knew he needed to be burped and had arrived just in time. She didn't even say hello.

"We'll get through this, you know," Val said over the baby's shoulder.

Talie nodded, although she wasn't so sure.

"Want some coffee, Mom?" Dana asked, coming up behind her.

"No, not yet." She sat in the chair Dana had vacated.

"I called my doctor's office this morning," Val said. "And received very little help for the effort. The nurse hadn't even *heard* of fragile X."

"Maybe you spoke to a receptionist," Talie said.

"When the doctor finally called me back, even he said he didn't know much about it. Of course, he's not a pediatrician, but aren't there any adults with this disorder?"

"The geneticist said there are probably a lot of adults misdiagnosed, since a cheap, reliable blood test for fragile X hasn't been around very long."

"A doctor ought to know a bit about it, you would think." Val sighed, shifting Ben in her lap and then looking again at Talie. "You seem to be handling this well, honey."

Talie felt instantly closer to tears after her mother's observation. So much for the theory that labeling something made it so.

Her mother wiped Ben's chin; he was drooling again. "I called my friend Ronnie this morning too, while I was waiting for the doctor to phone me back. Ronnie's been such a comfort to me, Talie; I wondered if you might welcome a visit from her."

Ronnie, the Elmwood Park expert on grief. Talie shouldn't be hard on her; the woman had experienced more than her share of loss, since she'd been widowed at age fifty. But that wasn't what made her a longtime expert. She'd lost her one and only child to SIDS thirty years ago.

Talie was already shaking her head. "No, Mom, not for a while. I just want to . . . adjust, I guess. I'm not up for company."

"But this would be more of a pastoral visit. You know, from someone who's experienced the worst of life."

She took Ben from her mother. "I don't think so. Not yet."

Val patted Talie's arm. "You think about it then. But it might be nice to talk to someone who's been through so much. I know she still grieves the baby she lost. A baby's death isn't something a mother gets over."

"Mom, you don't understand, do you?" Talie's voice wasn't much louder than a whisper, but the reproach was unmistakable. Perhaps she should have let the moment pass, knowing they were all just trying to cope. But the words were out and she couldn't call them back.

"What do you mean?"

She couldn't stop now. "I mean that Luke and I feel exactly like Ronnie must have felt thirty years ago. We feel like we lost a baby too. We thought we had a son who would grow up with big dreams—maybe not our dreams, but at least his own. Somebody we could nurture until he was out of the nest, ready to build his own. This diagnosis feels like the death of the baby we thought we had."

"Of course it does, honey," said Val. "I didn't mean to make it sound like Ronnie suffered more than you."

"Grief is grief," Dana said.

"If you ask me, Ronnie got the better deal," Talie muttered.

"Better deal? But honey, she only got to love and take care of her baby for three short months."

Talie leveled a hard gaze on her mother. "Her baby is in heaven, Mom. She didn't have to watch him grow up and struggle every day to learn the simplest thing. Her baby's battle ended the day he died. Mine and Luke's will outlive us. Who's going to take care of Ben when we're gone? He'll need care for the rest of his life, if he's anything like—"

She cut herself off. They didn't know about Royboy, Willie, or Ellen Dana. She glanced at the journal beside her on the table, knowing she'd have to tell them but unsure how.

Her mother reached for one of the napkins on the table, wiping away tears. "I'm sorry I ever brought her up. I was only trying to help."

Luke put an arm around Talie, and his touch communicated more than words. She handed Ben to Luke then faced Val. Her mother's sob forced her own tears to escape and they clutched one another, each offering apologies over the other's.

At last Val took another napkin and handed it to Talie. "This is not going to tear this family apart," she pronounced. "In fact, my prayer is that it draws us closer. Need does that, you know. Or should. We need each other now. And God."

Talie let out a little breath of air, not exactly a huff. A resentful one.

"God is still God, Talie," Val said. "And He still loves every one of us. Me, you. Ben. Dana."

Talie raised a watery gaze her mother's way. "I . . . know. . . ."

She guessed her mother saw her struggle, the one that might not doubt God was God, only that He was good.

Talie glanced at Dana. Had any of it sunk in yet? Did she realize how personal the ramifications were? what it all meant to her . . . and to Aidan? "I suppose you have some questions, Dana."

Dana shrugged. "It's hard to believe any of this. If we're carriers for mental retardation, how come we're not affected at all? We both graduated magna cum laude."

"Nonsymptom carriers," Talie said, as if a term could possibly explain anything.

Dana stared at her. Talie could hear her sister swallow once, hard. "How are you so sure this affects both of us?"

"It came from Dad. Genetically speaking, it's a certainty."

"But how do you *know* it came from Dad? If it came from Mom, the same fifty-fifty statistic would still apply, wouldn't it?"

Talie picked up the journal. "It's in here, Dana."

"What is?" Val asked.

But Talie didn't look at their mother. Instead, she stared at Dana.

Dana broke the gaze and took the journal. "There are relatives in here who are handicapped, aren't there?"

Talie couldn't deny it; Dana must see it in her eyes. The truth was sinking in.

"And you didn't tell us? You didn't connect Ben's delays to what's in here?"

"Look at the date, Dana: 1849. I didn't think anything that happened so long ago could possibly have anything to do with—"

"But Ben's delays . . . wasn't that enough?"

"I already told you I didn't want to believe it. I wanted him to be okay."

"And so you kept this to yourself all this time."

It was more accusation than observation.

If there had still been sympathy in Dana's gaze, it was blotted out by anger. "You knew before I started dating Aidan that something might be in our family."

Another accusation, this one entirely unveiled.

Talie stood, putting her hands on Dana's shoulders. "I . . . I didn't believe it at first. I didn't want it to be true. I only finished reading the journal last night. I kept hiding it away, out of sight and out of mind."

Dana shook her off, turning away. She went as far as she could without leaving the room entirely, going to the picture window on the other side of the living room.

Luke stood and said he'd take Ben in the bathroom for a diaper change. Talie didn't blame him; even the sour air that would accompany a soiled diaper was preferable to the tension in this room. Their mother sat still. If Val understood the depth of the battle, she said nothing to indicate she might have a side.

At last Val pulled Talie to her feet, directing her toward Dana. Talie didn't want to follow but knew if she didn't, her mother would pull her along anyway. Just like when they were kids. Kiss-and-make-up time.

"I don't know the details or what's in that journal. I've never seen it before today, but I assume it came out of that box with the family Bible in it." Val paused, looking between her daughters. "It's plain to see you're both hurting right now. But there's no malice here. Not on God's part to you, Talie. And not on Talie's part to you, Dana. The world is full of sorrow, and there's no reason any one of us should be spared. We're not in heaven yet, girls. Remember that, both of you."

Neither daughter said anything. Talie couldn't think of a thing to say, and she guessed Dana wasn't ready to talk. The anger was too fresh.

Maybe Dana was righteous in that anger. Maybe she'd never understand why Talie had put off telling her. Maybe all Dana would remember was that Talie could have warned Dana before she'd gotten serious with Aidan but had chosen denial instead. Talie might have been wrong, but she'd had no idea how wrong until receiving this diagnosis.

"I'm going to Talie's," Val said. "I plan to stay the day and babysit because I want them to go out and get their mind off of things. Go shopping, go to a museum. Maybe dinner. Did you tell me on the phone yesterday that you and Aidan are seeing a movie tonight, Dana?"

It looked as though ice stiffened Dana's spine. "Aidan and I won't be going out tonight."

She glanced once more at Talie, who felt the icicles aimed her way, despite their mother's reconciliation attempt.

How could she tell Dana—make her believe—that she would do anything to make it all untrue?

Talie turned when she heard Luke returning with Ben in one arm and a small blue plastic bag holding a heavy, disposable diaper in the other. They took their trash with them when they left, especially the odorous kind.

That was when she noticed Dana's wall arrangement for the first time. The clock, the black-and-white photographs blown up and framed in the weathered windowpane. But a shadow box in between drew her eye and kept it riveted. A cross, not much bigger than the palm of Talie's hand, hung inside. It was edged in iron.

Talie neared it.

Luke must have noticed it as well, but Talie didn't turn around. She heard Ben's noises close in behind her.

"Do you see it?" Talie whispered.

"It looks like . . ."

"Dana," Talie said, louder now, "where did you get this cross hanging on your wall?"

"From the attic. It was in Dad's things. Why?"

Talie looked at Luke, who stared back with the first hint of light she'd seen in his eyes in days.

"This has to be it. Where else could it have come from, if your dad had it? Look," Luke added, bending closer, "there's the middle, polished smooth from everybody's thumb."

Dana approached. "What are you talking about?"

Talie turned to her sister and smiled. The gesture felt odd, as if the muscles used for that had already hardened. "Read the journal, Dana. And remember: all and whatever."

38

I have been remiss in recording events of the past few days. But I must confess it is far more satisfying to be living the love Peter and I share instead of simply writing about it. While I know these events are forever engraved upon my heart, I want this written account to be complete for those not yet born. Yes, I can happily write of that hope now! This journal and whatever it has to offer might someday be held in the hands of our children, Peter's and mine, and every generation after as God so chooses to bless. It has been three days since my world was crushed and revitalized all in one evening. Three days of joy the likes of which I have never known before, reveling in the love Peter is so eager to give.

I told Peter everything—from the worst of Royboy's weaknesses to the horrible day my parents and I found Percy and the others in the ruins of the hunting lodge. I cried as I told him, and Peter held me close with tears of his own. Again and again I offered him freedom from his proposal, but again and again he flatly refused.

Both Beryl and Christabelle are thrilled with our plans to marry, but of all my relatives, Dowager Merit's response was the most unexpected. She had been the one to warn the Hamiltons about me, which had led me to conclude that she would not approve of the match.

But upon seeing us together that morning after the ball, the dowager took my hand and whispered, "He needed to make an informed decision, my dear. And so he has. It is not impossible for you to give him a son to carry on. You have healthy male cousins to prove that. See that you do, for England's sake—no matter how many children you must bear." Then she kissed my cheek and gave her blessing for all to hear!

The night before we left for Ireland, I met with the Hamilton family in the drawing room to pray. Between requests for a safe journey, I sensed in Lord Hamilton's voice a sincerity to seek and follow God's guidance even as he asked Him to guard the future of the Hamilton legacy. I prayed we would all put His will before our own.

When we departed Hamilton Hall, Peter sat beside me in the carriage taking us to the train. He held my hand, and though our smiles were inspired by each other, we easily shared them with everyone around us. Even with Beryl, who sat opposite, next to Millie. Berrie asked to come with us to

Ireland, and no one, not even Lady Hamilton, could think of a reason not to allow it.

Once settled and on our way, Peter immediately moved to kiss me. Dear Berrie teased him about asking the driver to hoist her and Millie up on the baggage rack to give us the privacy we obviously wanted. But of course Peter was the gallant gentleman even Beryl knows him to be.

It was not until we neared the long lane leading up to the manor house that my excitement was dimmed by the reality that Peter would at last see for himself all the evidence of the curse. I was certain Mama would make sure Royboy would not be the first person our guests would meet. But I still found no words to prepare Peter for what he would eventually see.

When I tried to express my concern to him, he placed a hand on my cheek and told me, with an unwavering smile, "You must not worry. I love you."

I leaned into his palm but could not return the smile. "'Tis your love I am wanting to keep."

"Do you think it is so fragile?" he asked me. "If it were the other way around and you faced this curse in me, would you be worried your love would suddenly disappear?"

"No. I know that I will always love you."

"Then know the same from me."

Before long they had all alighted and been greeted by boys Cosima knew from the village who had obviously been hired as footmen. And there, standing on the stone steps of the manor that had housed Kennesey blood for generations, stood her parents.

Cosima ran to their open arms, and they pulled her between them for a lung-constricting hug. In the exuberance of the embrace, Cosima lost her hat, and one of the footmen ran after it when it was picked up by the wind. Cosima hardly cared.

"Papa." She called him the name she'd used as a child, then looked at her mother saying, "And Mama. How I've missed you both!"

She turned and, with one hand in each parent's, led them to Peter and Beryl, who stood before the coach. "Mama, Father, this is Miss Beryl Hamilton and her brother, Lord Peter Hamilton, baron."

She saw her mother look toward the empty carriage as if expecting someone else to emerge. Perhaps Sir Reginald?

After polite greetings, they went inside. As Cosima expected, the manor was in full use. They were led to a large room near the front of the manor, one Cosima hadn't been in since long before she'd left only months ago.

All of the furniture shrouds were gone, and the green and white room glistened from the labor of a good cleaning and the freshness of a thorough airing. As hats were taken, tea was offered, and soon they sat talking about something more meaningful than the lovely day and the comfort and safety of their journey.

"Hamilton," said her father, not in an address but rather as if mulling the name. "Tell me, are you related to Lord Graham Hamilton, viscount?"

"Yes, sir, he's my father."

Her father's brows lifted, but she wasn't sure if he was pleased or dismayed, since some of the color left his ruddy cheeks.

"Mama, Papa, Lord Hamilton has accompanied me home with the hope of getting to know our family better," Cosima began slowly, watching her mother's eyes begin to dance with happiness. "Although I've told him about . . . our family . . . he believes we might . . . that is, we've been considering the *possibility* . . ."

Peter, sitting in the chair closest to her, set aside his tea and reached for her hand. "I've come with every intention of marrying your daughter, Mr. and Mrs. Escott. Forgive my bluntness, but I'm not as uncertain as Cosima seems to be at the moment."

"Marry Cosima?" said her father. "I must say I find it no surprise. I saw the moment Cosima introduced you that she holds you in high esteem. But Cosima will have to advise her mother and me on a few things first." He gazed at his daughter. "I'm glad Lord Hamilton has presented himself to be blunt. I shall be the same. How is it that you met Lord Hamilton, Cosima, and whatever happened to the bloke you left with?"

"Please, sir," said Beryl, "I wonder if I might answer your question? Since we're being blunt today, may I say I've traveled with them two days and they've left me out of nearly every conversation? I've been with Cosima from the day she arrived in London, so I may know more details than Peter himself. May I?"

Cosima's parents looked from Beryl to Cosima, as if for permission, and she gratefully nodded. She enjoyed the sight of her parents listening while drinking her favorite tea. Mama had remembered which to serve.

Beryl's voice, so like her mother's, told the tale as if it were from a Dickens novel. That Cosima's parents approved already was obvious from the start.

Cosima would have reveled in it all, from the love she felt to the plans she and Peter hoped to make.

Except for one thing: Peter had yet to meet Royboy.

39

Lying in bed beside Luke, Talie waited to hear her husband's even breathing. He always fell asleep before her, even prior to the many worries keeping her awake at night these days.

But tonight the even breathing didn't come. Instead he seemed more silent than ever, except for an occasional intake of breath.

"Luke?"

He turned onto his back. "I'm sorry. Did I wake you?"

"No, I wasn't asleep. You . . . okay?"

He lifted his hand to his face, and she realized he'd been crying. "I noticed something tonight when I was putting Ben in his pajamas." His voice was so steady; maybe she'd been mistaken about the crying. "When he yawned and opened his mouth really wide . . . I saw his palate for the first time. It's so high, so narrow." Luke let out another breath, as if he'd been holding it. "I guess I've been pretty stupid, Tal. All this time, deep down I didn't really believe anything was wrong. Like Dana said today, it's all pretty hard to believe. Even the blood test didn't convince me. Or the journal. Tonight was the first time I really *saw* something. Evidence that it's true: there really is something wrong with him. Something we can't fix."

Talie put her head on his shoulder, and his arms went around her. Tears fell freely from her eyes, dampening his T-shirt. In a moment she felt him tense and shudder with tears of his own for the son they'd thought they had but lost, for the son they did have who was so different from the one they'd thought they knew.

"Lord—" Luke spoke at last, in a voice that wasn't steady anymore—"help us in our unbelief; take away our lack of trust in Your goodness and help us to remember You want what's best for us. That You can give us the strength to get through all and whatever." He breathed deeply, adding, "God, I want this taken away, for all our sakes. . . . I want to understand . . . but I don't. . . . "

He stopped and Talie joined in. "We need Your strength, Lord, because ours is failing. We know we're to thank You in all things . . . but this . . . help us, Lord, to find a way."

Prayers didn't end the tears, but Talie felt as though the Holy Spirit was there, crying alongside them.

After a while, when Talie thought Luke must be sleeping, his quiet voice betrayed him as awake. "Did you ever think of God's love and goodness? I mean really dwell on those things, Talie?"

She didn't answer because at that moment she wondered if she ever had, in some special way that he meant. Lately God's love seemed hard to hold for long. And His goodness? To her own shame she'd questioned that more than once.

He brushed a kiss on her shoulder. "Remember sermons we've heard about the reason God let us have free will . . . to teach us to love? Without *choosing* love, it's not really love."

She remembered but didn't say anything. God loved her; she'd known that forever. She just didn't feel it.

"I have to remember that now, Tal," Luke whispered. "Because if I don't, I'll start doubting God is really good. And if I doubt that . . . well, I can't . . . I won't let myself."

Talie's heart beat hard. "I *do* doubt it, Luke. A good God who loves us gave us . . . this?"

She heard him breathe evenly beside her, though her own breathing was erratic.

"That's just it. Wasn't it because of His goodness that He gave us this free will to begin with? The one that had to come with all the bad stuff in order to learn the good? And a way out of the bad stuff . . . through His Son?"

Talie didn't want to argue the philosophical nuances of their faith. Nor, though, did she want to feel the way she was feeling. As if God didn't love her the way He loved others. Others with healthy kids.

"Isn't the way He loves us the way He wants us to love Ben?" Luke went on. "The way He wants all parents to love their children? Unconditionally?"

"I do love Ben that way, but . . ." She didn't want to say it. She didn't want to reveal the worst about herself, even to the man who had promised to love her until the day one of them died. Maybe especially to him. And yet she felt compelled to continue. "But Ben may never love us back, Luke. He may never be able to show it if he does or know how to say the words."

"So . . . our love should be based on what we get in return?"

"No, of course not. But isn't it harder to love someone who can't love you back?"

"I guess that's what will make our love more like God's. He sees every rotten thing we've ever done in our life and loves us anyway. If Ben is here to live what everybody on earth would call a meaningless life, without productivity, without cognizance, then it's those around him God must want most affected, touched, changed. Because He loves us."

"Funny, I thought we were loving each other and Him well enough before all this." But of course it wasn't funny at all.

Luke turned Talie to him. His face hovered above hers, earnest. "I'm struggling with all this too, Talie. But Ben will be able to show he loves us. Somehow."

She couldn't help but smile, to hang on to what she saw in his eyes. He might be struggling, as he claimed, but there was something beside that struggle that gave her hope. Something she couldn't define, except maybe . . . strength. "That'll be enough then."

40

There is an old Irish proverb that says, "Happiness follows simplicity." Perhaps, if I may bend this proverb a bit, happiness follows the simple. Royboy is almost never without a smile. There are days I need to learn from Royboy.

I am sitting in the morning room, and as I write I can see Peter and Royboy from the window. They are playing a rather unconventional game of tenpin, with Royboy rolling the ball from an illegally close distance to the pins. Peter resets them whenever Royboy hits any, cheering him on every time he does not. Royboy rarely knocks any over, but I see my brother's happiness in the familiar flap of his hands. His mouth shapes into what I call the "fish-face O" to make sounds only Royboy can achieve. . . .

"Tea still hot?"

Cosima looked up to see her father enter the morning room. It was still early, just past ten. Father was dressed like any English gentleman, with white drill trousers, polished shoes, a dark blue morning coat, and a waistcoat with the collar kept in place against his neck by a small, white cravat.

"Yes," she answered, holding up her cup and taking a sip.

Her father took tea but ignored the ham and eggs kept warm over a lit trivet. He joined her on the settee near the window. "Peter has proven himself a fine young man in the two days he's been here."

Cosima nodded. She had no doubt of that.

"I suppose you know he's asked to speak to me this morning."

"He said he wanted to," Cosima replied. "I didn't know when."

Her father lowered his tea and faced Cosima rather than the window. "My guess is he wants to inquire how I decided to marry your mother, given the circumstances were somewhat similar. You should know I want to be perfectly frank with the boy."

Cosima looked at him and smiled, placing a hand on his wrist. For a moment she considered his choice of words—not that he *intended* to be frank, only that he *wanted* to be. "Neither of us would have you be any other way, Papa. I've held nothing back from my own perspective. If Peter is to marry me, I'd rather have him expect the worst and be delighted if it doesn't turn out so bad, rather than the other way around."

Shifting his cup to one hand, he put his free hand over hers. "Have I told you, Cosima, how proud I am of you?"

Sometimes it was good to feel like a child again, under a parent's approval. "Thank you, Papa."

Soon Peter and Royboy came in. Both were dressed comfortably, the only way Royboy ever dressed. Peter's white linen shirt matched Royboy's, as well as his casual dark trousers. After good-morning greetings, they helped themselves to breakfast. Cosima made sure Royboy used a plate and utensils and reminded him about not stuffing his mouth. He behaved so well she wasn't sure if she was relieved or worried. So far Peter had seen only the positive end of Royboy's spectrum.

Decla came for Royboy after breakfast. He had to be taken to the privy on a regular basis or he would forget until too late. After that, as Decla had been doing since Royboy's birth, she would serve as tutor and nurse, spending time reading and playing what games he could enjoy. Decla had patience with Royboy that outlasted most others'.

The room quieted once Royboy was gone. Cosima decided she should leave in order to give Peter and her father privacy.

"I would like to write a letter, Father, Peter. So, if you'll excuse me . . ."

Both Peter and Cosima's father rose the moment Cosima did, but Peter, next to her, lightly touched her hand. "Must you go?"

"Perhaps now would be a good time for you and my father to speak. I've no wish for my presence to influence the questions— or answers—in your discussion."

"But I imagined you would be part of it," Peter said. "This is our decision together, not mine alone. I think you should be aware of each piece that goes into the future we decide."

Cosima was eager to stay but looked at her father. "Father?"

"I have every intention of being honest, with or without your presence."

"Very well."

They settled in the white wicker chairs that overlooked the expansive back lawns and crops beyond. Cosima had missed this view: the green plots separated by darker green hedges, rolling hills that lay so meticulously designed.

But as she took her seat and sent up a familiar prayer of thanksgiving, she added one more plea. *Please, Lord, help all of us hear and say what needs to be heard and said.*

"Sir," said Peter as he pulled his chair closer to Cosima's, "I find I'm in need of fatherly advice since my own father seems to have lost the common sense I credited him with. In any case, I would perhaps value your counsel more, since you've faced and lived what Cosima and I might see before us. Cosima told me there were rumors about her mother even before you married, and yet you married."

"Yes, that we did. Though I must say . . ." His voice drifted off as his gaze fell on Cosima. "Some of what I say may be hard for you to hear, coming from your father. I don't think it's easy for a child to think of a parent as anything but that and not simply a person like everyone else, full of flaws."

Peter reached over and took Cosima's hand. "I believe the best thing is for you to hear this, no matter how hard."

She shook her head and glanced between the two of them. "Swooning and fits—is that what you expect if you're both honest in front of me?"

Peter grinned. "Either one sounds feasible to me, given my knowledge of Beryl's and Christabelle's behavior."

Cosima smiled, knowing he jested. She welcomed his attempt to calm her, knowing they would discuss things most other people never had to face. "Let me assure both of you I'm quite up to all and whatever I need to hear."

"Very well then, Cosima," said her father. "I shall start by telling you that when I first met your mother, the last thing I intended was to consider marriage."

Cosima looked at him, surprised, but dared not say a word for fear of either of them thinking she was already failing her own declaration.

"I'd come to Ireland to escape all thoughts of marriage, you see. Just twenty-two years old. I came because it was the one place my parents would disapprove of most. I know you're both acquainted with my mother, and I assure you I have no wish to influence your feelings for her. Yet I cannot help but give you my opinion: She is demanding, narrow, judgmental. Adheres more readily to rules than any form of grace—does not, in my recollection, know the meaning of that word.

"My mother introduced to the family the woman my brother John was to marry. Little did any of us know, but there was an initial misunderstanding, and Meg thought it was I she was to wed. I'm afraid I encouraged the misunderstanding when I guessed what she believed, and I invited her to meet me in an empty drawing room. I don't know if I was more attracted to her than I was eager to best my older brother, but that was the beginning of what ended up being a rather nasty break in the family. My mother found us—simply talking, you understand, but alone. Quite unseemly.

"Despite the embarrassment to Meg, she and I became friends, though she agreed to marry John. So they became engaged. He was, after all, the heir and I, as the second son, a mere commoner. And my mother is a hard woman to refuse. She had chosen Meg to be the next viscountess, and neither John nor Meg had much to say in the matter. I didn't blame them—John or Meg.

"All should have been fine, except that one day when Meg and I were alone, we kissed. It meant nothing, really, only an experiment, as we were merely close friends to that point. I thought it odd to have a friend in a woman, and perhaps she thought it odd to have a friend in me. It was a nice enough kiss, and I believe if we'd married we would have continued to be friends. But unfortunately my mother heard of my transgression and chose to humiliate me in front of John, accusing me of trying to steal his fiancée and him of being blind.

"It was a minor incident compared to some of the arguments we had over the years, my mother and I. She had so little grace toward the flaws of others. But that disagreement was the last. I left and have never been back."

"Do you know, Father, that Grandmother has paid someone

to give her reports of you? She must have cared, all these years, and missed you."

He nodded. "There were times I missed her as well."

"But did you know? About the reports, I mean."

"Yes, Melvin handles them. Wrote some of them myself, in fact," he said with a smile. "Wanted to make sure the details were correct." He addressed Peter. "Now what does all that have to do with the decision you must make, Peter? I hope, for one, to let you know what sort of mood I was in when I first met Cosima's mother. Women were, at that point in my life, more trouble than tolerable. I had decided not to marry but instead to make the most of the investment money I brought with me—yes, to find fortune in the very place I knew would irk my mother most.

"That was when I learned of this estate, Cosima. Your mother's father had made it known he was willing to sell his land since it appeared his heir—your mother—was reluctant to wed. Her younger sister had married and moved north. At that time your mother had plans to join her and take her brother, Willie, with a hefty sum at her disposal, since her father intended to bequeath her whatever proceeds he received from the sale."

He leaned back in his chair and stretched his legs before him. "And so I came here first as a prospective buyer. The villagers thought I was interested in the land through marriage and not purchase, and so they quickly told me tales of Willie, the brother considered the village idiot. A harsh title, but his all the same. A harsh memory, too, of villagers perhaps overeager to spread their tales of a Kennesey curse.

"I met your mother for the first time on a morning like this." He looked out the window as if he were no longer in their presence but alive in another day, long before Cosima was born. "The sun shone on her hair, and it glistened like gold. She had a basket of flowers in one hand and a sketchbook in the other, and as I came up the lane, she dropped them both in the wind. We scrambled to catch the papers, and as I handed them back, I was struck—I barely saw the drawings, which might otherwise have impressed me. All I saw was her."

Cosima and Peter exchanged glances. She thought they both understood what her father had felt that day so long ago.

"As I said, I'd been warned of the fact that she had a brother who was feebleminded. I was also told her sister had married years before and had a small child suspected of being the same. There were rumors of others on her mother's side, another set of cousins also afflicted. Those two had been hidden away in an institution, but if that branch of the family had hoped to escape the stigma, they were wrong. No one forgot, and they made sure I knew it all. If I married a Kennesey, I might face the same.

"I was frightened, I suppose, in a way. But I was young and foolish too." Cosima's father looked at Peter and added, "Perhaps like you. Full of youthful invincibility. In my case, I further reasoned that since it was not my intent to marry, having a family was unnecessary to me. But I was raised in the strictest home, where breaking the rules was unthinkable, and so there was no question that if I wanted to keep company with Cosima's mother I should marry her. And why not? I thought. Unlike you, Peter, I had no legacy, no responsibility nor even old hopes for the future. And so, rather flippantly, I suppose, I shrugged off the warnings and asked Cosima's mother to marry me. What had I to lose, since a family had never been my goal?

"'Twas perhaps a mix of love and lust in the beginning, I grant you, but before long the love was the stronger of the two. We had our Percy and then you, Cosima, and for a very short time I thought life could be no happier. Willie was with us, but we had plenty of help to care for him. Tales of institutions were grim, and we gave no thought to sending him away where he might be mistreated. Do you know, in some places patients are herded to an open room where a visitor might, for a fee, view and laugh at those who cannot help themselves? That is no place for a human being made in God's image—on either side of the viewing wall, if you ask me. There was no choice but to keep him, you see. He was a kindhearted soul.

"And so our little family was established, and our farm grew more prosperous. It seemed to us people didn't talk anymore of the Kennesey curse. We were happy, and happy people are less often the subject of gossip, or perhaps happy people simply notice it less. We had friends and went to parties and lived a life more simple and serene than I imagined possible.

"Until Percy showed signs of being slow-witted after all. 'Twas the curse again, and it sent your mother into an insufferable depression. That was the worst of it, perhaps worse than realizing I had a son incapable of carrying on. A son I loved more than I ever expected. It seemed once I had my family there was now nothing more important to me. Still, I had Cosima to carry on for us, who is bright and healthy, and I've always found comfort in that. For your mother, though, it was unbearable. She loved me, you see, and wanted to give me a healthy son."

He took a sip of tea, as if the words had sapped his mouth dry. "We lived this way for what seemed forever, but in retrospect I recall it was only a few years. Cosima, do you remember the days your mother never left her room?"

She shook her head. "No, Papa."

"A memory no doubt plucked from your brain by the Lord Almighty."

"What brought her out of it?" Peter asked.

Cosima's father shrugged. "To this day, I cannot say. It was a slow process, to be sure. She began eating again, allowing my company. We were like strangers, and we visited as if I were courting her. It took time, but we regained what we'd lost."

"Did she blame herself for the way Percy was, Father?"

He nodded. "But after a while and after she began reading

her Bible again and returning to church, I think she accepted that the Lord God is ultimately in control. That He is still good, even though we live in a world that sometimes isn't. One day she looked at me and said perhaps it was a blessing to have Percy, since it made her long for the day he will be whole, in heaven. Can something making us long to be with the Lord be so terrible?"

Cosima's father looked at Peter. Resting his forearms on his knees, he entwined his hands together and stared a long moment before speaking. "We've had to face a future for our sons that no parent would choose. There were times, for both of us, that we believed joy would never be a part of this household again, not only when we realized the curse was upon us, but also after we lost our Percy. Rowena was wrong to have done what she did, even if she thought she could somehow remove the curse with her action.

"With time, though, we learned to live with the invisible scars. And Royboy . . . he is limited, that's true, and a sad life for us to see what he's missed. But we love him because he is the purest kind of person, one who trusts implicitly, who offers unlimited grace even when we're cross with him—sometimes unfairly cross. In Royboy, I've found the grace my mother never could give me."

He sat back, rubbed his palms on his knees, and looked away then back again. "Does he add to our lives? Not in the way most would want, but in a way that makes us remember how blessed we are to have a sound mind." He sighed then spoke with a lighter tone. "You know, I've never considered myself a funny man. But in my son I have a ready audience, whether I'm witty or not. He may not be able to tell me the love he feels, but he shows it in his smile and ready laugh, every day of his life. I'd give *my* life to have him whole, but as that cannot be, I accept him as he is and wait, with my wife, for that day he will be whole. In heaven."

For a while no one said anything, until her father continued. He looked at Peter pensively. "I suppose we could have tried to hide away our feebleminded sons, like some do. But it seems to me 'tis God who directs where a child is placed. If a soul is given to the care of a family, it is up to that family to see the blessing through the burden. Perhaps families like ours need a bit more help in the day to day, and it's all right to seek that help. But in a way that honors everyone, even a child like Royboy."

He stood, going to the window nearby and looking out rather than at Cosima or Peter. "You should know—both of you should know—that asylums are not the answer should you have children like Royboy. Ill fed, mistreated, shut away, and forgotten except by those who would ridicule them or wait at the viewing wall for them to do something outrageous. . . ."

"Oh, Papa!" said Cosima. "You mustn't think, even for a moment, either one of us would consider such a thing."

Peter stood, and Cosima watched the two men she loved most in the world face each other. "Sir, my duty as a father, should God bless me as such, would be to provide the best care to any child the Lord gives me."

Cosima's father nodded, placing a hand on Peter's shoulder in silent acceptance of his words.

Cosima came to stand beside Peter, and her father took a hand of each of them. "Royboy is not what any father prays for. Does not every parent look into the face of his child and think, *Ah, you'll be the one to make the world a better place?*" He looked at Cosima and smiled. "In you, Cosima, I've not been disappointed."

Cosima looked at Peter, who was silent. He offered a grim smile.

"I've but one real piece of advice for you, young man," Cosima's father said, still looking at Peter but stepping back, folding his arms before him. "As you make your decision, ask yourself what wife, what child—indeed, what part of life— guarantees happiness? Could another woman, one without a curse? I think, son, there are never any guarantees."

41

"All and whatever."

Talie repeated the words as she pressed in Dana's phone number early the next morning. They hadn't parted on friendly terms yesterday morning, but at least the cross was a reminder that God hadn't abandoned them. Talking and praying with Luke last night had helped. Maybe Dana needed a reminder too.

The phone rang so many times Talie was afraid Dana wouldn't answer. Talie glanced at the clock. Seven-thirty. It was too early for Dana to have left for church, and there was no way she'd sleep through the ring right next to her bed.

Five minutes later Talie tried again, and Dana answered on the second jingle.

"I tried reaching you a few minutes ago," Talie said. "Were you in the shower?"

"No. On the phone with Aidan—I still am, but I clicked over to ask if he can stop by to see Luke before church. He can be there in a half hour. Is that okay?"

"He wants to talk to Luke?"

"Yeah. So is it okay? I have to let Aidan know." Dana's tone was curt.

"Sure, we'll be here. We're going to the nine o'clock service though. Will you be coming here, too, or will we meet you at church?"

"I . . . don't know . . . on either count. Look, I have to go."
Then Talie heard a click.

So much for making this easy.

Aidan tapped at the door thirty-five minutes later. He was alone.

Talie had wondered if he would wait until Monday before
coming to Luke for counsel. After all, if Aidan was going to
follow in Luke's footsteps, he might as well glean advice from the
newest expert on marrying into a family like Talie's. Evidently
it couldn't wait that long—either that or he didn't want to have
such a personal conversation in the workplace.

When she'd told Luke that Aidan was coming, Luke had
frowned. Though he said nothing, she imagined his thoughts. *We
don't even know how to make it through a day without doubting God,
and we're supposed to be of use to somebody else?*

Talie invited Aidan in and offered him coffee on the way to
the kitchen.

"No, thanks," Aidan said. "I hope it was okay for me to stop
by this early."

"It's fine, Aidan. I understand, and so does Luke."

Luke sat at the table with coffee in front of him. They were
ready for church, even Ben. He was happy in his high chair,
making noises and occasionally laughing over some unfathomable
joke. He often laughed or cried without visible reason, and Talie
much preferred the laughter.

"I can leave you two alone if you prefer," Talie said.

"No, Talie," said Aidan. "I guess I'd like your input too. If you
don't mind some frank guy talk while I spill my guts, that is."

She found a halfhearted grin, poured herself a glass of orange
juice, and sat down. Aidan took a seat on the opposite side of the
table, glancing out at the patio. Summer was winding down, but

the flowers Talie had planted didn't know it. They grew tall and abundant as if life never changed except for the better.

"You know what I thought when I became a Christian?" Aidan asked.

Talie knew she was here to listen, that Aidan really only wanted Luke's advice. But Luke didn't respond.

Aidan stirred his coffee. "I thought with God on my side, how could I lose?"

"There are lots of promises in the Bible," Luke said. "Not one of them offers an easy life."

Aidan let out a breath and scrubbed his face with one swipe. "So what good is it to become a Christian? I cleaned up my life . . . stopped swearing, drinking, even sex . . . and what have I gotten in return?"

Luke cast an unimpressed gaze at Aidan. "Gave up all that, did you? Almost as much as Jesus gave up when He left heaven for a cross."

Luke's sarcasm wasn't lost on Aidan. He bent his head toward his knees, clasping his fingers behind his neck. "I know. I'm as selfish as they come." He gave a brief laugh and looked up at Luke. "And you want the truth about everything I gave up? I don't even miss it . . . well, except the sex." He glanced apologetically at Talie, as if he'd forgotten she was in the room. "But even that has an upside. This relationship with Dana, it's different from anything I've had. It's probably the first really unselfish one I've been in, and it's *better*. But now . . . I don't know what God wants out of this. Dana's ready to cut me off because she thinks it's best. For me."

"Is it?"

"I don't know."

Luke stared at Aidan. "When you get married, do you want kids?"

"Sure."

"Then walk away."

Talie's gaze flashed to Luke. Had she just heard what she thought she'd heard?

Aidan didn't welcome the advice; Talie saw that right away. He looked offended at first but after a moment just pained. She watched him run a hand over his face again, as if to wash away the impact.

Finally Aidan looked at Luke. "I guess I thought decisions would be easy as long as I stayed on the straight and narrow."

Luke offered no response. No comfort, no wisdom.

"I know you're in a tough spot right now too, Luke." Aidan's gaze touched Talie. "Both of you. I shouldn't be sitting here complaining about what I'm going through."

"I don't think you're complaining, Aidan," Talie said gently. "This isn't easy on you or Dana either. It's one of those unexpected bends in the road. Those are the worst."

"What do you think, Talie?" Aidan asked. "Same as Luke?"

She'd vowed to stand beside her husband, to support him in all things so long as he never put himself or his desires outside of God's will. But this? "Well . . ." She looked between the two of them, knowing it would be impossible to support Luke right now, at least fully. "Peter Hamilton didn't walk away from my grandmother Cosima."

"We can't all be Peter Hamilton." Luke's voice was firm now—not angry but clear and succinct.

For a moment Aidan looked confused; then his brows rose. "Dana gave the journal to me to read last night." He leaned back on his chair. "*After* telling me to cut and run. Run fast, she said, and don't look back. She said she'd rather I left now, just have it over with and not drag it out."

"Maybe she's right," Luke told him.

Talie wanted to scream, to shake both of them. Hadn't the journal taught them anything?

Or was *she* wrong? Did she expect too much?

"I don't think we should do anything right now," Aidan said. "Break up or think about marriage."

Talie wasn't sure that was an answer either. "Dana's right about one thing. It'll just get harder if you drag it out and end up separating anyway."

Luke pushed away his half-empty coffee cup. "I used to think what you thought, Aidan. If we served a good God, He wouldn't let bad things happen . . . not *really* bad, not like this. So now we all head off to church to worship a God I suddenly doubt is good, because He didn't care enough to spare my family from this."

Talie put a hand over one of her husband's, feeling his struggle as real as her own. If ever he needed her full support, it was now. And yet . . . his advice to Aidan still stung.

"You're always telling me we can't pick and choose what we believe the Bible says about God, Luke," Talie whispered. "We have reasons we believe what we do: the prophecy, the history, the science, the wisdom."

He grabbed her hand and squeezed, nodding. "And it says He's good. I guess we're just going to have to trust Him on this one."

"You're right, Luke," Aidan said with a smile growing in place of his frown. "Dana once told me sometimes obedience is enough . . . no matter what we feel at the time."

Talie put Ben's shoes on him. The sturdy baby oxfords were still pristine since they had yet to get much wear. He didn't have the balance for walking, but since reading some of the literature on fragile X, she no longer expected that, at least for a few more months. She hoped he would be walking by age two.

Aidan had left for church five minutes ago. Luke and Talie

went out to the garage to follow. She didn't want to bring it up, but something inside wouldn't let it go, no matter how she tried.

"Luke," she said once they were in the car and on the way, "I was a little surprised you told Aidan to walk away. I thought love is stronger than fear; that's what Cosima's journal said anyway. You don't believe that?"

He sighed as if tired of the topic. She was too. "Look, he wants kids. If he didn't care about being a father, I'd have said to stick it out, no problem. But he wants a family, and Dana probably won't want to risk having any. At least not until they can come up with an ethical way to guarantee a healthy baby."

He was quiet then, and Talie refused to look at him. Her bottom lip quivered, but she clamped down on it to keep it steady.

Luke shifted his hands on the steering wheel, and she saw from her peripheral vision that he glanced her way. "She's seen what you've gone through, Talie. Ben's not even two years old. Raising him is only going to get harder. He'll get bigger, but his mind won't progress."

He paused, and Talie thought he might expect her to say something, to concede or agree. But she couldn't.

"You've said yourself you can't think about Ben's future," he told her softly. "Why would you subject Dana to that?"

"But . . ." She withheld her protest. He was right, of course. Logical. Aidan was young, smart, good-looking. Of course he could find someone else.

And Dana? What was she supposed to do?

"I just can't believe you don't want Dana to be happy with Aidan."

"I do want Dana to be happy. Both of them."

As Luke directed the car into the church parking lot, Talie fell silent again. For the thousandth time she rubbed one palm over her middle, looking down as if by some miracle she might see inside and know if the new baby was all right or not. Everything was a mess, no matter which direction she turned. Unless maybe . . . up.

But just now the power of prayer wasn't much comfort either.

They went inside, and Talie hoped to find Dana and Aidan together. They spotted Aidan by the fountain, and she joined him while Luke took Ben to the nursery. When he came back upstairs they waited to find seats until the last possible moment before the service.

Dana never showed up.

42

Lord and Lady Hamilton sent word today that they are on their way here.

Both Peter and Beryl have tried to assure me that their parents must have had a change of heart. Why else would they come to Ireland? I want to believe them, but thoughts of Lady Hamilton grabbing Beryl and Lord Hamilton nabbing Peter were the first images to cross my mind, and I must confess that they have not quite faded. . . .

Beryl's call that a carriage was coming up the lane rang through the foyer, and just inside the blue room, Cosima exchanged glances with Peter. She saw his smile and automatically returned one of her own, but inside she quaked.

"Go outside and greet them as they approach," Mama said. "Your father and I will wait here."

Cosima nodded, and Peter took her hand. They left the blue room to join Beryl, coming down the stairs.

Beryl had a sparkle in her eye as her gaze caught Cosima's. "Oh, it'll be wonderful, Cosima," she said. "They've come with blessings; I'm convinced of that!"

Cosima nodded and smiled but remained silently wary.

Outside the sun shone through an opening of oppressive, gray clouds. The Escott lane was wet and hard to manage, and the rented carriage, pulled by an unmatched pair, splashed through ruts and bounced along to stop at last before the ancient stone porch.

Cosima felt Peter's grip on her hand tighten ever so slightly, and she looked up at him.

"It doesn't matter," he whispered, his eyes alight. "Whether they're here with blessings or otherwise, our future is decided."

"Yes, but will they want to be part of it?"

"We'll find out, won't we, now that they're here?"

Footmen once again familiar on the Irish Escott estate met the carriage and performed their duties, one near the horses to prevent any unexpected movement and another at the ready with footstool and gloved hand to assist in debarking.

Lady Hamilton was the first to step down.

"Mama!" Beryl breathlessly flung herself into her mother's embrace. Over Beryl's shoulder, however, Lady Hamilton's gaze went to Peter. Cosima searched for sadness and condemnation but could see no hint of either directed at Peter. She wondered if that gaze would change when it came Cosima's way.

Lady Hamilton's eyes did not leave Peter for what seemed a long time, and Cosima worried anew. Heavens, if Lady Hamilton couldn't look at her . . . Then it was there, shifting from Peter to Cosima even as Lady Hamilton still held Beryl.

Lady Hamilton smiled—absent of sadness or condemnation. Just a simple smile, a little like her old self, before she knew of the Kennesey curse. Yet she made no move toward Cosima or Peter.

Christabelle exited the coach, and as Beryl shouted with glee, she released her mother to clutch her sister.

Lady Hamilton at last came to Peter and Cosima. "I've missed you," she said, her voice as tentative as the look in her eyes.

Awkwardness hung as heavy as the clouds, yet Cosima sensed something different in Lady Hamilton. No longer aloof but not really herself either.

A moment later Lord Hamilton stepped down.

Peter moved forward, hand extended his father's way. "Father."

Lord Hamilton accepted Peter's hand in both of his with a vigorous shake. "Son."

Suddenly rain fell, huge droplets splattering from the sky.

"Let's get inside," Peter said.

Cosima turned to the house to lead the way. This was not the gentle rain that had descended earlier but an onslaught of wind and stinging rain they'd do well to escape.

Movement from the far side of the lane, closer to the house, suddenly caught Cosima's eye. It was the muddiest portion near a corner that always took the longest to dry, where few plants would grow.

She stopped. There was Royboy, standing in soft mud amid the trimmed arborvitae, his trousers heavy with wet earth, his hands and face no longer smooth and white but covered in a thick layer of ooze. Royboy's smile revealed a bit of white teeth behind his blackened face. That he was marred of mind couldn't be more obvious. If only she'd rushed in, maybe they wouldn't have seen him. . . .

She tried to turn abruptly away, not draw the others' attention to him. But it was too late.

Lady Hamilton was aghast. Cosima looked back at her brother, unable to bear the expression on the other woman's face any more than she could bear the guilt of her own shame. She'd been embarrassed by Royboy as never before.

She couldn't leave him there. Where was Decla? Cosima's mother had left explicit instructions that morning: Royboy was to be kept under a close eye. It might not have been the first time he'd slipped away, but perhaps it was the worst.

"Go inside, please," Cosima urged, not even daring to look at Peter. Ignoring the rain that now fell in torrents from clouds ripped open in the sky, she stepped in the direction of her brother.

"I'll get him," Peter offered.

But Cosima turned to him with more force than she thought she possessed, her hand landing on his chest. "No." Her lips were tight. "Take your family inside."

"Cosima——," he said, her name a surprised entreaty.

Hot and unwelcome tears contrasted the cool rain on her face. She looked up at Peter, certain his parents watched and heard every word. "I'll get him, Peter. It's my curse, after all. Perhaps it's best your parents have met him this way."

Then she strode forward, feeling them watching. It must be disgust filling them, making them ignore the rain drenching each and every one. She did not hurry. She no longer cared if she was soaked.

She'd failed. The profound, utter embarrassment at the sight of Royboy revealed her failure. Failed as his sister, failed as a child of the most loving and forgiving God. She'd failed as someone who could accept a future of children just like Royboy.

Shame had no place in a family of Royboys. Amid all of the unfair whispers and stares, the rumors and shunning of those in the village, she'd always clung to the comfort that God's Word was full of acceptance for the outcasts. Clung to the knowledge she'd done nothing to deserve a curse; nor had her mother, and not Royboy. How could she have failed so miserably?

There might have been some shred of dignity left if she lived without shame.

Cosima reached Royboy, and he flapped his hands. He was evidently excited by the storm. She took one of his muddy hands in hers, wishing she could apologize to him in a way he would understand. But she knew finding the words would be as impossible as it would be for him to comprehend them.

He greeted her with one of his high-pitched utterances and pulled on her as if intent on staying in the mud and rain.

"Royboy, come inside," she said, but his slippery hand fell easily from hers. Reaching for him again, another hand intercepted hers.

She turned, startled by Peter's close presence.

Royboy accepted Peter's outstretched hand.

"Come in," Peter said gently and put an arm around Cosima, leading the way.

They were sodden by the time they stepped inside the foyer, but so were all of Peter's family. Maids were already present, offering linens.

Cosima started to lead Royboy away. She wanted nothing more than to be with her brother and not with Peter's family. A range of thoughts and emotions assailed her, trying to ease her guilt. If they hadn't been so eager to condemn her back in England, perhaps she wouldn't have felt this shame. Was this how it would be? Would she give them grandchildren she could not possibly want them to share? ones they wouldn't want anyway?

She needed to get away, escape the feelings too strong to hide. She couldn't look at any of them, not even Peter.

"I'll tell someone to get Decla," he whispered to her.

"No, I'll take him."

"All right," said Peter. "We'll all have to change from these wet things anyway and give my family a chance to settle in before we meet back down here. Perhaps we should wait and meet your parents then."

It was too late for that, however, as both of Cosima's parents emerged from the blue room.

Cosima eyed her parents' faces, warm with welcome until they saw Royboy. Her father's face seemed to stiffen before her eyes, and her mother's became exasperated.

"Good day to all of you," said her father, who recovered first. He stepped closer to Lord and Lady Hamilton. "Welcome to our rainy Ireland, but you know, without all the rain we wouldn't have such an Emerald Isle, as it's called."

"True enough," said Lord Hamilton, and the two of them shook hands.

Cosima tried to slip away, Royboy at her side.

Lady Hamilton's voice stopped her. "Cosima," she called, "is this your brother?"

Cosima felt her heart drop to the pit of her stomach. With one deep breath, she turned back. "Yes—just the person," she managed to say, "not all the mud."

To her surprise, Lady Hamilton laughed. She stepped closer. "I'm pleased to meet you, Royboy."

"How do you do." It was a line that had become as rote as any other in his vocabulary. He said the words but did not look at Lady Hamilton. Instead he stared somewhere in the vicinity of the wall behind her.

"There's quite a bit of rain today," Lady Hamilton commented.

"Rain today," said Royboy. "Yes."

Cosima started to pull him away again, and he seemed willing to follow.

But Lady Hamilton took Cosima's free wrist. "Cosima—" her voice was hushed—"I'm pleased to meet Royboy, pleased to be here with you and Peter. I've missed you both so much, and . . . I wanted to tell you something I've learned."

Cosima looked at her, curious. "Learned?"

"Yes . . . about myself. Here I am, as old as I am, and I realized I have yet another flaw. One would think I shouldn't still be learning about myself by now."

Cosima said nothing, wondering if Lady Hamilton could possibly be nervous, the way her hands fidgeted.

Lady Hamilton's gaze fluttered downward. "For most of my life, I've had a weak faith."

A moment ago Cosima could barely look upon Lady Hamilton. Now she studied her, trying to read behind her words. "What do you mean?"

"I suppose this is neither the time nor the place, but I find myself so eager to unburden myself I cannot wait. I must ask your forgiveness, Cosima. The Lord God has done nothing but whisper to me since the moment I began acting any differently toward you. I was wrong and unwilling to listen to the words God Almighty put upon my heart."

"What words are those, Lady Hamilton?" Cosima asked. For once, Royboy wasn't trying to pull away. It was as if he wanted to hear as well, although she knew that couldn't be true.

Lady Hamilton paused. "I've always been so sure of what I believed." She smiled and put a hand over her heart. "I thought I held it all in here, but found I didn't after all. Not really. I used to profess that God is the creator of all and the owner of all. We're here by His grace, and all we have is not really ours but His. On loan, for a time. What we've been given—from the possessions we have to the children we bear—are simply put into our care, not through anything we've done but by His generosity."

She placed a hand on Cosima's wet shoulder. "You see how I've failed in proving that faith, don't you, dear? When it came to a test, I failed. I thought Peter was mine. Now I see that I need to trust the faith He's given Peter, and I need to trust Him as well. Can you forgive me for my lack of faith, Cosima? A lack of faith that obviously hurt you?"

"I . . . have nothing to forgive. You acted only out of love for Peter. I understand that. I've tried to talk him out of marrying me as well."

Lady Hamilton laughed. "Yes, I know! Your behavior made it so much more difficult for me to cling to all of my silly ways. You and Peter are the ones God used to remind me what faith really is: trusting that God wants only what is best for us."

Royboy tried to squirm free of Cosima's grip, but she held fast, only to let go a moment later when Peter joined them and Royboy stood next to him. It must be as clear to Lady Hamilton as it was to Cosima that Royboy had become attached to Peter even in the few weeks since they'd met.

Peter stood between Cosima and his mother, a curious but hopeful light shining in the brown depths of his eyes. His gaze settled on Cosima. "Weren't we right, Beryl and I?"

Cosima's heart soared. "Yes, Peter," she said with a nod. "I'm happy to learn you were both *absolutely* right."

43

The church service ended, and Talie glanced at Aidan as the three of them walked out of the auditorium. He probably hadn't heard a word of the sermon.

"We're going to get Ben," Talie said. "You're welcome to come back to our place if you want."

Aidan shook his head. "I'm going to Dana's."

Talie and Luke exchanged glances.

"I have to return the journal, at least," Aidan said, as if defending the visit.

Talie put a hand to his arm. "I'm so sorry, Aidan."

He tilted his head. "For what? For me, because your sister is dumping me?"

"No. I should have said something sooner—about the genetics. I denied it as long as I could. Too long, as far as you and Dana go."

He patted the hand she rested on his forearm. "I'm not going to blame you for giving me the time to fall in love with Dana while she still wanted to date somebody. What's the old saying? It's 'better to have loved and lost than never to have loved at all'?"

She pressed her hand downward. "Are you sure it has to be lost, Aidan?"

"Talie—" Luke's reproachful voice was like a sting to the deepest part of her heart.

She never took her gaze from Aidan's. "I want you to pray about *all* the options—not just how you and Dana will get through a breakup."

Talie and Luke picked up burgers on their way home from church. Even fast food was acceptable since she couldn't taste it anyway. It wasn't the most nutritious meal, but it was certainly the most convenient, especially when cooking a traditional Sunday meal was the last thing Talie felt like doing today. Only happy families sat down to formal Sunday dinners. Old-fashioned, Norman Rockwell families.

Talie started to take a bite of her burger but thought she might be sick. Right now *no* food, nutritious or otherwise, appealed to her. That morning her mind had found a new source for uneasiness, and she hadn't been able to shake it during the entire church service or since. A single thought had erupted like a germ in her brain, multiplying and festering inside her head until it spread to her heart.

One question demanded an answer: Did she love Luke enough to let him go?

44

My life has taken so many unexpected turns these past few months that I begin to feel nothing can surprise me. And yet this evening has proven once again that one never knows what will happen next.

I sat with Peter at dinner, at one end of the table near Beryl and Christabelle, while both sets of parents were at the other end having their own conversation. We had just finished the last course. I could not help but send more than a few glances my parents' way. Who were those two people hosting this dinner, so congenial and at ease with their guests? They laughed and exchanged stories as if they were not a bit like the two most private people I had known all of my life. It was a sight to behold, especially considering Peter's parents seemed to find them charming.

Then Melvin arrived in the dining room and made the most startling announcement. . . .

"Sir Reginald Hale," Melvin intoned, much like the proper butler whose role he had taken on.

Cosima cast a startled gaze toward the door as the announced man confidently entered, hat held in his gloved hands, an easy smile upon his face. What could possibly have induced Reginald to make the long trip to Ireland? And uninvited?

The man in question bowed a greeting, then briefly scanned those seated at the table until his gaze settled on Peter.

Clearly Peter was as shocked as Cosima. Coming to his feet, he looked from Reginald to Cosima, then back to Reginald. "Reginald." He offered no greeting beyond that, rather stood silently as if waiting for the man to explain his unexpected appearance.

Reginald's smile was so familiar it was as if nothing had ever changed. "I've come in peace, Peter. In repentance and the deepest desire to set things right between us."

Peter folded his arms. "I can't imagine why. You've proven you're no friend to me and less than that to Cosima."

"I've come to beg forgiveness." Reginald now turned from Peter to Cosima. "From both of you. I am deeply sorry for whatever heartache I may have caused." He looked back at Peter. "It was only temporary though, wasn't it, chum? If it hadn't been for me, no doubt you never would have met Cosima."

"But why did you lie to me, Reginald?" Cosima asked.

His gaze went momentarily to the floor. "Only to keep you from talking to anyone about . . . about the curse. So long as you believed I'd already received counsel from someone as honorable as Peter, you had no reason to ask me to speak of it to anyone. I worried others might not approve. Some people actually believe in silly curses, Cosima, and as I made quite clear from the beginning, I was willing to overlook that. As Peter obviously does."

"But you told her a lie," Peter said. "Reginald, I have no use for lies."

"Of course, man! I never did lie to you, though, did I? And

I only did what I did to achieve my goals. I see the error of my ways now, and that's why I've come. To ask your forgiveness and let both of you know I wish you the best."

Peter seemed to be studying his old friend, as if trying to decide whether or not to believe him. Once lied to, Cosima thought, trust was not so easily won back.

Then Peter looked at her. "His wrong hurt us both, but he's correct that it was temporary. Selfish motives seldom have a good result. But it was you he wronged most, Cosima. Say the word and I shall send him away. I can't think why he endeavored to travel here without proper invitation."

Cosima took a deep breath. She'd thought she hated Reginald when he'd betrayed her, but with her heart so full of love for Peter it was difficult to find room to hate anyone. So many images of Christ's forgiveness came to mind that she knew what she had to say. She should not hesitate. And yet she did.

Reginald, however, looked so hopeful and friendly that her hesitation ended.

"I've been forgiven so many times," she said. "'Twould be wrong of me not to offer the same to you, Reginald."

He walked forward, stopping next to her chair. For a moment she thought he might bend down and embrace her for the very first time. She was relieved when he only took her hand, but he shook it so thoroughly it jarred her all the way to her shoulder.

Cosima's mother stood. "We've just finished our dinner, Mr. Hale, but we can have something brought in for you if you like."

He was already shaking his head. "No, but thank you. I do wonder, though, if I might beg use of the lovely room I had the last time I was here. I plan to return to England tomorrow, but it's a bit late to start back tonight."

"Yes, of course. But, oh dear, that particular room has already been given to Peter. I hope another will do." Cosima's mother sent a footman for Melvin, directing him to have a room prepared. "You'll join us for tea and cake, though, won't you, Mr. Hale? If it's stopped raining, we plan to enjoy it on the veranda. The setting sun is a lovely sight from there."

"Of course." He bowed again.

While her parents led the way, Cosima moved to meet Peter, but Reginald came to her side before they reached each other.

"You are most kind to forgive me, Cosima. I wonder if I might speak to you again before I depart tomorrow?"

Peter was there, taking her hand in his. "What about, Reginald?"

"I'd like to speak to both of you, actually," he said, smiling broadly. "Only to reestablish our friendship, of course."

Cosima could see no good in such a notion. "I don't think—"

"But you mustn't refuse me, Cosima. Before I left England, I spoke to the dowager. She was very plainspoken, as you might expect. I need only regain your friendship and all of London will welcome me with the favor I've always wanted." He paused, attempting to coax a smile from her with one of his own. "You'll do this for me, won't you, Cosima? And give us a foundation right here, tonight?" He looked at Peter. "The three of us. I will wait for you in the library at eleven, for just a half hour of companionship, nothing more. To see if my future might be salvageable?"

He was gone before Cosima or Peter could refuse, catching up to Cosima's parents on the way outside.

Beryl approached them before moving toward the rest of the party. "I heard all of that, and if you ask me it's preposterous that your grandmother said any such thing, Cosima."

Peter nodded. "It doesn't seem likely, does it?"

Cosima frowned. "He must be desperate to reestablish friendship."

"Indeed," Beryl said, then harrumphed. "Without Peter's

endorsement and connections, his businesses will be half what they are today."

"I suppose that's why he wishes to speak to me, too," Cosima said. "To help persuade you back to a friendship with him."

"You should do just the opposite, Peter—personally *and* professionally," Beryl said.

"It would be the end of him were I to sever professional ties with him." He offered a half smile at Cosima. "What of the forgiveness we just offered?"

"Forgiveness is one thing," Beryl said before Cosima could reply. "Keeping him under the prosperity of your wing is quite another."

Peter led them on the same path to the veranda the others had taken. "We'll see him and decide after that."

45

"There's something I want to talk to you about, Luke," Talie said quietly, then put her straw in her mouth and drew hard on her vanilla shake. The action eliminated the tremble in her lips, and she hoped to swallow away any weakness in her voice. She must be strong, for Luke's sake.

Over his king-sized hamburger, he looked at her. "Shoot."

Since she'd first had the idea to broach this topic, she'd been unable to come up with a good way to begin. She'd hoped a way would come with the moment, but with that moment here, the words didn't come after all.

A prayer for wisdom was in order, except the whole subject was such a miserable one she hadn't talked to God about it, not even at church.

"I was wondering . . . well . . . thinking, I should say . . . that with this fragile X business . . . Ben being the way he is, and not knowing if the new baby will be all right—"

Luke set aside his hamburger and looked at her with brows gathered in concern. "Are you regretting we didn't go ahead with the amniocentesis?"

"No." She paused again. "This isn't about the amnio. It's something . . . harder to talk about."

He took another bite of his hamburger, then some fries. He

was behaving so naturally she knew he hadn't a clue what she was about to offer him.

"I don't know what could be hard to talk about between us, Tal," he said. "We've done just about everything there is to do with each other: laughed and cried and everything in between. What's up?"

"It occurred to me, Luke, that you . . . well, you're a very attractive man."

He smiled and raised his brows. "And that's hard to say?"

She shook her head, not calmed by his easy attitude. She knew he was grappling with everything; that had been clear last night. But somehow he was able to get around it better than she and appear as if he had the strength to face the days. She would miss that strength.

"You know how I feel about you, Luke. You're it for me. But I . . . I was thinking, because of fragile X . . . maybe I'm not *it* for you. Or maybe I shouldn't be."

"What do you mean?" He was still eating. The topic hadn't made an impact.

"I mean maybe you shouldn't have married me. Maybe you should get out while you're still young and start over with someone who can give you healthy children. Someone who isn't a carrier of a disease."

Luke's mouth momentarily dropped open, revealing a half-chewed portion of burger. He shut it instantly then dropped the handful of fries suspended midway from the tabletop. "What are you *talking* about, Tal?"

She turned from him because she couldn't look at him anymore, at his concern and confusion and love so obvious in his eyes. She didn't deserve him; there was no doubt about that. And he deserved so much more than she could give him.

Talie raised a hand to her face, surprised to find it wet. Before she could answer his question he rose and came to her, lifting her into his embrace. His arms felt familiar around her, secure and welcome and exactly what she needed.

Luke held her tight, pressing her cheek to his chest. "Talie, Talie," he whispered.

She couldn't speak. She had planned to say many things. But none of them came out. She just sobbed in his arms.

He stroked her hair, then pulled back and raised her face to his. "I love you, Talie. You used to know what that means. What about our vows? Good times and bad, sickness and health. What kind of love do you think I have? So shallow I'm going to bail out?"

"I only know you deserve better than what I'm bringing to this marriage."

He held her at arm's length. "What are you talking about, Talie? Why should something you have no control over, something you had no choice in, outweigh all the other things we have? We were born with two halves of the same brain, remember? Can't separate that."

"But it's your brain I'm thinking of, Luke!" She was calmer now. The tears had stopped. "You deserve to have children, sons just like you."

"Oh, come on, nobody can guarantee that. What if we had daughters? Think any of them would be like me?"

"Maybe."

"Not in the way you're imagining—some little clone walking around here who could inherit all my best traits—even if we have perfectly healthy boys. That's never a guarantee, Tal, even without a genetic disease. Aidan is proof of that; remember his story? Besides, who knows what's in my genes? Maybe I'm a candidate for cancer or diabetes or stroke or something. Maybe I'll die young, and you'll think you never should have married me because you signed up for a long life together."

She stared at him, none of his protests making an impact.

"Maybe you should follow your own advice and get out while you're still young."

He gazed down at her. "My own advice?" He paused. "That's what this is all about? My advice to Aidan."

She didn't deny it. That was, after all, the truth.

"Talie, I had reasons for what I said to Aidan."

"Of course you did. He wants healthy children, and you know how much it hurts not to have that happen."

"Yes, that's part of it." He let go of her, pulling a chair away from the table and sitting, resting his forearms on his knees, looking at the floor. "All through church this morning I asked myself why I gave Aidan that advice." He offered a grim smile. "Now that this has come up, it's almost as if God was trying to tell me something, so I'd be prepared to give you a coherent answer. And I do have answers, Talie. It might have something to do with how hard this has been for us, but that's not all. Aidan's faith is still new. What if he decides God isn't protecting him the way he expected? I think he knows Christians aren't automatically excused from pain and suffering—otherwise it wouldn't take any faith at all to come to God, just logic—but I don't know if I'd add such a heavy decision as this to someone whose faith isn't even a year old."

Luke stood again and took Talie into his arms again, rubbing her back. "Besides, I couldn't have told Aidan to go ahead and marry Dana even if I wanted to. That would be adding peer pressure to his pros-and-cons list. And I'm not going to judge him if he does decide to get out. In fact, by my telling him to do that he'll have to be *more* certain if he does stay in this relationship. If he asks her to marry him, it won't be because others think he's unchristian or some kind of schmuck to get out now. I did it to strengthen whatever decision he makes, not to hurt Dana."

Tears filled Talie's eyes again. "Earlier, you sounded so logical. All logic and no love."

"You know I get that way sometimes. . . . Like I said when I told you to read the journal, I can't live up to Peter Hamilton."

"That . . . that was part of my thinking, Luke. Maybe you don't want to. I'm giving you an out so you don't have to."

He held her at arm's length. "But I *want* to, Talie. I want to be noble and faithful; it's just not easy. Not as easy as it seemed to your great-great-great-grandfather."

"I don't think it was easy," she said. "Not at the time. Not for any of them . . . I read Cosima's guilt and identified with that right away."

He shook his head. "It wasn't about either guilt or setting a bar so high no one could reach it. It was about rising above all that. Faith above fear."

"I guess I saw the guilt more than you did because I fell into the same trap myself."

Luke put a hand on each side of her face. "Your guilt and my fears of not living up to expectations will get us into trouble, Talie. We'll have to remember that—both of us—when it comes to Ben. I love you. I'm not bailing out. I love Ben, too. How could I leave either one of you?" He brought one hand to the child growing in her womb. "Or this one? We don't know the reasons for any of this, Talie, but we do know the facts. God gave us these two kids, and we're meant to raise them. With His help. And we will. Together."

46

Just a short time ago I believed my heart might never again beat at a normal pace. Even now, my breathing remains erratic. It is my hope that by recording what took place tonight, revisiting the event while knowing the outcome, I might better realize the truth that God's hand never left us. Not for a moment.

Although we had not formally agreed to meet Reginald, there was really no question that we would go. I met Peter at the top of the stairs at eleven o'clock. Everyone else had withdrawn for the night, and the manor house was quiet and dark except for the few high sconces my mother insists upon keeping lit. Oftentimes Royboy wakes during the night, and it is easier to go after him with a light showing the way.

I could not suppress a breathless laugh. . . .

"If either of our parents knew we were out here, they'd see us wed on the morrow instead of next spring."

Peter drew her into his arms. "Then perhaps we should make a little noise."

Cosima couldn't laugh again though she might have. Peter's mouth came down on hers just as her arms went around him.

It wouldn't have been much of a scandal, headed as they were to her father's library rather than any improper place. But there was something exciting in the atmosphere, in the quietness and secrecy. And she had to admit that as the time approached to speak to Reginald at last, she had grown more curious. Was that all he wanted—to preserve his friendship with them? It seemed impossible to honor that request, not when Reginald's motives seemed more driven by greed than affection.

The library door creaked as Cosima opened it. Single sounds always seemed magnified at night. Peter stepped in front of her and pushed the door the rest of the way.

The room was dimly lit with two lamps in opposite directions. One, her father's favorite reading lamp, stood tall from the floor behind the comfortably cushioned leather chair in the corner.

The other oil lamp sat upon her father's large mahogany desk. It was here Reginald sat, in her father's high-backed chair. Reginald's blond hair was the only bright spot in the shadows, his head rising only two-thirds as high as her father's would. Reginald looked something like a child, playing at being a grown-up.

"Welcome," he said as if this were his library. He stood, walking around the desk and stopping in front of it. "I knew you would come."

The room wasn't as large as most others in the manor house. Books lined only one wall, the desk another, a settee and pair of chairs nearby. Two smaller shelves with plants sat on either side of the door directly behind Cosima and Peter. Though they were only four or five paces apart, Cosima couldn't see Reginald's eyes clearly. She saw only the whiteness of his teeth behind his smile.

"You said you wanted to reestablish our friendship—" Peter's voice was terse—"but I'm not at all sure that's possible, Reginald."

Reginald laughed, only he didn't appear amused or surprised by Peter's words. He sounded odd, uneven somehow. He walked back behind the desk, turning from them to the window. During the day her father took advantage of the natural light while he worked, but now it was dark, and Cosima caught a glimpse of Reginald's reflection, broken by wooden muntins.

"As a matter of fact," he said, "I came here to do . . . something . . . something very important." He swayed for a moment, as if he were dizzy, but then steadied himself with one hand pressed to the glass. His other hand slid beneath his jacket, disappearing from Cosima's reflected view.

She wondered what task he had in mind. Maybe achieving his goal, whatever that proved to be, would bring him back to his old self. Obviously reestablishing his friendship with Peter wasn't all he had on his mind. "Perhaps we can help you."

His shoulders shook after she spoke, as with laughter or tears. He turned toward them, and with his face now illumined by the lamp on the desk, Cosima saw his gaze was lit with mirth. When he collected himself, his smile was more of a smirk than a friendly gesture. He no longer looked himself.

He slowly withdrew his hand from under his jacket. Cosima watched, at first curious about the shiny object between his fingers. Then horrified.

A pistol, held loosely in Reginald's hands, caught the light. Not aimed anywhere, merely held as if it were an object of some interest. And indeed it was.

Instantly Peter moved forward, hands outstretched as if to take the weapon away. "What are you doing with that?" He stopped when Reginald waved the small gun their way, though not directly at either Peter or Cosima.

Reginald chuckled. "Protecting your ladylove, Peter? No

need." He moved away from the desk, stopping in front of the settee, where both Cosima and Peter were in his full view.

Cosima watched, transfixed by the weapon in his unsteady hands.

When Peter moved again, putting himself between Reginald and her, Reginald shook his head as if Peter's behavior were unnecessary. "I did not come here to kill her, my *friend*. No, no. I merely wanted witnesses."

Then he aimed the narrow, shiny barrel at his own head. He held the gun straight and sure, as if to pull the trigger.

Peter lurched forward, but Reginald stumbled back, out of reach, quickly regaining firm footing.

Reginald grinned as his brows lifted. He swung the pistol around, facing Cosima as he took two steps nearer.

Peter pulled her away, so that they were now in the center of the room and Reginald nearest the door.

"Or perhaps I *should* kill Cosima." Reginald smirked, looking at Peter. "Sentence you to a life without her. Surely there would be some satisfaction in that."

"Reginald, if you think you've been the spurned lover, think again," Peter said. "Cosima was never really yours—"

"Do you think I do this because of *her*?" Reginald's voice took on a higher pitch, almost as if it belonged to someone else. "She was mine, yes—but only as a tool, Peter. A tool to use against you."

Reginald took a single step closer, waving the gun between the two of them. It was ivory handled, Cosima noted, its barrel short and silver. Cosima had never seen anything so small yet so terrifying.

"You have no inkling, have you, Peter? All these years, you've believed a lie." Reginald used the pistol as an extension of his hand, pointing from Cosima to Peter as if the gun were nothing more than a harmless finger. "You should realize something about this man you hope to marry, Cosima." His eyes grew more glee-ful by the moment. "He fails to see the worst in people—even when it outweighs the best. This, contrary to what someone of your sensibilities might believe, is a great flaw." He straightened and pointed the small, deadly barrel directly at Peter. "You see, it's landed him here today, with lives in jeopardy. Even yours." He swung the gun her way.

"Reginald—" Peter raised his hand, taking a step toward Reginald.

"Be still!" Reginald commanded, tripping backward. His grip on the gun doubled with both hands on the hilt. "Hear me out, Peter. You'll let me tell you the truth at last."

"Tell me, Reg." Peter's voice was calm, almost gentle. Cosima spared a glance from the gun to Peter, struggling to mimic his control. "I want to hear what you have to say."

Reginald shook his head. "No, Peter. You don't. But I fully intend to tell you anyway. I can say it now. The truth is, I'm no friend to you. Never have been." He smiled, and for the barest second he looked like his old self again, friendly and calm.

"That's not true, Reg. You and I have shared good times, worked together, helped others."

"But I've *hated* you." One brief laugh punctuated the state-ment. "All this time I've hated you—only you never knew."

"That can't be true, Reg. I don't believe it."

He waved the gun again. "What more can it take, Peter? Here I stand with a gun pointed at you and your ladylove, and you *still* don't believe the worst of me? Foolish." He cocked his head Peter's way but looked at Cosima as if to label Peter in her mind.

His gaze returned to Peter. "Let me help convince you, my friend. Do you remember Nan? Of course you do; you almost wed her." Reginald looked at Cosima again. "You should thank me for this, Cosima. Had I not acted, Peter might not have been available for you."

Cosima glanced at Peter, but his gaze was riveted on Reginald. Her mind jumped to what Beryl had told her long ago, her suspicion that Reginald had paid a man to seduce Nan away from Peter. Perhaps Beryl was right.

"It was so easy," Reginald said, as if recalling a favorite memory. "I knew I wasn't handsome enough to do it, but it wasn't hard to find that young man, clean him up, buy him a fine suit of clothes, and school him in the fine art of *limited* talking. Then I threw them together—much as I threw you and Peter together, Cosima. Results are so predictable when you put two healthy, physically appealing people together. Of course, they should both have some sort of need to fill. That's where you made it easy, Peter. You didn't fill Nan's needs. I don't know why—perhaps it wasn't your fault. Perhaps it was Nan's nature. Vain enough to enjoy the attention of any handsome man."

He looked at Cosima again. "In all fairness to Nan, I should tell you it was only a kiss that ended her future with this Hamilton heir. One kiss, so perfectly timed I knew then how brilliant I was. I had invited Peter and his father, of course, to Hyde Park for an early morning ride. I needed him there at a precise time, you see. In time to witness his fiancée and my hired man holding hands as they strolled. The kiss was an added, unexpected bonus."

"It doesn't matter if you orchestrated that, Reginald," Peter said. "I've awakened many a morning grateful that marriage did not take place—even before I met Cosima."

"But you *didn't* realize it until Nan was seduced by another man. One I set up!"

Peter said nothing, only nodded, and Cosima breathed again. Best to keep Reginald appeased.

"And now here is Cosima." Reginald's tone was once again affable. "My strategy worked yet again. Put two attractive, healthy—well, *healthy* is not the correct word in Cosima's case. But when I put you together, you followed the plan as if under my direction."

Abruptly, he wagged the gun back and forth between Peter and Cosima. "It was all my doing, putting you together. Only you were supposed to come away with me, both of you, to Gretna Green. You were supposed to marry before Peter knew about the curse, so there would be no way out. You were to come back to Hamilton Hall with the marriage already consummated so that even your narrow-minded parents would wait to see if the first of your feebleminded children could be growing in her belly. They may have insisted on a divorce despite their declared *faith* and convinced you that was best. But my hope, my design, was that your legacy, Peter, might be feebleminded children."

Reginald guffawed, as if he'd told a monumental jest. At last he stopped to breathe deeply, and his eyes shone with that uncanny brightness, the sparkle of a tear in one eye. He stared at Peter, blond brows lifted. "Only here you are, Peter, know-ing everything and ready to proceed. That," he added, "was *not* my design. I really only wanted to kill your legacy. But now you make me want to kill you, too."

"*Why*, Reg?" Peter asked, and Cosima knew he was as bewil-dered as she.

Reginald took a step back, stopping abruptly as if surprised when he hit the door. The gun barely quivered, however, so secure was it in his hand. Aimed at Peter's heart.

If Reginald heard Peter's plea for understanding, he chose to ignore it. He faced Cosima. "I knew about you all along, Cosima. About Royboy and Percy and your aunt . . . everything. I knew before I ever sent my man to inquire about your hand. Rachel told me."

He uttered a short laugh. "Rachel, another sinner like me, only she is the daughter of a duke and so is free to do as she pleases. She hates you too, by the by," he said to Peter. "I suppose you never knew that, but she does. You never noticed her when she desperately wanted you to. Now she's engaged to a man who bores her when all she really wanted was you. Sad, isn't it? Nan is now married to her second choice, some fop her father fished up who didn't mind the minor scandal of a quietly broken engagement—so kind of you to do so; at least she wasn't ruined socially."

"Rachel told you about me?" Cosima asked. For a moment her curiosity outweighed her fear of his pistol.

"Yes." Reginald spoke as if they were sharing nothing more than a pleasant discussion. "She read your grandmother's reports—without the dowager's knowledge or permission, of course. And Rachel, I might add—" he looked again at Peter— "is far more astute than you. She saw me for what I am, Peter. Not a friend but someone who hates your place in society, hates you because you have it all and you have it too easily. Born into aristocracy. Born with a face any woman would admire. Born with intelligence and aspiration yet with a path easily paved by your father and his before him. All you had to do was be born, Peter."

Silence followed. All Cosima heard above the pounding of her heart was breathing. Reginald's deep, erratic breath, as if he'd run a race.

"You're right, Reg," said Peter quietly. "I've had more blessings than anyone I know."

Reginald sucked in suddenly, as if kicked. "Blessings! Oh, we shan't forget *your* faith, shall we? That's something else you were born with, Peter. A capacity unlike anyone I know to believe in God Almighty."

"We're all born with that capacity, Reg," Peter said softly.

"Oh no, not like you. Look at you, standing there protecting a woman who could very well mean the end of the Hamilton legacy. You don't even care. You stand there believing it was God who brought you together when really it was I. *I* brought you together, not out of love but hatred. But you aren't afraid.

You'll marry her thinking God—who you think *loves* you so much—will spare you from feebleminded offspring. Or worse, you'll have your tainted brats and still love the God who let this happen. You'll find a way to feel His blessing, even when you die and have children who can do nothing for you, none to carry on."

"Having a child born less than perfect isn't a sign that God doesn't love me," Peter said. "It only means we live in a decaying world. Perhaps He designed me for this purpose, Reg, to be a father to such a child. You said it yourself. Life has been too comfortable for me. Maybe He wants to teach me something I can learn only by facing what others would avoid if they could. If life was easy we might not think we need Him."

Reginald shook his head. "There you are, Peter—more evidence of your delusion that God loves *you*. Loves you like an individual, as if He cares about every little detail of your puny life."

"He does. He died for me. I'd say He loves me very individually. And you, too."

"Me! Oh, that's rich, Peter! God loving me? With a gun in my hand, ready to shoot someone He *does* love?" Reginald lost his smile and held the gun high. Cosima gasped. His taut hand gripped the gun as if he would use it.

Suddenly the door at his back moved—ever so slightly but unexpectedly.

Reginald turned and Peter pounced, taking advantage of the break in Reginald's attention.

Cosima pulled at Reginald's free arm, not strong enough to have much impact. He stretched his other arm out, as if to keep the gun from Peter. But Peter's reach easily matched Reginald's, and he grabbed the gun away just as the door behind them flung open and both of them nearly toppled to the floor.

A high-pitched squeal sounded. Royboy!

His noise was never so welcome. Peter thrust Reginald away,

the gun now secure in Peter's grip. Reginald fell and lodged against the half-open door.

Royboy pushed again, still unable to get in. "How do you do."

Peter grabbed the knob, pulling the door wide enough to let Royboy enter. Reginald slid away from them, slouched with his head between his knees.

"Well-timed, Royboy," Peter said, patting Royboy on the back.

Royboy flapped his hands, speaking words Cosima couldn't understand. Immediate danger had passed, but she was awash in heat and ice while her limbs tingled as if the blood in her veins had stopped but now rushed to its duty.

Knowing full well her brother preferred a simple smile to any form of touch, Cosima nonetheless cast her arms around him in a hug so tight he couldn't squirm free. His stiff response steadied her trembling. "Royboy! Well done!" She freed him, adding, "You—you saved our lives."

"Yes, saved lives. How do you do," replied Royboy. "How do you do."

Peter emptied the bullets from the pistol, and they landed in his palm. He looked far calmer than Cosima felt. Her heart still beat so fast she was afraid she might fall to the floor in a heap beside Reginald.

"It's true." Peter smiled and placed a hand on Royboy's shoulder. "God used you tonight, young man!"

With another squeal, Royboy flapped his hands, looking as pleased as if he had understood. And perhaps he had.

47

The doorbell rang just as Talie put Ben down for a nap. By the time she came downstairs, Luke was already headed to the front door. "Expecting somebody?"

She shook her head.

Luke opened the door to Aidan—with Dana at his side. They were holding hands. Smiling.

Talie came up beside Luke, ushering in the obviously happy guests. Her heart thumped, knowing they would be here together like this for only one reason. Aidan hadn't taken Luke's advice. "This is a surprise," she said.

"Surprised that we're here or that we rang the bell?" Dana asked.

"Both."

"We won't stay long; we're on our way to Mom's."

"Do you want to call her and ask her to come here?"

Dana shook her head. "No, we wanted to tell you guys something and then share some of the same news with Mom—sort of a modified repeat performance. And we're going to drop off Cosima's journal for her, if that's okay with you."

"Sure. It's her turn to read it." Talie led them into the living room, where her offer of soda was declined.

"We just wanted to thank you for our talk this morning," Aidan said. "It helped me put things into perspective."

"Obviously," Luke said, his tone skeptical.

"I suppose Aidan told you about what was said?" Talie asked Dana.

"Yes."

"Luke didn't want peer pressure adding to Aidan's decision," Talie explained.

"We thought as much," Aidan said. "Thing is, he missed one important point. About life not being about us. Our dreams are puny compared to the plans God has for us. So He's led us somewhere we didn't expect to go. I don't see any good reason either one of us should turn our back on the love God gave me and Dana for each other. We have a challenge, okay. Everybody has them. So we face them with the belief that God put us where He wants us and that His ways aren't always our ways."

Talie and Luke exchanged a glance.

"You're right," Luke said, then winked at Talie. "What was I saying about new faith . . . being the strongest kind?"

Talie laughed, feeling no need to explain the words to Dana and Aidan. She looked at her sister, knowing she had to apologize to her the way she had to Aidan earlier. "I'm so sorry, Danes. If I hadn't been so bent on denying anything was wrong with Ben, I wouldn't have stuffed that journal away. I was trying to control everything . . . even the truth. . . . I never should have kept it a secret—"

Dana held up a hand and Talie stopped rambling.

"You always did want to prepare me for what's ahead in life," Dana said. "I've just been too pigheaded to listen most of the time."

"What was it you called it that day so long ago?" Luke asked Talie. "What your dad was, what the journal was to you—a call back?"

"Call back!" Dana repeated the words as if they were familiar. "You did tell me that once, when we were in high school, and I've never forgotten. You said you were my call back, so life would be easy for me."

"Too bad that can't happen," Talie said.

"Yeah, well, life's not supposed to be easy," Aidan said. "Not on earth, anyway."

"I guess we'll have to do what Cosima's father said: find the blessing through the burden." Talie caught Luke's gaze. "I think I'm learning to do just that."

Five Months Later

Ben's squeal rang out in sync with the baby's high-pitched yelp. Kipp, named for his first American forebear, had found his voice—and his brother, Ben, delighted in it. Ben sat on the floor near the baby's seat, flapping his hands and laughing over the noise.

Talie looked up from helping Dana address her wedding invitations. Even before they'd received the test results on the blood taken from Kipp's umbilical cord, Luke and Talie had been convinced Kipp was unaffected by fragile X. His palate was wide and low, his ears small and close to his head. And though he weighed a hefty pound more than Ben's healthy birth weight of eight pounds, the circumference of Kipp's head measured exactly in the middle of the normal range. Most important, Kipp already made long-lasting eye contact.

Still, Talie's gaze often fell on the envelope she'd received weeks ago. It rested on the kitchen desk, just beneath the telephone where stacks of mail tended to build. She had no intention of filing that letter away just yet.

Results from the fragile X test on Kipp Hamilton Ingram: Negative.
She was indeed blessed.

On this day, June the seventh, eighteen hundred and seventy-four, I watched my son depart for America. Kipp, my youngest, revels in the freedom that comes with being the son without a legacy. He always told me a legacy would bring only responsibility and limitation of options, and he was glad to have been born without one. He says America has the greatest resources in the world and its people are the greatest resource of all. He wants to be one of them, to help bring change to a changing world.

I have no doubt our Kipp can do it. Especially with the reminder he carries in his pocket, the sure knowledge that he can survive all and whatever—no matter what he finds in the New World.

Our other children, Branduff, Clara, and Mary, accompanied us to the dock to see Kipp off. I suppose Lord and Lady Hamilton felt this way when they saw their sons travel, wondering if they would ever see them again. My four wonderful children, together for what may be the last time.

I watched my beloved husband, still handsome though near fifty. Never has there been a man more willing to suffer for the Lord our God. And yet the Lord has sent him only blessings, even in Mary, who is simple and yet never without a smile. In her limitations we lean on God's grace and love, and we are bound together as a family ever tighter each day.

When Mary was three years old and we began to suspect the truth about her, the Lord brought me closer to Him than anytime before. He spoke to me in the apostle Paul's words: "My grace is sufficient for thee: for my strength is made perfect in weakness. Most gladly therefore will I rather glory in my infirmities, that the power of Christ may rest upon me."

I seldom think of the curse anymore. The tongues of the villagers have long since quieted. Beryl, of course, had much to do with that. Even without her early work at the school, I believe her endlessly optimistic smile would have won them over. Her letters are full of challenges and blessings to this day; she will never stop working, not until the Lord calls her to His side.

Nor do I often think of Reginald Hale, who disappeared that night both from our lives and from the society he once coveted. I still pray he will one day discover the individuality of God's love, if he has not already.

Instead when I recall that I was once viewed as cursed, the Lord brings to mind a verse from His Word, a verse that is etched upon my heart: "The Lord thy God turned the curse into a blessing unto thee, because the Lord thy God loved thee."

And I praise Him.

A NOTE FROM THE AUTHOR

The Oak Leaves is a book I thought I would write "someday." *Someday* when I'd accepted fragile X in my life, in my son's life. *Someday* when I could find something good to say about being a mom to a permanently handicapped child. *Someday* when I understood why God allows things like fragile X.

As of today, I've made some progress toward that someday, but I am by no means there. As I wrote *The Oak Leaves*, I did find good things to say about being a mom to a special-needs child. Like Royboy, my son and so many other fragile Xers offer the smile of God—full of grace toward others. Without fragile X in my life I would never have written this book, never have experienced the joy of expressing some of the emotions God put in all of us—love and disappointment, hope and struggle, side by side. Of course it meant revisiting some of the painful moments in my own life to give my fictional story authenticity: the denial, the diagnosis, and the reeling from that. But it is something many have faced with me. This book is for all of us who've survived.

I pray anyone who goes through this diagnosis or one like it will know that joy will eventually return and that you will find a great many things to rejoice in along the journey of life. Most of all, I pray you will know you are loved by the God who created you and your child.

If you would like to know more about fragile X syndrome, please visit www.fraxa.org or www.fragilex.org. I pray for the day the "curse" in this book will be made obsolete by a cure.

Maureen Lang

ABOUT THE AUTHOR

Maureen Lang has always had a passion for writing. She wrote her first novel longhand around the age of ten, put the pages into a notebook she had covered with soft deerskin (nothing but the best!), then passed it around the neighborhood to rave reviews. It was so much fun she's been writing ever since.

Eventually Maureen became the recipient of a Golden Heart Award from Romance Writers of America, followed by the publication of three secular romance novels. Life took some turns after that, and she gave up writing for fifteen years, until the Lord claimed her to write for Him. Soon she won a Noble Theme Award from American Christian Fiction Writers, and a contract followed a year or so later for *Pieces of Silver*, followed by its sequel, *Remember Me*.

Maureen lives in the Midwest with her husband, her three children, and her daughter's dog, Bunubi.

Q & A about Fragile X

Why did you write *The Oak Leaves*?

Mostly to bring attention to fragile X syndrome and let others share in this life experience. Even though I believe one of the most difficult things in life is to face a serious diagnosis for your child, it was helpful to me to look at how it changed my life—and try to find something good to say about it. At the time of the diagnosis I questioned many things, not the least of which was why a good God would allow this to happen to those He supposedly loves (my husband, my son, my other children, our extended family, myself). Writing this book helped me to assimilate all the sermons I've heard about how God gave us free will in order to teach us to love. Free will brought all kinds of havoc—but without it, we'd all be robots without the faintest idea of what it means to love God or each other. And that would make the world a far different place than one in which we have to face evil and disease.

How much of the story is true? Did you find a journal from your family and learn that fragile X had been in your family for generations?

Although fragile X must have been in my family for at least three generations before it displayed itself in my son, the journal and everything else in *The Oak Leaves* are pure fiction. However, like Talie, I had recently found out I was pregnant again when my son was diagnosed. I went through the remainder of my third (and final) pregnancy not knowing whether I would have a healthy baby or another fragile X child. (Like Talie's son Kipp, my new baby turned out to be unaffected.)

In the story, why did it take so long for Talie to receive Ben's diagnosis?

This is where fact and fiction are more similar than you might expect. In my son's case, several years ago, it took nearly ten weeks to receive the diagnosis. The test still takes a matter of weeks, although not normally the six weeks or so that it took for Ben (and rarely as long as the ten weeks it took for my son). Not all genetic screening labs do the specific test for fragile X syndrome, and those that do will often wait until they have a sizeable "batch" of blood samples and test them all at once. Another factor that can delay results is having two or three different doctors involved. In both my case and Talie's, a lab, a geneticist, and a coordinating physician all took time to review the results before passing the information on to the parents.

I've met someone with fragile X, and he was much higher functioning than Royboy, the fragile X child portrayed in _The Oak Leaves_. Why did you choose to present someone with fragile X as being so limited when many fragile X children can do much more, especially with language?

I created the character of Royboy to match my own son as closely as possible, because my son is the fragile Xer I know best. But as portrayed in the book through Percy and Royboy, there are varying degrees of affectedness. Many fragile Xers attain good language skills, can read to a limited degree, and even play some sports. This unfortunately has not been the case for my son. He is considered "low functioning" on the fragile X scale.

Is it really possible that fragile X could be passed down from Cosima's generation to Talie's without showing up more often than it did?

Yes. Fragile X can be passed silently down through generations in a family before a child is affected by the syndrome. Essentially, there is a variable factor in the DNA of a fragile X carrier that typically increases with successive generations, increasing the risk that a carrier will produce an affected child. Occasionally, though, the factor (and risk) decreases, only to begin increasing again in a later generation.

It also depends on whether the carrier is male or female. As Talie learned, every child born to a _female carrier_ has a fifty-fifty chance of receiving the affected gene. (The children who receive the fragile X gene might be cognitively affected or might simply be unaffected carriers.) A _male carrier_, like Cosima's son Kipp, who is himself unaffected by the gene will pass on carrier status to all of his daughters. His sons will be free of the disorder altogether. It's never been documented that a father can produce a child who is a full mutation (that is, severely affected). Therefore, any children Cosima's carrier son (Kipp) would have had would have been cognitively unaffected. It could conceivably have taken another two or three generations for the mutation to show up again, and that is what is portrayed in *The Oak Leaves*: It affected Ellen Dana Grayson, then disappeared until Ben was diagnosed.

Want more?

The story doesn't end with *The Oak Leaves*.

Look for Maureen Lang's next book, **coming summer 2008.**

Turn the page for an exciting preview!

Visit www.tyndalefiction.com for updates.

The wooden box didn't easily open. Despite having been tucked away in an environmentally regulated place, the ancient varnish seemed glued shut from having been closed so long. Gently, Rebecca rocked the lid until it loosened.

"There." She glanced at Quentin without removing the wooden top. "Shall I, or would you care to do the honors?"

"Afraid of Pandora's box?" Quentin teased.

"Not at all. I simply don't want to steal the moment of excitement. It's your family's history."

Quentin shrugged. "I confess I'll be interested to contact this American relative who inspired our search, but beyond that I haven't nearly the fascination for the past that you—and the American, I presume—have. Lift it."

Rebecca obeyed. Inside, tied as neatly as the classic volumes with which it had been stored, lay a stack of letters. The one on top was addressed in a neat, feminine script. To Cosima Hamilton.

"Not *from* your great-great-great-grandmother, but *to* her," Rebecca said. She realized she'd reverently whispered only after the words left her mouth.

"From whom?"

Untying the ribbon, Rebecca gently opened the yellowed envelope. Whatever wax had once sealed it had long since dried, leaving behind only a faintly blue shade on the tip that any wax had ever been present.

" 'Loving greetings from Berrie,' it begins." Rebecca looked up again. "That must be Beryl Hamilton, your great-great-great-grandfather's sister. A note on a recipe from Cosima called her sister-in-law Berrie."

"Are they all from her?"

Rebecca carefully glanced through some of the other envelopes. "The handwriting appears to be the same. I believe so."

"Read one," Quentin invited.

Rebecca glanced down the page of the hefty letter, seeing the writing clear and apparently flawless. "It goes into some detail."

"Let me," he said, reaching for the letter and setting aside his cup. "It's the only way I can prove to you I'm not bored by the topic, historical though it is, and at the same time give you a chance to eat."

Rebecca put the letter into his outstretched hand, took a bite of the creamy chicken, then pushed it away and settled back in her chair.

She knew exactly what Beryl Hamilton had looked like and suspected Quentin remembered her portrait too. It hung in the gallery, next to the one of Christabelle and her brother Nathan Hamilton.

Berrie was forever young in Rebecca's mind, and lovely too. With dark hair like her oldest brother, Peter, Berrie had the kind of hair Rebecca wished she had. Instead of errant curls, Berrie's looked smooth and obedient. She didn't have Peter's dark brown eyes; rather, Berrie had unimaginably blue ones that had somehow survived all the way down the line to reside in Quentin today.

Rebecca had no trouble whatsoever imagining Berrie Hamilton writing that letter.

April 6, 1854

My Dear Cosima,

Do you recall I once feared most that I should find myself before the judgment seat of God with an unlit lamp? There I might have stood, having been ordained with some talent— surely I had one, I convinced myself of that—and yet not using that with which I had been blessed.

Yesterday, with only the first of the many students I hope to house, I proved the depth of my incompetence. And 'twas with your own, sweet brother Royboy! Did I think I would make a difference? Did I believe I knew what I was doing? . . .